HERE'S TO US

Also by

BECKY ALBERTALLI and **ADAM SILVERA**

What If It's Us

Also by

BECKY ALBERTALLI

Simon vs. the Homo Sapiens Agenda

The Upside of Unrequited

Leah on the Offbeat

Yes No Maybe So (with Aisha Saeed)

Love, Creekwood

Kate in Waiting

Also by

ADAM SILVERA

More Happy Than Not

History Is All You Left Me

They Both Die at the End

Infinity Son

Infinity Reaper

BECKY ALBERTALLI
& ADAM SILVERA

HERE'S TO US

BALZER + BRAY Quill Tree Books
Imprints of HarperCollins*Publishers*

Balzer + Bray is an imprint of HarperCollins Publishers.
Quill Tree Books is an imprint of HarperCollins Publishers.

Here's to Us
 For information address HarperCollins Children's Books, a division of HarperCollins Publishers, 195 Broadway, New York, NY 10007.
www.epicreads.com

ISBN 978-0-06-307163-6 (hardcover)
ISBN 978-0-06-315773-6 (international edition)
ISBN 978-0-06-314258-9 (special edition)

Typography by Erin Fitzsimmons
21 22 23 24 25 PC/LSCH 10 9 8 7 6 5 4 3 2 1
❖
First Edition

For David Arnold and Jasmine Warga,

the first stars in our growing universe

PART ONE

CLEAR THE SLATE AND START OVER

CHAPTER ONE

BEN

Saturday, May 16

What if we do?

This question lives in my head whenever I think about him.

I feel like I've been lost for a long time, like a box with its shipping label torn off en route. But I think someone's finally found me.

He's cut through the box's heavy duct-tape seal and cracked it open.

There's light and air.

Good-morning texts and sleepovers.

And Spanish and kisses.

Mario Colón.

Right before I entered the train station, Mario texted me

a photo of himself in the dentist's chair. He's wearing a white T-shirt with denim overalls, one strap hanging loose, like the Puerto Rican Super Mario reboot this world deserves. His olive skin is smooth because he apparently doesn't grow any body hair, which bums him out sometimes because he thinks he would look great with Lin-Manuel Miranda's beard. His dark hair is curly, and that bright office light is really catching the glow in his hazel eyes. His tongue is hanging out from the corner of his lips, and even when he's being silly, it makes me want to kiss him, like that first time when we were working together on our creative writing homework.

And the fifty other times since then.

I self-consciously swipe through to the photo I sent him in response. I usually take a dozen selfies before I feel one is Mario-worthy since he's clearly out of my league, but I had to be quick when my train was pulling up. I angled the phone above me, making sure the T-shirt he made me was visible. For his high school graduation, Mario's parents gave him a T-shirt printer because he wanted to add some flavor to his clothes. Last week he surprised me with *The Wicked Wizard War* shirts that have the same lettering from the cover Samantha created for me to use on Wattpad. The T-shirt was such a thoughtful gift. It even has me judging myself and my photos a lot less than I normally would.

Mario and I met at the beginning of freshman year in

our creative writing class, and at first, I was sure he'd turn out to be a Very Serious Fiction Writer or an amazing slam poet. Neither. Mario is a screenwriter who's been writing scripts since he was eleven years old, often getting in trouble in middle school for formatting his homework assignments like a TV episode.

He was the first person after my ex, Arthur, I zeroed in on. I would notice when he wouldn't come to class, I'd admire how he pulls off overalls, and I really liked the turtlenecks he wore during winter. And he was confident about his work in a way that I couldn't wrap my head around—always proud but also never cocky.

At the time, there were still too many what-ifs in my head about Arthur for me to even try to get close to him.

Now the what-ifs are about Mario.

What if we become official boyfriends instead of just friends who kiss and hang out?

I'm headed to Central Park to catch up with my best friend, Dylan, and his girlfriend, Samantha. It's my first time seeing them in person since the holidays, since they didn't come home from school for spring break. We were supposed to have a game night yesterday, but Dylan claims he was feeling extremely jet-lagged, even though there's only a one-hour difference between Chicago and New York. I let it go, because Dylan has always been dramatic that way.

I spend the rest of the train ride jotting down ideas in

my pocket-sized notebook for an upcoming chapter of my fantasy novel, *The Wicked Wizard War.* I finished drafting the book ages ago, but it became clear that my story was all over the place. Too many exciting moments were being reserved for sequels that may never happen, and all the characters inspired by my friends and ex-boyfriends needed to be more fully developed and accessible to people outside my circle.

My forever mood: writing is hard.

Mario once asked me if there's anything I've ever wanted to do besides writing. Writing is the only thing I'm good at. Even if some other dream did call out to me, I don't know what I would do without all the love my friends and strangers have shown my wicked wizards. Arthur used to talk about the characters like they were mutual friends. And Dylan loves the world so much he's been fantasizing about a real-life drag bar where all the drag queens are dressed as different fantasy races like elves and trolls, which is a thing I've never remotely expressed interest in.

I love connecting with people over words.

And I'm really loving connecting with Mario over words in both English and Spanish.

He's another white-passing Puerto Rican like me, but his parents actually raised him bilingual, unlike mine. He incorporated a lot of Spanish into his film script and said he hoped that no studio would force him to translate it for people; he wanted others to put in the work that his parents had to do themselves growing up. It really inspired me to do the damn work myself—and I practically screamed "¡Sí, por favor!" when he offered to be my personal teacher.

I'm pretty pumped to see him.

Today's hangout with Dylan and Samantha is going to be a bit of a juggling act since Mario will also be joining us. He's not my boyfriend, but he's also more than a friend. Things get really tricky in that space. Like when I wake up thinking about him and want to say good morning just because, but that can sometimes feel too intimate. Or when I'm wondering what's the best way to introduce him to my friends even though they know the gist of our relationship. Or even how words like "relationship" can feel too strong, sort of unearned when you compare them with actual relationships.

I don't know. That's a problem for One-Hour-in-the-Future Ben.

But I have to get Mario's beautiful face out of my head, because I'm about to miss my train stop. I jump out of my seat and cross to the platform right as the doors are closing. I've got to make sure I'm not late. I'm putting those days behind me. In our creative writing class, Mrs. García would call this "character growth."

I leave the station and walk down to the Central Park West entrance on Seventy-Second. It doesn't take me long to spot Dylan and Samantha. They're on a park bench, playing that game where you have to stare into each other's eyes and slap the other person's hands before they can retract them.

Samantha slaps Dylan's hands. "Gotcha! Four–one. You suck."

"Hey," I say as I walk around the bench. "Can I get in on this?"

Dylan smiles. "There's always room for you in our bed."

"I didn't say anything about your bed. I—"

Dylan shushes me as he stands and pulls me into a hug, patting the top of my head. "Missed you, buddy."

"Missed you, too. Exhausted by you already."

Dylan's hair has grown to the point where he's finally been able to master that man bun he's been working on, which looks really great on him—and if you ask him, he's the only person pulling it off. He's rocking a new Kool Koffee shirt and blue jeans. "There's a cute little café in the park. Get ready to drink all the espresso shots, my little coffee bean. Coffee Ben? Ben Bean?"

"I vote none of the above," Samantha says. Her blue-green eyes wow me as much today as when I first met her behind that counter at Kool Koffee. Her dark hair is braided into a Pinterest-ready crown that I should include in my book. She's wearing a navy shirt tucked into white shorts, and she's got a silver key hanging from her neck. "Hi, Ben," she says as she pulls me into a hug.

I'm relieved Dylan hasn't converted her into someone who aggressively nicknames me.

"Welcome back, guys."

Samantha's eyes widen at my shirt. "Oh my Greek goddesses, I love it!"

Dylan grins when he notices. "Those wicked wizards are going to wizard so hard one day."

There've been a lot of changes since Dylan read the book last summer, pre-college, but his support never really died down. Every now and again I'll get a text from him asking what's up with Duke Dill, the character I based on him. Dylan has been cheering me on to get a literary agent already, but I've become a bit of a perfectionist lately.

I don't want to let anyone down.

This love is the kind of pressure that gets to me.

"I want a shirt, too," Samantha says, feeling my sleeve. "Did you make that?"

"Mario did," I say.

"Super Mario!" Dylan says. "I hope he's not tired of people calling him that because you know I have to do it."

"He actually loves it."

It's the kind of thing I would find annoying after some time, but not Mario. The closest I've seen him to getting upset was when our classmate Spikey gave Mario some harsh critiques on his script, but Mario ultimately shrugged it off because Spikey was just out for blood after Mrs. García called his Civil War short story "historically impossible" and everyone laughed.

"So when is Super Mario popping out of a sewer pipe?" Dylan asks.

"Soonish. He's coming from the dentist. You're stuck with me until then."

"Fantastic," Samantha says as she loops her arm with mine and we begin our stroll through Central Park. "So things are going well with him?"

"I think so?" I feel a little stupid talking about Mario with Samantha and Dylan. There's no confusion about their relationship. Whereas Mario and I are more like a question mark paired with an exclamation point—there's uncertainty and excitement.

"We need to figure out your couple name," Dylan says. "I think 'Bario' has a nice ring to it, though 'Men' is chef's-kiss perfection. Because you're both dudes and—"

"How was dinner?" I interrupt, turning to Samantha.

"Good save," she says. "It was fun. Thanks for asking. I think we bounced back from Christmas."

Samantha's parents really love Dylan, but when the O'Malleys found out during the winter break that their daughter was sharing a room with him in Chicago, shit hit the fan.

"Dylan was on his best . . . well, better than usual behavior," Samantha says. "I'm sorry again we had to cancel on the escape room."

"Don't worry about it. We have all summer."

Dylan wraps his arms around my shoulders. "Big Ben, we know the escape room is your big ploy to get locked in a room with me for an hour. You don't need excuses, okay?"

"Dude, your girlfriend is right here."

"Oh, please, get him off me for an hour," she says.

Dylan winks. "See, the missus is cool with it."

I stop at a pretzel cart because all I've eaten this morning was a bite of a toasted bagel with jelly that Ma made for me on my way out of the apartment. In true Ben Alejo fashion, I dropped it on the subway tracks while taking that selfie for Mario, and a rat ran off with it; if I gave a single damn about TikTok, I probably could've gone viral.

"Do you guys want one?" I ask.

"I filled up on fruit," Samantha says. "Dylan had leftover duck for breakfast."

"Shhh," Dylan says. "There are ducks in the park."

"Do you think the ducks are going to attack?"

"A good old-fashioned quack attack, yes."

Samantha shakes her head. "Why do I . . . why do I *anything* with you?"

"Because the D Machine is too irresistible."

"Gross, man," I say.

"Oh, that just stands for the Dylan Machine. I call my friend downstairs the—"

Samantha claps her hand over his mouth. A true hero of our times.

"D—uh, Dylan, do you want coffee?"

Dylan looks around. "From where?"

I gesture at the pretzel cart.

"Very cute, Ben. You know I'm not drinking that bastard coffee." Dylan turns to the vendor. "I mean no offense to you, good sir, and great offense to the clowns who loaded your fine cart with that mess."

The vendor stares at Dylan as if he's speaking another language.

"You're hyper enough anyway," I say.

"We pregamed with a Dream & Bean double espresso."

"Duck and coffee for breakfast. Figures."

"Stop acting like this is day one of knowing me."

It's definitely not day one. We've been best friends since elementary school, though ever since Dylan left for college, the distance has had an impact on us.

"You better not have a caffeine crash before lunch with Patrick," Samantha says.

"Patrick," Dylan says and spits on the ground. "Get better best friends, babe. Do you see Ben going on and on and on and on and on and on about how he's swimming with dolphins and hugging monkeys?"

"I'm not doing those things," I say.

"Neither is Patrick," Samantha says with a side-eye. "Patrick took a gap year to travel with his cousin."

A gap year sounds great. Gap *years* sound even better.

"Join us for lunch, Ben. You'll see how extra this guy is."

"Are you really calling someone extra, D?"

"That should give you a sense of how extra-extra this guy is!"

"I can't. I have work in a couple hours."

"Tell your boss that royalty is in town."

"You know I can't."

My boss is my father. Pa got promoted to manager at Duane Reade during the holiday season. He hired me in April to work the cash registers and help out with stocking the shelves. Beginning work right before finals only made classes harder, but I didn't get a ton of sympathy from my parents, who worked full-time during college.

"You'll meet Patrick some other time," Samantha says. "He's home for the next two months. Maybe we can all do an escape room together."

"You're not locking me in a room with Patrick for an hour," Dylan says.

"Even more incentive for you to solve the puzzles sooner." Samantha playfully elbows me. "We can totally invite Mario, too."

"Maybe." My phone buzzes. "Speaking of Super Mario." I read his text, saying that he's walking over now. "He's on the way. Should we camp out here so we're easier to find?"

Dylan stares into the distance and points at the Belvedere Castle terrace. That spot always feels like it was plucked out of a fantasy novel and dropped into Central Park. "Tell your boy we'll be there."

"He's not my boy."

"Yet."

It's funny, the last time Dylan and I were at Belvedere was shortly after I met Arthur at the post office. We hadn't gotten each other's names before a flash mob separated us, but I couldn't stop thinking about him, so Samantha did some Nancy Drew-ing using some details from my conversation with Arthur to figure out the best way to find him. She discovered a meetup for Yale students happening at the Belvedere Castle, and since Arthur had mentioned wanting to go to school there, I gave it a shot. Dylan decided we needed pretentious code names to attend the event, and he chose Digby Whitaker for himself, which I only still remember because I gave that name to a scholar in *TWWW.*

I came here looking for one boy two years ago, and now I'm asking another to find me here.

Without even looking, Dylan's hand finds Samantha's and they go upstairs together.

Holding hands is a simple act, I get it, but it's really nice to see a couple two years in who still like each other—*love* each other. I've never personally experienced that. It gives me hope that someone will feel the same way about me.

We climb up the terrace and stop in our tracks. Normally it's pretty chill up here, just people posing with the park in the background. But today there's a wedding happening. It's intimate, only a dozen casually dressed people and a band playing a soft instrumental version of "Marry You" by Bruno Mars. I'm about to drag Dylan and Samantha away so we don't photobomb the event when the bride begins marching out.

I'm frozen in my tracks.

I think I know the bride . . .

Back when I met Arthur at the post office, that flash mob was actually a proposal for the teller who was helping me send my first ex, Hudson, a box of his things. It was too pricey, and this woman wasn't sympathetic to me. But she's glowing now with a black silk wrap around the shoulders of her simple white dress, smiling with a big lip ring.

First Belvedere Castle and now this woman. It's like the universe is flashing Arthur Seuss's name in Broadway neon lights.

I haven't spoken to Arthur in months, but I have to tell him.

I record a quick video of the bride walking toward the groom on my phone. Dylan and Samantha snuggle together as they watch. I open my chat with Arthur—the last text I got from him was on my birthday, April 7. I didn't respond because, well . . . yeah. I didn't have it in me then because everything was going so well for him with his new boyfriend, and I wasn't trying to pretend my birthday was a happy one. I should've said something, though, because now I feel weird saying anything.

It's like we don't know each other anymore.

I go on Instagram, where I've had his profile muted for my own sanity. It hurt too much to go online and find pictures of Happy Arthur and Happy Mikey being Happy Arthur-and-Mikey. I needed to create some space for myself; life was stressful enough with school and feeling cramped at home and lonely without Dylan or a boyfriend of my own.

Going to Arthur's profile is like ripping off a Band-Aid.

His blue eyes are piercing as ever in his circular profile picture. The most recent pictures on his feed include one of a box in his dorm room, then a Stacey Abrams quote ("No matter where we end up, we've grown from where we began"), a throwback of young Arthur with his mom, and Arthur and Mikey holding up a *Playbill* in their college's theater—which sends blood rushing into my head. Then my chest tightens when I see a selfie of Arthur holding up the postcard of Central Park that I gave him when we said goodbye two summers ago; written on the back is a sexual scene between our *The Wicked Wizard War* characters, Ben-Jamin and King Arturo, for his eyes only.

Why is he taking a picture with that?

I read the post:

Arthur Seuss's upcoming tour stop—New York City! May 17

He's coming back.

Tomorrow.

He used a postcard from our past to announce his future.

There's a lot of love in the comments from Mikey and his best friend, Jessie, and his former colleague Namrata. I'm the only asshole in New York who hasn't shown any excitement. I feel weird liking it now. Though what if this is the best first step to reconnecting? Knowing our luck, we're bound to bump into each other at some point. The only time New York kept us apart was when I was here and he wasn't.

I like the post. And even though I'm standing still, my heart is racing like I'm running.

Before I can leave a comment, Dylan snatches my phone. "Love is happening, Ben!"

"We can't even hear them—"

"*Feel* the love, Ben, *feel* the love."

"I actually saw this proposal happen."

"Really?" Samantha asks.

"The day I met Arthur. Remember that flash mob I told you about? It was all for these two."

During the chaos of that moment, I left. My breakup with Hudson was really fresh, and even though I had a fun debate about the universe with Arthur, I wasn't expecting anything to come out of that. Not once did I think I was going to fall in love with the boy wearing a hot dog tie.

"That's some luck stumbling into their wedding," Samantha says.

More like the universe at work.

"They're so young," I say. "What are they, early twenties?"

"Engaged for two summers," Samantha whispers, like she's trying to hear the vows. "Must be real."

"My parents got married young," Dylan says. "That all worked out."

"Your mother hates your father," Samantha says.

"She hates that he chews with his mouth open, never replaces the toilet paper roll, lies about his taxes, and wakes her up in the middle of the night to talk about his dreams before he forgets them. But she doesn't hate *him*."

I know his parents—there's a little hate going on there.

I can't believe I'm witnessing the Post Office Woman's wedding. When they exchange their first kiss as married people, we cheer for them like they're old friends, even though she was really rude to me. I never thought this would be the first wedding I'd attend. Maybe I can use this in a story one day.

Then, suddenly, everything goes dark as hands cover my eyes, and a familiar voice says, "Guess who, Ben Hugo Alejo."

"Someone very super," I say.

Mario removes his hands. "Don't you forget it."

I spin and take him in. This is one of those days where I'm kind of breathless at how effortlessly beautiful he is. He's not just photogenic, he's beautiful IRL, too. His hazel eyes are so pretty, even if they didn't instantly catch my attention like Arthur's blue eyes. But the closer Mario and I have gotten the past month, the more they strike me. Some attractions take more time to grow and aren't any less great because of it.

"The Mario to Ben's Luigi," Dylan says.

"The Duke Dill to Ben's Ben-Jamin," Mario says, going straight in for a hug like he and Dylan already know each other. We've talked about how our Puerto Rican parents have raised us to be very affectionate, even with strangers, something we're trying to be more mindful about out of respect for other people's personal boundaries. Though these two seem magnetized to each other. Mario turns to Samantha. "And you, world-renowned book cover designer."

Samantha smiles. "That's me."

Dylan stares. "Thank God you're not blushing. But also, my love, how dare you? Look at this beautiful man. Blush for him! Don't let this beauty go unblushed for."

Mario turns to me. "He's everything you described him to be."

"I have a way with words."

"Indeed you do."

How can he make three words ignite me?

I want to be so close to him right now. The kind of close that's not allowed in a public park. Now all I can think about is how I didn't even get a kiss from Mario when he arrived. Or a hug. It's this little reminder that we're not boyfriends where that stuff feels a lot more automatic. I want to be with someone who can't keep his lips off me or whose hand always finds mine as if they were never supposed to be apart. But with Mario I can't always tell if he even wants to be kissing me and holding my hand. Sometimes he points out cute guys on the street like he's encouraging me to go for it. Like it wouldn't bother him. I would totally be uncomfortable if he flirted with someone else in front of me.

Then there are the times where the energy shifts between us. These moments where we can forget that we don't need to be boyfriends to enjoy each other.

"What's up with the wedding?" Mario asks. "Friends of yours?"

"A friend of Ben's," Dylan says.

"Really?"

"Long story," I say.

"Tell me later?"

"Tell you later."

"Estupendo." Mario claps. "I brought presents. But none for the bride and groom." He reaches into his backpack and pulls out two *The Wicked Wizard War* shirts.

Samantha's jaw drops. "You're the best!" She puts the shirt on over her own.

"I had to get you one so you don't sue me." Mario turns to Dylan. "And I didn't want you to think I wasn't thinking of you." He winks, but it's kind of awkward. It's more like he has something in his eye. And somehow it charms me even more than a perfect wink.

Dylan puts on his shirt. "Oh my God, I'm blushing. Look!" His cheeks are red as he breaks into a laugh. "Mario, there's something really incredible about someone who looks like you making clothes when you should be naked every day."

"Now you're trying to make me blush!" Mario says.

"Oh boy," Samantha says. "I think we've lost them, Ben."

"Think so."

Mario pulls out his phone. "I got to get a picture of you three in your shirts."

"Only if you're in it with us," Dylan says.

"Yes!" Samantha says.

"You got it," Mario says.

I wrap my arm around his side as Dylan and Samantha cuddle up with us. I really like holding him, and even after he takes the selfie, I hang on to Mario for a little bit longer. We all look at the picture together and the sunlight is working in everyone's favor like the world's most generous filter.

Everyone looks so happy, and I hope this is the first of many documented memories this summer. And maybe the more I share my world with him, the more he'll want to be part of mine and let me into his.

This is every relationship. You start with nothing and maybe end with everything.

CHAPTER TWO

ARTHUR

Saturday, May 16

My clothes are on the floor, and Mikey's in my bed. Well, he's *on* my bed. He's propped against my pillow pile, wearing flannel pajama pants and his glasses and nothing on top, with a full face of finals-week stubble. Not that I'm complaining. Scruffy Mikey is my favorite Mikey.

Still, he's a beacon of order and symmetry, and you can tell at a glance which of my boxes he's packed. They're the ones lined up evenly against the foot of my bed, filled with neat piles of towels and sheets, each one labeled in Sharpie. *Arthur linens. Arthur textbooks.* Right now, he's taking down my photographs, lumping all my blue poster putty into one egg-sized mega-wad.

I plop down beside him. "You know what this looks like?"

"Poster putty?"

"Let me give him an eye hole." I poke my finger into the putty and look back at him expectantly.

"Poster putty with an eye hole?"

"Mikey! It's the blob guy from *Monsters vs. Aliens*!"

"Ah." He globs another little wad of putty onto its head, like a toupee.

"Yeah, now he looks like Trump." I quickly flatten him into a pancake and toss him onto my nightstand. "Much better."

"Such activism," says Mikey.

"Hush." I lean in to kiss him. "Guess what."

"What?"

"I'm bored."

"Thanks a lot," he says.

"Of *packing*." I push his bangs off his face and kiss him again.

"You know, we're never going to finish if you keep doing that."

I just smile, because Mikey's so thoroughly Mikey. He still gets flustered when I kiss him. Sometimes he'll clear his throat and say, *Well then*. Or he'll check the time or ask whether the door's locked, and for weeks I thought that meant he was looking for excuses not to kiss me. But now I get it. Mikey's one of those people who gets what he wants and then panics.

I rest my head on his shoulder and survey the room: piles of books, scattered papers. All my big hoarder energy. Mikey, of course, packed up his entire room four hours ago.

"Thanks for being here," I murmur.

If he wanted to, he could be in Boston already. But we both know there was never a universe where Mikey didn't stick around to rescue me.

I roll up a yellow-striped polo shirt I stole from a box of my dad's high school heirlooms and shove it into my New York bag—a giant camp duffel bag, already bulging with shirts, jeans, and books. Dragging everything onto the train tomorrow is going to be An Experience, but at this point I'm just hoping I actually make it to New York. Which won't happen until I clear my thirty metric tons of shit out of this dorm room.

I nudge a cardboard box aside with my foot, hands in my hair. "What am I forgetting? Chargers, shirts, jeans—"

"Underwear?" Mikey says.

"Underwear."

"Work clothes? Suit and tie?"

"Suit and tie? So I can look like Chad from corporate?" I shake my head. "Michael McCowan, this is queer off-Broadway theater! I'll be laughed off the stage."

"Off the stage?" Mikey squints. "You're an intern to an assistant."

"Intern to the *director's* assistant. Do you even know how many people interviewed for this job?"

"Sixty-four."

"Exactly. Sixty-four," I say, feeling just a little sheepish. So maybe I've talked Mikey's ear off about my internship once or twice or possibly a few hundred times. But can you blame me? It's my ultimate top-tier pie-in-the-sky dream job. I don't think I've even fully processed it yet. Starting in less than a week, I'll be working for Jacob freaking Demsky, Lambda Award–winning playwright and two-time New York Innovative Theatre Award–winning director. How could I not jump for joy, at least a little?

I was kind of hoping Mikey would do a little joy jumping, too. Or just, you know, try not to look like Eeyore whenever I mention it.

I mean, I get it. Of course I get it. We had our whole summer mapped out perfectly: living in Boston, staying in Mikey's sister's guest room, working at a day camp. Not exactly a résumé game changer, but I wasn't in it for my résumé. I was in it for Emack & Bolio's ice cream, Union Square Donuts, and day trips to Salem and Cape Cod on the weekends. I was in it for Mikey.

But then Jacob Demsky announced his internship, and I

couldn't get it out of my head.

Yeah, the stipend was less than half of what I'd be making as a camp counselor. But I could always save money living in Uncle Milton's apartment. Missing that time with Mikey would suck, but it's not like I'd be moving to the moon. And it was just for the summer. Also, there was no point even worrying about the logistics, because Jacob was never going to pick me. Every queer Broadway nerd in the country would be vying for this, and some of them probably had more impressive theater credits than *Beauregard and Belvedere* in Ethan's basement.

Still. I poured every bit of my heart into that email and pressed send.

Then I mostly tried to put the whole thing out of my mind. I focused on Boston and Mikey and frantically teaching myself how to make yarn looms, because, wow, I was not born with camp-counselor skills. But I was going to be a camp counselor. In Boston. Because Boston was real, and New York was a pointless secret email sent into the abyss.

Until two weeks ago.

I'll never forget the way Mikey froze when I told him I'd been offered a Zoom interview.

I study him now for a moment. Mikey Phillip McCowan, my pale-shouldered nervous wreck of a boyfriend. He's sitting with his knees tucked up, hugging them, not looking at me.

"Mikey Mouse," I say quickly. "Put on 'Don't Lose Ur Head.'"

If any album can pull a smile out of Mikey, it's the original cast recording of *Six*.

He grabs my phone off the charger, tapping in my password to unlock it. But then his face sort of . . . stalls out. He stares wordlessly at my phone screen.

He's definitely not smiling.

My heart kicks into high gear. "Everything okay?"

"Yeah. Yes." He taps the screen a few times, and Anne Boleyn's voice jumps to my wireless speaker. Normally Mikey sings along under his breath, but now his mouth's a sullen straight line.

It's like the air pressure changed.

I run my hand down the edge of one of the cardboard boxes marked for storage at my bubbe's house. "I should probably bring this down to the car."

"What if you just . . . don't go?"

"To the car?"

"To New York."

I stare at him, and he stares back through his glasses, his eyes plainly serious.

"Mikey." I shake my head. "I have a job—"

"You had one in Boston, too," he says softly.

My stomach twists. "I should have told you sooner. Mikey, I'm so—"

"Stop. You don't have to apologize again." He shakes his head, cheeks flushed. "I'm just not ready for tomorrow."

"Me either." I sink onto the bed beside him.

"I wish you were still coming to Boston."

The song switches—"Heart of Stone." I take Mikey's hand, lacing my fingers through his. "Well, luckily it's just two months."

"Ten weeks."

"Fine, ten weeks. But it'll go by so fast, I promise. We won't even have time to miss each other."

He smiles sadly. "I kind of miss you already."

I look up at him, so startled I lose my breath for a second. *I kind of miss you already.*

I mean, I know Mikey's into me. I've never doubted that. But he's not usually quite so direct about it.

"Me too. But at least I get you back in two weeks." I nudge him sideways. "And I'm taking you to every single one of my favorite places. Central Park, Times Square, Levain Bakery, you name it."

Mikey's brow furrows.

I narrow my eyes. "What?"

"I didn't say anything."

"You made an eyebrow face."

Mikey disentangles our hands. "It's just . . ." He pauses, rubbing the back of his neck. "Did you go to those places with Ben?"

"Oh. Well, yeah." I feel suddenly flustered. "But that was two years ago. Ben and I haven't even talked in ages. Since February."

Mikey shrugs like he doesn't quite believe me.

But it's true. It's been months since Ben and I have talked or even texted. I even tried FaceTiming him on his birthday in April, but he didn't pick up. He didn't even return the text I sent later.

Mikey's looking at me now with his basset-hound eyes. "Are you going to see him?"

"You mean Ben?"

"You'll be in the same city."

"Mikey, seriously. I haven't talked to him since February. He doesn't even know I'm coming."

"I think he knows."

There's something about the way Mikey says it.

"What do you mean?"

The song switches again. "I Don't Need Your Love." I swear I can hear Mikey's heartbeat change tempo. He leans sideways, gropes around for my phone, and passes it to me. The Instagram notification pops up the moment I tap the screen.

@ben-jamin liked your photo.

It's the first time Ben's liked one of my photos in months.

My heart leaps into my throat. I've been trying not to let the Instagram thing bother me. It's normal for people to drift, right? Especially when it's your ex-boyfriend.

I just didn't think it would happen to *us.* To Ben and me. I kind of thought we were indestructible.

And in the beginning, we were.

I'll never forget that first week back home after leaving New York. Ben and I talked every single night until our phone batteries died. And for the rest of senior year, we never went more than a day without texting. I used to walk around the house on FaceTime so often, my parents started shouting, "Hi, Ben," whenever they saw my phone. Then sometimes Diego and Isabel would shout back, and the four of them would be off and running with some side conversation. Ben and I complained about it constantly, but I think we both secretly loved that our parents were lowkey obsessed with each other.

I mean, I liked to think Ben and I were lowkey obsessed with each other, too.

And I thought college would be the same. Or better. Definitely better, because at least I wouldn't have to deal with my mom's knowing looks every time I stepped out of my bedroom. For the record, that's a barrel of laughs: trying not to be in love with your ex-boyfriend when he rants adorably about story structure over FaceTime *and* having your parents see right through every single denial. All the boyfriend-related parental teasing without the actual boyfriend.

So. Privacy was good. And Wesleyan's proximity to New York was even better. Just over three hours by train—two if I left my car at Bubbe's house and took the train from New Haven. It's not that I expected our relationship to pick right up where we left off—not necessarily. But Ben seemed really happy I was moving closer. He brought it up constantly for months.

Of course, once I was actually *in* Connecticut, things got weird really fast.

We still talked all the time, and Ben was always saying he missed me. Or I'd wake up to rambling *remember when* texts. But when I mentioned train schedules, he'd change the subject so fast it made my head spin.

Once he sent me a screenshot of my own Instagram selfie, followed by a single heart-eye emoji. Which led to two hours on FaceTime with Ethan and Jessie, trying to pinpoint the most casual-yet-effective way to say, *Um, I think you're joke-flirting, but in case you're also real-flirting, might I remind you that I have a single dorm room.*

It was bewildering and infuriating, and I was a Ben-addled mess all over again. I thought about blocking his number. I thought about showing up on his doorstep. I was surrounded by cute boys with loud opinions who liked kissing, so I tried that. But I always ended up alone in my dorm room, poring over Ben's texts.

Until Mikey.

@ben-jamin liked your photo.

I can't stop staring at the notification. Of course, it doesn't say which photo he liked. Could have been my packing-day post, sure. But it could have also been the Stacey Abrams quote graphic I reposted last night, or Sunday's throwback photo for Mother's Day, or anything, really. I want to click into the app so badly my fingers are twitching, but I can't do that in front of Mikey.

That little heart icon.

I wish I knew what it meant.

Probably nothing. Maybe his finger slipped while scrolling. Maybe he doesn't even know he liked it. I wonder if he'll unlike it as soon as he realizes. I don't know if that would make the notification go away or if I'll get a new notification or—

I realize with a start that Mikey just spoke. And I didn't hear a word of it.

"Wait, sorry." I swallow guiltily. "What did you say?"

Mikey looks at me. "I said if you want to see him, you should see him."

"Mikey, I haven't even talked to him since—"

"February. I know." He's blinking a lot. "You said that. A few times."

I blush. "Well, it's true."

February 12th, to be exact.

And I hate it. I hate how far I have to scroll to find Ben's texts. I hate not knowing if he finished his last *TWWW* revision, or whether his parents followed through and made him get a job like they threatened. I hate not knowing what he had for breakfast this morning.

I hate that it's my fault. I'm the one who made it weird. I guess it started when Mikey and I got back together, on New Year's. But I can't blame Mikey—it's not like he asked me not to be friends with Ben. He just always got kind of prickly and distant when Ben's name came up.

So I stopped bringing his name up.

And I guess that made Ben feel like a thing I was hiding.

"Mikey, Ben liking one Instagram post doesn't mean we're suddenly best friends again," I say, aiming for the space between casual and jovial. But even I can hear the defensive edge in my voice.

I glance sideways, and Mikey's doing this tic he has sometimes, where he pinches the bridge of his nose behind his glasses. He used to do it a lot first semester. I don't think it even hit me until now that he'd stopped. He shuts his eyes for a moment. "Can I be really honest with you?"

"Of course." I scoot an inch closer.

The music's stopped, and the silence feels boundless and thick. When Mikey speaks at last, his voice is flat. "I know you haven't talked to him. And even if you did, I trust you, Arthur. You'd never cheat. I know that. I'm just scared."

I press my thigh against his. "Of what?"

"I don't know. I guess I feel a little threatened by him. He was your first love. Your big Broadway love story."

"Two years ago. And I haven't seen him since then. You know that."

He nods quickly. "It's just, what happens when you *do* see him again?"

"But why would I? I don't even think he thinks we're friends at this point."

Mikey looks at me strangely. "Do *you* think you're friends?"

My cheeks go warm. "I mean, we were? I don't know. He's my ex. We dated for a few weeks, a million years ago. But I'm with you now. And, Mikey, I really, really like you. I really like us."

And I do. I really like him. I like Mikey's face and his voice and his weird nerdy brain, and there are times when I find him so endearing I almost can't stand it. And we're so good together. We barely fight. Yeah, he's been a little moody about New York, but I know we'll work through that. We always work through stuff. Because we're mature grown-ups in a mature grown-up relationship, and everything's good and chill and solid. And I'm happy.

"I like us, too," Mikey says.

I take his hand again and squeeze it.

Here's the thing. Ben was my big Broadway love story. But I was sixteen. That's just what falling in love at sixteen feels like. Just because it's different now doesn't make it less real.

I study Mikey's face for a moment. "Okay, I want to show you something. I was going to wait to surprise you in New York, but . . ."

I stand, stretch, and quickly tug my shirt down, winning a fleeting smile from Mikey. My messenger bag's propped against the edge of my bookcase, packed and ready. I grab it and bring it back to the bed, unzipping the smaller front pouch.

Mikey watches me curiously.

"Wait for it . . ." I root around until I find a short stack of paper, folded in thirds. Then I pass it straight to Mikey, who hesitates. I nudge him. "Open it."

He does, and then pulls the papers closer to read, his eyes going huge behind his glasses. "Wait, for real?"

"Two weeks from tomorrow. It's the matinee. But the seats are terrible, just so you know."

Mikey stares at me, dumbfounded. "We're seeing *Six*?"

"We're seeing *Six*!"

"Arthur, that's—it's too expensive. You didn't have to do that."

"I wanted to say sorry for ruining our summer—"

"You didn't ruin it."

"I did." I lean my head on his shoulder. "And I wanted to do something special, you know? For us."

"Arthur." His voice sounds choked.

"And it wasn't expensive," I say quickly, lifting my head to meet his eyes. "I mean, it was, but I get a discount. Internship perk."

"Why don't they skip the discount and raise your stipend?"

"Doesn't work like that." I kiss his cheek. "Sorry, you're just going to have to suck it up and see the best show on Broadway with me. And you know what?"

His lips tug up. "What?"

"You were right. I do need a tie. Chad from corporate is going to Broadway." I stand again, scanning the room. "Now I just have to figure out where I packed them."

"Cardboard box by your desk. Label says *Arthur: Fancy.*"

My hands fly to my heart. "You made me a fancy box?"

"I did." He looks at me for a moment, smiling faintly. Then he stands, grabbing his shirt off the floor. "Okay, how about you finish up? I'll go drop off my key and grab us some food on the way back?"

"Mikey Mouse, you're my hero." Even after he leaves, I can't help but smile at the door.

But a moment later, I reach for my phone.

@ben-jamin liked your photo.

Apparently my heart's going for a jailbreak from my rib cage. Over an Instagram notification. It's the most ridiculous thing.

But I tap the notification, and moments later, I'm staring at my official New York announcement post from last week. It's a selfie where I'm holding a postcard of Central Park, the one Ben gave me the last time we saw each other in person. There's even a handwritten Ben-Jamin and Arturo scene on the back. But of course, the only person who would possibly recognize the postcard ignored the post entirely, like he always does.

Liked by **@ben-jamin** and **others.**

Until now. The day before I leave for New York.

CHAPTER THREE

BEN

Sunday, May 17

The best thing about Pa being my boss is that now I get paid when he tells me what to do.

I've been able to put my Duane Reade checks toward what I hope will be my next job—mega-best-selling author of *The Wicked Wizard War*—by buying a writing program to help me keep all my world-building thoughts organized, and purchasing the domain name for the series website. I'm dreaming big here, but Mario has been an excellent hype-man, saying that my series could be the next big thing. It would be epic to have a franchise of movies, and I can write spin-off comics and play video games set in my world. And of course Pa and Ma won't have to work anymore if they don't want to, even though I'd love to boss Pa around at my eventual amusement park.

But until then, Pa hands me a basket of pregnancy tests and condoms. "Here's some more for this aisle."

"Shouldn't condoms go elsewhere? Let's create a Not-Family Planning section."

"By all means, go for it. I'm sure corporate wants all their floor plans restructured by their new manager's nineteen-year-old son."

"Nepotism for the win."

I still can't believe my first official job is working for Pa. I thought it would be something like unboxing shipments at a bookstore. But when Pa told me they were hiring, I applied because I was positive all I'd have to do was stock shelves while listening to music. Nope. It's a lot of memorizing where different items are in the store as quickly as possible because customers hate it when you can't spit out the answer at Google-search speeds. And it turns out that working the cash register stresses me out. One time I didn't give a customer his correct change, and he asked to speak with my boss. I stupidly called my father Pa in front of the customer, who snapped at Pa for not doing a better job at teaching me how to count. I blushed and Pa bit his tongue, and we were both upset for the rest of the shift.

It's pretty clear why I prefer unboxing things in the back room when given the chance. No customers plus bonus time to think about my worlds—real and imaginary.

I pull out my phone.

"No phone while working," Pa says.

"I'm just checking the time. Lo siento."

"Está bien. You meeting with that boy later?"

He's talking about Mario. "Just Dylan," I say.

"It's never 'just' Dylan, even when it's just Dylan. He's a lot."

Pa approves of Dylan way more than he does Mario. He thinks I deserve more commitment, but Mario and I have only been playing around in a romantic space for a little over a month. There's still so much Mario and I haven't talked about. Like his own history with past boyfriends or whether he's even looking for a new relationship. I'm not a fan of Pa judging Mario for not being my official boyfriend.

Pa taps my shoulder. "If I offer you a penny for your thoughts in Spanish, will you understand that yet?"

"No," I say.

"Was that an English 'no' or Spanish 'no'?"

I stare at the condom boxes some more.

Pa snaps his fingers. "Benito, talk to me."

"We're at work."

"I'm your father before I'm your boss. Except when you want to leave early or need an unscheduled day off."

He doesn't understand that this is one of the problems. He's my father and my boss. He might want to have a conversation right now, but I'm pretty burned-out and need to breathe. Everything would've been so different if my family had money like Dylan's so I could've gone away for school. I'm not airing out any of this to Pa while we're wearing our blue Duane Reade vests. Or even at home. I need my space.

"I'm okay," I say.

Pa sighs. "If you say so. Wrap it up with the wrap-it-ups and you can clock out early."

"Thanks."

Pa does his exaggerated cough to get me to speak in Spanish. He's been pushing for more out of me ever since I turned Mario into my personal Duolingo. That's the other reason Pa gets weird about Mario, though he'd never admit it. He had the chance to teach me himself. Now I'm turning to someone else.

"No one needs Spanish lessons to say gracias."

"Every little bit counts."

"Gracias, Pa."

He squeezes my shoulder. "Ese es mi hijo." Static rasps from his walkie-talkie before Alfredo's voice asks for Pa for assistance at the cash register. "Don't forget to say bye before you leave."

"Don't you mean adiós?"

Pa bows slightly in gratitude and heads to the front of the store.

I have this instinct to apologize for closing myself off, but I shouldn't have to. I should get some time to figure out my feelings in peace.

I shelve the condom boxes, thinking about another consequence of still living with my parents. Last month Pa was doing laundry and found a condom sleeve in my jeans pocket. It led to this big conversation where he asked if I was sexually active or not. He was shocked when I told him that I'd had sex with Hudson, Arthur, and Mario. Pa got really fidgety because I don't think any of the articles he read about how to talk to his son about sex could've prepared him for what to say when you find out your nineteen-year-old son has had sex with more people than you. All he could really say was how he was relieved condoms were always involved, and that he would tell Ma for me if I wanted. I didn't mind her knowing, but I still couldn't look either of them in the eye for the rest of the night.

I'm about to turn my attention away from the condoms and to the pregnancy tests when I hear my best friend.

"Aha! I should've known I'd find you here," Dylan says.

"Why's that?"

"Because you must be stocking up for more sex marathons with your boyfriend."

"He's not my boyfriend." And right as Dylan opens his mouth, I add, "And we don't have sex marathons."

"How are you not bumping butts with that perfect

creation every chance you get? I told Samantha that I bet Mario was created in a lab by some horny Dr. Frankenstein, and she did not disagree." Dylan lets out a low whistle.

"Yes, he's beautiful," I say while stacking more pregnancy tests, which unlike the condoms did need restocking; the math here speaks for itself.

"Hot," Dylan says.

"It's more than just sex for us," I say while carrying the extra condoms to the back room.

"I know, Big Ben. I saw you guys together. You're definitely going to be the Luigi to his Mario, just jumping down each other's pipes and"—Dylan stops talking as a customer with a child passes us in the aisle—"just—"

"No need to finish that sentence," I say.

I go into the back room, clock out, and change out of my khaki pants and white polo to jeans and a blue V-neck that reminds me of the shade of nail polish Mario sometimes wears. When I come out from the back, Dylan is reading the blurb of a mass-market romance novel. I pause in front of him, thinking that will get his attention, but he keeps reading, muttering the summary about a schoolteacher and a marine falling for each other.

"Am I gay if I buy this?" Dylan asks.

"What do you think?"

Dylan pauses. "No?"

"Correct."

"Awesome. What's your employee discount? Fifty percent?"

"No."

"Seventy?"

I'm truly shocked we're on line buying this book, but it works out in his favor when Pa calls us up to the cash register he's working.

"Dylan, welcome back," Pa says.

"It's an honor to be welcomed back, Diego." Dylan salutes.

Pa's polite smile reminds me of whenever he's exhausted by customers but has to hide it. He turns to me. "You didn't have to get in line to say bye."

"I didn't."

Dylan steps up to the counter and sets down the romance novel.

"This for Samantha?" Pa asks.

Dylan shakes his head. "Diego, Diego. Surely you're more progressive than that."

"You're the one who asked if buying the book meant you were gay," I say.

"I am the reader of romances," Dylan continues. "This is what makes me so wonderful with the ladies"—he wraps his arm around my shoulders—"and your son."

"It appears college didn't make you any more mature," Pa says.

"Oh, believe me, Diego, I've been plenty mature at college."

The other cashier, Donny, accidentally scans a shampoo bottle multiple times while eavesdropping on Dylan's insanity.

Pa bags up Dylan's book. "Please leave."

"You'll be seeing more of me soon," Dylan says, throwing the bag over his shoulder and walking toward the exit.

"Why did that come off as a threat?" Pa asks.

I shrug. "See you, Pa."

"Te quiero, mijo."

"Love you too, Pa."

Pa coughs.

I sigh. "Te quiero, Pa."

In our family, we always say that we love each other before we leave home, go to bed, hang up the phone. My parents have always made it clear that we might have some economic challenges from time to time, but we'll always be rich in love. And I get it—but if love was cash, I wouldn't want to spend it all in the same place. Maybe I want to invest in a cute guy with the name of a cartoon plumber.

I leave Duane Reade and Dylan is waiting outside for me. The block is always crowded with people because it's right next to a couple subway stops and right across the street from Union Square, where people are playing chess, walking their dogs, reading, and riding skateboards. It's one of my favorite parts of the city—*was* one of my favorite parts of the city. Even Union Square is losing its shine because of how often I see it now. A couple weeks ago, I was meeting up with Mario around here and I unintentionally walked straight into work, making it all the way into the break room before I realized what I was doing. I was on total autopilot because this is my life now.

"What should we do?" I ask.

"You mean without the missus and the mister?" Dylan links his arm with mine and leads me toward the subway.

"He's not my mister," I say.

"Not with that attitude he won't be."

Every day, my feelings for Mario grow. I keep trying to play it down to protect myself after having been burned by guys I loved. First Hudson and I had that massive argument and he kissed some stranger before we could make up. Then Arthur, whose love for me seemed to crash into a wall once he met Mikey, who seemed so much more compatible with him. Now it's my turn to be with someone who is more compatible with me.

"To uptown we go," Dylan says. "I got to pick up some cookies for Samantha's parents' twenty-fourth anniversary."

"That's a strange anniversary to celebrate."

"Text that to Samantha immediately! I said the same thing. It's not twenty, it's not twenty-five. What's their angle, Ben? They just in it for the cookies?"

"What's Samantha doing?" I ask, ignoring the question.

"She's—" Dylan stumbles in front of the MetroCard machine. "She's going to Skype with Patrick." He spits on the ground.

"You could hate on Patrick without spitting every time," I say as we swipe our way onto the platform.

"He leaves a bad taste in my mouth."

"I don't get why you're at war with him."

"He talks about Samantha like he's known her forever."

"D, they grew up together. They *have* known each other forever."

"Forever is a lot longer than nineteen years, Benzo. Do you need more summer school?"

"Do you want to pick up these cookies by yourself?"

"Ooh, feisty. Dylan like."

The train arrives, blasting us with wind and drowning out Dylan's next sexual advance. We hop on, squeezing onto a bench while the train takes us uptown. Dylan catches me up on how great things have been with Samantha. There were some rough patches when they first moved away because, no matter how much they loved each other, they still had to adjust to living together. Samantha had to get used to Dylan being Dylan 98 percent of the time and how to be there for him on those 2 percent days where he was off. And Dylan had to learn how to sit in silence while Samantha was studying and how to give her some space just because.

We get off the train as I tell him about how much I'm hating my non–creative writing classes and how expensive school is in general. Walking through the Upper West Side doesn't help. There's a group of people standing outside a café with shopping bags. I'd bet a dollar that someone there just bought a shirt that costs more than I make in two weeks of work. I would feel like such a fraud walking around any of those stores. Who needs them anyway? I'd much rather pay Mario to customize clothes for me.

"I am parched, my fine Bengentleman," Dylan says in a pretentious accent. "I hope Levain does iced teas or perhaps a crisp seltzer water."

It takes a second for the name to sink in. At first I think it might be some character from a fantasy novel. Then I stop above a sewer grate, feeling like I'm going to melt through it as I realize where we're going. "Levain Bakery?"

"See, you are smart. I take back the summer school comment."

"That's where—" I feel like I'm being thrust back in time, two summers ago. "That's an Arthur spot."

"And?"

"And I'm sure he's going to be in there with his boyfriend, buying cookies and—"

"And you'll be with me!"

"But you're not my boyfriend."

"Whose fault is that, Mr. Hard-to-Get?"

I take a deep breath as we approach the bakery. There are millions of people in New York and billions of things to do, and I'm still nervous I'm about to bump into Arthur. He's always been an absolute believer in the universe pushing people together, whereas I had more doubts about destiny and shit like that. If we step into Levain and find Arthur, I'll change my tune about the universe. I'll become a total believer, but I draw the line at knocking on doors and sharing the good word.

We get on line, which is trailing out the door. I tiptoe and peek ahead to see if I spot Arthur. I don't, but I'm not ruling out that he's here. He might be too short to notice.

"It's not the end of the world if you bump into him," Dylan says, eyeing me. "You love him."

My chest tightens. "What? No I don't."

"Whoa, Mr. Defensive. I'm not saying you're *in* love with him, but I am saying you love that little firecracker. In the right way that doesn't have you cheating on your boyfriend."

"Mario isn't my boyfriend." My feelings about Arthur would feel simpler if Mario were though. "You know how exes get so competitive, right?"

"Uh, yes. Harriett literally told me that she was more important because she had tens of thousands more Instagram followers than I do. Is it too late for me to text her that one Samantha is worth a million Harrietts?"

I glare at him.

"Way too late," Dylan says. "Back to your thing. Why is he Public Enemy Number One?"

"He's not my enemy, but it sucks how much it feels like Arthur is winning everything. Great college, a boyfriend, a cool summer job in New York. What do I have?"

"Your sexy best friend."

"That's not new."

"My man bun is, and I don't believe you're giving it the love it deserves."

"I don't know, D. Sometimes I feel like my life is moving so slowly that it's like it's not moving at all."

"Like this line." Dylan peeks ahead. "How long does it take to choose a cookie, people?"

"Thank you for your undivided attention."

"Say what now?" Dylan winks. "The war between exes is a complex one, but do not forget that Arthur would burst into flame like a vampire hit by the sun if he took one look at your boyfriend."

"Not. My. Boyfriend."

The comparison game about appearances is stupid. I'm into Mario for different reasons than I was into Arthur. Not better ones. Nothing was instant with either of them. I wondered about Arthur a few times after first meeting him at the post office, but I wasn't putting up his face in coffee shops. And I clocked pretty quickly that Mario was really cute, but it still took months and a whole writing assignment to get closer.

One day I hope I don't have to work so hard for something to feel easy.

I'm sure Arthur and Mikey got it good. Sometimes I think about them singing show tunes together and how Arthur doesn't have to introduce Broadway hits like *Hamilton* to someone like Mikey so they're free to talk about more obscure off-Broadway shows. Stuff for the real theater fans, not ones like me who listen to a cast album because a cute boy wanted me to while he read my manuscript. That experience with Arthur was really special and intimate. It's upsetting how that's nothing but a moment in time; I'm nothing but a blip for him. I liked his Instagram post and he still didn't bother reaching out to let me know that he's in New York. Really, that's how I find out he's in New York? *Instagram?*

It's fine.

I'm going to stop obsessing about the past.

I'm going to keep my eyes on my own paper.

On my own life.

Like how tomorrow I get to spend time with Mario. I'm going to help him with some errands before we hang out at my place. Watch a movie, work on some Spanish, maybe even more. I totally see how this looks like a date to most outsiders. But it's different with Mario. Everything is different with Mario.

Sometimes I feel like we're a clock with one hand stuck on eleven, never quite meeting in the middle at twelve.

I hope we'll find our time.

We finally get into Levain Bakery, where the smell of freshly baked cookies is powerful. Dylan informs the cashier that he's here to pick up an order, but of course we can't leave without treating ourselves, too. I get oatmeal raisin and Dylan gets dark chocolate peanut butter. He holds up the cookie like a fist to the sky.

"You could beat someone to death with this," he says.

"No you can't," the cashier says.

Dylan stares at her suspiciously, taking a step back. "I hope you have a great and cheery day." He carries his box and heads for the door, whispering, "She's definitely tried killing someone with a cookie, Ben. Do we report this?"

"What do you think?"

". . . No?"

I hold open the door and the universe takes a swing. It's not the punch I was expecting, but that might be a few breaths away.

Arthur's best friend, Jessie, is standing outside. She seems just as surprised to see me.

"Ben! Oh my God, hi!" Jessie hugs me, and once again, it's like I'm being sucked back in time. She hugs Dylan next.

"You guys! It's like a reunion special."

"Can it be one of those reunions where there's a catfight?" Dylan rubs his palms together. "Where's Arthur? Bring him out, let's get this Battle of the Exes started. Ben, I love you, but my money is on Arthur. There's something scrappy about him."

Jessie laughs and rolls her eyes. "Arthur is still unpacking at the apartment. I'm on cookie duty. Do you guys remember that night at Milton's? Feels like ages ago."

It does and it doesn't.

It was Arthur's birthday at his uncle's apartment: we split a Levain cookie; I got to know Jessie and Arthur's other best friend from home, Ethan; Dylan and Samantha came through with a *Hamilton*-themed cake; Arthur's coworkers Namrata and Juliet surprised him; and at the end of the night, Arthur and I cuddled up in bed while he read the *TWWW* chapter where I first introduce King Arturo.

I remember all that joy like it was yesterday.

"So much fun" is all I say.

"I'm surprised we didn't get in trouble that night," Jessie says. "Arthur's parents didn't come this time, so we can have more house parties."

"Count me in," Dylan says.

Jessie grins. "Arthur is going to be so jealous I bumped into you both."

"Wish him luck from me on his New York do-over," I say.

"And let him know I miss his raw sexual energy," Dylan says.

Jessie laughs. "I should get in and get out."

"Smart," Dylan says. "I think the cashier might be a murderer."

Jessie's laugh seems forced this time. "I'm in awe of Samantha for putting up with you. Girl's got stamina."

"Oh, you don't even know—"

I drag Dylan away. "Bye, Jessie. Have fun this summer."

Dylan almost drops the box. "What's the rush?"

"Because that whole thing was weird for me, D. You should know that."

"It's not like it was Arthur."

"No, but it's going to get back to him. How do you think that looks? I like his Instagram post yesterday and today I'm hanging around a bakery in his neighborhood. He's going to think I'm trying to get his attention. I don't want any weirdness, especially since he has a boyfriend." I hold up a finger. "If you tell me that I have a boyfriend, too, I'm going to beat you to death with your cookie."

"It won't work," Dylan sings.

I head back toward the train station, wishing that whole experience hadn't shaken me so much. I want to be happy for Arthur, but it's hard when I feel like he wasn't even ultimately happy with me. I was just someone to entertain him until he found someone who fit better. But that's okay.

I have someone who fits better with my life, too.

Instead of worrying about bumping into my past, I'm going to keep building my future.

CHAPTER FOUR

ARTHUR

Sunday, May 17

Arthur Seuss: fallen hero. Conquered warrior. Lost the last shred of his dignity at the hands of a fitted fucking sheet.

I sprawl back on Uncle Milton's bare mattress, breathing like I've just run a marathon. This is like the time I tried to squeeze into my bar mitzvah blazer last year because Ben couldn't believe I'd worn pinstripes. Did I get a cute selfie out of it? Sure. But I basically had to birth myself out of it afterward. And at least then I could sort of get the second sleeve on without the first one popping off, which is more than I can say for this shitshow of a bed.

I need Jessie. Of course she left for a "quick takeout run" an hour ago, which is enough time to confirm what I've always suspected: I'm *laughably* unequipped to live alone.

But I guess the universe knew that all along, because Jessie's summer housing fell through the exact same day I accepted Jacob's offer. Fast-forward a week, and here we are: Manhattan roommates. Glamorous legal adults doing glamorous legal things in the city that never sleeps.

Okay, so far it's mostly been a lot of putting socks away and looking for wall outlets and breathing heavily on my bare mattress for completely nonsexual reasons.

But it's almost glamorous. It *will* be glamorous. I just need to do one quick panic selfie for Jessie where I'm bundled into the sheet like it's a full-body shower cap. Death by linens 😱 SOS

She writes back instantly.😁 It's probably turned the wrong way, check and see if it has one of those top or bottom labels.

My bedsheet has its own grindr profile now??

But sure enough, sliding my fingers along the inside seam yields a full set of satin tags: *Top or Bottom* and *Side.* Guess which genius had it flipped around for half an hour.

Ten minutes later, my room looks like it sprang out of one of Mom's *Real Simple* magazines—more than worthy of the triumphant Mission Accomplished photo I'm about to snap for Jessie. But as soon as I pick up my phone, it starts buzzing with a FaceTime request.

Mikey. I press accept, smiling at his awkwardly close-up face on my screen. You'd think a boy who inherited his brother's old smartphone at age eight would know how to operate a selfie camera by now. But even Bubbe is better at video chatting than Mikey. It's pretty fucking adorable, actually.

"Check it out. Good bed, right?" I flip the camera to show off my handiwork. "Only thing missing is you, naked—"

Mikey clears his throat loudly and scoots backward, cheeks flaming. A second later, his niece, Mia, pokes her head into the frame.

"Neigh, kid!" I flip back to selfie mode, grinning frantically into the camera. "Look! Hi, Mr. Horsie!" I tilt my phone upward, catching the giant horse painting centered above Uncle Milton's headboard. "Hiiiiii, Mia!" I add in this fucked up quasi-British horse voice.

Mikey looks amused. Also, vaguely alarmed.

"Hi, Author," says Mia. Mikey murmurs something into her ear, and she looks back up at me. "Arrrrrrthurrrrrr," she adds, enunciating her *r*'s like a pirate and earning a fist bump from Uncle Mikey.

He's so good with her. When I met Mia in person on New Year's, she was too shy to speak to me. But Mikey never pressured her—he just held her and let her bury her face in his shirt while we talked. It made me melt. I couldn't stop staring at him all night, couldn't stop thinking about kissing him, even in front of his family.

It's strange knowing I could be with them in Boston

right now, living out this domestic-fantasy summer with my unbearably sweet boyfriend. If I think too hard about it, it aches a little. Maybe more than a little.

I swallow it back. "Mia! How old are you now?"

She mutters something shyly, too soft for me to hear.

"Sixteen?" I ask.

She giggles. "No!"

"Seventeen?"

"No!" Mia looks incredulously at Mikey before turning back to me. Mikey holds up four fingers behind her back.

"Okay, okay," I say. "Hmm. Are you . . . four?"

"And a half!"

Mikey makes an *oops* face and shrugs.

"Of course!" I smack my forehead. "Wow. I miss you. How are you guys?"

Mikey pauses. "We're . . . okay."

"Just okay?"

"Mimi, want to go find your dad?"

"No," she says promptly. No bullshit, just a rock-solid *nope*. Because Mia McCowan Chen is an icon.

"Go find Daddy," says Mikey. Mia scowls and disappears from the frame.

"What's up? Did something happen at dinner?" I try to remember if anything was off about Mikey's texts last night. It's hard to tell with him—no matter how good I get at reading his face, he's still so mysterious in writing. I meant to FaceTime him last night from Bubbe's house, but Bubbe always makes such a big scene about dinner, and then Jessie got in from Providence and we stayed up half the night talking in my mom's childhood bedroom.

"Dinner was fine." Mikey rubs the bridge of his nose. "We found out this morning—my brother eloped."

"Robert did what?" My jaw drops.

"And he told my parents via text message."

"He did *not*."

"He did!"

"Nope. That's too much, even for Robbie."

Mikey cracks the tiniest smile. He gets the biggest kick out of my iron-jaw memory for random personal details. I can tell you Ethan's top five most cursed insects, Ben's ex-boyfriend's zodiac sign, you name it. I may not be able to get through a page of a book without having to reread every third paragraph, but at least I remember my second-grade teacher's husband's name. It's my vaguely creepy superpower. But I'm starting to think it's not such a bad skill to have. Mostly because my boyfriend's big, loud, tight-knit family is his whole entire world, and I could basically write a book about every single one of them.

"My parents are freaking out," Mikey says. "Laura's been over there since ten, and apparently Mom hasn't stopped crying. It's a mess."

"I thought your parents liked Amanda!"

"They do—"

"He didn't run off with some other girl, right? Or guy?" I gasp. "Did Robert marry a guy? That is—oh my God, that is the most epic way to come out. Why didn't I think of it?"

"He's straight," Mikey says. "I mean, as far as I know. And everyone loves Amanda. They're just upset about the elopement."

"Is Amanda pregnant?"

Mikey shakes his head. "No, it's just the whole wedding thing is really important to my parents, you know? They went all out for Laura and Josh—invited basically everyone they'd ever made eye contact with." He pauses. "Which is probably why Robbie and Amanda bowed out."

"Probably. Wow." I shrug. "At least it's kind of romantic. An elopement!"

"Well, Laura thinks they actually did it because of health insurance. Amanda just turned twenty-six—"

"Right. And she's working freelance now. That makes total sense."

"Literally how do you remember this stuff?" Mikey smiles for real. "You know you don't have to keep tabs on my brother's girlfriend's job details, right?"

"Brother's wife. She's your sister-in-law now."

Mikey looks momentarily taken aback. "Yeah."

"So, not even a tiny wedding, huh?" I lean onto my

pillows, holding the phone aloft. "No first kiss, no cake? Nothing?"

"They can still kiss and eat cake."

"True. But. I don't know. Aren't you a little sad you don't get to watch Robbie's face when Amanda walks in? That's what I'd do—"

"I know," Mikey says. "You sent me that BuzzFeed list four times."

"And I'm going to *keep* sending you grooms blown away by their beautiful brides until you actually start appreciating them."

"Is that a threat?" He wrinkles his nose and smiles, one of my all-time favorite Mikey expressions. But a moment later, his face falls. "I can't believe there's already family drama. I've been home less than twenty-four hours."

"Well, if you ever need an escape from the drama, I'm here."

Mikey just looks at me.

"Okay, fair enough. But if you want *different* drama . . ."

The front door of the apartment thuds shut.

I glance up. "Jessie's back!"

A moment later, she's in my doorway, holding a giant double-chocolate cookie in one hand and a white paper bakery bag in the other. "Arthur, you will *not* believe who I just saw at Levain Bakery." She scoots in beside me, eyes landing on the screen of my phone. "Oh! Hi, Mikey."

"How's it going?" He shoots her a stilted half wave.

"Good, good."

I smile back and forth between them. God, I love awkward people. I think I collect them.

Jessie hands me the bag, and I inhale happily. "This smells. So good."

She pats my shoulder. "You're welcome."

"So who'd you run into?"

"Right." She nods quickly. "Namrata."

"At Levain? No way! I thought she was living downtown these days."

"Who's Namrata?" asks Mikey.

"She was one of the summer associates at the law firm when I worked there. But she's a real associate now. Wow, Jess, what are the odds of you running into her the day before you start work?" I shake my head, smiling. "Way to go, Universe!"

"Anyway, I'm gonna go eat this." Jessie jumps up. "Cookie lunch?"

"Cookie lunch." I turn back to Mikey. "I should probably go, too."

"Warm cookie. I get it," he says.

I smile. "Keep me posted on your parents and Robert?"

"Deal." Mikey pauses. "I miss you."

"Miss you too, Mikey Mouse."

I hang up and head out to the living room, where Jessie's

settled in at the dining table with her cookie and two glasses of milk.

"I fucking love you, Jessie Franklin," I say.

She smiles up at me. "You didn't tell me I'd need a spoon for this cookie."

"A spoon? Toughen up." I plop into the chair beside her and bite into my cookie like a hamburger. It's so warm and gooey and rich. So New York. And here I've been living off Usdan Marketplace dining hall cookies for a year. "You have no idea how much I needed this."

"Had a feeling."

"I can't believe you saw Namrata. How's she doing?"

"No clue." Jessie shrugs. "I didn't see her."

"Wait—"

"I saw Ben," she says plainly.

The whole world grinds to a halt.

"Ben . . . like *Ben*? Alejo?"

Jessie takes a bite of cookie and nods.

"But you said—"

"Yup."

"So why didn't you . . . ?" But Jessie looks pointedly at my phone, and my cheeks flood with heat. "Oh."

Jessie pauses. "So how's Mikey?"

"Great! I mean, he's fine." My head feels foggy. "Why was Ben at Levain Bakery?"

"Getting cookies?" Jessie says. "So weird, right? He was

with Dylan. It honestly took me a second to place them. Did you know Dylan has a man bun?"

"Did Ben look different?" I squint, trying to remember the last time I saw a selfie of him. He usually posts pictures of buildings and graffiti and boring stuff, like pigeons. I guess he still hasn't figured out that his face is the best view in New York.

Nope, nope, nope. Delete that thought.

"Nah, he looked the same. I think I just wasn't expecting to see them. Dylan says he misses your raw sexual energy."

"I miss him, too!"

I don't think I've talked to Dylan in a year, maybe more. But I knew about the man bun because I still follow him online—he and Samantha are definitely my favorite Instagram couple. Last week, Dylan posted about a fort they made in Samantha's dorm room—basically just a blanket spread across two stacked piles of cardboard packing boxes. But they'd pushed Samantha's bed underneath so they could spend their last night of school under a canopy, and if that isn't peak romance, I don't know what is. Of course, I spent the whole week thinking about how I'd replicate it with Mikey on *our* last night—I even bought glow-in-the-dark stars from the toy store on Main Street so we could pretend we were sleeping outdoors.

But in the end, I never even mentioned it to Mikey,

even though I'm sure he would have humored me and gone along with it. I guess I just kept picturing him looking at me with a wait-why-are-we-doing-this face. Or asking if it was really worth the extra cleanup we'd have to do in the morning. Talk about the ultimate self-answering question. If your boyfriend asks whether your romantic gesture is worth doing, it's not worth doing.

I don't know, maybe Mikey would have been super into the whole fort idea. He's not the type for spontaneous romantic inspiration, but he's pretty persuadable, especially when there's no PDA involved. And he likes to make me happy. He *does* make me happy. And so what if dating Mikey isn't exactly one big surprise party. Love doesn't have to be like that. It doesn't have to be showy or maudlin or larger than life. Love can be a pile of folded laundry and a full tank of gas, or your steady, sweet boyfriend spending an extra night at school to help you pack up your dorm room. Anyway, not every single relationship is going to be—

"Ben Alejo," says Jessie, and I almost knock over my milk. "On day one. How random is that?"

"Totally. Totally random," I say, nodding. Okay, wow. Now my head's spinning. Windmill brain, dreidel brain, *giant fucking tornado* brain. Because yesterday, Ben liked my post about moving to New York. And suddenly he's hanging out at Levain Bakery, in my neighborhood, *on my moving day*? Talk about a neon sign from the universe. Unless—

"Did Ben say anything?"

Jessie tilts her head. "Anything?"

"About me." My cheeks go warm. "I don't know. I was just wondering—I don't even know if he knows I'm here."

"Oh, definitely. He called it your New York do-over."

My lungs stop working. I open my mouth and then shut it.

Jessie raises her eyebrows. "You okay?"

"What? Yeah, of course. I'm just . . ." I pause. "Do you think I should text him?"

"Absolutely not."

"Because of Mikey?"

"Yes! Art, come on—"

"Oh my God." I laugh. "I'm not talking about a booty call. I'm talking about a friendly, platonic 'hey, what's up, we haven't talked in a sec—'"

"Not a good idea."

"Why not?"

"Arthur, two seconds ago we had to *lie* about me running into Ben—"

"We?" I look at her incredulously. "That was you!"

"Yeah, because how many times have you told me Mikey gets weird when you talk about your New York summer?"

"You think I don't talk about that summer with Mikey?"

"You literally just had to explain to him who Namrata is."

"Okay, not sure why my boyfriend needs to know every coworker from two years ago."

"I'm just saying, Mikey's clearly already sensitive about Ben. Why would you want to add that to the mix right now?"

I shake my head. "You're overthinking this. I'm not trying to hook up with him! I just want to say hi, okay? I'm in his city! He was one of my best friends—"

"He's your ex," Jessie says.

"*And* my friend! Those aren't mutually exclusive concepts." I shove another bite of cookie into my mouth, chewing it roughly. "Just because"—I swallow—"you don't talk to Ethan—"

"This has nothing to do with me and Ethan." She stands abruptly, pressing both hands to her stomach. "Wow, this cookie is dense."

I nod vaguely, but my brain's already miles away. Jessie running into Ben has to be some kind of sign from the universe, right? That's not a thing that happens in New York. Not without celestial intervention. Am I supposed to just ignore that?

Mikey would understand. I'm not saying he'd be thrilled at first, but he trusts me. As he should. Because as far as personal lines in the sand go, cheating on my boyfriend is up there with voting Republican and murder. Plus Mikey did say I should see Ben if I want to see him. Which isn't to say I, you know, *want to see Ben.* I just mean it doesn't have to be a big deal. Honestly, *not* texting Ben would be weirder because then I'm actively avoiding him, thus *proving* I still have feelings for him. And I don't. Have feelings for Ben.

So why shouldn't I text him?

What if I just . . . did?

CHAPTER FIVE

BEN

Monday, May 18

I was the reigning champion for Most Likely to Arrive Late until Mario came along.

I check my phone, clocking him at twenty minutes late. So far. I'm not trying to be that guy who nags him about being on time. Hudson definitely wasn't a fan of my chronic lateness while we were dating, and Arthur took it even more personally. But Mario and I aren't dating, so I shouldn't even be putting him in the same sentences with those two. Mario is a friend who I like—actually *like*—and I can't act like he's my boyfriend until he becomes mine.

If he even wants to.

The thing is, everything we're doing today is for him, and now it's going to derail our entire evening. I've tried calling him a couple times, but no answer. It's not even going straight to voice mail, which would at least probably mean he's on the subway.

I call again because I feel like an idiot waiting around like this.

"Lo sé, lo sé, lo siento," Mario says, out of breath. "I swear I'm like fifteen minutes away . . . twenty tops."

"Twenty minutes? What happened?"

"I had to stop my brothers from killing each other over our PlayStation, but I'm in a Lyft now making up for lost time! I packed up my uncle's stuff and I'll mail it at that post office on Lexington. Then I can go straight to the barber from there before Francisco cancels the appointment."

"Yeah, we can't have you walking around without a haircut."

"I cannot rock a man bun like Dylan."

I'm sure Mario could pull off any look. "All right, but the later you are, the later we're going to be to our movie."

"It's on Netflix," Mario says.

"Yeah, but my parents are going to be home by eight. So it'll be all Netflix. No chill."

"Or maybe no Netflix and all chill," Mario whispers, like he doesn't want the driver to hear.

I've got to cut this conversation short because I can't walk around like this. "Ándale, Colón."

"Lo tienes, Alejo. Meet me at the post office."

I pull up the directions on my phone and make my way over. My entire life in New York and I still don't know the city like other veterans. It's not like I'm going anywhere, so I have all the time in the world to master the grid. Though I wouldn't have to worry about this at all with Mario at my side. He's like my personal GPS, and we always joke about how I wouldn't stand a chance in any apocalypse. I guess we'll have to see how I do after he leaves for his trip to Los Angeles this weekend.

Mario's uncle moved to LA a few years ago and started a production company. Close Call Entertainment focuses on jump-scare horrors, creepy science fictions, end-of-the-world thrillers. Mario's favorite genre has always been suspense—maybe I should read between the lines there—and I know he's looking forward to spending some more time with his uncle, who has always felt like a second father to him, and is eager to show Mario the ropes on the TV side of things.

I turn the corner and time seems to slow down when I see the building ahead.

This is the post office where I first met Arthur.

I'm being catapulted to memory lane at a time when I'm trying to go down new paths. But Mario mapped out all these destinations—the actual ones, not my metaphorical ones. Of all the post offices in this borough alone, I can't believe he randomly decided on this one. And it's unbelievable how much the universe seems determined to make New York feel even more suffocating to me.

I stand outside, heart hammering like the post office is a haunted house. But after a minute or so, the heat gets to me.

The Ben who steps inside doesn't even feel like me. It's a Third-Person Ben who walked in here two summers ago with a breakup box and met the person who would become his next boyfriend. It's like I can see Past Ben walking through the post office with Past Arthur right behind him, fresh off a conversation about twins in romper outfits they saw before entering the building. Then Past Arthur calls Past Ben's box a "big package" and Past Ben notices Past Arthur's hot dog tie. And they talk about the universe until a flash mob splits them up.

Fast-forward to almost two years later and I'm me, standing alone in the post office waiting for a different boy. It must've been a lot easier for Arthur to get over me. He got to return home to Georgia and then go to school in Connecticut, two places I've never been. Meanwhile I had to act like I didn't see Arthur-sized footprints all over the city we walked around together. I can't tell you how many times over the past few months I specifically avoided Dave & Buster's in Times Square. I'm never in the mood for the tourists swarming Madame Tussauds and McDonald's, but that arcade is where Arthur and I had our first of many first dates.

I don't regret those dates. But I don't always like thinking about them.

It's not lost on me why I'm having trouble trusting people. For all I know, Mario is guarding his feelings, too. And if he laid everything out on the table, I still might not know how to feel. Arthur was a bighearted open book that didn't have a happy ending. Just because someone says they love you doesn't mean they'll never say it to someone else. Between me and Arthur, I should've understood that better than anyone as the one with more dating experience.

It's okay.

I'm working on my own character development. I didn't rush into a relationship, or even try to force my way back to Hudson just because he was familiar and I was lonely. I lived in my loneliness and I got uncomfortable, and now I have to make sure I don't let my character building go to waste because I'm too needy with Mario.

I don't want to lose sleep over a broken heart ever again.

I go wait by the counter with all the mailing slips, right under the air conditioner. I grab the pen that's chained up with a rubber band like it committed some crime, and begin drawing on the back of someone's abandoned receipt. I've been dreaming more and more lately about what the book cover for *The Wicked Wizard War* will look like. Samantha's drawing from a couple years ago was great for Wattpad, but I don't think it's going to fit the book anymore. Last

Monday I spent the afternoon at the Strand bookstore with Mario, and we studied different cover art and discovered we have complete opposite tastes. We played a game where we randomly selected ten books, took notes on our phone apps on whether we liked the cover or not, and there wasn't a single one we agreed on. I honestly don't know if I wanted different results because it just got funnier and funnier the more we disagreed.

This is something I really like about us—we can have different tastes and still be interested in each other.

My phone vibrates. It's either Mario with an update or Dylan sending another random TikTok of people popping their pimples.

But it's neither.

It's Arthur.

I legit spin around like I'm going to find him inside the post office.

This is his first text since April, when he wished me happy birthday. The first text since he arrived in New York.

Hey, heard you ran into Jessie 🙂

It's a brief message, which bothers me. I want more. It seriously took him a whole day to text that? Was he having some major cookie hangover with Mikey?

Maybe they were chilling. Let's call it what it is—maybe Arthur and Mikey were having sex. Picturing your ex with someone else is really hard. It's one of those things you don't want to think about, but the thoughts don't care what you want. It's especially hard to not think about those things when you're writing a book with a character inspired by that person.

There's a chance to make things right for never texting Arthur back after he wished me happy birthday. I wish he would've told me himself that he was coming to New York, but maybe he was taking the hint when I never got back to him. But he's reaching out now, so it's my turn.

I take a picture of the post office and send Arthur two texts.

Happy, Universe?

CHAPTER SIX

ARTHUR

Monday, May 18

Jessie steps out of the dressing room in a herringbone suit made for someone half a foot taller. "Cool, I look like three kids in a trench coat," she says.

I laugh. "You do not."

She eyes me skeptically.

"First of all, it's a blazer, not a trench coat."

Jessie puffs her cheeks out and exhales noisily, and I instantly feel the pain of a thousand suburban-mall boyfriends. "What do I do? I can't show up at a law firm like this."

"You know you don't actually have to wear suits, right? Just go business casual."

She looks despairingly into the mirror. "What does that even mean?"

"Business casual? I don't know, like, a blouse or a button-up. Something like that. Just dress like Meghan Markle in *Suits*."

"So you're saying I *do* need a suit?" Jessie looks bewildered.

"No—yeah, no, that's just what the show's called. Meghan's solidly business casual. You know what? Let me just pull up my Meghan board—"

"Why do you have a Meghan Markle Pinterest board?"

"Because she's my birthday twin. You know that." I stand, grabbing my phone from my back pocket. But I stop dead in my tracks the moment I see the screen.

Two notifications. Two texts. Texts from—

"Jess." My voice comes out choked. "Ben wrote back."

Jessie yanks my phone from my hands. "You texted him? When?"

"When you were in the dressing room. It's not a *thing*."

"Are you going to tell Mikey?" she asks.

"Already did."

"You told Mikey you texted Ben?"

"Yes! Go check if you want."

Jessie narrows her eyes, like she's looking for the catch.

"It's fine! Why do you have literally no faith in my relationship?"

"What?" She pauses, startled. "Not true. I just think you should be careful. I don't want you to do something you'll regret."

"Jessie, I'm not going to cheat. That's so *completely* not—"

"I know! But, Arthur, cheating's not the only thing that can strain a relationship, okay? Here." She hands my phone back. "Just take it. But use it responsibly, okay?"

"So I should delete the nuclear codes from my Notes app?"

"Just don't blow up your relationship with Mikey. I kind of like him."

I smile. "I do, too."

Now I'm thinking about how Mikey surprised me this morning with a video of him and Mia singing "New York State of Mind"—hands down the cutest thing that's ever happened in the history of music. I played it for Jessie over breakfast, and half a croissant fell out of her mouth when Mikey hit the A4 in the second verse. It was the first time she'd ever heard his singing voice outside of group vocals. Mikey's just always been really shy about solos. But fucking look at him now. I haven't been this proud of anyone since—well, since Bennace the Menace uploaded his final chapter to Wattpad.

Ben.

The minute Jessie steps back into the dressing room, I tap into my messages.

Definitely a sign from the universe! And speaking of the 🪐, guess where I am at this very moment

Ben's second text is a photo. And my brain completely derails.

"Holy shit."

"Uh-oh. What?" Jessie peeks her head out the side of the dressing room curtain.

"Ben's at the post office."

"Okay."

"Jessie, the *post office.* It's—"

"It's where you met. I'm familiar with the legend."

"No, I mean it's two blocks away. Ben Alejo is *two blocks away.*"

Jessie's eyes flare wide. "Oh."

I press my phone to my chest, only half aware I'm doing it. My heart's pounding so hard, I swear it might crack the screen.

"Should we go say hi?"

"You mean should we ambush your ex-boyfriend?"

"It's not an ambush!" I laugh, but it comes out breathless. "I just think it would be cool to see him. It's been two years—"

"So make actual plans with him, like a normal person."

But I'm shaking my head before she even stops talking. "You don't get how Ben and I work. Jess, this is the universe at play. Ben said so himself!"

"Yeah, but—"

"And it's not an *ambush*. It's a surprise!"

I mean, when Dylan was in the hospital, I tore through half of Manhattan to be there. And Ben was pretty fucking fine with that ambush. I don't think I'll ever forget the look on his face when he saw me in the waiting room.

Jessie purses her lips. "Arthur, I—"

"Okay, you know who you sound like?"

"Who?"

"You sound like you before New Year's! *Arthur, you're doing what? You're flying where? Can't you just talk to him when you're back at school?*"

"Well, I'm glad it worked out that time!" Jessie says. "But you can't pretend it wasn't risky. Showing up at Mikey's parents' house? What if they'd taken a weekend trip somewhere?"

"It was a Tuesday—"

"That's not the point. Just because last time you got lucky—"

"Lucky?" I scoff. "Give me a little credit, please. That was an A-plus grand gesture!"

"So maybe let's *not* make a grand gesture for your ex-boyfriend."

"Jessie!" I press my forehead. "You want me to have a chaperone? Come with me!"

"I didn't say you needed a chaperone." Jessie grips the dressing room curtain, staring me down for what feels like an hour. Then she sighs. "Okay, look. Go to the post office. I've got a few more things here to try on, and then I'll go see what other stores are on this block. Just text me when you're heading back this way, okay?"

"You don't have to do that. I can wait for you—"

"Arthur. Go!"

"But—"

"Now. Or you're going to miss him."

"Right. Okay." I nod quickly and exhale.

And with that, I'm off and running. I know the way there by heart.

Everything about this place is just like I remembered: white stone, green trim, and the words *UNITED STATES POST OFFICE* in raised capital letters. And those glass double doors—I'm half convinced walking through them will transport me right back to that summer. Back to being sixteen, in my ridiculous tie, dumbstruck by this boy and his *face* and his big cardboard box.

Meeting Ben made the rows of PO boxes look like gold bricks. The fluorescent lights became sunshine. Ben just had this way of making the whole world feel zoomed in. I didn't even learn his name that day, didn't get his number, had no clue where to find him. Still, it felt like New York had finally cracked itself open for me.

It's funny to look back on it now, knowing everything

that came next. I feel like a time traveler, popping in from the future.

Of course, my heart's flat-out decided I'm sixteen again. It's beating so fast, I can hear it. Now that I'm here, I can barely wrap my head around this. *Ben.* My legs feel weak and loose, almost spindly. My fingers find the door handle, and suddenly I'm drifting down the ramp toward the lobby.

Toward Ben. For the first time in almost two years.

Everything's so scrambled and strange. I didn't know I could still *feel* like this.

And then I see him leaning against a self-service kiosk, empty-handed and aimless. No boxes, no packing slips, not even a book of stamps. But he looks perfectly at home. I guess he kind of always does. His hair's grown out a little, and his royal-blue pants are bolder than anything I've ever seen him in. But mostly I'm just mesmerized by his profile and the way his hair curls up around his ears. Things I knew but forgot. Funny how time always blurs out the details.

He turns toward me and visibly starts. "Arthur?"

My heart jumps into my throat. "Sorry. I'm—I was just. When you texted, we were—I was right there. Two blocks away. Sorry." I wave my hands uselessly. "How are you?"

Ben laughs. "I'm good. Holy shit. Arthur."

And the next thing I know, he's hugging me and I'm hugging him back, and it's as familiar as breathing. The way he smells, the way the toes of our sneakers touch, the way

I fit beneath his chin. Maybe these last two years were all a dream. Maybe I've been here in Ben's arms this whole time. Maybe I never left.

I feel like bursting into tears. I feel like—

Mikey. I have a Mikey. So I can't—I can't feel this. And I don't. Because there's no *this* to feel. And my brain already knows that. Just need my lungs to catch up.

Ben disentangles and studies my face, and I stare back. I can't help it. "I *missed* you," I blurt.

Ben hugs me again. "Me too. Sorry I haven't been—"

"No, it's my fault," I say. "I was kind of wrapped up in stuff. School, you know."

"And Mikey! How are things going with that?"

Wow, okay. Jumping right in with the boyfriend stuff. But that's great! Just a couple of old friends discussing our love lives. Maybe this time we can even skip the part where we ghost each other for three months.

Ben looks at me expectantly, and my cheeks go warm. "Yes! Mikey! He's good."

I can't decide if Ben's freckles have multiplied. Maybe I've just gotten used to only seeing the ones that show up in pictures.

"That's really great."

"How are you? How's school?"

"Fine. I mean, I'm writing a lot. Not, like, for school. Just wizard stuff." He waves his hands dismissively.

"Just wizard stuff? You know you're talking to someone who's read *The Wicked Wizard War* three times, right?"

"Aww. Really?"

"Ben, I've literally read other people's *Wizard War* fanfiction."

"I have . . . fanfiction?"

"You most certainly do." I blush, remembering a story I discovered last fall about Ben-Jamin and King Arturo getting locked in a dungeon together. Not so heavy on the plot, but the prose was *very* descriptive.

I clear my throat, ignoring the heat in my cheeks. "So why'd you take *The Wicked Wizard War* off Wattpad?"

"Oh. I mean, I'm revising it. Adding a few things," he says vaguely.

"Let me know if you need someone to look at your new stuff!"

Wow, I love how cool I'm playing it. Love how I'm not being an obvious fucking fanboy for my ex-boyfriend. Hey, maybe I'll be the world's first person to enter into a parasocial relationship with someone I've literally had sex with.

"Thanks, that means a lot. Seriously." He studies me for a moment, smiling. "Oh! Wait, you won't believe who I ran into in Central Park—"

"Please tell me it was the twins."

"No!" He laughs. "Wow, good guess. But no. So I'm hanging out with—friends, and we stumble upon this wedding, right? And when I get closer, I realize, no joke, it's the couple from the flash mob proposal."

"Shut up."

"Dead serious." He rubs his cheek, grinning. "I was like, how do I know them, how do I know them—oh SHIT."

"The universe! When was this?"

"Saturday! Just happened. I actually caught a video—I've been meaning to text it to you."

Ben steps back toward the self-service kiosk to let a Black woman wearing a Baby Bjorn walk by, and I drift along beside him, a light flickering on in my brain. *Saturday.* That's the day Ben liked my photo.

Nostalgia, I guess?

Maybe it was just the universe reminding him I existed.

I study his face. Now he's talking about how the bridesmaids wore pants and how Dylan had Opinions about the street vendor coffee, and I keep nodding along, but my brain's miles away.

Because how is Ben allowed to just show up with that face? It's pretty rude, to be honest. Yes, Ben, we all know you're gorgeous. You don't have to knock people over the head with it.

Or maybe it's just me. I don't even know if he has this effect on most people, but something about Ben Alejo's face makes my brain light up. It just does, and I've never understood it. Honestly, it made the Mikey stuff harder at first, because things weren't quite so instantaneous with him. I mean, I'd definitely *noticed* Mikey. I'd seen him around campus a lot—this sweet-faced boy with grandpa glasses and Elsa-blond hair. But it wasn't a stop-me-in-my-tracks all-organs-on-deck situation. And I guess that made me wonder whether my attraction to Mikey was even real.

I used to try to stack up the proof of it. I spent all of fall semester studying Mikey's mouth and his jawline and his dark blond eyebrows and lashes. The way he printed all his readings for class and highlighted almost every line. I found him so irresistible sometimes, but other times I'd swear I was talking myself into it. And there were always sparks when we kissed, but afterward I'd feel so strangely relieved. Like I could never quite trust the sparks would be there next time. I remember wondering if things would all click into place if I'd just ask Mikey to be my boyfriend. One last leap, and I'd be sure. But if I *wasn't* sure, how could I ask him that? I kept putting it off a week, and another week, and another week after that, until it was December. And I still wasn't sure.

Which felt like its own kind of answer.

So I broke up with him, though even using the word "breakup" felt ridiculous. Can you even call it a breakup if it wasn't really a relationship to begin with? Even though Mikey was perfectly stoic when I told him, I cried the whole night. I felt like a monster.

But then again, waking up alone in my bed the next morning felt kind of . . . right. And the next day felt even more right. I walked around campus that whole week feeling like I'd just stepped off a too-fast treadmill. Discombobulated and dizzy, but also kind of blissfully untethered.

And then it was winter break.

At first, it was my parents who made it weird, Mom especially. She was so full of Gentle Concern it was almost aggressive. Basically, neither of them let me out of their sight for a week. We did the menorah lighting at Avalon and the Fantasy in Lights at Callaway Gardens, and they both spent the whole time watching me warily, like at any moment I might remember to collapse into a big messy gloom-spiral meltdown.

But this wasn't anything like my breakup with Ben. I was a year and a half older and wiser, for one thing. "Plus," I reminded Mom as she pulled into the parking deck at North Point Mall, "I wasn't the one who got dumped this time."

Mom put the car in park and turned to look at me strangely. "You weren't dumped last time either."

She was right, of course. My breakup with Ben was completely mutual. Technically, verbally, on paper, and any way you looked at it.

I don't know why it always felt like Ben dumped me.

The point is, Mikey was different. I felt fine, for the most part. Maybe my heart did a little jolt every time I scrolled past his name in my texts, but it's not like I was moping or pining. Sometimes I'd even go hours without thinking about him.

Until Christmas Eve.

I swear, it hit me out of *nowhere*. My parents were watching *Home Alone* for the twenty billionth time while I swiped through TikTok and texted memes back and forth with Ethan. But then Macaulay Culkin walked into a church.

I think I stopped breathing for a second. It was like a cartoon anvil crashing down.

The choir was singing "O Holy Night."

And suddenly, all I could think about was that night in October, when my friend Musa roped a bunch of us into waking up before dawn to watch some meteor shower. Not going to lie—at first, I was really grouchy about it. I was only half-awake, it was fucking freezing, and I didn't really get the point of meteors to begin with.

But then we got to Foss Hill, and something shifted in my head. Lots of people were out there lying on blankets with extra blankets on top, like the world's biggest sleepover. And it was really nice tucking in right beside Mikey, gazing at the sky and holding hands under the covers. He told me about his niece, and what it was like to have much older siblings, and how lonely he was when they all left for college. In the month or so that I'd known him, I'd never heard him speak this much at once. It was the first time I'd noticed his very faint accent, the lilt in his voice on the short *o* sound. It made me want to kiss him every time he said Boston.

He talked about Christmas and how much he loved it, and how he used to sing with his church choir. He hated when they did "Joy to the World" because it was too melodically simple, but "O Holy Night" was his favorite. So I told him how we used to sing that song in school chorus, and I loved when the notes got really high at the end, but I'd always have to mouth the word "Christ" instead of singing it, because I didn't want God to think I was a bad Jew.

Mikey turned to face me when I said that. "A bad Jew?"

"For cheating on him with Jesus."

I was hoping to make Mikey laugh, but he didn't. He just gazed at me, half smiling, like he was starting to realize my brain was just one big surprise egg full of mystery weirdness, and maybe that wasn't such a bad thing at all.

I tried to memorize the lines of his face in the starlight. We'd kissed a few times before at that point, but something about that moment seemed to cut deeper than kissing.

So there I was two months later, on the couch between my parents, thinking, *O holy fuck.*

I *missed* him.

Which is how I ended up in Boston a week later, begging Mikey for a do-over. To let me get it right this time. To be actual, official boyfriends.

Mikey McCowan, my actual, official boyfriend.

Therefore, Ben Alejo is welcome to mail his eyes and freckles and his fucking cute bright blue pants straight back to the universe. Return to sender.

"And the weirdest thing," Ben says, "is that I didn't even know you were going to be here until literally that day. I don't know how I missed that."

"It's—yeah, it's recent. Kind of a surprise job offer."

"Well, I'm glad you're back," he says, smiling so fondly at me that I blush.

"Yeah, me too."

Ben starts to speak—but then his eyes drift up and his mouth snaps shut, and a dark-haired boy appears out of nowhere. He drops two boxes on the ground next to Ben. "Sorry, sorry! Don't be mad. I'm here!"

He grabs both of Ben's cheeks playfully and kisses him quickly on the lips.

Every molecule of air leaves my lungs.

"Hi!" says the boy, extending his hand. "Mario."

Mario. My head's spinning. Mario? I've never heard Ben even mention the name Mario when he wasn't talking about Nintendo. And I've never seen this guy in my life. He's not in any of Ben's photos on Instagram. Believe me, I'd fucking remember that, especially if the guy looked like this.

Because this boy is holy-shit-level cute. Or hot. Probably hot's the right word. He's got these big hazel-brown eyes and a movie-star face and a wide-open smile, and he's wearing half-buckled overalls over a tank top, like he just wandered off someone's backyard chicken coop in Brooklyn. He's got really nice arms, too. Not in a jacked-up bodybuilder way, but he definitely looks like he's seen the inside of a gym. And he's at least half a foot taller than me. And—

I realize with a start that I'm supposed to shake his hand. "Hi! Arthur. I mean, *I'm* Arthur." I blink.

"Wait. Arthur like *Arthur*?"

Okay, so Ben's new boyfriend knows about me, which is just . . . so funny. Hilarious, even. Mario knows me by name, and I didn't even know he existed.

Ben smiles uncomfortably and shrugs, and Mario's whole face lights up.

"No way!" He hugs me tightly and kisses my cheek. "So nice to meet you. Holy shit. Are you here on a trip, or for the summer, or what?"

"For the summer," I say. To Mario. To Ben's boyfriend. Because Ben has a boyfriend. "I have an internship with this queer director and playwright, Jacob D—"

"Jacob Demsky?"

"You know Jacob Demsky?"

"Dude, JD is a legend. You're seriously working for him?" Mario clasps his hands together. "Arthur, congrats! That's insane."

"Thanks! I'm—yeah. I'm excited." Out of the corner

of my eye, I catch Ben looking nervously back and forth between Mario and me like we're the crossover series he never asked for. "Sorry, you've got stuff to mail. I don't want to keep you," I say, gesturing vaguely at the boxes by Ben's feet. "Anyway, I should run. I'm meeting my friend . . ."

"No, you're good! I'm just so glad to finally meet you." Mario hugs me again. "Seriously, don't be a stranger. We should all hang out sometime."

He smiles, and it's so plainly sincere, it almost catches me off guard.

"Okay." I glance back at Ben, who looks as dazed as I feel. "Okay, yeah. That sounds great."

Just me and Ben and his boyfriend. Because Ben has a boyfriend. Which is *absolutely* fucking fine, because I have one, too.

I have a boyfriend. I have a Mikey. And before I even step out of the post office, my phone starts dialing his number.

CHAPTER SEVEN
BEN
Monday, May 18

The last time I watched Arthur walk away was two summers ago.

I'm reliving that deep uncertainty in my chest all over again. Back then I wasn't sure who we were going to be after breaking up, and I'm not sure who we're supposed to be now that he's back in town with his new boyfriend.

Texting him that picture of the post office wasn't meant to be an invitation for him to come surprise me, but I can't exactly blame him. I did send a believer in the universe a picture of where we met. I practically conjured him here like the summoning spell in my book.

"The ex is back. He's really, really cute," Mario says with a smile. "¿Cómo estás?"

"What do you mean? I'm fine."

I'm maybe a little defensive. But I don't want him freaking out that I'm freaking out on the inside and hoping that he can't tell.

"I believe you, Alejo. I just know it's weird seeing exes for the first time."

Weird is an understatement. "Have you ever bumped into exes before?" I ask.

Mario has never talked about his dating history. I've totally respected that even though I've been really curious.

"Totally," Mario says as we get on line. "I ran into Louie outside a movie theater and—"

"Louie?"

"My first boyfriend."

First boyfriend implies there's a second out there. Maybe more. But that's not what I'm fixed on right now.

"Please tell me his name is short for Luigi."

Dylan is going to love this detail more than he loves Samantha.

Mario laughs and shakes his head. "Lo siento, Alejo."

Dylan is going to hate that more than decaf coffee. Maybe even more than Patrick.

"What happened when you bumped into Not-Luigi?"

Mario grins, like he's transported back to that moment. "I was so happy to see him, but strictly as a friend. It helps that we were only seventeen when we dated and it only lasted two months. Nothing serious."

Nothing serious? Arthur and I were seventeen when we dated. It wasn't even for two months, but I would definitely say it was serious. Not that I have to defend how that summer once felt like everything to me. How after our time together I wished I could have jumped through my phone screen while on FaceTime with Arthur and slept next to him in his bed. How I wished his family had moved to New York for good.

I'm sure we would still be together if I hadn't been so out of sight, out of mind.

That doesn't matter anymore.

Eyes on the prize, Alejo.

"Arthur seems really cool," Mario says.

"He is."

Arthur did seem cool, but the Arthur I knew had no chill. Maybe he's grounded himself a bit. But would someone who's grounded hurry to surprise their ex-boyfriend? I don't know. I really don't know who Arthur Seuss is these days.

I tried to stay in touch, I did. But talking about Mikey got too hard. I was in this tough place where I had to support Arthur like a good friend even when I was still working through my own feelings for him. Then they broke up and it gave me hope that the door on us wasn't completely shut. But ever since they got back together, it's been clear that we aren't the great love story I thought we were.

A teller window opens and I help Mario unload the boxes before stepping aside so he can handle his business. I look around the post office, wondering what straight-out-of-a-movie thing will happen. Another flash mob proposal? Then it quickly hits me. The straight-out-of-a-movie thing already happened.

My ex-boyfriend bumped into me with my potential next-boyfriend.

Mario charms his way through the rest of his transaction and we go outside. He taps the empty shopping cart. "Your chariot awaits, Alejo."

"No way. I'll push you."

"No, no, no. I got this."

"Is this some weird macho thing you're doing?"

Mario steps around the cart and rests his hand on my shoulder. "Hold up, Benjamin Hugo Alejo. Who taught you 'macho'? Do you have another Spanish tutor?"

"Uh, 'macho' is an English word, too."

"Sure, but you said it in your Spanish voice. Don't think I can't tell the difference."

I don't know if he can tell the difference. But I definitely know when Mario's voice shifts from friendly to flirty. My face flushes while chills run up my arms, and it always takes me an extra few seconds to find my next words.

"Tengo una pregunta."

I stare into his hazel eyes as my heart hammers. Of all the questions.

Maybe he's going to ask if he can be my boyfriend.

"¿Sí?"

"Do you think hanging out with Arthur would make things less weird? Maybe even meeting his boyfriend? I'll shut up if this is too much for you."

So he's not asking to be my boyfriend. He's pointing out how weird I'm being since bumping into my ex.

Mario removes his hand from my shoulder and looks away. "Never mind. I'm shutting up starting now."

"Please don't shut up," I say. "Hanging out with Arthur and Mikey might be good for me."

"If you want some backup, I can go with you. Maybe Friday before I fly out on Saturday?"

"Yeah. That would be fun."

Translation: double date.

"Any chance you've also met your ex's new boyfriend?" I ask.

Mario smiles and pulls me into a hug. "I'm afraid I haven't crossed that road yet, Alejo."

I rest my chin on his shoulder, breathing in his shampoo and not wanting to move. I pull back from him and we stare into each other's eyes again as we smile together. I'm not normally the best at initiating affectionate moments with Mario because I don't want to risk rejection, but I'm so grateful for how compassionate he's being that I feel magnetized to him. I kiss him and linger on his lips long enough so he knows that I'm not trying to be mistaken as a friend. I'm nervous when we stop kissing, wishing we could live in that space where we're locked into each other.

"Otra vez," Mario says.

I'm searching my mind for the translation. "I got nada."

"Again," Mario says.

I kiss Mario—*otra vez!*

"Your chariot still awaits," Mario says.

I step into the cart, squeezing my knees against the metal. It's totally uncomfortable, especially as Mario breaks into a sprint. We're laughing and I'm sure that we're going to flip over and break our faces against the sidewalk, but Mario is being careful with me.

Once he stops to catch his breath, I text Arthur.

hey good "bumping" into you. you guys want to hang out with me and Mario on Friday night?

I hit send, not trying to spend forever on a message to Arthur. I want to enjoy every minute I have with Mario.

CHAPTER EIGHT

ARTHUR

Tuesday, May 19

"Mikey Mouse, why am I awake?" It's barely six in the morning, but of course my early-bird boyfriend is a freshly-showered ray of sunshine.

He perches on the foot of his bed, smiling. "Did you sleep at all?"

"My front-facing camera says no," I say, peering closer. "Though my pillow creases say yes? Oof—" I stop short. "Wow, okay, your screen just did a big murdery camcorder lurch. Are you—"

"Murdered?" He pops back into frame. "No, I was putting on a sock."

He's so cute, it's almost unbearable. It just hits me out of nowhere sometimes. Mikey, who once wrote a fifteen-page essay on Cold War American opera, but can't hold a phone and put on a sock simultaneously.

"Okay, I need first-day outfit advice. I'm leaning toward the suit-and-tie thing—"

Mikey raises his eyebrows. "Chad from corporate, is that you?"

"Hush. I'm just talking about the first day. First impression. I'm thinking—"

"Jeremy Jordan *Supergirl* vibes," he says with me, and I laugh.

"Exactly." I pause. "And you're sure—"

"It's not going to make you look like a baby tax accountant."

I bite back a smile. "You think you can read my mind now?"

"Am I wrong?"

His deadpan expression makes me gooey inside. Maybe it's just the fact that Mikey never used to tease me. Now he's the world's gentlest shit-talker, and I honestly can't get enough of it.

"So what's on the camp agenda today?" I ask. "Scuba diving? Archery?"

"You realize these kids are in preschool, right?"

"I did scuba diving in preschool!"

"Arthur, you're literally scared of fish."

"Because I was scarred for life from scuba diving." I pause. "Wait, it might have been snorkeling. Anyway, I should go get dressed!"

"Call me when you get home? Can't wait to hear how it goes."

"I'll give you the full minute-by-minute summary. You, Mikey Mouse, are going to know more about Jacob Demsky than his own husband."

"I definitely already do."

I laugh. "Miss you."

"You too," he says softly.

There's this pause, which is a thing that's been happening more and more lately, and I never quite know what to make of it. I guess it's the part of the conversation where you're supposed to say *I love you*, but Mikey and I haven't really gotten there yet. I'm not opposed to it, exactly. I guess it just feels kind of soon. Though in a way, that pause makes it feel like it's already out there. Like it's a placeholder for an "I love you" that's pretty much a foregone conclusion.

We hang up, and I drift through my morning routine—shower, teeth, shirt buttons. And the tie, because at the end of the day, I'd rather be Chad from corporate than a "snappy casual" bar mitzvah boy. At least it gives me a chance to show off my half-Windsor skills—born from hours of YouTube tutorials, culminating in flawless senior prom looks for me, Ben, *and* Dylan: my greatest high school accomplishment, hands down. Of course, now I'm stuck with the memory of Senior Year Ben's eyes lighting up my phone screen the moment he tugged that last loop and realized he'd nailed it.

Kind of like how he lit up when he saw me in the post office yesterday.

I squeeze my eyes shut, trying to force the image out of my head. It's unnerving how often Ben's been haunting my brain lately. I'll be sitting here minding my own business, mooning over my actual boyfriend, and then Ben just pops in out of nowhere, in a million different disguises. There are Bens on every hundred-dollar bill, every postcard of London. Even the mayor of my college town is named—what else?—Ben. He's just perpetually *there*, and I don't know how he does it. He's like a volcano, always just an earthquake away from erupting.

Sometimes I wish I had twenty ex-boyfriends, just so I'd know whether this was normal.

What's weird is how much this job feels like a first date—the way I'm so amped up and nervous, so desperate to make a good first impression. Jacob's assistant, Taj, texted me subway directions two days ago, and at this point, I think they're basically tattooed on my brain. I luck into a seat, which is great, because it means I can use the ride downtown to sneak one last peek at my script binder—sticky-tabbed and feverishly annotated, even though Jacob didn't *technically* ask for notes. But that's how hard you have to ride when it's your dream job. I turn to the title page, and as always, those no-nonsense Courier capitals make my heart beat faster.

PLAY IT AGAIN
By Jacob Demsky

The play itself is so different from what I expected. I guess I thought it would be some kind of experimental multisensory performance art, like the dance concert Mikey and Musa dragged me to once at Wesleyan, where all the dancers emerged from a giant spandex womb, and the ushers handed out bags of dirt to sniff at critical moments. But it's not like that at all. It's just a story—conventional, linear, almost disarmingly sweet.

It's about a pair of queer New Yorker best friends and the baby they're platonically coparenting. I've probably read it at least a dozen times at this point, but I couldn't stop myself from diving in again if I tried. But I'm barely past the second scene of Act One when we hit Columbus Circle, my transfer point. And from there, it's just a few stops to the rehearsal studio.

In related news: I work at a rehearsal studio—an actual, legitimate, off-Broadway rehearsal studio. No, it's not the iconic ten-story one near Times Square, where you run into *Hamilton* cast members on the elevator. But I'm pretty sure our studio's better anyway, for about five million reasons, beginning with the fact that it's in the East Village, aka hipster central. I don't think a single city block has ever contained so much sheer coolness. There's a pair of heavily tattooed guys speaking Spanish, a woman with a crocheted mandala pattern stretched across the spokes of her wheelchair, and a dapper-looking Black guy with gray locs and a reusable coffee mug. I'm surprised I haven't sprouted a full beard and pompadour yet, just from breathing the air here.

I pace around near the front entrance of the studio for a moment, trying to calm my nerves. I'm still about fifteen minutes early, enough time to do a lap around the block if I want, just to scope out what's here. I actually think I'm near Ben's neighborhood. Not that Ben needs me showing up on his doorstep on what must be a very erotic Tuesday morning with Mario.

It's just funny, I guess, because he spent so much time talking about how much he wanted to try being single. He kept insisting he needed "Ben Time," and saying he wasn't going to date anyone unless he was all in. It was this whole thing with him, how he'd rather be single than half-ass something just for the sake of being in a relationship. So clearly he's full-assing Mario. But I guess that's how it goes when you meet a guy who looks like that.

But you know what? I have my own full-ass adorable boyfriend. Mikey McCowan, of Boston, Massachusetts, who absolutely needs a selfie of me in front of the rehearsal studio. Discreetly, of course, so I don't give off those just-flew-in-from-Georgia vibes on day one of my East Village avant-garde life. I'll just angle my phone upward at chest level—

"Want me to take a picture of you?"

I look up with a start to find a guy with swoopy dark hair, clear brown skin, and a perfectly symmetrical face—early, maybe mid-twenties, I think, and South Asian. There's something weirdly familiar about him, which means he's probably an actor, maybe even a semi-famous one. But more than anything, it's his outfit that leaves me speechless. Specifically, his tie and suspenders. His *floral* tie and suspenders. Pure fucking genius. A revelation.

"Happy to do it," he says, holding his phone up while I gape at him. "Smile!"

I grin like a dumbass, because apparently East Village Avant-Garde Arthur is highly susceptible to commands from cute guys in floral suspenders.

"I'll text it to you," he says, already tapping his phone screen. I nod mutely, waiting for the part where he asks for my number. But instead, he just looks back up and smiles, and my phone buzzes in my hand. One new text message, photo attached, from—

"Oh, you're Taj!" I shake my head, feeling the heat rise in my cheeks. "God. I'm so sorry. I'm—of course you are. Your hair was—"

"Failed experiment. Though my partner thought I looked like Johnny Bravo." He laughs, wincing a little.

"Well, I'm Arthur," I blurt, and then my cheeks burn all over again. "Which you already know. Clearly." I lift my phone in what I assume is the universal gesture for *you just texted me and I'm an actual clown.* "Sorry, I'm just, uh—"

"So nice to finally meet you in person," Taj says. "Should we head in?"

"Yes! Amazing. And me too. Back atcha."

Back atcha. How do I sew my mouth shut again?

Taj holds the door for me, and I scramble into the Lafayette Rehearsal Studio lobby, which looks just like the virtual tour I took twelve times online. It's an older building, with velvety green carpet and ornate gold frames—but there are big windows, too, and the air has that just-cleaned citrus smell. Taj heads straight to the bank of elevators in the back, presses the button, and smiles down at me. "How are you feeling?"

I inhale. "Good. I can't believe I'm here. Jacob's my favorite director on earth. I feel like I'm dreaming."

"Jacob's great," Taj says. The elevator doors slide open, and he lets me step in first. "The show's great, too. I'm so psyched."

"Oh God, I know. I'm so sad I missed the table read. I had a final exam Friday morning. I'm in school. College. Obviously. Hopefully obviously?" I rub my cheek. "I don't know how much Jacob told you about me."

"You just finished your freshman year at Wesleyan, right? I graduated from Yale two years ago."

"Wait, really?" I gasp. "My bubbe lives in New Haven!"

Fucking fantastic, Arthur. Way to name-drop *your grandmother* before you even step off the elevator. Always a winning career move.

"Very cool. New Haven's great," Taj says as we reach the fourth floor. "All right. You ready?"

I nod and shoot him an extremely chill smile.

"Seriously, don't stress—everyone's super nice. I'll introduce you around."

The studio's brighter than I expected, and the high ceilings and mirrors make it feel bigger than it is. Only a few people are here so far, bustling around with clipboards and pushing chairs into place. My gaze lands on a Black guy with a pierced septum and a "Trans Rights Are Human Rights" shirt—he's talking to a tiny retro-femme white woman and a guy with brown skin and huge eighties glasses, who looks barely older than I am. The hipster energy is off the charts.

"He/him, right, for pronouns?" Taj asks, and I nod. "Okay, the actors aren't getting here until eleven, but I can introduce you to some of the PAs. And Jacob, of course." He gestures to a group of people chatting near a bank of music stands, one of whom turns suddenly in my direction—and even if I didn't know him from our Zoom interview, I'd recognize Jacob in a heartbeat: baby-faced, with blond hair and big blue eyes, just like his pictures. He lights up when he sees me, and jogs over. "Arthur, hi! I see you've met Taj. Excellent. He'll take good care of you." He turns to Taj. "Oh, you know what? Stacy needed backup on the props inventory. Maybe get Arthur started on a spreadsheet?"

"No problem."

"Oh! And if you can catch Justin, ask them if we can move more toward a green palette for Amelia. But I'm liking that vermilion for Em."

I nod along with Taj, even though I have literally no clue who Justin, Amelia, and Em are. Or what vermilion is. Also I'm dressed like Pete Buttigieg. Am I nailing this yet?

"So, good news." Jacob turns back to me. "We're officially confirmed at the Shumaker Blackbox Theater. Fifty seats, and it's this accessible, amazing space. You'll love it. I'll give you the tour at some point. But feel free to ask me anything now. We're so glad you're here!"

My heart pounds. "Thank you—so much." I take a deep

breath. "I'm kind of freaking out right now. It's *such* an honor to meet you."

"You're so sweet." Jacob pats my arm. "Okay, so today, maybe just try to get acclimated. Taj will get you started on the prop chart, and then we'll introduce you to Stacy when she gets back. Oh! And do you have a hard copy of the script?"

"Yes!" I hold up my binder.

"Great! So, why don't we—" He stops short, gaze drifting past me. "Oh dear *God*."

I whirl around to find the pierced septum guy holding what appears to be a bald Chucky doll.

"Oof," murmurs Taj.

"If I ever write another show involving a baby," says Jacob, "please kill me."

"Is that the prop baby?" I ask.

"Yeah, no. Absolutely not." Jacob lets out a tired-sounding laugh, running a hand through his hair. "Okay, I better go deal with this."

"And I'll get you logged in," Taj says, turning to me—but then he pauses. "Actually, you know what? You want to grab some coffee before the actors get here?"

"Oh! No thanks, I'm good. First-day jitters. Can't have caffeine, or I'll turn into Sonic the Hedgehog. Or a vibrator."

Hello, yes, hi? I'd like to speak with a manager, please,

about the possibility of me voluntarily bursting into flames? Because I, for some unknowable fucking reason, decided to refer to myself as both a Sega Genesis character and a sex toy on my first day of work. Also, I can't stop staring at those suspenders. And that *tie*.

"Got it," says Taj after about ten hours of excruciating silence.

I text Jessie as soon as he leaves. I could pull off a floral tie, right??

No response. I'm guessing she's currently drowning in legal files or fighting with the copy machine or taking Starbucks orders, and God I'm so glad I'm not a law intern anymore. I'm not saying entering props into an Excel sheet is the pinnacle of creativity—intern life is intern life. But if I'm stuck picking up someone's iced coffee, it might as well be Jacob Demsky's.

And then it hits me like an anvil: Taj wasn't asking me if I wanted to get coffee. He wanted *us* to get coffee for Jacob and the crew, maybe even the actors. Which means I'm officially the most useless assistant's intern on earth. Is this my legacy? Arthur Seuss, trailblazer in the realm of forgetting basic tasks like offering to get my boss's coffee?

I'll just have to make up for it by dazzling Taj and Jacob with the best props log in the history of theater. The blank template Taj gave me is really basic, but I bet I could replicate the grid in the design app Samantha's always hyping on Instagram. Maybe I could even import images to go with each prop, just for the wow factor. I want Jacob to know how seriously I'm taking this. My bare-minimum-effort days are over. I'm putting all my kiss-ass teacher's pet energy into the universe.

I'm so in the zone that I don't even hear Taj's footsteps until I'm hit with the scent of his coffee. "Oh, wow." I glance up to find him peering at my screen, his brow furrowed. "Is this—"

"What do you think? Obviously, it's all the same info, but I wanted to give it a little bit of extra punch. You know?"

"Um. Yeah, okay. I see that. It's definitely got the punch."

I bite back a proud smile.

Taj rubs the bridge of his nose. "So. Um. Typically, the props team likes to stick to their standard templates, just to streamline the process."

My stomach drops. "Oh. Um—"

"This is really impressive," he adds quickly. "I'm just—you know. Wondering if you also happen to have the other version . . . ?"

"Totally! I mean, I don't have it yet, but I can go back. God. I'm so sorry. I didn't realize . . ." I stare at my hands.

"Oh! No. I'm sorry. I should have clarified. You were just—this is a *fantastic* chart. It's just—"

"It will take me ten minutes. I'll do it right now." I'm blinking so fast, my eyelids are practically fluttering. But I can't. I can't cry on the first day of work. It's just. I haven't even been here an hour, and I've already messed up. I already need a do-over.

This really is like a date.

CHAPTER NINE
BEN
Friday, May 22

"Knock, knock," Dylan says outside my bedroom door without actually knocking.

"One sec."

I'm standing shirtless in front of my open drawer. I want to wear one of the shirts Mario made for me, but that feels like a strong choice of wardrobe on my way to hang with my ex and his new boyfriend. Will it come off like I'm trying to really push how much Mario cares about me even though we're not official? Or is it more than enough that Mario's already hanging out with all of us on his last night before he leaves for his LA trip?

It's stupid caring this much.

I don't need to seem like I'm in competition with Arthur.

I'm going to walk into this hangout with my head high.

Speaking of pride, I choose my favorite shirt Mario made for me after we started our Spanish lessons: a plain white tee with a Puerto Rican flag stamped onto the chest pocket. I had joked with him that sometimes it felt like people wouldn't be able to tell that I'm Puerto Rican unless I started wearing the flag like a cape, and he made this shirt and told me it was more subtle. I feel seen when I wear this.

"Knock, knock," Dylan says again. "You have five seconds to pull your pants up."

"Come in," I say.

"Really? You still have like three seconds," Dylan says, still outside my door.

"Move," Samantha says, letting herself in. "Hey, Ben."

Samantha is twirling her key necklace around her finger and dressed in black and white—black tee, white vest, black jeans, and black-and-white sneakers. She's got a Cruella de Vil intern vibe, and it really works for her. Then in comes Dylan, following like her loyal puppy.

"Not just a single date, or a double date, but a triple date!" Dylan says. "This is a first in the history of the world."

"We went on a triple bowling date with my friends back at school," Samantha says.

"That didn't count. Your friends had no chemistry. At best that was a double date." Dylan turns to me. "Ashleigh was always on her phone, and Jonah was the absolute worst, Big Ben. He was such a show-off at the bowling alley."

"So he was a better bowler than you?" I ask.

"Yes," Samantha says. "And Ashleigh was dealing with a family emergency, but Dylan's right: Jonah is pretty insufferable."

Dylan beams. "Did you hear that? She said I'm right."

"A true first in the history of the world," Samantha says.

Dylan hops onto my bed and bounces. "I'm right!"

"Get off," I say.

Dylan leaps off and eyes me suspiciously. "Why? You hiding Arthur under here?" He looks under the bed.

I blush. "Why would I be hiding Arthur?"

"Because keeping Arthur out in the open would be downright disrespectful?"

"There's nothing going on between us."

I've only exchanged a couple texts with Arthur since we saw each other on Monday. The first was one when I suggested the hangout, and then earlier today to confirm the times for tonight and see if he was cool with Dylan and Samantha tagging along.

"Don't be weird tonight, D. I don't want to make anyone uncomfortable."

"Me? Weird? May I be insulted, Fun Police?"

"Sure."

I pocket my wallet and lead everyone out of my bedroom.

My parents are snuggled up on the couch watching the second season of Netflix's *One Day at a Time.* Ma has probably watched every episode like four times, but it's the first time she's getting Pa through the series. They've invited me to join, but I usually prefer to go to my room to write or FaceTime Mario. Watching family shows often makes me wish my life were simpler, like I could go through the ups and downs of living with my parents over the course of thirty minutes.

"What's the plan, Benito?" Ma asks as she covers her lap with a blanket.

"Just hitting Times Square."

"Times Square?"

"Hasn't Arthur been there already?"

"Yeah, but he loves that area. Mikey probably does, too."

I wouldn't be surprised if they've spent every night in New York seeing a different show. Meanwhile I'm over here earning paychecks and giving my parents money for rent and groceries.

"Well, have fun," Ma says. "You too, Samantha and Dylan."

"Gracias," Dylan says like a true white person.

We leave and make our way to the subway station,

getting on a train just in time to see a duo of boys with dark brown skin shout, "Showtime!" The beat kicks in and Dylan tries to clap along—though he's so off-rhythm, I'm this close to grabbing his hand. To be honest, I don't always pay attention to the subway shows, but these boys are on another level. I can't help but watch them flip down the aisles and spin around the poles with the upper body strength of superheroes. We tip them a few dollars before we transfer to our next train.

When we arrive in Times Square, I'm so aware how it doesn't cast its magical spell on me. The lit-up marquees blend in with the traffic lights. All the Broadway billboards may as well be posters for bus stops. I'm feeling this all the time around New York now. Every morning I wake up to the city shining a little less brightly. But this glamour isn't for residents like me. It's for people like Arthur and Mikey, who will probably be skipping down the street any moment now and singing some show tunes that I won't know.

I check my phone to see Mario is running a few minutes late because he got caught up packing for his flight. I was thinking about spending the night at his place, but he's taking off really early, and I know how important rest is to him. Thankfully we got to scratch some itches while my parents were working yesterday afternoon.

"I'm starving," Samantha says.

"Hot dog?" Dylan asks, pointing at the vendor on the corner.

"Maybe a pretzel," she says.

Dylan approaches the cart. "My good man, what's your pretzel rate?"

"Why are you talking like that?" the vendor asks.

"So you don't mistake me as a tourist."

"You sound like a tourist."

"From where?"

"The past."

Dylan glares. "How much for the pretzel? My woman is starving and I need to put food on the table."

"Five dollars."

"I see. And after I hand over my main man Lincoln, will you be immediately arrested for your crimes?"

The two lock into a staring contest. Samantha and I roll our eyes.

"Four dollars," Dylan haggles.

"Five."

"Four dollars plus a dollar for a soda."

"Seven."

Dylan leans in. "You're embarrassing me in front of my woman. Come on, one family man to another. Help me out."

"You're a child."

"How dare you? I have a beard."

Samantha steps in with a five-dollar bill. "One pretzel, please."

The vendor takes her cash and hands her a pretzel. "Have a great evening."

Samantha takes a huge bite, mumbles her thanks, and walks off.

Dylan glares. "Enjoy prison, man."

We catch up with Samantha, who is devouring her pretzel. She goes on about how they're so much better than the ones on campus, and Dylan jumps in about his favorites (chicken tenders, pepperoni pizzas, beef patties) and the banes of the cafeteria (hot dogs, fries, tacos). I have nothing to add to this conversation, which is great since I'm focusing on tonight.

Still waiting on Arthur and Mario.

No, correction: Mario and Arthur. Mario comes first these days. I think about him when I wake up. I hope he's behind every text. I would cancel on everyone else to hang out with him. I get that I should make more time for Arthur while he's in town, but his trip isn't based around hanging out with me. It wasn't the case back then and it won't be this time either.

Then Arthur is the first person I see making his way through the crowds. I'm surprised he's not holding Mikey's hand, though it's possible they got split up from all the foot traffic. Not seeing them all over each other is a good way to inch into this experience. But when Arthur turns to talk to someone, it's not Mikey. It's Jessie. I didn't realize he was inviting Jessie, but that's cool with me.

This is the same area where we met for our first first date.

"Hi!" Arthur says, beaming. "Wow. Dylan! Samantha!" He hugs them. "It's so great to see you."

"It's even better to be seen by you," Dylan says.

"Hey again," I tell Jessie.

"Hey, hey." Jessie kisses Samantha on the cheek. "I listened to the podcast you sent me. Hilarious."

I like that Samantha and Jessie didn't lose touch after our breakup. Things shouldn't have to be complicated for them, too.

"Hey, Arthur."

"Hey, Ben."

We hug, but it doesn't last long. That's fine. Cool even. We already got the wow-great-to-see-you-for-the-first-time-in-two-years hug out of the way.

"Where's Mario?" he asks.

"He should be here soon. He got caught up packing for his trip to LA tomorrow."

"How long is he going to be gone?"

"A week."

Here I am talking about Mario's schedule to my ex-boyfriend.

I've got to stop only thinking about Arthur as my ex-boyfriend. He's more than that. We're friends. It doesn't matter that he was the last person I loved. That was years ago.

"Hola hola hola hola," Mario calls from behind me. He pinches my sides and hugs everyone he knows before introducing himself to Jessie. "I'm sorry I'm late, I was packing and—I'm here now." Mario smiles at me and flicks the Puerto Rican flag on my shirt's pocket and winks. "Nice shirt, Alejo."

"Gracias."

Mario finger-snaps at Arthur. "Where's Mikey?"

Arthur seems confused. "Boston."

I wonder if everything is okay. "When did he leave?"

"He was never here . . ."

"I thought he was in town with you . . ."

"Just us," Jessie says. Her hands fly to her mouth for a second. "Oh no, this is mortifying. Did you mean to invite Mikey and not me?"

"No—I mean yes, but of course we're happy you're here!"

This is a disaster. How did the lines get crossed here? I guess not paying closer attention to Arthur's Instagram posts is a good start. I've just been assuming everything about Arthur and Mikey in New York—Broadway shows, skipping hand in hand while singing show tunes, sharing a bed.

I feel a little lighter. Like I'm not the only person in the world whose life isn't perfect.

Arthur's boyfriend not being around shouldn't be comforting.

"Sorry to miss Mikey," I say.

"He's visiting next weekend. You can meet him then."

"We'll have to send him a group photo," Mario says. "But first we should go do something more exciting than standing on a corner in Times Square."

Jessie points at the Regal Cinema theater down the block. "Movie?"

"Oh my God, yes, I would kill for a slushie," Samantha says.

Mario shakes his head. "This is the first time you're all hanging out in years! You can't catch up during a movie."

"You've never been to a movie with that chatterbox," Dylan says, pointing at Samantha. She smacks his arm and he feigns pain.

Mario scans around us. "How about Madame Tussauds? We can pose with different wax icons or—wait, Dave & Buster's!"

Arthur looks at me and turns away so fast he must have gotten whiplash.

Dave & Buster's is where Arthur and I had our first date. It shouldn't be a big deal, though I admittedly haven't been back since we were last here. But if this is something Mario wants to do, I don't want to avoid it because of my history with Arthur.

"Please tell me they still have *Mario Kart*," Dylan says. "We need a picture of Mario playing *Mario Kart*. Iconic."

"Pac-Man?" Jessie asks Samantha.

"Pac-Man," Samantha says.

Arthur looks frozen.

"This cool with you?" I ask.

He nods like a bobblehead. "Absolutely. Bring on the claw mach—"

Mario grabs my hand and kisses my cheek. "I challenge you to *Guitar Hero*."

He drags me down the block before I can see Arthur's reaction. I'm sure it's weird to see some other guy kissing me again.

On the way to Dave & Buster's, Mario apologizes again for being late and goes on about how excited he is for his trip. I don't tell him how excited I am for him to be back already so I don't look needy. But that's the truth: I like Mario and I like being around Mario. His energy is like sunlight you soak in.

We enter the building and ride the escalator up to the gaming level. We catch the very end of a P!nk song as a Rihanna track kicks in. The arcade is lit up with air hockey tables and pinball machines and dancing platforms. The bar is crowded, which is a win for those of us who are here to play games. Mario and I go in on a Power Card together, each putting in fifteen dollars, and we'll share the credits. If we get separated throughout the night, we'll always have to find each other; I'm looking forward to these little check-ins.

Dylan is playing *Speed of Light*, where the objective is to hit as many blinking lights as possible; it's got a Whac-A-Mole vibe to it. And Dylan is failing spectacularly at hitting any lights. Unlike Mario, who is an absolute pro when he steps up. It's like he has a sixth sense for where the next light will appear.

"He's amazing," Arthur says, appearing at my side. "Does he play this a lot?'

"It seems that way, but I don't know. I haven't been here since I came with you."

"Why not? I didn't make it weird for you, did I? Is it weird that I'm asking that? I don't want this to be any more weird than I've already made it by bringing Jessie. You said 'you guys' in the text, and we both figured you were talking about us. I didn't realize you thought Mikey was here, too."

"Oh, so you're not a mind reader?" I ask.

"Unfortunately, I'm not Ben-Jamin after he drinks the telepathy potion."

Arthur grins, like he's still so proud to be one of my

biggest fans. Maybe even the biggest fan.

"Not Ben-Jamin's finest hour. It's probably for the best that we don't know everyone's every thought."

"Probably."

It's already pretty clear I don't have a handle on what's going on in Arthur's life. I'm sure reading his mind will only tell me just how little he thinks about me.

"Anyway, I should've been clearer about Mikey. I just figured you'd be spending your summer break together."

"We were supposed to be in Boston, but I lucked into this gig, and hello, New York. Arthur Seuss is officially on Broadway. Off-Broadway, but I can cough my way through that off."

"You don't have to pretend to be flashy, Art. I'm proud of you."

"Thanks, Ben."

His eyes are still so blue. I'm getting lost in them when Mario's cheering shifts my attention.

Dylan is bowing down before Mario. "You truly are super!"

Mario holds his head high, playing along before turning to me. "Did you see that?"

I check the scoreboard. "You destroyed Dylan's record."

"Not very hard," Samantha says.

"You give it a shot," Dylan says.

Samantha rises to the challenge, moving with efficiency through the game as if she's still back at Kool Koffee and multitasking between steaming milk, pumping flavored syrups, and ringing people up. Mario records her as she dominates on what I guess is her very first time playing this. She's an absolute natural.

"Super Samantha!" Mario cheers when she beats his score. "Arthur, you up?"

Arthur shakes his head.

"Come on, Arthur, you got this."

"I absolutely will not have that."

Mario is about to go into full hype-man mode until I grab his shoulder to rein him in.

"Let him chill," I say.

"Backing off," Mario says.

Jessie and Samantha go off to bowl, laughing.

I see the photo booth where Arthur and I took pictures on our first date. I wasn't as comfortable in that moment as I'd like to have been; even Arthur was able to tell. I was still dealing with my Hudson feelings, and we'd also taken pictures in that very photo booth. It's like Dave & Buster's is this romantic time machine that sucks me back every time my heart is excited about someone new.

I spot four empty *Mario Kart* seats and tell everyone to claim them. Dylan and Mario race there, and I love how much fun they're already having together. You always hope your friends and crushes like each other. No concerns for Dylan, but I'm not sure what Arthur's early impressions are. I sit next to Mario and Arthur takes the seat on the end, placing me between them; I don't need to be a mind reader to know that Dylan is thinking up a crude joke about this.

Before the start of the race, we all choose our characters. Mario's choice is obvious. Dylan goes for Bowser and promises pure chaos on the tracks. Arthur selects Toad, which isn't actually a toad but instead a tiny humanoid who looks like a thumb with a mushroom cap.

The timer is running low, and I have to decide who I'm going to be.

"Choose Princess Peach so Mario-Mario can rescue you," Dylan says to me.

"Wrong game," I say. "There's no teams here."

"I'll let you win if you want," Mario says.

"Game on," I say, choosing Yoshi. I've always had a soft spot for that green dinosaur.

Dylan leans forward, winking suggestively. "You know there are levels where Mario rides Yoshi, right?"

"Shut up, D."

Bringing up sex as I sit between Mario and Arthur bothers me.

I do my best to focus on the race. Dylan is honoring his

promise and knocks me off course with a red turtle shell. Mario has a strong lead on all of us. What isn't he good at? As Yoshi recovers, I'm sure that I've fallen completely behind. Then I see Toad bumping into every canyon wall, and I laugh at how horrible Arthur is at this game.

"First time?" I ask, keeping my eyes on the road.

"I don't know what gives you that idea," Arthur says as he's driving the opposite direction of everyone else.

We haven't even completed our first of three laps when Mario passes us again in the middle of his second. He's so concentrated on the game, like he's going to get a real gold trophy out of this. Or like he has something to prove. As cute as it is watching Arthur prove why he should never be trusted with a driver's license, I'm playing to win and praying for a miracle that will slow down Mario—his character falling off the map, being struck by lightning, or hit by a series of blue turtle shells. But everything is smooth sailing for the Marios.

"Congrats," I say, wishing I'd at least managed to come in second place. But at least third place is better than sixth like Dylan's. And yes, better than twelfth like Arthur, but there's something adorable about that.

"Group selfie, guy gang," Mario says, stretching his arm out and leaning close to me.

For the picture, Dylan holds his mouth open like he's

roaring. Mario beams with the kind of smile you have when you're your dentist's favorite patient. Arthur moves closer to fit into the picture and he leans his arm on my shoulder.

And I smile, feeling my cheeks go warm at his touch.

CHAPTER TEN
ARTHUR
Friday, May 22

It's too much. Beyond too much, all of it: the laser beeps and synth music, the blinking neon lights. The fact that this entire night feels like one big inside joke I'm not a part of.

I don't know why I thought this would be fine. I was even kind of looking forward to it—just a couple of chill, casual friends having a chill, casual evening, and I'd be one of those mature, friends-with-my-exes kind of guys. Plus, if things somehow went south, I could always just disappear into the Midway with Jessie. Basically foolproof, right?

Wrong. Jessie ran off with Samantha an hour ago, Ben and Dylan are ten levels into an alien invasion, and my ex-boyfriend's new boyfriend may or may not be planning to murder me with the sheer force of his charm.

"I was there for a week after Christmas," Mario's saying. "High sixties and sunny the whole time. Fucking incredible. Ben didn't even—"

"FUCK!" Dylan slams his palms down.

"Suck it," says Ben. "Suck. *It*."

"—until I showed him the pictures."

I tune out, because I don't need to hear about Mario's sexy California pics. Nor do I need to bear further witness to the good news of Mario's biceps. We get it, Mario, you work out. It just sucks, because I was kind of liking my face today. Even my outfit felt right: rolled-up sleeves, light sweater vest, and my brand-new blue floral tie. Taj said I looked like the manic pixie dream child of Joseph Gordon-Levitt and Zooey Deschanel in an alternate-universe sequel of *(500) Days of Summer*, and I guess my brain just kind of took that and ran with it. All day, I've felt like I was living in a movie, like there was something gold-filtered and poignant about me. I'd scratch my head, and it would feel like I'd choreographed it. You could almost hear the Smiths playing in the background.

Until Mario walked in. Biggest record scratch of my life.

Indie dream boy? Nope! Just an eighteen-year-old dumbass from Georgia with a farmer's tan and a bold new zit on my jawline. And those two-dozen flickering LED TV screens aren't exactly serving me the flattering mood lighting I'd hoped for. But I bet they hit like golden hour sunlight when you're Mario's height.

Can I just teleport to Boston? That's all I want. A regular couch night with Mikey. He'll reel in animated sharks on *Animal Crossing*, I'll watch Broadway *Miscast* videos on YouTube, and then we'll brush our teeth and turn the lights out and definitely not have sex, since Mikey won't even masturbate when his sister's home.

But who cares? I just want to wake up beside him.

I could call him. I could hide inside some racing game or sneak out to the lobby, and maybe that's all I'd need to feel centered. My boyfriend's sweet, dependable face.

But what would I even say to him? How would I explain tonight to Mikey? I don't mean Dave & Buster's, or even the fact that I'm here with Ben. Mikey knows about that, and he's fine with all of it. I guess Ben's not such a threatening concept when there's someone like Mario in the picture.

Now Mario's winding into some anecdote about their writing class and Ben's manuscript and something Ben said once during peer critiques, and I swear, every other word out of his mouth is Ben's name. And he keeps touching Ben's arm. Which is fine, I guess, though I'm not sure why he thinks distracting Ben midgame is going to end well. This is a boy who, as legend has it, once turned down a *blow job* in favor of beating Dylan's high score on *Candy Crush*.

A blow job from Hudson, for the record. Ben's never

turned down a blow job from me. Not that he ever had much of a chance to.

But none of this is relevant. Blow jobs definitely aren't relevant. That's not even a concept that applies to us now, because Ben has a boyfriend, and I have a boyfriend, and everyone's settled. And happy. I'm happy! I'm just a little off my game today, but so what? It's not like Mario's stopped talking long enough to notice.

"So I'm like, you know what? I'm gonna go home after this and knock the rest of it out tonight. However long it takes. I'll just sleep it off on the plane tomorrow."

I smile vaguely, like I have any clue what's getting knocked out here. "Definitely."

"I feel good, you know. Like I know where I'm going with it, so now it's just diving in to get the words down." He yawns and stretches. "Oh man, sorry. I was up so late—"

Having sex with Ben, I think.

"—pinning down the beats for the climax," he says. And it takes me a full fucking minute to realize he's talking about a screenplay, not a sex act. Is Mario's face interfering with my brain waves? Is this just what happens when you meet your ex-boyfriend's new boyfriend?

I sneak a quick glance at Ben and Dylan, and they're both leaning in so close to the console, I can't tell if the goal is to crush the aliens or make out with them. No chance of this mission ending anytime soon.

I just need to step away for a minute. My brain needs a factory reset.

"I have to phone call." I shake my head, wincing. "I have *a* phone call. To make."

"Ah. Checking in with the boyfriend," Mario says knowingly.

I nod, a little too quickly. That's right. Checking in with my very perceptive boyfriend who's going to last, what, ten seconds before asking me if I'm okay? At which point I'll trip all over myself explaining how I'm *totally* okay, not even remotely upset, because why would I be upset, and if I seem moody, I'm just tired. LOOK, I'M YAWNING! NORMAL YAWN.

Yup, that'll reassure him.

Five minutes and one Very Casual Mikey Text later, I'm spiraling at Ethan from inside a race car. Guess who's hanging out with Ben's new boyfriend 😬

Two seconds later, my phone buzzes with an incoming call. Ethan doesn't even wait for me to say hello. "You're seeing Ben?"

"I'm not *seeing* Ben! I'm with a group of people at Dave & Buster's —"

"A group of people, including Ben."

"And Ben's boyfriend," I remind him. Ben's boyfriend

Ben's boyfriend Ben's boyfriend. I blink down at the steering wheel, feeling dazed and off-center. It's like I'm standing outside my own brain.

"I didn't know Ben had a boyfriend," says Ethan.

"Not just a boyfriend. An extremely hot boyfriend. Definitely hotter than me."

"Whoa. Good for Ben."

I almost drop my phone. Good for Ben? Does Ethan even remember our breakup? I cried the whole way back from New York. Couldn't sleep. I was a zombie for *weeks*. I went through so many pints of ice cream, Dad started calling me the Dairy King. Even remembering fall of senior year makes my stomach lurch.

"I can't believe you just said that."

Ethan laughs. "Why? You have a boyfriend. Why shouldn't he?"

I scoff so loudly, a kid with a pubestache turns to stare at me through the driver's side door. I wave him off and turn back to Ethan. "Did you miss the part about him being hotter than me?"

"No?"

"You're supposed to say I'm hotter!"

"But I've never met him," says Ethan. "How would I know?"

I smack my forehead. "Because Mario's not your friend and I am!"

"His name's Mario? Yikes, that does sound hot."

"Oh, believe me, I fucking know. This is my second time experiencing his hotness in person," I say. And then I'm instantly paranoid that Mario's somehow overhearing all of this. Or Ben. God, I don't know which would be worse. But when I glance up, it's just Pubestache staring me down and, inexplicably, flicking his tongue into the V of a backward peace sign. Not exactly the hand gesture I'd use to describe my sex life, but okay.

I grace Pubestache with a classic hand gesture of my own.

"I'm still stuck on the fact that you're hanging out with Ben's boyfriend," Ethan says.

"Not on purpose! It's the universe's fault."

When I look up again, Pubestache has evidently decided to share his gifts elsewhere, leaving my view unobstructed. And suddenly, all I can see is the dual-rider motorcycle game. The one I played with Ben once on our first first date.

I squeeze my eyes shut. "I can't believe Ben's having a do-over date of our first date. Right now. With his new super-hot boyfriend—"

"He's not that hot! You're hotter!" Ethan pauses. "How'd I do?"

"Very convincing." I grip the steering wheel. "It's not weird to feel weird about this, right? Like, Ben was weird about my boyfriend. I can be weird about his."

"What's weird is you using the word 'weird' four times just now."

"Well, it's a weird situation!"

Ethan laughs. "It's really not! You're just jealous that your ex has a new boyfriend. That's the most normal thing in the world."

My chest squeezes. "You think I'm jealous of Ben?"

"I mean—"

"Seussical!" Dylan's face pops up next to the game screen, and I almost fall out of my seat.

"Gotta go, I'll text you," I say, jamming the end-call button so hard it almost bends my finger back. Already, Dylan's squeezing into the driver's seat beside me.

"Seussical, hear me out. I need you. I love you. I want to spend the rest of my life with"—he yanks me out of the race car—"the tiger you're about to win me in the claw machine."

So now I'm walking dazedly behind him like he's some sort of overly caffeinated Pied Piper. He weaves me past a bank of coin pushers, takes a sharp left next to *Pac-Man*, and there they are. Ben and Mario, side by side, but also sort of facing each other. Mario's speaking, and Ben's laughing, and there's just something about the way they look against a backdrop of stacked stuffed-animal prizes. It's like they're posed for some kind of whimsically romantic photo shoot. It kind of knocks the air from my lungs.

They look really, really good together.

"Step aside, gentlemen! The king of Clawlandia has arrived," Dylan says, bowing, and I legitimately can't tell if he's drunk or if he just has a drunk personality. "Look, Seussasaurus, I'm not saying you have to win this li'l guy to prove your love for me. But. I need you to win this, or I'm going to assume it's all been a lie—"

"Remind me why you're pinning this on Arthur and not Samantha?" interjects Mario.

"Because Samantha is garbage at claw machines, and we don't need this to end in tears."

"Her tears or yours?" Ben asks.

"Irrelevant."

Ben smiles at me, and my brain's too slow to keep from smiling back.

"Arthur! Eyes on the prize." Dylan taps the claw-machine glass, pointing to what appears to be a ball of neon-orange synthetic fur with two snow-white penises sticking out of its face.

I lean in. "That's supposed to be a tiger?"

"Seussical, come the fuck *on*. A *tiger*?" Dylan looks dumbstruck. "Wow, so what's a T. rex? A lizard? I guess Mufasa's just a lion to you?"

"Well." I pause. "Mufasa *is* a lion—"

"He's the goddamn *king* of the lions. And this motherfucker is a saber-tooth. Equally majestic. Equally legendary.

I'm naming him Sabre with an '-re.'" Dylan kisses his fingertips. "For that extra touch of class. Say-bruh."

I peer through the glass for a minute, then turn back to Dylan. "He's kind of—"

"Delicate but fierce," says Dylan, "with the face of an angel."

"No, his face is the worst thing to happen to saber-toothed tigers as a species, including extinction. I was *going* to say he's too jammed in there. He's not winnable."

"Oh, you. So modest."

"No, I mean there's literally no way that claw will pull that tiger up."

"Thank you!" Mario looks triumphant. "That's what I said! I'm telling you, they rig the machines. You can't win."

"Maybe *you* can't win," I shoot back, which sounded so cheeky and playful in my head. But out loud, it's sharp and intense, practically a declaration of war. Ben's eyes widen, just barely, and Dylan visibly chokes down a laugh.

Mario just smiles. "Cool. Prove me wrong."

All three of them move in closer to watch, which makes my heart speed to double time. I've never been good at ignoring an audience.

"Fine." I peer through the glass, considering my options. Then I glance back at Dylan. "I can get you that bear."

Dylan looks like I just asked permission to punch him. "I ask for a saber-toothed tiger, an ancient beast with dignity and power, and you offer me a valentine bear?"

"Okay, first of all, this bear *radiates* dignity and power. Look at his face. Second of all, if you don't want him—"

"Whoa. Didn't say I don't want him," says Dylan.

Ben leans closer to Mario. "Why is this the most exciting standoff I've ever witnessed?"

"The tension," Mario murmurs back. "The stakes."

Cool, glad I can provide such thrilling entertainment for Ben and his new boyfriend. Is that why I'm here—to feed them anecdotes to whip out for all the other couples at future dinner parties? *Babe, remember that little guy you dated who thought he could win claw machines?*

I turn back to the machine, staring down my target through the glass. Fifteen seconds on the clock. The bear's just a few inches behind the prize chute, so that's good—less ground to cover means the claw has less opportunity for a premature drop. *Twelve seconds.* His back leg is wedged under something, but his other limbs are loose. Even better, the satiny plush heart he's holding doesn't seem to be fused to his chest. *Nine seconds. Eight. Seven.* I'm going for it. *Four seconds.* If winning this ten-cent valentine bear is how I wipe the smug smile off Mario's face, consider it won. *Three seconds. Two seconds. One second.*

"He's too far back," Mario says—but he's wrong. The claw descends in the exact right spot, evenly framing its target.

I don't blink. I don't even breathe.

The claw closes, grazing the bear's face and torso. Then it pauses for the barest split second before starting to rise again. Empty. Of course. Unless—

"Oh. My. God." Dylan presses his palms to the glass.

The claw lifts the bear by its valentine heart and carries it safely to the prize chute before releasing it. For a moment, I'm frozen in place, like a dancer holding a jazz-hands pose after a big Broadway number.

"*Holy shit.* You fucking did it. Are you guys seeing this?" Mario slams his palm into mine in the most forceful high five of my life, and then—before I even realize it's happening—he hugs me. "Incredible. I can't believe I doubted you."

"That's what I'm talking about. One and *done*." Dylan squats in front of the prize chute. "That's right, come to papa."

Ben shoots me the tiniest smile, and my stomach flips like a pancake.

"Just look at the little guy! He's so cute," Mario says, and I whirl around, blushing. *Little guy?* Okay, but he's looking at Dylan. Not even Dylan. It's the bear. Mario's talking about the bear.

"You know what I'd love?" Dylan says. "For goddamn once, I'd like to see a valentine with a little creativity. I'm not buying what he's selling. Haven't we evolved past *I love you beary much*? Hello?" He flicks the bear's heart. "Where's that energy for *I bearly love you*?"

"That's not a valentine; that's a breakup gift," says Ben.

Mario elbows him and laughs. "That's your breakup move, Alejo? You win the guy an asshole bear, and it's done?"

Nope. Absolutely not. No one, literally no one, asked for Mario's hot take on Ben's past breakups. And I can tell from a glance that Ben feels weird about it, too. It's actually bizarre how much a year or two of FaceTime can teach you. I can read Ben better now than I could when we were dating.

Dylan jumps into the fray. "Are you calling my bear an asshole, Super Mario?"

"Your hypothetical asshole bear? Definitely," says Mario. "This bear, on the other hand? Total fucking sweetheart. Dylan, you're a lucky dad."

And I guess I've been possessed by some kind of Pick-Me-Cool-Ex demon impulse, because suddenly I'm grabbing the bear from Dylan and thrusting it at Mario.

Dylan's jaw drops. "WHAT?"

Which is when I realize, with dawning horror, that I just gave my ex-boyfriend's new boyfriend a teddy bear. With a heart. That says *I love you beary much.*

Has my whole entire life been leading up to the complete and utter shame of this moment?

"I'm—God, I'm *so* sorry. You don't have to . . ."

I reach for the bear, but Mario whisks it away. "Hey, now. I didn't say you could have it back."

Dylan looks stunned. "I have never been so offended in my entire life. You just kidnapped my *child*."

"You *just* said you weren't buying what he's selling," says Ben.

"Bennifer, why are you making this about capitalism?"

Mario presses the bear to his chest, heart to heart. "Arthur, you've made me the happiest man alive."

"I'm . . . glad things are working out for you two," I say to Mario.

But my eyes drift to Ben.

CHAPTER ELEVEN

BEN

Saturday, May 23

It's been raining all day.

I swore Mario's flight was going to be canceled this morning, but the plane was able to make it out of New York before things got really bad. Still, I was tracking his flight throughout my shift this morning to make sure everything was okay. Before I could check a sixth time, I got a text from him letting me know that he'd landed safely and was already on his way to meet with his Tío Carlos. I liked that he wrote to me. He didn't have to, but he did. That put me in a pretty great mood for the rest of my shift.

Up until Dylan texted to cancel on our plans to eat Taco Bell and talk about everything that happened at Dave & Buster's that we couldn't talk about in front of Mario and

Arthur. I don't know why he's treating the rain like it's acid, but I'll let him have his cozy night in with Samantha. I get how rare it is for them to see each other since they live in the same college dorm room, are bouncing back and forth between their respective families' homes, and are still inseparable while out and about in the city.

Totally get it . . .

I'm in my room working on *The Wicked Wizard War* rewrites, really in my head over some feedback from my teacher about my early pages. Mrs. García thinks the story would benefit from more backstory about Ben-Jamin, but other early readers thought I was info-dumping too much. I'm torn about whose critique to pay more attention to. Yes, she's my teacher and has given me so many helpful tips—I wouldn't have been able to fix my plot's bridge without her. But Mario and others felt Ben-Jamin's origins were slowing down the story and didn't ultimately serve the central plot.

It's times like this when I don't even want to deal with this book. Like I'll never know how to make it everything everyone wants it to be. Like it'll never be good enough for people.

But I've already put so much time into it that I want to cross the finish line. I still remember how amazing it felt to complete the very first draft, and to upload the final chapter on Wattpad. But the book has also changed so much—it changes as my life does. Hudsonien used to be a major relationship for Ben-Jamin, but as I've aged up the characters, Hudsonien is more backstory than main plot. The same goes for King Arturo, who doesn't embark on epic journeys with Ben-Jamin anymore. King Arturo is still a pivotal character since he needs assistance tracking down a jeweled scepter as blue as his eyes and Ben-Jamin is the wizard for the job. I've gotten rid of all the kissing though—it felt weird writing about that since I'm no longer kissing his namesake.

Feels even weirder making Mario read about it.

I can't thank Mario enough for how cool he was about the hangout. There's no way Hudson could've gone the entire night without flipping out, and Arthur would've been really insecure. And I don't blame them. But it feels nice that as I'm building something with Mario, my friendship with my ex-boyfriend won't be an obstacle.

I need to hear his voice. See his face.

But I can't right now.

I use the Forest app when I'm writing to measure how many minutes I'm actively working and to stay focused. Depending on how much time I spend on the app, I grow more trees for my forest. If I click out to check Instagram or call a cute guy, a tree dies. I'm trying really hard to let the ambient sounds of ocean waves keep my imagination afloat, but right now I would personally go outside with an ax and chop down a tree to call Mario. I'm at the start of this chapter where I'm thinking about writing Mario in as the new love interest—Mars E. Octavio, a swordsman with a charming smile and powers to understand any language, human or beast.

I exit the app—lo siento, dead tree—and try Mario on FaceTime. I smile immediately when he answers.

"Well, well," Mario says. "Your timing is perfection."

"Really?"

Mario smiles. He's wearing those blue overalls that he painted Saturn on with rainbow rings. He holds up a bag of groceries. "Carlos sent me to the store because there's been a change of plans tonight. There's someone he wants me to meet."

Immediately, my heart sinks. Is his uncle introducing him to some other guy?

"Oh, cool. Who?"

"Close Call Entertainment is working on this android thriller and the writer is coming over. I might get to pick his brain on some things," Mario says. I'm immediately relieved it's just a work-type thing. "Carlos didn't want to tell me until I got here so I wouldn't freak out."

"That's so amazing." I'm embarrassed by how I was panicking over Mario meeting another guy. "So is Carlos going to cook?"

"I am, Alejo." Mario stops on the corner of the street and looks both ways before crossing. "I'm going to make this pumpkin soup for everyone while my uncle cleans up the backyard. Everything will be cozy and I will not lose my mind over speaking to a cool screenwriter. Also, I love it here—look." Mario flips the camera and shows me the bright blue sky and sunlight bouncing off a shiny black building.

"We've got some exciting weather here, too," I say, aiming my phone toward my window and showing him the rain.

"Still?!"

"Still."

We shift our cameras away from our skies and back on ourselves.

"Pop quiz, Alejo. ¿Como se dice 'rain' en español?"

I know it's a double-L word, but it's not coming to me as quickly as I'd like. Then I remember how I thought it sounded like it would be a gorgeous spell to use in *TWWW*, or even a character name. "Lluvia?"

"Bien hecho."

It feels weird being praised for such level-one vocabulary. I'm nineteen and learning what rain is for the first time. Even though my parents have spoken Spanish their entire lives, they didn't teach it to me. I was willing, but between all the jobs they've worked they didn't really have the time. Even though I know that speaking Spanish won't make me any more Officially Puerto Rican than I already am, every new word I learn makes me feel less like a fraud.

Anyway, better to start with the basics now with the goal of being fluent in a few years.

"Alejo, my uncle is calling. He's probably going to send me back to the grocery store to get more stuff. Can I call you later tonight?"

"I'll—"

"You'll be asleep! Three-hour difference. I'm in the past and you're in the future."

"I'm in *your* future," I say. Then I shut up because I realize how this sounds. My face runs so hot I need a lluviastorm to cool me down.

"Yeah, you are," Mario says with his weak wink. "Te veo luego, Alejo."

"Catch you later, Colón."

We hang up and I stare out the window. Dark cloudy skies. The same view of my neighborhood I've had my entire life. Same shoe repair store. Same park entrance down the block. Same apartment building across the street that's clearly nicer than ours.

Whenever this world bores me, I go back to creating my own.

I write about Ben-Jamin finding Mars at a campfire that appears out of nowhere in the forest. The attraction is there, but the chemistry takes a while to grow, and I'm able to work in some solid slow-burn metaphors about magical potions brewing across full moons. Ben-Jamin needs Mars's powers to communicate with a serpent known as a wavesnake that lives underwater, but I realize I'm undoing my measured pacing by making Ben-Jamin and Mars kiss in a field of crystal flowers. I need to slow it down. Don't give the reader everything right away.

I hope I'm not misreading the Mario vibes.

Maybe Mario should switch from tutoring me in Spanish to Marioish so I can become fluent in understanding him better.

I go through our WhatsApp chat, where he sent me a bunch of pictures from last night at Dave & Buster's. I wish I had been bold enough to ask him to take photo booth pictures with me.

I come across the group selfie after our game of *Mario Kart*. I remember the heat on my face with Arthur leaning on me, but the glow of the arcade conceals my blushed cheeks. The lights expose Arthur's forced smile. I could be overthinking it, but I know what Happy Arthur looks like: sitting on the curb in Times Square while we listened to music, the day we finally decided we didn't need another do-over date, and when I kissed him for the first time.

Friendships are two-way streets. He shouldn't be the only one walking toward me. I have to meet him in the middle.

If Arthur can hang out with Mario, I can be better talking about Mikey.

If I can't, I'll lose him again.

And I want Arthur in my life.

I should keep writing. I know I should, but I have to reach out to him.

I send Arthur a quick text: Between Mario and Mario Kart and Dylan and his Dylan-ness I feel like we didnt get to talk much. Do-over hangout?

There. I've put it out into the universe and now I wait to see—

Arthur has texted back already: Do-over hangout!

CHAPTER TWELVE

ARTHUR

Monday, May 25

The line outside the diner's already halfway down the block, but it barely even feels like I'm waiting. The weather's mild and sunny, I've got the whole day off work, and I'm on literal Broadway—the street *and* the district. Plus, the Winter Garden Theatre is practically within spitting distance, and I'm not even going to try to be cool about it. If I have to crouch to get that perfect low-angle shot of the marquee, so be it.

Which is exactly how Ben finds me: popping a squat on the sidewalk. He peers down at me with an expression that's half amused and half disturbed, and I jump up so quickly, I almost conk his chin with my skull. "Sorry! Hi!"

"Hi! Yikes. Am I really late?" He surveys the line, looking vaguely distressed.

"Not at all. It's not even open yet."

"But why are there so many people here?"

"Because it's Eileen's Galaxy Diner. Ben, it's a landmark! Have you never been here?"

His face falls. "Have you?"

"No," I say quickly. "I mean, maybe once? Years ago, though. I don't even really remember it."

Ben looks at me like he's never seen someone so full of shit in his entire life.

"Fine, it was two years ago and I remember everything, but so what? It's amazing! The waiters *sing*. It's like a full Broadway performance while you're eating."

"Yeah, that's why I suggested it. It has extreme Arthur energy."

"And New York energy." I peer around happily, taking in the souvenir shops, yellow cabs, and pretzel stands, the impossibly huge billboards. "God, I love New Yorkers. You guys embrace every single moment. Just look at all these people." I gesture down the line. "No one's pissed they have to wait, no one's driving around Alpharetta or wherever, looking for a place with parking, because God forbid—"

"Alpharetta, Georgia?" An older white woman ahead of us turns around, clasping her hands. "Don't mean to interrupt, but are y'all from there?"

"Yeah! I mean, I'm from Milton, which is pretty much—"

"Oh, I know it well. We're from Woodstock." She gestures to a guy wearing an FDNY T-shirt. "Bill, you won't believe where these gentlemen are from. Milton, Georgia!"

"Well, how about that?" says Bill. "And you know, the young lady with the big puffy sleeves up there? She's Australian!"

"Big New York energy," Ben whispers.

"Shh!" I elbow him, and he elbows me back, and I can't believe how different this feels from Dave & Buster's, or even the post office. I spent all week reminding myself that the awkwardness between us was normal. Seeing your ex for the first time in almost two years isn't exactly a chill situation, and meeting his new boyfriend? Whole new level of weird. But in this moment, it's almost hard to remember the awkwardness ever existed. I feel as instantly at home with Ben as I always did.

The line moves quickly, and before I know it, we're seated in the middle of a bank of identical rectangular tables, all barely an elbow's distance apart. "Well, this is cozy," says Ben, glancing sideways.

"You mean the fact that I could literally reach out and pull that lady's ponytail?"

"That's definitely what I meant. Touching strangers' hair."

We smile at each other.

"So," I say.

"So." He cups his chin in his hand. "No Jessie, huh?"

I make a face. "She's at work."

"On Memorial Day?"

"Can you believe it? She's there catching up on paperwork. It's tragic."

"I would cry."

"Oh, me too, for sure. I love my job and everything, but—" I stop short, looking up at Ben. "Wait, how do I not know what you're up to this summer? Are you working?"

"A little. Mostly just writing, though." He leans forward. "I want to hear about your fancy theater internship. Your boss is kind of a big deal, right?"

I sit up straighter. "Kind of, yeah. I mean, I don't know how many people outside the queer arts scene have heard of him, but he's won a bunch of awards."

"Wow. Is he pretty hands-on? Like, do you get to talk to him and stuff?"

"Oh, definitely. Like, I mostly work with Taj, his assistant, but Jacob's really chill. I ask him questions all the time."

"That's so fucking cool," Ben says. "You must be pinching yourself. Your actual dream job."

"I know." I bite my lip. "I'm kind of bad at it though. I'm constantly messing up."

Ben smiles a little. "I doubt that."

"For real! It's because there's so much organization involved—like spreadsheets and keeping track of things, and I suck at that. Like, you should see Taj. He sorts emails into folders. He has a *bullet journal*."

"I don't know what that is."

"It's just a fancy journal and organizer. I don't know, he has a whole system for it. He's just so on top of everything. Like, you ask him when a package is arriving, and he's like, 'Want the tracking number?'"

"I hate tracking numbers," Ben says.

"Me too!"

"Okay, so what about your role? Is it mostly the spreadsheets, or do you ever get to do director stuff?"

"Director stuff?"

"Like yelling into a megaphone? I don't know." He clocks my expression and laughs. "Is that not a thing?"

"Oh, it's my whole job. Just yelling in megaphones. For hours." He wrinkles his nose at me. "Yeah, no. It's more the spreadsheets . . . I basically just do whatever Taj tells me to do. Like on Friday I had to go through all this makeup inventory to get rid of all the expired stuff. That kind of thing."

"That doesn't sound too bad," Ben says.

"Until I squirted it on Jacob."

"Um. What?"

"Like, Jacob came over to ask us something, and I'm holding this bottle of foundation made for the whitest of white people. And I guess I was just antsy or something, because I don't even realize I'm pressing up and down on this bottle pump until this goopy blob splooges out and lands on his thigh—"

"Hiiii! Welcome to Eileen's Galaxy Diner. I'm Kat. Can I take your drink order?" I look up to find a ponytailed waitress smiling sweetly as she sets a pair of menus on the table. "Or should I come back once you're done talking about—"

"Makeup!" I say quickly. "Not—you know. The squirt was makeup. The kind you rub on your face? Like, for skin?"

"Should you be rubbing foreskins on your face?" Kat asks.

Ben laughs so hard he can barely order his coffee, and he instantly declares Kat to be his all-time favorite waitress. I grab a menu, mostly to have something to hide behind. Scanning the list of options makes me hungry already—omelets, grilled cheese, milkshakes.

But then I look at the prices.

"Um. Ben?"

His eyes pop up adorably over his menu.

"I forgot how expensive this place is."

"Yeah, that's kind of how it goes with these tourist-trap places."

"We don't have to eat here. Why don't we go grab bagels or something?"

"No, look! They have bagels!" Ben flips his menu around, pointing.

"I mean a bagel that doesn't cost double digits."

"Arthur, it's fine. I knew what I was getting into."

I study his face, trying to read between the lines of his expression. He seems sincere—but I'm never quite sure how to step when it comes to money stuff with Ben. It would be so much easier if I could just pay for his meal—but that feels so *boyfriendy*, like I'm trying to encroach on Mario's territory. Not that Mario seemed territorial. Honestly, Ben's probably the one feeling territorial, now that I've apparently confessed my love for Mario via claw-machine teddy bear. Because I'm—I can't emphasize this enough—a full goddamn disaster.

"So, what's up with Mario?" I ask.

Ben looks taken aback. "You mean—"

"Sorry." I blush. "I just mean what's he up to today? Why is he not having fancy bagels with us?"

"Oh!" Ben says. "He's in LA. Visiting his uncle."

"Oh, right! He mentioned that."

Kat shows up with Ben's coffee. "Are you guys ready,

or do you need more time to . . . ?" She waves her hands around vaguely.

"Ready!" I shoot her a nice big not-talking-about-splooge-and-foreskins-this-time smile. I end up going for the challah French toast, which sounds great until Ben orders something five dollars cheaper off the appetizer menu. So then I go around in circles for a second, trying to decide if changing my order would make Ben feel more or less self-conscious.

"Why are you making your panic face?" Ben asks as soon as Kat leaves.

"What? I'm not!" I clasp my hands and tuck them under my chin. "Anyway! How's the coffee?"

Ben studies me for a moment before answering. "Decent. I've had better."

"Coffee snob. You've clearly been spending too much time with Dylan."

He laughs, but there's this edge to it.

"Wait, is everything okay?"

"Yeah, no, totally," Ben says quickly. "He's just—I don't know. He's been sort of distant lately."

"Distant?" I tilt my head, thinking about Dylan's claw-machine antics. "Like distant from reality?"

Ben laughs. "It's kind of hard to explain."

"Well, talk me through it."

"It's just . . ." He pauses. "I mean, I'm probably reading

way too much into things. I'm sure he's just busy. Which is great, because so am I."

"You've got Mario now," I say, nodding—but the look on Ben's face sends my stomach into free fall. "Okay, I feel like that came out weird."

"No—"

"I just mean that I'm happy for you. Mario seems awesome, and I'm glad you have a boyfriend who makes you happy."

"Oh—that's not. He's not my boyfriend."

"He's . . . not?"

"Not officially," Ben adds, and I'm pretty sure he's speaking English. But there's this lag before the words sink in. It's almost like I'm waiting for a live closed-captioned translation.

Did Ben just say Mario isn't his boyfriend?

It doesn't compute. I'm not trying to be dense, but I saw them kissing—in broad daylight. Which is what you do with your boyfriend, not some random guy you're hooking up with. Okay, there might have been a modest amount of daylight kissing before Mikey and I were official, but not at the goddamn post office. I'm sorry, but there are two and only two reasons to kiss at a post office. Either you just got proposed to via flash mob, or you're saying goodbye to your first love before you head back home to Georgia. Anything else is just gratuitous PDA.

"Arthur?"

I look up with a start. "Hmm?"

"Why are you doing big eyes?"

"Those are just my eyes."

Ben raises his eyebrows. "You think I don't know what your eyes look like?"

My heart leaps into my throat—which makes no sense whatsoever. *Eyes*, Arthur. This isn't an intimate statement. He's not talking about your dick. Strangers on the subway know what your eyes look like.

"I'm just saying, you don't have to be scandalized about it," Ben says. "It's what Mario and I both want. Things are good, we have fun together, and we make each other happy. We just haven't quite reached the no-I-love-YOU-more stage like you and Mikey."

"Wait, *what*?"

"Hello, New York!" booms an amplified voice. I whip around sideways in my seat, craning my neck—there's a waiter with a microphone standing directly behind me on the booth divider. "Looks like you've wandered into Eileen's Galaxy Diner!" Cheers erupt from every corner of the dining room. "I'm Blair, but I'm about to turn the microphone over to my friends Kat and Dana—"

I glance back at Ben. "Our Kat?"

"Who are going to—okay, Dana's dropping off some drinks, but *then* they're going to dazzle you with their extraordinary talent. Are you ready, Dana? Yes! Okay! This is . . . 'Dance with You' from *The Proooom*!" Blair hops off the divider as the opening notes of background music start to play. When I turn back around, Kat's standing a few feet behind Ben, clutching a microphone in both hands. Ben twists his chair sideways, which gives me the perfect profile view of his mouth falling open when Kat starts the first verse.

"Holy shit." He turns back to me. "Are they all this good?"

"Pretty much."

"Okay, well, *I'm* impressed."

I laugh. "I am, too! I just mean everyone here's amazing. You'll see."

But the truth is, I don't even notice when the vocals switch to Dana. I can't keep the music in focus; I keep drifting back to what Ben said about Mikey. The no-I-love-you-more stage? Does he really think Mikey and I are that serious? Obviously we're serious in the sense that we call each other boyfriends and have sex sometimes. But *love*? And for Ben to just assume that?

There's an explosion of cheering when the song ends. Kat shows up with our food a minute later, and I'm treated to yet another intriguing performance: Ben Alejo in the nonverbal role of Fanboy Visibly Losing His Shit.

"I can't believe you're having your Broadway awakening at this very moment."

Ben grabs a mozzarella stick. "If you say so."

"Pretty sure I know the hip hooray and ballyhoo when I hear it."

Ben looks at me blankly.

"'Lullaby of Broadway'? From *42nd Street*?"

"Oh, does the awakening come with a full encyclopedia of obscure Broadway references?"

"Did you just call *42nd Street* obscure?" He tilts his palms up. "Ben, it won a Tony. And then the revival won a Tony."

"I'm sorry?"

"Unacceptable. I'm making you a playlist. No, you know what? I'm making you a whole *playlist* of playlists. One for ballads, one for love songs—" I feel my cheeks go warm. "Oh, and just so you know, Mikey and I haven't discussed that yet."

Ben holds his mozzarella stick aloft. "The playlist?"

"No, the I-love-you thing. We haven't said it yet."

"Oh!" He blinks. "Sorry, I just figured—"

"No, you're fine. Yeah, we're just . . ." God, I don't even know how to finish that sentence. But Ben's looking at me, waiting to hear the rest of my bullshit. "Like, I've thought about it. Obviously, I love him. I just don't know if I'm—" I stop short.

"If you're in love with him?"

I shove a giant bite of French toast in my mouth, scanning the room as I chew. Maybe a waiter's about to break into song right now? Maybe a nice, loud, full-ensemble number? Anyone?

"You don't have to answer that," says Ben.

I swallow. "I know."

Something flips in my chest when our eyes meet.

I quickly look away. "It's just hard to pin down sometimes. I always thought love was a certain feeling, and it's either there or it's not. But with Mikey, it's just . . ." I tilt my palms up, looking back up at Ben.

He doesn't reply. He just furrows his brow and watches me.

"But I don't actually think it's supposed to feel like Broadway, you know? It's not a rom-com. It's just, I don't know. Real life. He makes me happy. And I love who he is as a person."

"He seems great."

"He is." I smile. "Like, he's really funny, but he's so quiet that hardly anyone *knows* he's funny. So you feel like you're in on a secret. And he's *so* smart. And he can sing—sorry, I know I sound like a checklist."

"No, I get it," says Ben.

"It's just . . . I think about it a lot, actually. I keep trying to add it all up in my head. Like at what point does all of this mean I'm in love with him?"

Ben wrinkles his nose. "Why are you trying to turn love into a math problem?"

"I'm not, I swear!" I laugh. "I just wish I knew is all? I keep waiting for it to click or something, and maybe that's not—I don't know. I'm probably doing this wrong. I'll probably look back in a year and say, 'Wow, I was in love with him the whole time,' right?"

I shift in my seat, feeling squirmy and strange. I've never said any of this out loud before, and now I wish I could snatch the words back out of the air. All these questions about Mikey, these tiny back-burner thoughts in my head. It's like they're highlighted and bolded, stamped all over my face: ARTHUR DOESN'T KNOW HIS OWN HEART.

The thing is, two years ago with Ben, there wasn't a doubt in my mind.

I shake the thought away, turning brightly to Ben. "Seriously, you should come meet him next weekend," I say. "Mario, too, of course."

"Right." Ben pauses. "Mario's still going to be in LA."

"But you'll be here, right?"

"Yeah. But . . . would that make things weird?"

"What? No way. I know Mikey would love to meet you! He's heard a lot about you. Not in an overshare way—"

"Of course not. Never."

"Shut up. I'm just saying." I grin. "It'll be fun! Universes colliding! You know, I actually think you guys will hit it off. You have a lot in common."

"We do?"

"Well, you've got me," I say. "And I'm a lot."

Turns out, Ben's startled laugh is still one of the best sounds on earth.

CHAPTER THIRTEEN

BEN

Thursday, May 28

Kool Koffee hasn't changed much over the past couple of years. Samantha's past regulars still recognize her, sitting at a table by the door with me and Dylan. It's like she's some celebrity visiting home, and she still remembers so much about them:

"Staying strong with that decaf, Brian?"

"You were so right about going away for school, Greg."

"Congrats again on the wedding, Stephanie!"

"Do we need to get you a disguise?" I ask Samantha. "Maybe some sunglasses."

"Ben, do we ask you to put on concealer to hide your freckles?" Dylan asks. "No, because we don't hide beauty in this house."

"We're in a coffee shop."

"It's an expression."

"For people who live together."

Dylan glares at me from over his double-espresso mocha with two pumps of caramel.

"Hi, I'm still here," Samantha says, waving. "Anyway, Ben, we keep getting interrupted."

"By your fans," I say.

"My adoring *friends*, yes. So why are you so nervous about meeting Mikey?"

It's been a few days since seeing Arthur at the diner, but the idea of hanging out with Mikey is still eating away at me. I've even had a couple dreams where I'm this third wheel as they make out in front of me. It's gotten me to the point where I wake up in the middle of the night and try to work, but my escapist world feels polluted with all the King Arturo scenes.

"I don't know how good I'm going to feel about myself after meeting with Mikey," I answer.

"Then maybe you shouldn't meet him," Samantha says.

"But Arthur met Mario," I say.

"Because you also thought Mikey was going to be there. And you had us."

I mess around with the leftover ice from my lemonade. "I want to be a good friend. And Arthur showed up even though he knew Mikey wasn't going to be there. I just think backing out now makes it look weird."

"Just lie and say you're working on your book," Dylan says.

"I mean, I am working on my book."

"Cute little lemonade break you're having."

I shift slightly, so that I'm face-to-face with Samantha. "I just don't think it's fair if Arthur can spend all night with my people and I can't meet Mikey."

Samantha nods. "Maybe you'll prove yourself wrong and Mikey won't make you feel inferior at all—not that I think he should."

"Definitely not," Dylan says. "I've written poetry about you. You think I'm writing poetry about Mikey?"

"Do you plan on writing any for me?" Samantha asks.

"Do you plan on letting a poet breathe? Everything in good time." Dylan hides behind his hand and mouths, "Help me write a poem."

"Write your own poem," I tell him. "Between us, Arthur said that he and Mikey haven't said 'I love you' yet," I add.

Dylan's eyes widen. "But they've been together forever in gay years."

"Please find me a calendar with gay years."

"You would love that, wouldn't you?" Dylan winks.

Samantha sighs and turns to Dylan. "I'm powering you down for two minutes." She pulls out her phone and sets a timer. "Any last words?"

"You'll regret this," Dylan says.

"I always do." Samantha kisses his cheek and presses start on the timer. "Ben, we don't have much time. I wouldn't spend so much energy obsessing over what Arthur and Mikey's deal is. That's for them to figure out and not for you to worry about."

She's right. Arthur could be telling Mikey 'I love you' this very second.

"I think I wouldn't be obsessing over this if things were clearer with Mario. But it feels like this unspoken agreement where we don't want to ruin a good thing by defining the relationship. It's just hard," I say.

Between his tightly sealed lips, Dylan murmurs, "That's what he said."

Samantha adds another thirty seconds to the timer. "Ben, you need to figure everything out with Mario. You deserve to know how someone feels about you. Dylan made his feelings really clear."

"The future wife business," I say. "Right in this very shop."

Samantha laughs. "Maybe he says too much sometimes. But at least I know what he's thinking." She turns to Dylan and twirls her necklace. "I love you."

"I love you, too," Dylan says.

He kisses her and adds another thirty seconds to the timer.

This is what I want in a relationship.

Now I need to figure out what I want in a friendship with Arthur.

What I don't say aloud is how much I miss Arthur. It's been months since I lost sleep over that, but not having him in my life has been weighing on me. There was a time when we were able to talk about little things, like what he was getting up to in college. But I kept my business to myself because I didn't want to hurt his feelings. Even stuff like noticing how cute Mario was when I started college. Maybe I shouldn't have held back—Arthur never did. And even after I muted his Instagram profile, I still had to dodge "How's Arthur?" questions from my parents. It's why I wrote our old love out of my book. It was all too much.

But I don't want to be scared of Arthur and his life anymore. And I don't want to bury him away like he has no place in mine.

CHAPTER FOURTEEN

ARTHUR

Friday, May 29

The escalator keeps churning out people who aren't Mikey. There should be a rule against that, something in the bylaws requiring one train-rumpled boyfriend for every dozen pantsuited strangers.

Nothing to do now but hang beneath the Arrivals/Departures sign, cradling a bouquet of impulse-buy bodega flowers. I should have gotten him something useful, like sunscreen or a MetroCard, but how was I supposed to resist two dozen roses for twelve dollars?

My phone buzzes with an incoming text, and I scramble to check it.

Sounds good, see you soon!

A perfectly normal text to receive from my almost-here boyfriend.

But it's not from my boyfriend.

I stare at the words, stomach fluttering faintly, until—

"Hi, sorry, I'm looking for Chad from corporate?"

Mikey's face, but he's not on my phone screen. I fling my arms around him so fast I almost smack him with the roses. "You're here!"

"I know!"

"I can't believe it. You were in *Boston*." I hug him harder. "Mikey!"

He laughs, short and breathless. "Long two weeks."

"You're telling me." I draw back to look at him, and his cheeks go instantly pink.

I can't kiss him. Mikey's so shy about PDA, and it doesn't get much more public than the main terminal of Penn Station. But him being here feels like the first few steps off a roller coaster, when solid ground feels brand-new.

Good. This is good. The math checks out. *Two weeks without Mikey* equals *I'm so fucking glad that he's here.* I'm feeling everything I'm supposed to feel. Nothing off-kilter. No weird doubts or unspoken questions. Nothing but—

Is it cool if we see Ben tonight?

Hey, so Ben's meeting us for ice cream.

It'll be fine. I'm not even worried, you know? We'll talk

it out on the subway ride home, and it will be sorted before we even reach Columbus Circle.

Except Columbus Circle comes and goes, and then Lincoln Center comes and goes, and then we're on Seventy-Second Street, turning the corner past Citarella, and I still haven't told him.

It's not that I was avoiding the topic. But the subway was crowded and sweaty, and Mikey looked so wide-eyed and overwhelmed. And now he's in the middle of telling me about this eighth-grade overnight choir trip, his only other time in New York. Chatty Mikey, his rarest and most fascinating natural form. No way am I going to derail this. I don't even cut in to tell him we've reached my building—I just take out my key and slip it into the lock while he talks.

But the minute we're alone in the lobby, I kiss him so hard he drops his roses.

I can hardly believe he's here. Real-life Mikey, in all three dimensions. In New York. In this building. It's like running into your math teacher at Publix, or seeing a bird fly in through your window. It just doesn't seem scientifically possible that I could be kissing Mikey in the same place I pick up mail for my great-uncle Milton.

When we finally resurface, Mikey's adorably flustered.

"Okay!" I say, slightly breathless. "That's the lobby."

Mikey picks his bouquet off the floor. "So far, so good."

On the elevator, we're weirdly shy around each other. Mikey keeps getting startled by his own reflection in the mirrored elevator walls, and I keep smiling down at my phone, thinking about how Jessie's not usually home for another hour or so. And, of course, we're not meeting Ben until nine. Which I'll tell Mikey about momentarily. For real this time. I'll tell him the minute we're settled in at home.

The elevator lands on the third floor with a ding, and I grab Mikey's suitcase. But the moment my hand grazes the knob of 3A, the door swings wide open.

"Hey! Sorry!" Jessie props the door open, smiling brightly. "I don't want to get in your way. Just dropped off my laptop. I'm meeting Namrata and Juliet for appetizers. Anyway, Mikey! Hi! I'm really glad you're here."

"Glad to be here." He smiles shyly.

"Remind me, what time are you meeting up with Ben?" she asks, turning to me.

My stomach drops. "Um. We haven't really . . ."

Jessie's eyebrows shoot up, the world's most crystal clear *What the fuck, Arthur?* expression.

Mikey doesn't say a word, even after she leaves. He just follows me into the apartment, where I jerk the door shut too loudly and then fumble around with the light switches. My heart's pounding so hard, I can practically taste it. "Hey. So. I was just about to tell you."

He's staring down at the floor, his expression inscrutable. When he speaks at last, his voice is as faint as a ghost. "You're doing something with Ben tonight?"

"We!" I say quickly. "Oh my God, not like, without you. Here, sorry, I don't mean to make you stand in the foyer." I laugh weakly, spreading my arms. "Welcome to Uncle Milton's apartment."

Mikey nods stiffly.

"Are you thirsty? I could get you some water or, I don't know. I think there might be Coke—"

"I'm fine." He looks pointedly away from me.

"Okay." I cross the room, sinking into the love seat, scooting to one side to make room. "Can we talk about it?"

He doesn't reply, but he sets his flowers on the table and settles in beside me, his back perfectly straight. When I take his hand, he doesn't pull away, but he doesn't lean into it either. There's no trace of the flustered softness from the lobby. I study his profile. "Mikey."

He's staring at his knees. "So we're seeing Ben. Tonight."

"I know it's not ideal. It's just, we have the show tomorrow afternoon, and then Ben's got dinner with Dylan, and then Mario gets back from his trip, and you leave so early on Sunday, so—"

"Tonight's the night. Got it."

"Not until later. And it's only for dessert, and I *think* you're going to like the place I picked." I squeeze his hand, but he doesn't look up. I hesitate. "I just really want you guys to meet each other, you know? It's important to me."

Mikey meets my eyes at last. "Why?"

"Because you're important to me? I don't know. He's my friend, and I want him to meet the guy who makes me really, really happy. Okay?"

His expression softens. "Okay."

"Mikey Mouse, I'm so sorry. I shouldn't have sprung this on you literally the second you walked in the door."

"Oh, I was still in the hallway." He smiles slightly.

"Well, you're here now." I kiss him on the cheek, then rest my head on his shoulder. "Do you even get how much I missed you?"

"Me too."

And for hours, we pretty much stay like that, tucked up on the couch. I mean, we make out a little, but it's strictly Disney Channel. We don't even bring up the possibility of sex. Maybe that's a waste of precious alone time, but it's nice. We order pizza, and I take out my contacts and put on glasses. By the time we finish eating, there's still an hour or so before we're supposed to meet Ben, but I talk Mikey into heading out early so I can show him Central Park on the way.

Of course, Mikey barely speaks the whole way down Seventy-Fifth Street, so my brain decides to fill the space with continuous word vomit. "There's an entrance at Seventy-Seventh, I think, if you want to pop in there, or we can just turn back at the Museum of Natural History. It's right up there." I point ahead, glancing sideways at Mikey, who smiles vaguely and nods. I take a breath and barrel on. "Did you ever see *Night at the Museum*? With Ben Stiller?"

"I . . . think so? I don't remember. I was pretty little."

"I refused to watch it until like sophomore year of high school, because I knew the whale would be in it, and Mikey, I was *so* scared of the whale."

"The whale?"

"Uh, the giant fucking whale hanging down from the ceiling?" I look at him incredulously as we step off the curb, into a crosswalk. "How do you not know about the whale? He's my nemesis. I'm gonna—okay, you know what, I think it opens at ten tomorrow, maybe? What time's our show, two?"

Mikey raises his eyebrows. "I don't want to make you see the scary whale."

"I would do it. Mikey Mouse, I would do it for you."

He laughs and then exhales, his shoulders rising and then falling. A moment later, he grabs my hand. I look up at him, startled. We just passed Columbus Avenue, it's barely sunset, and we're surrounded by people. Which doesn't bother me in the slightest—but Mikey?

He squeezes the tips of my fingers. "This okay?"

"Yeah. God. Of course." I study his profile. "I just. I don't want you to feel uncomfortable."

"I don't." He draws in a big shaky breath.

"That didn't sound comfortable."

Mikey laughs. "No, I'm good. Sorry. Yeah."

We walk in silence for a moment, our hands still twined together. When we reach Amsterdam Avenue, I nudge him. "That's my warm-cookie bakery," I say, pointing to Levain.

"Is that where we're meeting Ben?"

"Nope. Almost there, though. We're going to be pretty early."

He nods quickly, lips pressed together.

"Don't be nervous!" I laugh a little, tugging him closer. "I promise he's not scary. You're going to like him."

"I know," Mikey says. "That's not—yeah. I'm fine."

"Are you ready to be more than fine?" I tilt my chin. "End of the block, on the right."

Mikey stares down the street, squinting, and his whole face lights up the moment he sees it. "You're *joking*."

Emack & Bolio's in white capital letters against a basic green awning. I don't think I'd have even noticed it if Mikey hadn't drilled the name into my head. It's his favorite ice cream place in Boston. His sister and brother-in-law got engaged there, and it's also where Mikey came out to his brother. When we started talking about summer in Boston, it was the first thing he mentioned.

"I had no idea this was here." He looks amazed.

We're almost thirty minutes early, so we settle onto a

bench near the front of the shop. Mikey's gone back to being quiet, and I can't quite get my head around his mood tonight. I don't *think* he's still upset about Ben. I mean, a minute ago, he was practically giddy over the Emack & Bolio's reveal—not to mention the unprecedented public hand-holding on the way here. But somehow our hands came apart in the transition from sidewalk to bench, and Mikey definitely made a point to leave a few inches of space between us.

Now he keeps stealing glances at me, almost like we're strangers checking each other out at a dorm party. But every time I try to catch his gaze, he looks abruptly away.

"Mikey Mouse," I say finally. "I can't tell if you're okay."

"I love you," he blurts.

I just stare at him, stunned.

"God. Sorry, I'm—" He exhales. "I've been working up the nerve the whole way here. I feel so—"

"Oh my God. Mikey. Don't be—don't be sorry, okay?" I press my hand to my chest, like it will help me catch my breath. I can hardly tell my thoughts apart from my heartbeats. *He loves me. Loves me. Loves. Me. Mikey, who turns red whenever I kiss him. Mikey, whose Valentine's Day gift was filling my car with gas. Mikey, who took the train in from Boston to see me. Mikey loves me.*

My brain can't hold the thought.

He closes his eyes and opens them again—and suddenly his face sort of freezes.

"I think Ben's here," he says softly.

I shake my head. "No way. He's never early. Ever—" But the word dies on my tongue.

Because there's a boy walking down Amsterdam Avenue wearing jeans and a dark fitted T-shirt, and it's unmistakably Ben Alejo. He looks up from his phone, breaking into a smile when he sees us.

He's twenty minutes early. "Mikey—"

"It's okay. Seriously." He starts to stand, but I grab his hand first and squeeze it.

"We'll talk later," I say, and it comes out slightly choked. "To be continued, okay?"

He nods wordlessly and adjusts his glasses, and it's such a familiar Mikey gesture, it makes my throat hurt. When I stand, my legs feel like rubber. Like Gumby.

People do this, right? Boyfriends and friends are supposed to meet. It's the most normal thing in the world. So why does it feel like I'm trying to squeeze two universes into one solar system? What are my lines here? How do I even phrase the introductions? Guy I lost my virginity to, meet the guy who just said *I love you* for the first time literally two seconds ago.

"Aren't you going to give me props for being early?"

Ben asks, smiling in this fake-proud way he does sometimes when he's *actually* proud of himself but feels weird saying so. When he turns to Mikey, his smile settles into something a little bit shyer. "Nice to finally meet you."

"Me too. I've heard . . . a lot about you."

Ben looks intrigued. "Oh yeah?"

"Hey!" I clasp my hands together so tightly, my knuckles turn white. "Anyone up for ice cream?"

CHAPTER FIFTEEN

BEN

Friday, May 29

Third Wheel Time.

I stare at the menu board as if it's just another night out with my friends, and not my first time meeting my ex-boyfriend's new boyfriend. His new boyfriend who has apparently heard a lot about me. That's not a huge surprise—this is Arthur we're talking about. Arthur who always has to fill the silence.

"There's so many flavors," I say.

"Mikey is a pro here," Arthur says, holding Mikey's hand like it's a balloon that he never wants to float away. "What do you recommend?"

"What are you into, Ben?" Mikey asks.

Hearing him say my name tightens my chest. Every

second he becomes realer and realer, and I really wish Mario or Dylan or Samantha were here with me right now.

"I keep it simple," I say. "I'll be good with strawberry."

"You have great taste," Arthur says. "In ice cream," he adds. "People, too, obviously. Not talking about myself—I mean Mario."

Mikey and I stare at Arthur. Normally I'd find this funny, but it's just really awkward.

Arthur points behind the counter. "Do you think they'll let me cool off in their fridge?"

"Doesn't seem sanitary," Mikey says.

Arthur nods. "Right."

I wonder if this hangout would feel easier if we just addressed the elephant in the room. Yes, Arthur and I were in love. Yes, Arthur and I broke up because we didn't think long distance would work. Yes, Arthur started dating Mikey and didn't let distance get in the way. If we're going to talk about all of this, it doesn't really feel like my place. They're the couple, and I'm an add-on tonight.

But I can distract. "You have any flavor recommendations, Mikey?"

Mikey stares at the menu. "Grasshopper Pie is certainly a choice, and I respect everyone's right to choose, but I personally won't be choosing that tonight."

"Me either," I say with a laugh.

Arthur laughs after, a little too loudly.

"I'm good with any fruit flavors," I say.

"Goa mango is the best," Mikey says, his eyes lit up. "My treat."

I'm suddenly self-conscious that Arthur has talked about how poor I am. "No, please, I got it," I say. "In fact, let me get yours as a welcome to New York."

"My treat," Arthur says. "You guys can go grab a table. Mikey Mouse, the usual?"

"Yup," Mikey says.

Mikey Mouse? It's a pretty cheesy nickname. (Shit, no pun intended.) I can't really judge given that Ben-Jamin is a pretty ridiculous name for a main character, which I can only get away with in a fantasy novel.

Besides, it's awesome that Arthur has his Mikey Mouse. I have my Super Mario.

Mikey and I settle into a table by the window where we can see a group of people laughing outside of a restaurant and hugging before going off in their own directions.

"So you have a usual?" I ask.

"The mud pie," Mikey says. "It sounds gross, but it's coffee-flavored with chocolate chips and crumbled Oreos. You can try mine if you want."

"Thanks, I'll let you enjoy it. So are you in New York often?"

"This is my first time in years, actually," Mikey says.

"Welcome back. Are you planning on seeing any shows?"

Mikey nods. "And some sightseeing."

Then there's an awkward silence. I know I haven't been comfortable with the idea of finally meeting Mikey. Now I wonder how he feels about meeting me. There's definitely some energy between them. I wouldn't say it's chemistry, exactly. (But don't take the word of a former chemistry summer schooler.) I can see that they care for each other, but I guess I always expected them to be shining bright like Broadway lights. It's possible I caught them off guard with how early I was. I just didn't want to be late and make it seem like I wasn't taking this meetup seriously.

It means a lot to Arthur, so it means a lot to me.

Still, this is Mikey's first night back in New York in years, and he's spending it having ice cream with his boyfriend's ex-boyfriend. It must feel like meeting a ghost of Arthur's romantic past. I was his first kiss, his first boyfriend, the first person he had sex with, the first breakup he cried over. But maybe he doesn't mind at all because he's so confident in their future.

I may have been the first, but he'll be the forever.

"Voilà, gentlemen." Arthur returns with all the ice cream, and his is the only one with a cone. "So what did I miss?"

Mikey and I start talking over each other and stop at the same time. Then he insists that I go and I insist that he goes. It's almost like we're both trying to not fight for the spotlight. Better to sink into the shadows.

"I was just telling Ben how excited I am to be back," Mikey says.

"It's going to be so fun," Arthur says.

Arthur adjusts his glasses, which really does make me rethink how people can't tell the difference between Superman and Clark Kent. Superman and Arthur are both attractive without their glasses, but when they are wearing them, it's a heart-pounding transformation. Not that I'm crushing on Superman; he's a comic book character. And not that I'm crushing on Arthur; he's my ex-boyfriend. It's possible to think someone is attractive without wanting to be with them, right? It's like when Dylan points out hot guys because he wants *me* to date them, not him. Honestly, the jury might still be out on that one.

I'm certain about my feelings, though, and when it comes to Arthur, they're completely platonic. Obviously.

"What shows are you planning on seeing?" I ask.

They tell me all about their plans, but I get distracted when Arthur and Mikey swap cone and cup, wordlessly, like they've done this a thousand times. And when Mikey's phone buzzes on the table, Arthur silences it for him. I would've thought that was passive-aggressive, but Mikey thanks Arthur. Maybe Mikey likes being present, and Arthur knows that about his boyfriend.

From the few times I looked at Mikey's Instagram, he wasn't posting regularly like a lot of the people I know. He's not trying to be some influencer or pretend his life is extraordinary or show off what he ate that day. He's real.

Man, Mikey is real.

And he's sitting right across from me.

There was a time when I wanted Mikey to be the worst person ever so I wouldn't have to feel bad about Arthur committing to him over me. But he isn't the worst.

I want to be happy for them. Arthur especially.

Happiness is tricky when it comes to the person who used to make you happy.

"I hope you guys enjoy the show. Don't be late," I say with a laugh.

Arthur does this cringe-smile and shakes his head. "That wasn't fun."

"What wasn't?" Mikey asks.

"I'm sure Arthur told you how I screwed up us seeing *Hamilton*."

"He didn't," Mikey says.

I suddenly wish I could reverse time, because I really didn't want to walk into any dating history territory. But that's hard when that's all Arthur and I really have.

"I was late getting to the theater and we missed out on those rush tickets," I say. I don't mention how Arthur and I sat outside on the curb, listening to music.

Mikey shakes his head. "That's heartbreaking."

"One of many reasons I've gotten better about not being late anymore," I say.

Everything I say feels wrong. Like I'm trying to let Arthur know that I'm a better person now. But this isn't about me trying to get back with him. I just don't know how to be friends with him when we never got to be friends first.

Not to mention the fact that dodging him on social media for months left me totally unprepared for the reality of Arthur having a serious boyfriend. I should have warmed up with pictures.

Then again, how serious can they be if they haven't said *I love you*?

"So you're a writer," Mikey says.

"I'm not published."

"You're still a writer though, right?"

"Yeah. I write about wizard stuff."

"He has hundreds, maybe even thousands of readers who want more from him," Arthur says. "As they should—I love that story so much."

Back to awkward. I really hope Arthur has had the

common sense to not tell Mikey about all the original romance stuff between Ben-Jamin and King Arturo. Or even the fact that Arthur inspired a character—though Arturo isn't the love interest anymore. I'm not looking forward to sharing that news with Arthur. But any concern about breaking Arthur's heart goes out the window when I see Mikey holding his hand.

"I took the story off Wattpad so I could rework it in school. I really want to get it published soon."

"What school do you go to?" Mikey asks.

"Hostos College," I say. I feel insecure again, wishing I had the grades and financial means to have gone to the New School creative writing program, or anything at NYU. But that's my truth. I did my best and my family does their best. I'm trying to be more comfortable with that. "I really like it. Great teacher, great classmates. There's even this guy Mario who became my partner on a project and now we've got a will-we-won't-we thing going on."

"He was the one with you all at Dave & Buster's, right?"

"He beat us in pretty much every game," Arthur says.

"Where's he now?"

"He's in Los Angeles with his uncle. Apparently it's amazing."

"Why didn't you go with him?"

I shake my head. "Kind of a big step since he's not my boyfriend. Besides, I got to work on my book."

"Yeah, but you can write anywhere," Mikey says.

Why is he pushing so hard on this? It's like he doesn't want me in the same city as Arthur.

"I don't really have book-a-flight-last-minute money."

Bringing up money makes me uncomfortable. It reminds me that no matter how much I try, there isn't much money to save. It makes me feel even more powerless. This is where a book deal would come in handy. We had a book editor visit Hostos to talk about publishing, and she gave us some realistic ranges to expect for a first-time deal. Even the lower-end advances would be life-changing for me. Maybe then I would have the money to go wherever I want, whenever I want.

Mrs. García once asked the class what motivates us to write, aside from being drawn to stories. The raw reason we push ourselves draft after draft. I was really nervous, but I raised my hand and told her I wanted financial security. To not be worried anymore about how I spend my money. To see something cool online and buy it because I can and want to and not because I need it. To take care of my family the way they've taken care of me. To repay Dylan for all the times he's given me money even though he's never asked for a dollar back, not even when he sees me get the occasional twenty in the mail from my abuelita.

As everyone finishes their ice cream and the conversation moves away from money, I'm ready to give them their space.

"I'll get out of your hair. Thanks so much for the ice cream, Arthur." I get up from the table and throw out my trash.

"You're not in our hair!" Arthur says, a little too brightly. "Walk back with us?"

"I'm—"

"I mean, you haven't even told me what Ben-Jamin's up to in the revision!"

Something tells me Mikey could live without that update, but Arthur looks so weirdly panicked that I just shrug. "Um. Sure."

But Mikey takes Arthur's hand as soon as we leave the shop, and it's kind of messing with my brain. I keep losing the thread of what I'm talking about, midsentence.

I'm not going to say it's the most excited I've ever been to arrive at Arthur's building, but it's definitely the most relieved.

I turn to Mikey. "It was really great to meet you. I hope you love the rest of your trip."

"Thanks, Ben." Mikey extends his hand. I would've gone in for a hug, but a handshake is more than respectable.

"Good luck with the writing. I'm sure it'll all work out."

I cross my fingers. "Here's hoping."

"Get home safely," Arthur says. "No fights with anyone on the train."

Two summers ago, we found ourselves being harassed by this homophobe on the train because Arthur and I were cuddling together. Arthur was really rattled, and honestly, I still tense up whenever I pass that subway stop thinking I might see him again. It's yet another thing about this city that haunts me.

"I'll do my best," I say.

Arthur and I give each other the world's quickest hug, like anything longer will be mistaken as intimacy.

Then he steps into the lobby with Mikey. I watch them for a few moments before I turn away because jealousy gets the best of me. I want a solid relationship like they have.

And I want it with Mario.

The next evening, Dylan drags me to the Upper West Side again for an early dinner.

The Earth Café seems really chill, and the entire time we're eating, Dylan keeps scoping the place like he's trying to invest in it. I don't get the comedy behind this bit, but I just let him keep inspecting every utensil, plate, and food temperature. But I draw the line when he tries ordering three different coffee flavors. He rebels by ordering one of every pastry for dessert.

He cuts a chocolate croissant in half. "Rate this from one to one hundred?"

"That's a wide range."

He takes a bite. "It's a solid eighty-seven." He takes a second bite. "No, eighty-eight."

I'm too full from my chicken salad to eat anything else, so I let him have at it.

This is our boys' night, since Samantha and Jessie are hanging out, but he's seemed really distracted all evening. I don't know what's up with him, but he insists everything is fine.

"So," I say. "Mikey was nice."

"Translation: boring AF."

"No, Mikey is a nice guy. He might be a little privileged, but not in a douchey way. I don't have anything bad to say about him. Does that mean he's good for Arthur?"

Dylan devours the second half of the croissant while he ponders the question. "I think Arthur needs more than someone nice. But I haven't met the guy."

"They must be a good fit. Arthur wouldn't force anything that wasn't working. Also, you have a thousand crumbs on you."

Dylan looks down at his shirt. "Say what you want about

your ex-boyfriend, but when it comes to my crumbs, you mind your business."

"Noted. I wonder if Arthur and me breaking up was a good thing for him in the long run."

"I care more about if it was good for you."

As Dylan eats a blueberry muffin, my phone buzzes.

I smile. "It's Mario," I say, and answer the call. "Hey!"

"Hey, Super Mario," Dylan says with a mouthful of muffin. He grabs his phone, probably to rate the pastries.

"Oh, you're out and about," Mario says. "I don't want to bother you if you're busy."

"No, it's okay. Dylan is acting like a food critic because . . . he's Dylan? Did you make it back okay?"

"Just landed a bit ago and headed home now. I'm still on LA time and I've got some extra hours in me. I thought maybe we could hang out and you can welcome me back to the future."

"I'm game!" I'm not even going to play it cool. "I'm with D. You cool with a group hangout?"

"The more, the merrier, as long as you're there, Alejo. Figure out the plan. I'm almost home and going to take a quick shower."

I can practically smell his ocean breeze bodywash already. It makes me wish we could have an evening in together, but my parents are home, and his house is never empty on Saturday nights.

"Te veo pronto," I say and hang up.

"What's that secret language stuff?" Dylan asks.

"Just saying that I'll see him soon since he's back. Where should we go?"

Dylan's eyes widen. "You know who's nearby, right?"

I know who he's talking about, but I shake my head. "No."

"Yes. We are in full-on Arthur Territory. You ready to party like last time?"

"I am so far from ready."

Dylan holds up his phone. "They're expecting us!"

"What?" I take his phone and see that he's texted Arthur, letting him know that we're in the neighborhood. "Are you doing some *Parent Trap* thing and trying to get us back together? He's with his boyfriend, D. We should leave them alone."

"If they're in it for the long term, they will have plenty of alone time."

"Why are you talking like you're a wise man of long-term relationships? You and Samantha have been dating for two years."

"Which makes me an expert compared to you and Arthur." He's not wrong there. "I think there's a great opportunity here for you to show off your boyfriend—I know, I know!—and spend more time with Arthur and his."

It would definitely be a different dynamic getting Mario and Mikey in the same room. It could even settle a lot of my insecurities. Prove once and for all that Arthur and me not being together opened the door to us finding better matches.

"A do-over double date," I say.

"Plus one, of course," Dylan says with a massive smile. "I've got to see this."

CHAPTER SIXTEEN
ARTHUR
Saturday, May 30

"They're coming . . . when?" Mikey looks slightly bewildered.

"No clue. Dylan just said they're on the Upper West Side, and apparently Mario's back in town?" I pass him a barely rinsed dish, still speckled with bread crumbs. "And then he asked if we were home, and I said yes, and he said they were on their way, and that was it. I can text him again if you want."

"It's fine," Mikey says without looking at me. I watch him rearrange the dishwasher for a moment, trying to dial my heartbeat down to normal.

"Hey." I grip the edge of the counter. "I haven't forgotten about what we talked about."

He flips a plate around, slotting it neatly beside the others. "Okay."

"Do you want to talk about it now? I was just going to wait for Jess to head out, but—"

"Later's fine."

"Later," I echo, ignoring the guilty twinge in my chest. It's not that there's anything wrong with talking later. It's just that the *laters* keep piling up on top of each other. First it was Ben walking us home from ice cream last night, and then it was Jessie and more Jessie, and then we slept, and then today it was the museum and *Six* and then *talking* about *Six*, and then dinner. So it's been kind of a lot. And now this, just when Jessie was heading out to Samantha's parents' house.

Right on cue, Jessie appears in the doorway, a weekend bag hitched over her shoulder. "Namrata thinks I should bring condoms and booze."

"Orgy etiquette on point." I press my palms together.

Mikey's eyes widen, and Jessie laughs. "Absolutely one hundred percent not an orgy," she assures him. "Samantha's friend Patrick's in town, so we're eating cupcakes and watching movies."

I shake my head. "I still can't believe you text with Namrata. She and Juliet acted like I was a little kid."

"I mean, you kind of were? That was two years ago."

Two years ago. The way Jessie says it makes my breath

hitch. She makes it sound like the Stone Age—but maybe it really was a whole other era. Me at sixteen, with all my high-octane feelings. I was like a human volcano. I remember every beat of that summer, everything I felt, everything I thought. It's right there, but I can't seem to climb back inside it. It almost feels like something I read in a book.

When I open the door ten minutes later, Dylan hugs me like he's returning from war. "Look at you. Haven't aged a bit. How long has it been?"

I count back to Dave & Buster's. "Eight days?"

"Right right right, but we don't count the night you gave my son away to Super Mario." He steps into the foyer, Ben trailing behind him.

"Mario's on the subway," says Ben. Then he turns to hug Mikey. "Hey, man, good to see you again."

"The famous Mikey! Aardvark's told me so much about you!" says Dylan.

Mikey's face is like a middle schooler being kissed on the cheek by an unknown elderly relative. Nothing but sheer polite panic. It's like looking at my own bar mitzvah album.

Ben turns to me. "Hope it's okay that we're here? Samantha kicked Dylan out for the night."

"She did *not*. I escaped in a blaze of glory. I don't fuck with that crowd."

"Who, Jessie?"

Ben rolls his eyes. "He means Patrick."

"I don't want to hear that name. I don't want to see that face." Dylan cuts through the living room, plopping onto the love seat. "That man is a goddamn bunion on the foot of my life. You know he and Samantha used to share a bed, right?"

"On family trips," Ben says. "When they were six."

"A bed's a bed!"

"You and I have shared a bed. Many times."

Dylan scoffs. "I'm supposed to find that reassuring? Benzo, every time you and I are within ten feet of each other, you can cut the sexual tension with a knife."

Ben shoots a quick smile at Mikey. "Would you believe he's sober?"

"Which is a *crime*."

"No. It's literally the opposite of a crime," says Ben.

Dylan ignores him. "Seussical, what's the drink situation here?"

"Right. Okay, water, obviously. Coke, milk, OJ, and . . . uh. I can scope out the other stuff." I stand.

A moment later, Ben does, too. "Need any help?"

"Oh!" I sneak a quick glance at Mikey. "Um—"

"Sweet. You two, hook me up with some Seuss juice. The Mikester and I are long overdue for some bro time." Dylan slides closer to Mikey, who looks terrified.

A minute later, I'm standing with Ben in my uncle's

tiny bright kitchen, trying to remember how conversations work. "So, um. I think most of the alcoholic stuff is—"

"Is this chocolate liqueur?" Ben holds up a bottle Jessie must have left on the counter. "Is this, like, up for grabs, or—"

"Yeah, no, definitely," I say, nodding a little too enthusiastically. I don't know how I forgot about this feeling—the way being alone with Ben makes my heart feels like it's buffering. My eyes flick to Mikey's bodega roses, now displayed in a metal pitcher I found in Uncle Milton's Judaica cabinet.

"Have you ever tried it?"

I shake my head.

"You should. It's like a Levain cookie in drink form." He pulls a spoon out of my uncle's cutlery drawer. "Godiva's the real deal. My mom got some in a gift basket once."

"And she gave it to you?"

"Thought it was chocolate sauce, so she spiked my ice cream. Okay, try this." He nudges a spoonful of liqueur toward me like it's cough syrup, but suddenly freezes in midair. I tilt my head away, flustered.

"Here." He hands it to me instead, and I bring the spoon to my lips. It's not technically my first taste of alcohol, but I'm pretty sure it's my first taste of alcohol not preceded by old people saying "borei pri hagafen." I swirl it around in my mouth for a moment, and at first I think it tastes like chocolate, but worse. But the more I sit with it, the more I like it, and by the time I finish the spoonful, I'm sold.

Ben looks at me expectantly. "What do you think?"

"It's so rich."

"Yeah. I mean, I think it's usually mixed in with something. Do you have any Bailey's?"

"Who?"

"Bailey's Irish Cream. Or bourbon. I'm trying to think of what would pair well with chocolate."

"How do you know all this? Is Mario a bartender or something?"

"Mario doesn't drink."

"Oh—"

"And he's twenty. He's not—oh, you've got vodka! That should work." Ben looks at me. "You're sure your uncle won't mind?"

"Yeah, it's totally fine."

"Okay, cool." He pulls up a recipe on his phone. "So we just need enough for four people, right?"

"Three. Mikey doesn't drink either."

I mean, technically, neither do I.

Though it's not that I *don't* drink. I just haven't yet. But once I tried a bite of weed brownie with Musa. Sure, it's possible we didn't know the brownie contained weed at the time, just like it's possible we immediately spit it out and spent the rest of the night panicking about failed drug tests and broken futures, but the point is, I'm not the baby-faced kid I was two summers ago. And maybe Ben needs to know that.

"Okay, try this." Ben passes me a glass full of what looks like melted chocolate. But as soon as I take a sip, I have to clap my hand to my mouth to keep from spitting it out. Ben's eyes widen. "You okay?"

"Yup! No, it's good!"

He takes the glass back and sips it. "Yeah, that's a little strong. Let me mess with the proportions." I watch him pour in more Godiva, trying not to think about the fact that Ben just sipped from my glass like it was nothing. Isn't that kind of like a gateway to kissing?

I jump back from that thought so fast, I almost fall flat on my uncle's kitchen tiles.

The moment my butt hits the couch, Dylan leans toward me. "I was just telling Mikelicious how you sang Ben that song about a rat."

"Great." I take a gulp of my drink.

"Look, in retrospect, it was a genius move. You've got the serenade, which is already a winner, but then you bring in the whole sexy rat angle—"

Ben shakes his head. "Rats aren't sexy."

"Rats are famously sexy!"

I take another swig of my drink.

Dylan pauses. "Oh, you know what? I'm thinking of rabbits."

"What if you spent less time thinking about animals' sex lives?" asks Ben.

"My point stands! Let's not forget what happened after karaoke—"

"Okay!" Ben jumps up. "Mario's downstairs."

"I can buzz him—"

"I'll just let him in. Back in a sec." Ben practically bolts out the door.

Dylan leans into the cushions, draping a casual arm on the back of the couch. "This is nice, right? Guys' night. Got my whole gay squad here. You two are adorable." He waves a hand at Mikey and me, and then he points at the door. "They're adorable. But you know who's not adorable?"

"Patrick?"

"Fucking *Patrick*." The next thing I know, Dylan's ripping into Patrick so hard, he could make an entire YouTube comments section blush. But Mikey nods along politely to every single word of it, even past the five-minute mark. Dylan's still going strong when Ben reappears in the foyer, Mario in tow.

"Oh shit, this place is huge," Mario says, and even though he's not being sarcastic, my cheeks flood with heat. I'll never see the world the way a New Yorker would. I can't even calibrate space like a New Yorker.

Mario takes the last empty seat, beside Mikey—of course we're configured all wrong. I hop up. "You guys probably want to sit together, huh?"

"Oh, we're fine." He settles in. "Hi! You must be Mikey. I'm Mario—I belong to that one."

He points to Ben, who looks as startled by his phrasing as I am.

I toss back the rest of my drink and practically leap from the couch for a refill. And even though I'm a little unsteady with the Brita filter, I manage to get water for Mikey and Mario, too. Though now I've got to walk back from the kitchen with three full glasses, which feels a little like walking blindfolded through an obstacle course. Except without the blindfold. And I guess the only obstacles are my own feet.

I return to find Mario in the middle of some story about his trip, but he smiles up at me when I hand him his glass. I sit back down beside Mikey.

"It was amazing just being there," Mario's saying. "I want to move there one day, you know? Write for TV, the whole dream."

"We've dabbled in TV," Dylan says grandly. "Me and Bento Box. Made some waves in the reality space in our time."

"*Being Bad Boys*?" I ask.

Mario grins. "Wow."

Mikey shifts uncomfortably beside me, and it occurs to me how quiet he's been. Overwhelmed by all of this, probably. I feel this sudden wave of affection for him—my wide-eyed lamb of a boyfriend. I lean in so close, I can almost hear his heartbeat. "You good?" I whisper, letting my lips rest for a moment on his flushed cheek. Mikey nods.

Ben stands, glancing down at my drink. "Grabbing a refill. Want me to top you off?"

My head snaps up.

"Your drink." His whole face lights up red. "I was—"

"That sounds great!" I throw back the rest of my drink with one frantic gulp, before shoving the glass into his hand.

Dylan ends up following Ben into the kitchen, and then Mario and Mikey start talking about Nintendo. So I just lean back against the cushions, listening to them compare notes about turnips and friend codes. It's the most animated I've seen Mikey all night. I'm not even surprised that Mario loves a wholesome nerd game like *Animal Crossing*, because that's the kind of cool person he is. He's so cool, he doesn't even care if he looks cool. He's the type who laughs loudly in movie theaters and sings at the grocery store and happily announces his favorite singer is Taylor Swift, because he just loves Taylor's music, probably because her music is fucking amazing and she's a goddius, which is a new word I invented just now that means both genius and goddess, but I think I'm skating past the point here, which is that Mario wouldn't even worry for a second that he's being too mainstream or basic. Also, even his phone case is cool without trying—just an old-school Mario with a raccoon tail, flying across a sky-blue background. He unlocks the screen now, leaning in toward Mikey. "Okay, wait, pulling up the app."

I rest my chin on Mikey's shoulder, looking back and forth between their side-by-side screens. I feel a little whirly-brained, like I'm being spun around a ballroom.

"Your phones are friends," I inform them.

Ben and Dylan emerge from the kitchen—though Dylan hangs back, pausing to type on his phone. But Ben presents me with a very generously poured glass. "Here you go. Top-shelf provisions."

"They are! Literally! My uncle keeps them on the top shelf. My great-uncle," I add hastily. "And he's great. He's a great great-uncle. Not a *great-great-uncle*, that would be his dad. I think." I pause to take a sip. "Or would that be my great-grandpa?"

Ben looks like he doesn't know whether to laugh or take my drink away.

"Okay, this is actually *so* good? Ben! You should be a bartender. Or—wait—you could write a book about a *wizard* bartender, and the drinks could be potions!"

Ben just looks at me. "Okay, so. I don't want to be the party police or anything, but . . . you know you're drinking that really fast, right?"

"I prefer 'efficient.'" I smile up at him. "And I'm fine. But I have to pee."

I spring to my feet, but as soon I'm upright, my stomach does a sea-monster lurch. I clamp my hand over my mouth.

Mikey looks up. "You okay?"

"Shit." Ben leaps toward me, grabbing my cup and setting it down on the coffee table. "Hey. Are you . . . ?"

I nod frantically, trying not to gag.

"It's okay. You're okay. Breathe." He presses his hand on my back, and I feel like someone pixelated my brain. But then Ben's eyes dart to Mikey, and his hand falls to his side. "Um. Someone should probably get him to the bathroom?"

"Oh!" Mikey jumps up. "Okay. Um—"

Ben points to it. "Back there."

"I know," says Mikey.

"I'm sorry. Mikey—"

"You're fine." Mikey slips his arm around my waist. "Let's just—"

"Hey, I think I'm gonna split," Dylan says suddenly.

Ben eyes him warily. "You okay?"

"Never been better. Gonna go rescue my woman from Satan's clutches."

My stomach wrenches again—I clap both hands over my mouth.

"I know, Seussical, I know. He disgusts me, too."

"Okay!" Ben turns to me. "Go with Mikey. You're

about to puke on the floor. And, D, promise me you won't kill Patrick."

"I promise you nothing."

Ben opens his mouth to reply, but I don't catch a word of it. Because, it turns out, I'm *still* a human volcano at age almost-nineteen.

Mikey gets me to the bathroom just in time.

CHAPTER SEVENTEEN

BEN

Sunday, May 31

Mario's family is out—his brothers on their way to an escape room, his parents at work—so I came over this morning to his house in Queens. I really wish I had my own place so I could have sex with my potential boyfriend whenever I want. Still, catching up with Mario after him being away was a really, really great way to start the day.

I shower alone, generously using his bodywash to keep that Mario smell around me a little longer. When I come out of the bathroom, Mario surprises me with a plate of scrambled eggs and a smiley face drawn in ketchup.

"What's this?" I ask.

"Late breakfast," Mario says. "Eat up."

I follow him back into his bedroom, which is the basement he shares with one of his brothers. It's definitely a man cave down here with gaming consoles, a beat-up couch guests use when they spend the night, minifridge for his brother's Snapple addiction, and a fifty-inch TV. Mario's workshop table where he makes his shirts is close by. I sit on his bed, where we've eaten a few meals together before, but it's usually something his parents cooked or that we ordered in. I know it's just scrambled eggs with McDonald's packet ketchup, but it was a choice he made. To take care of me.

"You're in a good mood," I say.

"How could I not be after all that?" Mario says, tossing my condom into his trash and burying it under rejected sketches for shirt designs. "I don't know, Alejo, I finally feel like I'm finding myself. It's like I'm getting closer and closer to becoming someone I've wanted to believe so badly wasn't some stupid dream."

"That also thanks to me or your trip?"

Mario leans in and kisses me. "Both. I wanted to talk to you about everything last night actually, but we didn't have the time."

"Sorry, I wouldn't have brought you to over to Arthur's if I knew."

"No apologies necessary. I had so much fun." Mario sits down. "I've been having a lot of fun with you especially."

"Same." My heart is pounding. I think this is the moment I've been waiting for.

"I like you more than I've liked my past boyfriends, Alejo. No disrespect to them, but they don't hold a candle to you. Tú eres amable. Tú eres bastante guapo. Tú corazón lo es todo."

I'm kind.

I'm really handsome.

My heart is everything.

No matter how much time I've spent alone building up my self-worth, I still welcome Mario's words about how much I mean to him. I believe him when he says my heart is everything.

"How do I say 'Are you trying to make me cry?' in Spanish?"

Mario smiles.

I grab his hand. "You're one of the most generous souls I know. And you're pretty damn handsome yourself."

"I seriously wish I'd started talking to you the moment you stepped into the classroom."

I'm glad he didn't. I was still deep in my feelings for Arthur and needed more time to open myself up to someone new.

"Everything in its own time," I say.

Mario stares at our held hands. "Except I messed up by

not acting sooner. Something has come up that's pretty exciting."

I'm tempted to let go of him, nervous what he's about to share. "Okay . . ."

"So Hector, that writer I met in LA? He shared his document for his android series so I could see what a proper pitch package looks like. It was so cool, and I was sold on the premise. But I thought his younger characters needed some work, and I gave him some ideas. Hector actually went and rewrote some scenes and said they shined brighter."

"That's amazing," I say.

I'm still waiting for the gut punch.

"Hector isn't sure if a network will buy the pitch yet, but if they do, he wants to hire me as his writer's assistant."

"That's so awesome—" I stop when I realize what he's saying. "The job isn't in New York."

He doesn't look up at me. "It would be in LA."

"You think you would go?"

"I would definitely go."

This is the kind of news that people ask you if you're sitting first before they tell you.

Why does everything have to be so damn hard for me? I've waited years to find someone right for me, he's finally confessing his deep feelings for me, and now he's ready to leave? It's shit like this that makes me not want to believe in the power of the universe. I keep meeting incredible people in this city who leave me behind and go on to lead better lives.

"What about college?" I ask. I know it's grasping at straws, but there's no way in hell he's going to stay for me.

"I'd be getting paid to learn in a real writers' room instead of paying the school to teach me."

"When would you know? If the show is getting picked up?"

"Maybe in the next couple of weeks."

"Weeks. Wow." He could be gone so soon. "Mario, are you sure you're not riding some high after all that LA sunshine?"

Mario finally looks me in the eye. "I think there's a version of me in LA that will be happier than I am now. That's worth chasing. Do you think you're at your happiest here?"

"No. I haven't been for a while. But you've made it better."

"And apart from my brothers, I'll miss you the most. You're one of a kind, Alejo. I think you would like LA."

"I don't have LA money or an uncle with a guesthouse."

"But you have a Mario who does. Maybe you could stay with me sometime?"

I don't know how to respond to that. The whole sentiment makes me feel like we've been dating the entire time and I zoned out when we made it official because I was too busy staring into his hazel eyes.

"Say something," Mario says.

This is a lot to take in right now. "I'm just thinking about everything I'm about to lose," I say. I can practically feel his lips on mine, the comfort of his head on my shoulder, the swelling pride whenever I understand him in Spanish.

"Hey, maybe I don't know what I'm talking about and Hector's script actually sucks," Mario says. "Then I won't go anywhere."

"I want you to win at life," I say. "Even if it means missing you."

"Don't miss me yet," Mario says.

He leans in for a kiss, and as much as I want to step back to protect my heart, I welcome his lips—because I know they'll be on the other side of the country soon.

CHAPTER EIGHTEEN

ARTHUR

Friday, June 5

You know those expectation-versus-reality memes? That's my professional life.

I love my job; don't get me wrong. I get to joke around with Taj and breathe the same air as Emmett Kester and Amelia Zhu. I'm even getting somewhat more chill around Jacob, probably because he's about as intimidating as a mall Santa—until you watch him flip a whole scene on its head with a single bit of direction. The whole process fascinates me—watching the story stitch together, piece by piece.

It's just that I thought I'd be doing some of the stitching.

"So you *think* you sent it?" Taj asks, managing to convey a hearty *Dear God, Arthur* in a single split-second arch of his eyebrow. Like I'm the biggest fuckup on earth.

"No, I sent it. Definitely." I lean forward, scanning the list of subject lines in my outbox. "I forwarded it to him on . . . Friday. Ha!" I point to last week's design budget log on my screen, silently thanking Past Arthur for not dropping the ball.

"Okay, cool. He probably just scrolled past it. Why don't you resend it, and I'll touch base with Jacob really quickly to make sure that's all he needs."

My phone vibrates against the vinyl of my tabletop workspace.

"Sounds good!" I say quickly.

I'm pretty sure it's a new text from Ben—he's been venting to me on and off all week about the weird vibes he's been getting from Dylan, which I'm a million percent here for. And not just because weird vibes are my whole entire brand. Honestly, the fact that Ben's confiding in me again feels really fragile and precious in a way I can't quite explain. I guess I thought we'd lost that forever.

I tap into my message app as soon as Taj leaves, and sure enough: You really didn't think he seemed weird on sat

Um, I write back, depends on what you mean by weird, I guess. Like he was chaotic, but that's kind of his baseline, right?

I mean, if Ben wanted to see actual chaos, he should have stayed for the part where I full-force had to pee but also full-force didn't want to stand up, so I just cried about it in Mikey's arms for an hour.

Yeah idk, maybe im reading too much into it? but also he was so glued to his phone, like hyperfocused, Ben replies, and I can't decide if I'm charmed or annoyed by the way he always frets over Dylan. Ben didn't seem to lose any sleep this week over the fact that I literally drank myself sick Saturday night. Not that I'd expect him to. Because that would be a very, very weird thing to expect from your ex. Very.

I write back. Maybe? I honestly didn't notice!

That's funny, Ben replies, u seemed so clear-headed and alert that night

I grin down at my phone.

Another Ben text comes in. Also the way he just randomly bounced at the end?

Well he had to rescue Samantha from 😈, I write.

Lol good point

Okay but for real, is Patrick that bad??

Ben responds with a shrug emoji boy. Never met him, probably never will

You know what you should do?? I write—and then I press send so he can sit in suspense while I outline my multiphase plan to gradually introduce a Patrick character into *The Wicked Wizard War* canon. Patricio, the roguish fiend who kidnaps Sam O'Mal, but is ultimately thwarted by Duke Dill's greatest ally, the legendary saber-toothed chimera warrior knight, Sir Sabre. I'll let Ben and Dylan decide which of Sir Sabre's three heads lands the fatal strike. Look, I'm not saying I'm a diabolical genius, but if the horns fit—

"So how's Mikey?" Taj asks, settling back in at his desk.

"What?" I look up at him. "Mikey left five days ago."

Taj's eyebrows are doing the work of a thousand winks. "I know. I'm just saying, you get the love crinkle when you talk to him. Right here." He pokes the corners of his eyes.

"That's not—" I stop short, heat rushing to my cheeks. What am I even supposed to say?

That I'm not sure I'm in love? That I've been avoiding the conversation for a week?

That it isn't even Mikey that I'm texting?

My phone buzzes, and I try not to stare at the screen. It's elementary school all over again. Me with my behavior card flipped from green to yellow, knowing I'm one chair tilt away from getting a note sent home. Me, fucking it up half the time anyway. All my report cards were variations on the exact same theme. *Extremely bright. Enthusiastic learner. Pleasure to have in class. A full goddamn mess with no impulse control.*

"So," I say, yanking my brain back to earth. I watch Taj scroll through a list of file folder icons, each one neatly labeled and ordered by year. "Everything okay with the budget?"

"Oh yeah. I'm just pulling some of the figures from the last few summers so Jacob can see it all side by side. He's talking about replacing the GDB again."

The GDB, otherwise known as the Goddamn Baby. Basically, the script calls for an onstage baby, but Jacob keeps getting creeped out by every doll the props master buys. So we keep returning them for refunds that sometimes take days or even weeks to process. It's wreaking havoc on the design budget logs.

"This isn't going to end in him bringing in a real baby, right?"

Taj laughs. "They've actually done that before on Broadway. There was a play called—"

"The Ferryman!"

"I can't believe you know that," Taj says.

My phone buzzes again—but before I can sneak a peek, Jacob materializes out of nowhere. "Are you texting the boy?" he asks, smiling.

I jolt up straight in my chair.

Jacob laughs. "I promise I'm not here to play phone cop. Write him back!"

Him. The boy. Jacob thinks I'm talking to Mikey, just like Taj thinks I'm talking to Mikey. Because why wouldn't I be? Why wouldn't I be texting my boyfriend who's in love with me, and who I maybe love back, which is a question I should definitely be able to answer by now?

"Okay!" Taj announces. "I've got 2016 through 2019. Ready when you are."

Jacob clasps his hands. "God, I love you."

My brain stops in its tracks.

"Be right back," I say, swiping my phone off the table. "Dressing room. Bathroom."

Taj nods solemnly. "Godspeed."

The whole way there, I'm barely aware of my own two feet on the ground. Because—

God, I love you.

Love.

It's such an imprecise word. That's the problem. Love means too many things. Jacob loves Taj for tracking down a bunch of budget spreadsheets. I love chocolate and *Hamilton* and my parents and Bubbe. I mean, it's pretty absurd when you really think about it, right? Here I am, floundering under the weight of the big do-I-love-Mikey question, when I wouldn't even blink if it was anyone else in my life. Do I love Ethan and Jessie? Of course! And I love my Wesleyan friends. I love Musa. It's not even a question. So how come it feels like one when I try to apply the concept to Mikey?

I mean, I love Mikey in the regular way. Obviously. It's just the rest of it that's foggy.

I'm so distracted, I don't even see Emmett stepping out of the dressing room bathroom until I crash into him head-on.

I stare at him, my jaw going slack. Emmett Kester.

I just full-on collided with a person whose face is literally on a Times Square billboard. Sure, he's a little off to the side, kind of tucked behind Maya Erskine and Busy Philipps. But that's because he's going to be in a TV show! With Maya Erskine! And Busy Philipps! And these days you can't even google him without tripping over another Out and Proud Bicons list or Twenty Queer Black Stars Under Thirty.

"I'm—*so* sorry," I choke. "I wasn't—"

"Hey. You're fine." He gives my arm a reassuring quick pat. "Arthur, right? I'm Em."

Emmett—Emmett Kester knows my name. He wants me to call him *Em*. And now we're just hanging out in the dressing room like a couple of dressing room bros, and there's absolutely no way this is real. I was still weeks away from working up the nerve to talk to the actors. Now we're on nickname terms?

"Hi! Yes! Sorry, I'm not usually such a disaster—" I pause, just long enough to spiral through a hyperspeed greatest hits montage, beginning with the time I complimented Ben on the size of his package. "Oh, and I'm Arthur! Really nice to officially meet you, Ben—*Em*."

My heart crash-lands somewhere in the vicinity of my stomach. Fuck. Fuck fuck fuck. Undo. Back arrow. Delete.

Emmett just smiles. "Nice to meet you, too. I'm sure I'll see you around."

After he leaves, I just stare at myself in the dressing room mirror, hands pressed to my scalding cheeks. I look like a little Jewish sunburned Macaulay Culkin.

I can't believe I called him Ben.

I take a few deep cleansing breaths and pull out my phone. Two notifications—two Ben texts. I tap straight into our text chain, scanning for the last text I sent him. It's from almost thirty minutes ago. You know what you should do??

Ben's reply, a few minutes later: ??

And a few minutes after that: the suspense!!

I scroll back down to reread the unsent message I'd been typing, about Patricio and Sir Sabre and Duke Dill, and it's so painfully try-hard, I can't even get to the end without cringing. I slam my finger down hard on the delete button.

Sorry, got pulled into work! I write, pausing for just a second over the exclamation point. But I think it's fine. Maybe even good. Nicely restrained, not too apologetic, nothing forced. I know it doesn't exactly alleviate the suspense (*the suspense!!*), but maybe leaving a little mystery isn't such a bad thing.

Lol it's okay, he writes back.

I guess it feels almost like a game with Ben sometimes, where the more I put in, the more I lose. I'm always the one who texts first and replies faster, and just about every text conversation we've ever had ends with me. Not just this summer. It's been like this for two years. I've been losing for *two years.*

Maybe I should just not reply. Quit while I'm ahead, for once.

But no. This isn't it. We're just starting to get our friendship back on track, and that's not a thing I'm willing to lose again. Plus, with Dylan's alleged weirdness, he clearly needs a friend more than ever.

I tap into our text chain again, filling the window with the kind of unfiltered sincerity I'm always trying to hold back these days. At least with Ben, I hold back. But this time, I press send before I can talk myself out of it.

Okay so I was going to make some joke about Dylan and his weird one-way rivalry with Patrick, but seriously I know you're worried about him and I just want you to know I'm up for listening if you ever really want to sit down and talk about it

Or stand up and talk about it? I add. Or stand on one foot and talk about it?

Ben writes back right away. Thanks, yeah, that's really nice of you, may take you up on that

You should! I feel my mouth tugging up at the corners. Name a date and I'll put it on the calendar, it'll be like scheduling therapy with a wildly incompetent therapist

What a compelling offer lol, Ben writes back—and just as I'm about to shoot back a clown emoji, he adds: okay what are you up to this coming Wednesday?

I stare at my screen for a moment, feeling like I just chugged a full bottle of chocolate liqueur. But I blink away the thought and start typing. Nothing, just work! Should be getting out around six

Cool, you're pretty close to me, right? Want me to meet you outside and we can figure out where to go from there?

Best plan ever, I write.

Because so what if Ben and I hit a few awkward notes last weekend. Maybe our friendship just needs one more do-over. I'll help him dissect and hyperanalyze all his interactions with Dylan, beat by beat.

And maybe Ben's the friend who can help me cut through my Mikey fog at last.

PART TWO

WE CAN TRY THAT

CHAPTER NINETEEN

BEN

Tuesday, June 9

Everything is going wrong today.

The moment I clocked in, some unsupervised child was sitting in a corner with an as-seen-on-TV cooking pot and mixing fruit punch and Sprite from the fridge to make a magical potion. I applaud the imagination, but this kid is banned from my future amusement park after this mess I had to clean up. Another customer yelled at me at the cash registers because she was short seventy-five cents for a deck of cards and I couldn't just look the other way. And I've got so much extra work on my plate because my coworker called in sick, even though his Instagram shows him having a picnic with friends by the Brooklyn Bridge. I'm so tempted to show Pa, but then I'm the person who snitches to his father to get his colleagues in trouble.

I'm starting to not care.

This job isn't who I am, and I'm not trying to be here forever.

I'm also not sure if I'm just talking about Duane Reade anymore when I think *here*.

In the nine days since Mario broke the news that he might get a job out in Los Angeles, I've experienced a range of feelings: pride that his brilliance is recognized, jealousy that nepotism for Mario means a job in TV and all I got was cleaning up Sprite–fruit punch potions at Duane Reade, praying to higher forces that the executives at the network hate androids so Mario won't have to leave.

I've been trying to focus on my own work instead of letting my selfish feelings get in the way. It's been harder to write lately. I keep staring at the same words, unsure how to fix them and make them right.

Everything is so confusing, and I don't know what my story is supposed to be anymore.

Maybe Mario is right that I'd be happier out in LA.

New home. New people. New life.

What I keep coming back to is how much it would hurt to say goodbye to Mario. If long-distance wasn't an option with Arthur—who was in love with me!—I can't count on a relationship with Mario surviving. I'm not ready for another round of sleepless nights, hating how lonely I am.

I'm not ready to let another amazing person slip out of reach.

I finish mopping up the aisle, put up a Caution sign, and go into the break room even though I'm still supposed to be out on the floor. Pa's office door is closed and the employee bathroom is empty, so I'm safe to FaceTime Mario before I change my mind. I stare at the wall that has my schedule for the rest of the week, wishing so badly that I could tear it down, quit, and not go home to my boss tonight.

"Alejo," Mario softly answers. The way he says my name simultaneously calms me down and excites me. He's in his bedroom and props the phone up against a stack of books as usual.

"Is it stupid that I miss you even though I saw you yesterday?"

"Not one bit."

"I'm scared of missing you even more when you're not a train ride away."

"Remember, it may not even pan out."

"It'll pan out. Or something will. You're going to move, and I'm going to miss you."

"We can do something about that, you know."

"I've been thinking about that, too." I look around the

break room. "I don't want to be here."

"When's your shift over?"

"I don't mean here. I think I mean New York."

Mario smiles and looks like he's holding back a fist pump. "You thinking about moving to LA, by any chance?"

"You said it yourself. I might be happier out there."

Then the door to the manager's office opens and Pa steps out. I hang up so fast you'd think I was watching porn on my phone. "I'm not on the floor so you can't be mad at me for having my phone out."

"You shouldn't be on the phone whenever you're on the clock, but that's not the problem. Remember, I'm your father first. Did I just overhear that you want to move to Los Angeles?"

"Yeah. I mean, yeah, that's what you heard. I'm still not sure if that's what I want."

Pa nods. "It's not that easy to pick up and go."

"You wouldn't know. You've been in New York your entire life."

"Because, Benito, it's not that easy to pick up and go."

"If I'm always going to be struggling, then why can't I struggle somewhere else?"

"There is a major difference between struggling under your parents' roof and struggling on your own."

"I wouldn't be on my own."

"You mean the boyfriend? You would move in with him?"

"He's not my boyfriend." No matter how true that is, it's the stupidest thing I could've said.

"Listen to yourself. Do you feel good about this? Does that make sense to you?"

No, it doesn't feel good or make a ton of sense.

But what if it makes me happy?

"Look, Mario doesn't even know for sure that he's going, okay? I'm not flying anywhere tomorrow—"

"I know you're not, because your mother would be on the first flight out to drag you back."

"Being treated like a kid really makes me want to stay, Pa."

"That's not what I mean to do. I want your life to be amazing, but you're making a gigantic mistake. You still have school and—"

"Then I make a mistake," I interrupt. It's my life. "Pa, I've had no adventures like my friends have. Dylan and Samantha got to leave the city. Arthur is really happy with his boyfriend at Wesleyan. And I'm stuck here."

"I'm sorry you feel so stuck here, but many people would love to be in your position."

"I know."

I'm tired of not being able to own my feelings because

someone else has it worse. I know I'm lucky to have a roof over my head and parents who love me and food on the table. I know, I know, I know. I can also want more for myself.

"Benito, I don't want you to make an impulsive decision that you'll regret. You haven't even brought this boy home to meet your family and you're thinking about leaving the city with him."

It's like he thinks Mario is just some fuckboy. But Pa does have a point that Mario and I need to sort ourselves out before I even entertain more conversations about Los Angeles. But for the first time, it's like my life doesn't feel light-years away. There's a map forming in my head with a circle drawn around Los Angeles. And I know the first move I have to make to get there.

"I'm going to head back out. Short-staffed," I say.

"We'll talk later," Pa says, following me out onto the floor.

Once a customer leaves the medicine aisle, I pull out my phone and find a text from Mario.

Everything okay?

Yeah, I reply. Would you want to come over for dinner with my parents later this week?

I don't know how I'm not sweating. I'm nervous and grateful that I didn't ask him this in person or over Face-Time in case he responds negatively. Though enough is enough. Mario and I need to figure out what this is before I figure out my next moves.

He responds before I can put my phone back in my pocket.

I read it and smile.

I'm in!

CHAPTER TWENTY
ARTHUR
Wednesday, June 10

Seeing Ben outside the rehearsal studio is like stepping through a wormhole. I don't know how else to explain it. Maybe it's just one of those ex-boyfriend things, but his face makes me forget what year it is.

"I've totally walked by this place a million times," Ben says, giving me a quick hello hug. "Didn't even put it together that you work here." He's dressed in way too many layers for June—a light gray sweater zipped over a blue polo shirt.

"You look very autumn collegiate," I tell him.

He laughs. "Wait—what?"

"Like—I don't know—like you're dressed for the big homecoming game? It's not a bad thing!"

It occurs to me suddenly that I've never seen Ben in the fall—not in person, at least. I've never stood with Ben in any season but summer, and the thought alone makes me lose my breath for a second.

"The homecoming game," Ben says. "You're so Georgia."

But when he steps into the intersection, I follow him, even though the walk sign hasn't switched yet, and if that isn't pure New York instinct, I don't know what is. It's funny how easy it is to slip back into that city headspace—dodging taxis, anticipating light changes, walking three times as fast as I do at home. I'm right where I left off two summers ago, like some parallel version of me never stopped crossing this street.

"So Dylan's being weird and distant," I say.

"We don't actually have to talk about that."

"But I want to." He scoffs a little, but I wave it away. "I'm your friend! I care about you."

Ben just looks at me, and I can't quite read his expression. But then he smiles faintly and says, "Okay, but I don't even really know where to begin."

"Just start at the beginning. You said it's kind of subtle, right?"

"Not to me, but yeah." We turn onto St. Marks Place, and Ben fidgets with the sleeve of his sweater. "Like, he's still Dylan, and it's still the Dylan show. But underneath that, he's always been real with me, and that's not happening now. I feel like he's been shutting me out for weeks." He shrugs, gesturing to a nearby plaza. "Anyway. Did you know there used to be a rhino sculpture here?"

"Rhino like *rhino*?" I point my finger out from my forehead.

"Okay, that's a unicorn." Ben tugs my finger-horn down a few inches, until my hand's resting on my nose. "Rhino. It was like a PSA about them dying."

"Sounds fun to look at," I say, trying to ignore my drumrolling heartbeat.

He laughs. "They weren't dead in the sculpture."

We pass Cooper Union and a bunch of restaurants and tattoo parlors, and I can't stop mixing up my past and present tenses. I'm sixteen years old, carrying a bag full of condoms, and every square foot of this sidewalk feels like holy ground. I'm walking past buildings I've never seen before with a boy who knows them by heart.

Ben's still bursting with stories. He points up a side street to tell me about a restaurant that serves latkes, which he pronounces like *lot-case.* And when we reach Tompkins Square, he tells me how he and Dylan ghosted each other for their very first playdate because their moms walked them to different playgrounds on either end of the park.

"Feels like some kind of metaphor." Ben shoots me a faltering smile.

"Do you have any idea what's up? Like, why he's shutting you out?"

He stares straight ahead. "I mean. I figured he was wrapped up in Samantha, you know? People always ditch their friends when they're in relationships."

I startle. "What—"

"But then he canceled plans again," Ben continues, still not looking at me, "so I asked why, and he was like, 'Oh, I have a doctor's appointment.'"

"Wait." I look up. "You don't think he's having issues with . . ." I trail off, not wanting to mention Dylan's heart condition out loud for some reason. But I point to my chest.

"Yeah. I don't know."

"Fuck."

He blinks. "Maybe I'm pulling this out of nowhere. He's probably just in Samantha world."

"Yeah, hopefully." I pause. "Not that I want him to ditch you. That's not—"

"I know, Arthur."

We're both quiet for a moment.

"Hey," I say finally. "Can I ask you something?"

He looks at me but doesn't respond.

I swallow. "Do you feel like I ditched you?"

"I mean." His brow furrows. "'Ditched' is the wrong word. Just, you know. Prioritizing, I guess? But that's normal."

I shake my head. "You should never expect to be ditched. If I made you feel like that—"

"You didn't. I make myself feel like that."

His voice is so soft when he says it. But the words reverberate in my head like he yelled them into a cave. *I make myself feel like that.*

Suddenly, all I can think about are those three months we didn't talk—and the fact that neither of us has mentioned it since. I guess it felt like there was this unspoken agreement where we pretend spring semester never happened. But maybe we should talk about it. Friends should be able to talk about their friendship, right?

"I think I fucked up," I say finally.

Ben looks at me. "What?"

"With you." Ben opens his mouth to reply, but I head him off at the pass. "I know it's been kind of weird between us, maybe? I didn't know whether it was okay to talk about Mikey stuff with you."

"You can talk about anything with me."

"Yeah, but." I pause, trying to sift through my swirling brain for something halfway coherent. "I just didn't know how much to say, I guess, and I wasn't trying to be an asshole—I'm not saying you were still hung up on me," I rush to add.

"What if I was?"

I freeze. "You mean—"

"Oh." Ben's cheeks turn bright red. "Sorry, I just mean, *so what* if I was? Like, it wouldn't have been your fault. I wouldn't want you to stop talking to me."

"I mean, I kind of got the feeling you *did* want me to stop talking to you."

For a minute, Ben doesn't respond—he just glances up at a park sign and steers us past a fork in the trail. But then he does this sharp little inhale. "I never replied to your birthday message."

"It's fine, seriously. I'm sorry—"

"No, this is on me. I meant to reply, but we hadn't talked in almost two months, and it felt so big, you know? And then I kind of built it up in my head, and the longer I *didn't* reply—"

"Ben, it's fine!"

He shoots me a quick smile and doesn't speak for a moment.

"Well," he says finally. "You guys seem really great together."

I blink, feeling slightly untethered. "You mean—"

"You and Mikey."

"Same with you and Mario. He seems like an amazing person." I wince a little. "Sorry, I don't know if that's a bummer to talk about."

Ben laughs. "Why would it be a bummer?"

"Because of California? It sucks that he's moving." I rub

the back of my neck, feeling my cheeks flood with heat. Maybe the Mario-moving-to-California topic is off-limits. Ben certainly hasn't mentioned it—not since he dropped the news in a random Sunday-night text. I'm so curious, though.

He hasn't said anything about a breakup. But where else could this go? Ben's made it very clear he's not a long-distance kind of guy.

"I mean, it's not a definite thing, but yeah. It sucks," Ben says finally. He presses his lips together and blinks. "Hey, can I ask you something?"

"Of course! Always."

He draws a quick breath. "Do you ever feel stuck?"

"Stuck? Like—"

"Not—I don't mean Mario. I don't know. It's just life in general. I'm not loving school. Not loving Duane Reade."

"Duane Reade, like the store?"

He looks away, blushing. "Yeah. Um." He unzips his cardigan, revealing a small embroidered logo. "So, I'm working there now. For my dad."

"Oh, okay! Cool."

He makes a face. "I mean, I need the money, but it's just kind of a frustrating job. And it's a little better in the summer, but when school starts up again, I'll have barely any time to get classwork done, much less work on my book."

"That really sucks." I pause. "Maybe there's a way to

make your book count for class credit or something?"

"I don't know," Ben says. "I don't know if I want to."

"No, yeah, I get that—"

"Honestly, I'm not even sure I want to be in college."

I look at him. "You mean—"

"Maybe." There's this edge to his voice. "I'm just saying, maybe college isn't for everyone."

"I know. I just thought you liked it. The creative writing—"

"Yeah, I like that class, but it's like . . ." He puffs out his cheeks. "I'm paying so much for tuition, and I barely even feel like I'm getting anything out of most of my other classes. Meanwhile, there are a million regular writing workshops that teach the exact same skills, but they're a fraction of the price. Plus, you don't even need any of that to be—"

"Of course not. I'm sorry. I don't mean to pressure you."

"You're not. I'm being—I guess I'm a little sensitive about this." He rubs the back of his neck. "Sorry, can we talk about something else? How's off-Broadway life? Are they letting you yell into megaphones yet?"

"I wish. Still in Spreadsheet City."

Ben makes a face.

"I mean, it's fine. I'm getting the hang of it. It's just boring—" I stop short, blushing. "God, you must think I'm the biggest asshole."

Ben lets out a startled laugh. "What?"

"The number of people who would kill to have my job, and I'm complaining that I had to forward an Excel file."

"Okay, well, it's me! You can complain about that stuff."

"No, I know. I'm just trying to have a better attitude about it. I really do love it. And everyone there is just so brilliant. Maybe I'll absorb all their genius somehow."

We turn a corner, swerving out of the range of water spraying from a fire hydrant. There's a group of kids running through it, shrieking and laughing, while Spanish music bursts from someone's phone on the stoop.

"And Taj is still cool?" Ben asks.

"Oh, totally," I say, thinking about the short-sleeved lace button-up shirt he wore today. And the fact that he just got back from a dreamy long weekend in Montauk with his partner. "He's, like, *exactly* who I want to be at twenty-five. And then the next step is to be a gay uncle like Jacob, with a British husband and a hypoallergenic dog—"

"Wow—"

"And then, for my final, most powerful form?" I pause dramatically. "Dorky gay dad of twin girls named Rosie and Ruby."

He laughs. "You're like a domestic gay Pokémon."

We pass an elderly couple who say hi to Ben, by name, in accented English. "That's Mr. and Mrs. Diaz from my building." He stops short beneath an awning, glancing at me with a quick, self-conscious smile. "And, uh. Speaking of my building . . ."

I look up, instantly recognizing it. "Wow. Been a minute, huh?"

"For real," he says. "You should come up. I guarantee my parents would flip their shit if you walked in."

Another wormhole. I'm here, straight from work, following Ben Alejo up the stairs to his apartment. I'm weirdly nervous—maybe just because it's been so long since I've seen Ben's parents. I wonder if they'll think I'm different than two summers ago. Maybe I am different. After all, you never really feel yourself changing until it's already happened.

The door to Ben's hallway spits us out right next to his apartment, where Isabel's balancing a bunch of grocery bags and fumbling for her keys. She gasps when she sees me. "Arthur Seuss. Oh my goodness."

"So good to see you!" I grab a few of her bags, and then almost drop all of them while attempting to hug her.

"Arthur—thank you." She squeezes my arm. "Oh, I can't believe it. How are you?"

"Good! You know, back in New York for the summer."

Isabel turns the key, pushing the door open with her hip. "Benito says you're working for a famous Broadway director!"

"I think he might be overselling me a bit." I shoot a quick grin over my shoulder at Ben, who grins back and tips his palms up. "It's not Broadway, but I love it."

"Which is all that matters," she says as Ben and I follow her inside. "Diego, you won't believe who's here!" She turns to me again. "Look at you. Even more handsome than before. I bet you're breaking boys' hearts left and right and back again."

I laugh. "Hopefully not."

I peer around the space, drinking it in. Whenever Ben and I FaceTimed, I'd picture myself sprawled on his bed or sitting at his little dining room table. It looks the same, down to the place mats. Honestly, the whole apartment looks the same, apart from a few tiny details—Ben's high school diploma now framed on the wall, a few new family pictures.

"Well, look who the cat dragged in," Diego says, striding toward me.

"Bags can go on the counter there, conejo," Isabel says. "Thank you so much."

Diego hugs me. "What on earth brings you here? Just in the neighborhood?"

"He works near here," Ben says.

"With a very famous director," adds Isabel.

Diego claps his palms together. "Is that right?"

I blush. "He's—kind of? In certain circles, I guess."

I start to unload one of the grocery bags, and Ben wanders over to help me. Diego watches us for a minute, eyes gleaming. "Benito, keep bringing these boys around. We've got Georgia here taking care of the groceries, California coming this weekend to make asopao de pollo. We've never even met the guy, and he's cooking for us."

It lands like a punch to the throat—for a moment, I swear I stop breathing.

"Asopao," Ben explains, as if the main course is the bombshell. He looks vaguely panicked. "It's a Puerto Rican rice stew. You can make it a lot of different ways, but Abuelita's recipe is with chicken—that's the pollo—and pigeon peas. Gandules."

"Nailing that pronunciation." Diego pats his shoulder. "Benito, I'm impressed."

"He's been working so hard," Isabel says, but I can't stop staring at the package I just pulled out of the grocery bag.

Pigeon peas.

Right. I didn't think the universe would find a way to have me unpacking the ingredients for Ben and Mario's big meet-the-parents dinner, but here we are.

"Now tell me, Arthur," Diego says, sidling up to me. "Have you met this Mario character? This one tells me nothing." Isabel shoots him a look and quietly murmurs something in rapid-fire Spanish. Diego's eyes flick to me, and he lifts his palms defensively. "Okay, okay."

Isabel squeezes my shoulder. "An-y-way," she says, drawing out all the syllables. "We're just so glad you're here. Why don't you join us for dinner tonight?"

"Oh—uh." I shake my head and set the peas down. "Thank you. I should—I better get home."

Ben's brow furrows. "Can I walk you to the subway?"

"It's fine—"

"At least let me walk you downstairs." He pauses. "Please."

"Arthur, you'll have to come back for longer next time. I want to hear how your parents are doing."

"They're good," I say, nodding quickly, already halfway to the door. "Really good to see you guys."

Ben follows me into the hallway, and our eyes meet as soon as the door shuts behind us.

I clear my throat. "So you and Mario are getting serious, huh? Meeting the folks."

His laugh fills the corridor. "Okay, it's actually not like that—"

"No, I'm happy for you! I guess you changed your mind about long-distance relationships, huh."

"Oh—"

"Sorry. Okay!" My face goes white-hot. "I'm heading out, but yeah. I'll see you!"

I'm pretty sure my throat's closing in on itself. But that makes no sense. He's not my boyfriend. Ben's not my boyfriend.

I guess I should be glad he finally found a boy who's worth the distance.

CHAPTER TWENTY-ONE

BEN

Saturday, June 13

Days later, and I'm still stuck on Arthur's expression the moment Pa mentioned Mario. I don't know why he thought it was okay to casually ask someone's ex about the guy who replaced him. I think I'd forget how to breathe for a minute if someone asked me about Mikey like that.

It just sucks, because everything up until that moment had been perfect. Walking next to Arthur again felt so right, as if we were picking up right where we left off two summers ago. Even talking about our own friendship stuff wasn't too bad. It was actually kind of a relief—like maybe things could finally be normal again between us.

But Arthur was so far from normal in the hallway, he couldn't even fake it.

I guess you changed your mind about long-distance relationships, huh?

Like, why would he just assume that? And if he's that weird about long-distance, how's he going to react when I tell him I'm thinking about moving? But I can't worry about this now. Especially when it might not even happen if that show doesn't get picked up. Why obsess over Arthur's forced smiles or watering eyes before it's time?

The table's already set for dinner, and Mario just texted to say he's walking from the subway right now. Which is absolutely fine, and nothing to freak out about in the slightest. It's not even like it's his first time hanging out here. Sure, Ma and Pa were never around. That's been intentional, especially after Pa found out Mario and I were having sex. The time alone with him has always been great. It's given me a taste of what life will be like when I get some space from my parents. What it could be like if I end up in Los Angeles with Mario.

Everything coming out of the kitchen smells great. We've got tostones slathered with garlic as an appetizer, pernil that's spending extra time in the oven for an epic crunch, and empanadillas that I always enjoy with a little hot sauce.

The doorbell rings. I tense up like the other two times I brought a guy home to meet my parents. It's funny how you flash back to the past when you're thinking about the future. Ma and Pa are always warm to my guests, but there was no competition between how much they adored Arthur over Hudson. And now Mario is here, ready to charm my parents as he does everyone else around him.

I get the door.

Mario is in his overalls and an unbuttoned plaid shirt. He holds up a tote bag with food. "Hola. I got some goods."

"Gracias. Entra."

The first time I ever let Mario into the apartment, I wasn't as nervous as I usually am with inviting people inside. I hadn't even been to his family's house yet, but I just knew that they weren't living large. Mario had so many stories about how his mother will sweep a mouse out of her home like a cartoon character, and how his brothers act like they're allergic to laundry, and how his father is the only one who knows how to fix the stove, but not well enough that the pilot light stays on. It was nice to not feel like my home had to be perfect. I wasn't self-conscious about kitchen cabinets that are older than I am, or our fridge that sounds like metal grinding when it's open for ten seconds, or how the occasional fly will set up camp in our living room like it's trying to join us for family movie night.

That comfort is rare to come by, and one of the reasons I've always thought we fit together.

"Ma, Pa. This is Mario."

"Hi, Mario!" Ma finishes drying her hands and gives him a hug and kiss on the cheek. "Welcome!"

Pa shakes Mario's hand. I'm glad Mario has no idea how affectionate Pa usually is—otherwise it might bother him the way it does me. "Thanks for coming over."

"Are you kidding? Thanks for having me. Ben was really hiding you guys from me."

Mario never once asked to meet my parents. All this time I've felt like we were hiding from them for max privacy. Not even just for sex. Like how nice it's been to rest my head on his shoulder while we lie down in my bed and he plays *Animal Crossing.* Or when our legs are tangled together as he sketches in his notebook while I edit *TWWW.* And so I could butcher whatever Spanish he was teaching me, and then thank him with kisses. But I never wanted to pressure Mario into meeting my parents either. It felt like too big a step. Maybe Mario was respecting my space just as much as I was respecting his.

"I'm sure he's ashamed of us," Ma says lightly.

"You know I'm not," I say. I haven't been ashamed of my family in years, and that was only because of money stuff. I snapped out of it when I realized I maybe didn't have the freshest sneakers or new gaming consoles on release days, but my parents have always been amazing to me and my friends, and the same can't be said for other people.

"Perdón. ¿Cuáles son sus nombres?" Mario asks.

Yeah, I didn't properly introduce my parents.

"Yo soy Isabel y este es Diego," Ma says.

"Mucho gusto," Mario says with a little bow. "It smells fantastic in here."

"Benito says you're going to cook asopao for us," Ma says. "Good luck impressing Diego. He hates whenever I make it."

"Mentirosa," Pa says.

"Mentirosa?" I ask.

"Liar," Mario translates.

"I guess you guys haven't reached the *M*'s yet in your lessons," Pa says.

"You do realize we're not going alphabetically, right?" I say.

"You're not?" Pa turns to Mario. "We're going to have to revoke your license."

Mario holds his hands up in surrender. "Let's see if I can earn back your trust with some food."

"Only because I have a big appetite," Pa says, inviting Mario into the kitchen.

Ma smiles at me and air-claps. "He's cute," she mouths.

I nod.

Ma turns on some music and everyone gets busy in the kitchen. It's crowded and we're all sweating within minutes, and Mario takes off his plaid shirt. I could spend all night watching him in nothing but his white undershirt and overalls. He's deep in a conversation in Spanish with my parents. I'm able to decode a word here and there about something involving numbers, but I give up because they're speaking so fast. I don't need a translator though to see my parents are genuinely laughing. That makes me really happy. And even a little sad that we haven't done this sooner.

Maybe there will be more opportunities like this in the future.

While I mix some iced tea, Mario translates his story for me.

In second grade, he was struggling with subtraction. He only wanted to solve addition problems, so he would draw vertical lines into the minus marks, turning them into plus signs. His teacher sent a note back home to his parents asking them to better supervise his homework.

That story is really cute, but I'm still blown away by how he's able to casually tell a story like that in Spanish so rapidly. More time with Mario should help me get to that level.

Once all the food is ready, we settle down at the dining table. It totally feels like a double date with my parents.

Everyone's exchanging stories, and as the bridge between Mario and my parents, I kind of know them all already. But I still pay attention when Mario starts talking about how his mother and father are both from Carolina in Puerto Rico and lived a couple towns apart but didn't meet until they moved here to the States. There are all these new details, like how his mother was shopping for crystals at a flea market in Queens when she bumped into Mario's father, who was shopping for his sister's birthday. Mario's mother helped him out, and after they got along, she asked for his number. They didn't even know about their Carolina connection until their fourth date. It's a really sweet story.

My parents ask Mario all about classes, and Mario and I quote our teacher's most popular notes, stuff like *Need?* and *I would cut* whenever something is running long in our works. They want to know why he's so willing to drop out of college, and he breaks it down for them the way he did with me. But it's tricky for my parents to understand because they're not creatives like we are.

"Following your heart can have its consequences," Pa says.

Mario nods. "I think it's less about following my heart and more about understanding that my heart is dragging me somewhere."

I never thought of it that way before. It's technically a choice to pursue his dreams, but deep, deep down, it's not. It's magnetic and inevitable. That's how it feels for me with telling stories. I didn't just wake up one day wanting to write—I just started doing it.

This is making a lot of sense to me. My parents are nodding along, too, like they've made peace with Mario's decision. Totally helps that he's not their son.

Once we've devoured dinner, Ma surprises us with churros with caramel dipping sauces. As Mario talks about the stages of getting a TV show picked up, I think back to that time I was out with Arthur and I introduced him to churros. It led to an important conversation between us about what it means for me to be white-passing and Puerto Rican, something I never had to educate Mario on since he's in the same boat. Arthur was really amazing about all of that moving forward. That's not a surprise given how big his heart is. And he taught me about Jewish stuff, too. I remember senior year, when we talked for three hours straight on Yom Kippur, because Arthur was fasting and needed me to distract him. He said Yom Kippur was all about owning up to your bullshit and vowing to do better, and I loved the way he laughed when I said it sounded like the ultimate do-over.

Of course, a year later, Mikey was the only distraction he needed.

Mario squeezes my shoulder. "Once Alejo here publishes his book, maybe I'll be able to adapt it for film."

"Yes, please," Ma says. "Benito, I promise to watch the movie without asking a million questions."

"¡Mentirosa!" Pa says.

It takes me a second. Then I remember the meaning. "Liar?"

"Ayyy!" Mario says. "¡Buen trabajo!"

Pa holds up the plate with the last churro. "Mario, my gift to you."

"Muchas gracias," Mario says. He splits the churro with me.

I catch my parents smiling.

It's getting late, so after we finish our dessert, Mario helps clean up the kitchen. He says bye to my parents, telling them in Spanish that he hopes to see them soon. Ma and Pa say they'd like that, too. That means a lot to me, especially coming from Pa.

I go downstairs with Mario, barely even thinking about the time Arthur burst into tears and kissed me on the second-floor landing, because he'd just Google Translated "estoy enamorado."

"I love them, Alejo," Mario says. "My parents are fantastic, but between all my brothers it's hard to get that kind of attention at home. I see why you wouldn't want to leave them."

"Too much attention can be a problem. I'm ready for some more privacy."

"Look, if this show moves forward, then LA could be a real chance for you to reboot your life. I meant it when I invited you there. I would really like it if you were out there with me."

"I think I would, too."

I kiss him out on the street and think about kissing him in Los Angeles, on streets where I've never kissed Arthur.

CHAPTER TWENTY-TWO
ARTHUR
Sunday, June 14

Jessie scowls into her light-up tabletop mirror. "Remind me why I'm doing this."

"Because Namrata talked you into it, and you can't say no to her." I smile back at her from the bottom bunk. "Jess, this is how lawyers mate in the wild. The junior associates set up their interns, who then become junior associates who set up *their* interns—"

"I'm breaking the cycle. No blind brunch dates for my interns. Mark my words." She squeezes a blob of makeup onto her fingertips with emphatic finality.

"You know how hard I'm going to laugh if this guy turns out to be your soul mate?" I tug up Jessie's pillow, pinning it against the wall with my head. "Okay, let's run through what we know about him. Grayson, age twenty, goes to Brandeis, from New York."

"Long Island. Montauk."

"Montauk! Taj was just there. His pictures were amazing." I press my palms to the top bunk's slatted bed frame. "You should have your wedding by the big lighthouse!"

"What a normal and reasonable thing to decide before I meet this guy."

"Hey, love is really unpredictable! You have to be ready."

"Big talk," Jessie says, "from a guy who still hasn't responded to his boyfriend's 'I love you.'"

I make a face at her. "That's different."

"Is it?" she asks, tapping little dots of light brown liquid onto her cheekbones. Jessie always says she doesn't know what she's doing with makeup—not that I can tell one way or another. But there's something so peaceful about watching her open and close all those tiny containers, humming along to her Phoebe Bridgers deep cuts playlist. I bet I could fall asleep on the spot.

Except every time I close my eyes, I start thinking about Mikey. *I love you, too.* I test out the words in my head. *I love you, too. I love you, too. I love you, too.* Four quick syllables, already on the tip of my tongue. How have I not erupted by now?

Mikey hasn't brought it up again—he hasn't even hinted at the question. But the longer it goes unanswered, the bigger it gets, and it's really starting to feel like some kind of weird final exam. *Question #1, worth your whole goddamn grade: Are you or are you not in love with Mikey?*

Probably? Possibly? Signs point to maybe?

I just want to hire some scientist to poke around in my brain and turn it into a PowerPoint. Run all the numbers and make graphs and just tell me how I feel.

I don't know what's wrong with me. I was so certain with Ben. Knowing I loved him was like knowing my own name. But this feels so slippery, like I'm scrambling to remember a dream. I know love is supposed to be different when you're older.

Maybe the certainty comes after you say it out loud.

"I just feel like it's pointless," Jessie's saying. "We'll both be back in school in two months. I'm not exactly looking for a boyfriend who lives an hour away."

"Better than a boyfriend who lives on the other side of the country."

"Not sure I'd call Boston 'the other side of the country.'" Jessie laughs—but then she looks at me. "Right. Ben and Mario."

"It just doesn't make sense. They're not even officially boyfriends."

"Well, maybe they are now. Dinner with Ben's parents sounds pretty boyfriendy." Jessie flips off her mirror light, glancing up at the horse-silhouette wooden clock on the wall.

Boyfriendy. I tuck my knees up, feeling dazed. Maybe Jessie's right—maybe their label status has changed since Ben and I last talked about it. There's no denying that taking a guy home to meet your parents has big-time capital-*B* Boyfriend energy.

"I should text him," I say.

Jessie freezes. "You mean Ben?"

"Yeah—I don't know. I just feel like an asshole for how I left things on Wednesday with all the Mario stuff." I paw around for my phone. "I should see what he's up to."

"I don't know if that's—"

The music drops off, and Jessie's phone starts vibrating beside me. "Um." I look from the screen to Jessie. "You're not going to believe this, but Ethan's calling you."

Jessie leaps for it, pressing accept. "Hey!" She sounds breathless. "Running late, sorry. Call you in five?" She pauses. "Yup."

I stare at her, stunned. "Since when do you guys talk?"

"Gotta go," she says. "I'll explain later. Love you! Don't text your ex."

Don't text my ex? When literally two seconds after I said Ben's name, Jessie got a call from *her* ex? Could the universe have been any clearer, or does Jessie need it carved on a stone tablet? THOU SHALT DIFFUSE THE AWKWARDNESS FROM THY PRIOR WEEK BY PLATONICALLY TEXTING THINE EX.

I've got the message window open before Jessie even reaches the foyer.

I was a weirdo on Wed—any chance you (and Mario!) are up for a do-over? Maybe central park? I press send, feeling so mature, I honestly have to sit here and bask in it for a minute. The proof's right there in writing: I'm the chillest, most dignified ex in the game.

At least, I'm chill until Ben starts typing. Lol, you weren't a weirdo! Would totally be into a central park do-over, but I'm supposed to help Dylan try on a suit for samantha's cousin's wedding, he's too scared to go to bloomingdale's alone.

Patrick wasn't available?? I ask.

LOL, Ben replies, LOL IN ALL CAPS

I grin at my phone screen. I forgot how much I love making him laugh.

Ben starts typing again. Wait how would u feel if we made it a group hang?? Maybe you could give me your take on the Dylan vibes

Oh, ok! Are you sure D would be cool with me third wheeling it?

Ben's response is instantaneous. You wouldn't be a third wheel! You should come—meeting at noon at the flagship store on Lex, men's formal wear near Armani.

It's the one near our post office 🙂, he adds.

Our post office.

And here I thought Mikey was the only boy who could knock the air from my lungs with three words.

Standing next to a bunch of Armani-suited mannequins, Ben and Dylan look like a pair of camp counselors crashing the Met Gala. When I reach them, Dylan's already mid-declaration. "I was there when she ordered it. I swear on the life of my ancestors, there is a suit back there with Digby's name on it."

"Empty promise," Ben says. "Your ancestors are already dead."

"We're not talking about *my* bloodline, Benstagram. This is about Digby Worthington Whitaker, five-time Yale graduate, tsunami cum laude. Show some goddamn respect."

"Is Digby Samantha's cousin?" I ask.

"Arthropod! That shirt!" Dylan lights up. "It's like *Stranger Things* meets . . . the sun."

"Ha, yeah. I guess it's pretty yellow." I fidget with the collar, cheeks going warm. "Thanks for letting me crash your shopping trip."

"Glad you're here, bro." He pats my shoulder. "Gotta go check on Digby's suit, but you make yourself comfortable.

Mi casta es su casta."

"Mi casa," says Ben.

"Yes, darling, it's *our* casta." Dylan rolls his eyes, smiling.

By the time he disappears into Men's Formal Wear, Ben's managed to extract a tag from between the buttons of a folded blue shirt. "Holy shit. Guess how much this costs."

"Fifty dollars?"

Ben tilts his palms up and gestures for me to go higher.

"A hundred?"

"Two hundred twenty-five," he says, "for a button-down shirt."

"Oof. Armani's not messing around."

"I don't get it," Ben says. "Why is this better than, like, Marshalls? Is it threaded with diamonds? Does wearing it give you an orgasm?"

"Hola, I'd like to place an order for one diamond-threaded orgasm shirt, please."

We both whirl around to find Mario in a loose blue tank top, looking like he teleported straight from the beach. He greets me with a kiss on the cheek, which catches me so off guard, I can hardly process the fact that he's here in the first place. I'm pretty sure Ben didn't mention he was coming, but I guess Mario's presence is the default setting now.

But before I can even cough up a real hello, Dylan reappears, carrying a black suit on a hanger. "Gentlemen, time to try this bad boy on for size. And by 'bad boy'"—he glances slyly at Ben—"I do *not* mean the suit."

"I'm not having sex with you in a Bloomingdale's dressing room," says Ben.

"Then we'll save it for Bergdorf." Dylan tousles Ben's hair. "Come on, I don't want to be the only one trying stuff on."

Ben shakes his head. "I don't have—"

"Don't you worry, Benji. I'll find you something hot."

"D, I don't even think I can afford socks here."

But Dylan's already prodding Ben toward the dressing room, leaving Mario and me to amble along behind them. Of course, I can't resist peeking at the price tags out of sheer morbid curiosity. "This one's *eight hundred dollars*." I gape at a mannequin wearing a three-piece suit in deep blue. "How fancy is this wedding? Is Samantha's cousin Jeff Bezos?"

"Damn." Mario high-fives the mannequin. "I see you, Mr. Literal Fancypants."

Minutes later, I'm following Mario into a space that could pass for a minimalist studio apartment, with its hardwood floors, hanging orb light fixtures, and framed black-and-white photos of off-kilter street signs. This isn't the kind of dressing room where you can see feet poking out under curtains, but it's pretty easy to tell which stalls Ben and Dylan are in from their voices. Especially Dylan. I settle onto one of the backless black leather couches beside Mario, who immediately cups his hands around his mouth and calls, "Where's my fashion show? I need some swagger."

"You can't handle my swagger," Dylan shoots back, and Mario opens his mouth to reply. But then the door next to Dylan's creaks open, and my brain flips to portrait mode. Everything blurs except Ben.

Ben in his dark gray suit with its unbuttoned jacket, scuffed sneakers poking out the bottom of slightly-too-long gray trousers. He's pink-cheeked and bashful, and the way he's holding his arms makes me think of penguins. I feel flustered just looking at him.

"Wow," Mario says softly. He's clutching his heart, but Ben just grimaces.

"I could pay half of our rent with this suit. It's ridiculous."

I clear my throat. "You did a half-Windsor."

He smiles and says "yeah" and then we just kind of stare at each other for a minute. Or ten minutes. Or ten hours. I don't know how to measure time when Ben's looking at me.

"Behold!" Dylan's voice booms through the stall door. He flings it open, revealing a suit that's somehow even fancier than Ben's. "'Tis I, emerging from my chrysalis, transformed by the forces of nature and beauty."

I give him a thumbs-up. "I like it."

"You *like* it?" He gapes at me. "You sound like my mom."

"Is that . . . bad?"

Mario studies him. "Love the suit. Are we open to constructive feedback on the bow tie?"

"I . . . do not know if we're open to it." Dylan swipes his phone out of his breast pocket and starts typing. "I'll have Samantha . . . text her cousin to find out."

"Ah," I say. "Difficult groom?"

"Absolutely," he says.

"Okay, here's how we do this." Mario hops up, turning to Dylan. "You come with me. We'll find some options and send photos to Groomzilla."

"Super Mario, I'm all yours," Dylan says—but then he whirls around to grab Ben by the sleeve of his jacket. "And where do you think you're going?"

"Back to the dressing room?"

"Absofuckinglutely not." He pokes Ben in the shoulder. "Don't you dare change out of that until Frantz sees you. I'll be right back."

Ben rolls his eyes and plops onto the couch beside me. But a moment later, he stands, removes his jacket, and sits stiffly back down. "I really didn't come here expecting to play dress-up."

"Well." I blush. "You look great."

"Thanks. I just feel so bad. This guy Frantz set us up in

here, and he was so nice. I hate that I'm making extra work for him for no reason."

"He'll understand. People try on suits all the time," I say. At least, I'm pretty sure those words came out of my mouth, in my voice.

I can't remember if I've seen Ben in just a button-down and tie before. And I think the last time I saw Ben in a suit was when we FaceTimed each other from our respective bathrooms before senior prom. It's just kind of a lot to take in.

When Dylan comes back, he's got four or five ties draped over his shoulders like a tallit. Mario jogs in right behind him—but he does a double take as soon as he sees Ben and me, yanking his phone out of his pocket. "Whoa!"

Ben tilts his head. "What are you doing?"

"You'll see." Still staring into the camera lens, he reaches forward and snatches the jacket from Ben's lap. "Now put your hands back how they were"—he snaps a picture—"because you guys"—*snap*—"are doing"—*snap*—"a spot-on"—*snap*—"reenactment of *La La Land* right now."

I laugh abruptly. "What?"

"Look how you're sitting." Mario does a chef's kiss. "And the outfits."

Dylan's eyes go wide. "Holy shit."

"Must be a sign." Mario leans forward to kiss Ben on the lips.

Ben smiles awkwardly. "Of what?"

"That you're going to love LA and never want to move back."

It doesn't quite compute for a minute. The words aren't stringing together. *LA. Never. Move back.*

Dylan's looking at Ben like he's never seen him before. "You're *moving*?"

Something pulls in my chest. Maybe it's my veins and arteries unplugging like cords from a socket. Maybe every valve of my heart is going dark.

"Um. Possibly? I guess it depends whether Mario's show gets picked up." Ben glances up at Mario. "It wouldn't be forever. Just to try it out. Change of scenery."

"What the fuck? Were you going to mention it, or nah?"

"Yes!" Ben flushes. "D, I kind of—I don't know, I just decided—"

"You *just decided* to move to California? You've never left New York. You wouldn't even visit me and Samantha in Illinois."

Ben looks at him incredulously. "You're mad that I couldn't—"

"I said I'd pay for it!"

"Well, I'm not cool with that!"

"Right." Dylan laughs sharply. "But you're cool with moving to *California* for this guy you've known for, what, two months?"

Ben looks like he might burst into tears. "We've been

in class together all year! And I'm not—I'm not moving for anyone."

I tune him out. It doesn't even feel like I'm here. I feel like I'm watching myself on a jumbotron from fifty yards away.

CHAPTER TWENTY-THREE

BEN

Wednesday, June 17

I've been summoned to Dream & Bean.

I get out of the train station and finish up my text conversation with Arthur as I walk down the block.

I think Dylan just needed to cool down, I say.

I've never seen him so upset, Arthur texts. You turned him into a real boy, Geppetto.

I laugh. And he's treating me like I'm some big nose Pinocchio! I didn't lie. I just didn't tell him yet. I stop outside Dream & Bean and snap a picture. Throwback!

Arthur is typing a message. Stopping. Typing. Stopping. Typing. The suspense is getting to me. The text finally comes in: Get Dylan an extra-large iced coffee to cool him down!

He must have deleted something. Maybe even paragraphs of something, and I can't help but wonder about the text that might have been.

Maybe it was about California.

I wish I knew what Arthur was thinking. He hasn't really said anything about it so far, other than letting me spiral about Dylan's reaction. If anything, he's seemed almost cheerful about it. Which makes sense. Or at least it doesn't *not* make sense. Except when I think about how stunned he looked at Bloomingdale's.

I can't help but wonder if there's something he's not saying. And of course he doesn't owe me a reaction. He's allowed to keep things to himself if he wants to. But the thing is, this is exactly how it started last winter. This is how Arthur and I lost each other. And when I think about losing Arthur again . . .

Maybe it's pointless. Maybe I should push him away now so I can get that loss over with already.

Okay, wow, I'm overthinking this. He's probably just busy at work, or being really extra about the wording of a joke, because it's Arthur, and that's who he is. And it's not a question. We're going to stay in touch, no matter what time zone I'm in. I'll send messages before I go to sleep, and by the time I wake up there will probably be half a dozen texts from Arthur describing everything about his morning from choosing outfits and what he and Mikey are up to. Then I'll walk him through my day with Mario.

Maybe Arthur-and-Ben-as-friends is the best us all along.

I send a quick text back: Going in. Wish me luck. Send rescue texts in case I need an out.

Aye, aye, captain, he writes.

I walk into Dream & Bean, and it feels like a walk down memory lane. Except this feels nothing like the time Dylan and I discovered Arthur's poster with my photo on the wall here. Dylan is sitting with Samantha in the corner table. His hands are folded and he makes eye contact with me before staring up at the ceiling like he didn't see me.

I roll my eyes.

I walk over to Samantha's side and give her a kiss on the cheek. "Hey. How are you?"

"Tired," she says. "Long night."

"Everything okay?"

"Some family stuff. I don't really want to talk about it right now."

"No worries. I hope everything gets better." I turn to Dylan. "Hey, D."

Dylan looks away.

I don't even bother pulling out a chair yet. "Dude, you—I quote—'summoned' me here to talk. Are you really going to not talk?"

"He will talk," Samantha says.

"Through you?"

"What do you think?"

"I think we're too old for this."

Samantha claps. "That's what I said. Sit and talk with me instead. Dylan can join us when he grows up."

Dylan turns to her. "I am grown."

Samantha pulls out her phone.

"Don't set a timer," he says.

"I'm not. I'm setting a stopwatch so I can have it on record how long you keep this act up."

"That seems rather childish."

"Pot, kettle." Samantha starts the stopwatch. Dylan eyes it but says nothing. "Anyway, Ben. This LA business. How long have you been thinking about this?"

"A while. I mean, sort of. Mario brought it up, but I've been feeling restless in New York. My life isn't changing at all, not like you guys. I know all that's changed is you two seeing each other twenty-four/seven, but that's nice. Even if I don't know how you survive this." I gesture at Dylan who looks like he wants to retaliate but remembers he's not talking to me.

"I survive this because it's not twenty-four/seven," Samantha says. "I take really long showers and practically beg my campus counselor to let me hang out with her longer."

"Sounds healthy," I say.

"Sounds healthy," Dylan mockingly echoes.

I lean in. "Oh, what's that? You heard me?"

Dylan says nothing.

Samantha shakes her head. "Ben, I think this is really sudden. You've registered for fall already and you love your classes and—"

"I only love my creative writing class. And Mario won't be there."

"But since when are you following Mario across the world?"

"That's really dramatic."

"Pfft," Dylan adds, like he's not being ridiculously dramatic right now.

"Fine, you're thinking about following Mario across the country. To a city you've never been to before."

"I don't have to stay there if I hate it."

"I personally think you'll love Los Angeles, but I'm not sure this is the right move to get you there."

"Is this an intervention?"

"It's a loving check-in. We want the best for you, even if Dylan's *childish* silent treatment says otherwise."

My phone vibrates. I almost don't check the text, but I'm glad I do. It's Arthur cheering me on and telling me to stay strong. It's like he's sitting in this empty seat next to me.

"I just want some support. I've always supported you two, even back when this one was calling you his future wife way too soon. I'm not trying to marry Mario, okay? I'm just thinking about spending some time in Los Angeles with him."

"Quitting school to do so," Samantha says.

"Yes, quitting school! I'm not on some scholarship like you, and this education isn't worth stressing my family's finances. These other classes haven't exactly been super useful with my writing. I can register for some local classes and not bankrupt my family."

Samantha nods. "I understand. Ben, you know that publishing a book isn't guaranteed to change everything, right?"

"What, you don't believe in me?"

"I—" Samantha takes a deep breath and turns to Dylan. "Cut it out. Your best friend is struggling and I'm not going to be the villain because you're being immature." She turns back to me. "Ben, I love you and I believe in you. You're an amazing and dedicated writer. I want you to have some magical story where you publish a book and your life changes in all the best ways. But I don't want your dream to bite you in the ass in the long run." She gets up and shakes her empty juice bottle. "Now if you'll excuse me, I have to use the restroom." She turns back to Dylan. "If you aren't talking to Ben about how badly you want to make sweet love with him by the time I get back, then you'll be making sweet love to yourself for a long time."

Samantha walks toward the bathroom line, dropping the bottle into the trash like it's a mic.

Dylan closes his eyes. "One cappuccino, two cappuccino, three cappuccino, four cappuccino . . ."

He was never a big fan of counting with Mississippis because he thinks no word should be that tricky to spell. It's always been stupid to me since he's not spelling the word when he says it, but Dylan is going to Dylan.

". . . ten cappuccino." He opens his eyes and hits stop on Samantha's phone's stopwatch. "Hello, Benjamin. I appreciate you taking time out of your day so we may converse like civil men."

I glare at him.

"I would like to speak with you about something I found rather upsetting if you're willing to dialogue with me about said matter."

"That's why I'm here."

"Once again, I appreciate your presence. So, the matter at hand was the discovery that you are considering a move to Los Angeles. Not from you, as one would expect between best friends for life, but instead by one Mario Colón. He dropped the bomb as if it were a plaything when I assure you that bombs are no toys."

"Take that up with him."

"I'm not particularly fond of him right now. He's taking my best friend away from New York."

"You don't even live here anymore."

"That could change! Chicago's winters are the worst!"

"You know where winter isn't the worst?"

"Don't say it—"

"Los Angeles."

"Damn you, Benjamin. You said it when I asked you not to, and I'm our worried our civil conversation is at risk of becoming uncivil."

This is giving me a massive headache. "D, why do you care? You talked this big game about how we were going to hang out all summer, and instead you've canceled on me a thousand times—"

"Falsehood! Falsehood!"

"And your reasons are so weak. Why should I have to stay in New York when you're not here? And even when you are, you're being weirder than usual?"

Dylan leans in. "There are forces at play here that I cannot speak to because I have been sworn to secrecy," he whispers. "The stuff happening in Samantha's family is huge, but that's her business and as her boyfriend I have been trusted with that and I can't abuse it. Not even to you, my freckled best friend who equates my canceling of plans to the same crime as moving across the country without telling me."

"I haven't moved yet. We don't even know if the show's getting picked up!"

"And when might that information be forthcoming, pray tell? Or should I ask Mario?"

"I mean, Mario thinks we'll know soon. Maybe a week or two? But even if Mario has to head out sooner, I don't think I'd leave until next month."

"Next month?!"

Samantha returns from the bathroom. "I don't see anyone making sweet love."

Dylan turns to her. "He's moving next month!"

Samantha takes his hand. "It's his life. We have to respect that."

"I might hate it and come back," I say.

"Oh, please, you're going to walk away from your hot boyfriend who probably makes the best sandcastles and surfs like an Olympian and looks hot all the time?"

"Mario can't swim, actually."

"What about the sandcastles, Ben? What about the sandcastles?"

I shrug.

Dylan sighs. "I guess let me know when you move to Los Angeles forever next month."

"We just all have to hang out some more," Samantha says. "Dylan and I are going to an open mic night on Friday. Why don't you and Mario join us?"

I nod. "That sounds fun." I pick up my phone, distracted as Dylan mutters something to Samantha. I type out Open mic night this Friday with Dylan and Samantha? and ask, "What's that, D?"

"Nothing," he says.

"He said that he's hoping the open mic night will trick you into loving New York again," Samantha says. "Which is not my intention. I just want to see you while we can."

My phone buzzes.

Sounds FUN! Where?

The world grinds to a halt.

I texted the wrong person.

"Um." I swallow. "I accidentally texted Arthur instead of Mario about Friday. Should I . . . ?"

"Oh, it's fine," Samantha says. "Invite them both! The more the merrier."

"Thanks."

I text Mario—for real this time—and he's immediately game. Just the five of us this Friday, hanging out.

What could possibly go wrong?

CHAPTER TWENTY-FOUR

ARTHUR

Thursday, June 18

I don't want to sound the alarms prematurely, but I'm pretty sure I'm being stalked by the state of California. First it was the *Clueless* GIF Jessie sent me at lunch. Then: a taxi ad for the *Real Housewives of Beverly Hills*, a busker singing "Hotel California," a guy reading *Big Sur* on the platform, and no fewer than four articles in my news app about a *Once Upon a Time . . . in Hollywood* spin-off. I don't know if the universe thinks it's being funny or what, but if I see one more palm tree or sunset or big white letter, I'm filing for a restraining order.

Though the real fucking winner is Ethan smogging up my brain with a link to Mario's latest Instagram post. Please tell me you've seen this

I flop on the couch, trying to imagine a world where I haven't checked this post five million times since Mario uploaded it. Since when do you follow Mario? I ask.

A moment later: lol since you sent me his feed?

I click into Mario's profile, pulling up the now-familiar post: Ben and me on the dressing room couch, cropped next to a screenshot of Emma Stone and Ryan Gosling on a park bench. Mario's caption says, "Spot the difference." It's already gotten almost eight hundred likes, and every single one feels like being stabbed by a needle. But what's worse is how I can't stop myself from scrolling through Mario's squares of unfiltered selfies and snapshots from LA: the La Brea Tar Pits, a stack of pancakes, the outside of a bar where an episode of *RuPaul's Drag Race* was filmed. It's a little too easy to plug Ben into every frame. Mario and Ben walking down the Santa Monica Pier, hand in hand. Ben's laptop next to Mario's on a patio table. It's like a bruise I can't stop poking.

People don't warn you that heartbreak is a chronic condition. Maybe it quiets down a little over time, or you can muffle it with distance, but the ache never quite dials down to zero. It's there lurking in the background, ready to flare back up the minute you let your guard down.

Ben's leaving New York. And it feels like he's leaving me specifically.

Which makes no sense. I don't even live here. And even

if I did live here, Ben's not my boyfriend. He's absolutely, unequivocally not—

Mikey. A photo pops onto my screen like I summoned it: a fish-face selfie with Mia in her dim bedroom light. It's the sweetest picture ever taken, and I feel so guilty I could puke.

But where does the guilt even come from? I haven't crossed any lines. And I won't. I wouldn't. Mikey knows about every single Ben hangout this whole entire summer.

I tuck my knees onto the couch and press the voice call button.

He answers in a whisper. "Hey, hold on a sec. Just leaving Mia's room." A moment later, a door creaks shut, and I picture Mikey padding down the hall in his crisp white socks. "Okay, I'm back," he says. "Can we FaceTime? I want to ask you something."

My stomach twists, but I smile through it. "Should I be nervous?"

"Why would you be nervous?"

"Because you said you wanted to ask me something, and questions are scary."

"This isn't a scary one, I promise." Mikey pops into video, smiling. He's at his desk now, with his phone propped up, camera angled up from below. All chin, forever adorably bad at FaceTime. "So my parents finally talked Robbie and Amanda into a wedding," he says.

"Oh! Wow—"

"Really tiny. Just dancing and cake in their backyard. But I get to bring a plus-one, so . . ." He smiles shyly. "Save the date for July eleventh?"

I pause. "Of this year?"

"I know, it's ridiculously soon. But apparently they've got our pastor lined up, and I think they've booked a tent already, too."

"Mikey, I can't," I say quietly. "I'm so sorry. The play opens that weekend. I have to be at work."

His brow furrows. "You don't think anyone could cover for you?"

"On opening weekend?"

"You're the assistant's intern."

My cheeks go warm. "Yeah, I get that you're disappointed, but please don't shit all over my job."

"That's not—" He shuts his eyes for a moment. "Arthur. I'm sorry. That came out wrong. I just miss you, you know?" His cheeks are flushed. "And it's not just the wedding. I guess . . . I feel like I'm the one putting in all the effort lately."

My stomach goes taut. "What do you mean?"

"I don't know. Just the day-to-day stuff, and FaceTime—"

"We talk every day!"

"Yeah," he says softly. "Because I call you every day."

I stop short. "I'm sorry. I didn't realize—"

"And it's like, you're so good at the big moments. Like New Year's. The theater tickets. But I feel like we get a little lost in between those things."

"Well," I say, "maybe I want more big moments from you."

"Like when I told you I loved you?" says Mikey.

All the air leaves my lungs.

"Sorry." He pinches the bridge of his nose. "I'm sorry. I shouldn't pressure you."

"No, you're right." I take a deep breath. "I'm so sorry. You've been so patient. I want to say it back to you. I'm just not—I don't know what's wrong with me. I keep getting in my head about it, and I end up thinking in circles."

Mikey nods quickly without meeting my eyes. We're both silent for a minute.

When I finally speak, my voice cracks. "I shouldn't have come to New York."

"Arthur, no! It's your dream job. I shouldn't have said anything." His voice shakes, and it makes my whole chest clench.

"Mikey."

"I'm gonna go." He tries to smile, but it doesn't quite hold.

"Mikey Mouse. Hey. Can we talk about this?"

"Tomorrow. I'm sorry. I'm not mad, okay?" he says. "I miss you."

Then he ends the call before I have a chance to say it back.

At work the next day, Taj ambushes me before I even put my bag down. "Ready for some fuckery? You're not going to believe this." He throws up jazz hands. "The theater double-booked us for the weekend of the tenth."

My mouth falls open. "Are you serious? Opening weekend?"

"Mm-hmm."

"Is that, like . . . a normal thing that happens?"

He lets out a choked laugh. "It's *so* far from normal. Marketing's already started. The posters. I'm losing my goddamn mind," he says, reaching for his bullet journal. Then he spends the next few minutes outlining the entire revamped production schedule that I forget on the spot, because it seems my brain only has room for two dates.

July 17th, our new opening night. And July 11th, the wedding.

When Mikey said to save the date, I guess the universe listened.

Taj leaves to find Jacob, but I barely register his absence.

I'm too wrapped up in what should be the simplest equation of all time: Mikey plus one.

I settle in at my table, chin in my hands, waiting to feel over the moon about this.

It's a good thing, no question. I like Robbie and Amanda, I like cake, I like dancing. I definitely like making Mikey happy. And who knows—maybe seeing Mikey in a suit will make it all click into place. We'll kiss under the stars and hold hands under the table, and I'll finally know for sure that I'm completely in love. That I've been in love all along.

But I'm missing something. I know I am. It's like there's a thought circling my brain, waiting for clearance to land. Something about weddings and dancing and blown-away grooms and the l'dor v'dor of it all. Generation to generation.

I think about my bar mitzvah, and how I missed the kiddush luncheon because I was crying in an empty Sunday school classroom. I'd managed to skip a line in my Torah portion, and even though my parents swore no one noticed, I knew that was bullshit. God noticed. And wasn't God the whole point? Did my bar mitzvah even count anymore?

I was a quaking lump of pinstripes and hair gel when Bubbe found me, and at first she said nothing. She just pulled a chair up beside me and rubbed circles on my back like she used to when I was little. But when she spoke at last, it felt like the first real adult conversation of my life. "It's not about the Torah," she'd said gently, and I'd looked up in scandalized amazement. "It's not! Your zayde was called to the Torah, and your uncle Milton, and my father, and his father, and so on. But your mother and I never read from the Torah. When I was a girl, it was unusual for girls to even read from the haftarah. *My* mother gave tzedakah and received a private blessing at home. There's no particular way a ritual has to look. You could have stood up there and done the Charleston, and it wouldn't have mattered, as long as you felt it right here." She touched both hands to her chest and smiled. "It's our link to the generations who came before us, and it's how we hold space for the ones who haven't been born yet. L'dor v'dor, Aharon," she said, using my Hebrew name, and I knew she was thinking about my great-grandpa Aaron. Bubbe was young when her dad died—even my mom never got to meet him. But that's who I'm named for, and Bubbe always says my heart is just like his.

Here's the thing: this isn't just cake, and it isn't just dancing. It's a *wedding.* Which means it's wrapped in every wedding that ever came before it and all the ones that haven't happened yet, too. Maybe even mine.

I press a hand to my face. Suddenly, I'm holding back tears.

I've been searching my brain, inch by inch, but I never

thought to zoom out. Now it's as clear as the X on a map.

I'm completely in love. I've been in love all along.

But not with Mikey. And when I think about the future, Mikey's not the one who's in it.

I must be time-traveling again. Every time I blink, another hour goes by—a full Friday workday, gone with no trace. I don't remember taking the elevator down, but here I am under the studio awning, waiting for the rain to die down. The plan was to call Mikey from home, but maybe I should do it now, before I lose my nerve.

Except my hands won't stop shaking. I don't even know what this conversation looks like. There has to be a script for this somewhere. I'm not the first guy on earth to break up with someone. It's not even my first time breaking up with Mikey.

The thought rips through me so sharply, I barely keep my grip on my phone.

I know I'm impulsive. And careless. But the way I've treated Mikey? The way I keep yanking my heart out of reach every time he tries to catch it?

I'm his first *I love you*, his first time having sex, his first kiss, his first everything.

I'm his Ben.

The rain hasn't died down at all, so I walk back into the studio lobby. Mikey's so easy to find in my contacts—his name's at the top of my favorites. I tap the call button and try to catch my breath while it rings.

I owe him this, I think.

But he doesn't pick up. So I shove my phone in a plastic bag and step straight into the rain.

By the time I reach my building, I barely care that I'm soaked. I press the elevator button so hard my knuckle cracks. And then I stare at the mirrored door, watching my lips move as I run through my lines.

Hey, can we talk?

Mikey Mouse, you deserve so much more than my bullshit.

You deserve the biggest, loudest I love you

With no hesitation.

But, Mikey, I don't think I can get there

Because. Because. Because.

How the fuck am I going to tell him this part?

Hey, Mikey, remember the exact thing you were afraid of?

The elevator spits me into my own hallway, but from the way my heart's pounding, you'd think I was walking a plank. Just a few steps until I'm there. I'll dry off and change clothes, and then I'll suck it up and call him. I'll rip off the Band-Aid.

Hey, Mikey, can we talk?

Hey, Mikey, you told me so.

I turn the key and push the door open. The living room

light's on. There's a suitcase in the entryway.

I feel like an old-timey film reel, a whirring countdown blinking down.

In all the months that I've known him, Mikey's never kissed me like this. It's so earnest, my knees buckle.

I blink up at him, dumbfounded.

"How's this for a big moment?" he asks.

CHAPTER TWENTY-FIVE

BEN

Friday, June 19

The New Town Street coffee shop in Tribeca is one of the best open mic spots according to Yelp—and Dylan, who has been here for the exact amount of time as the rest of us. I don't have anything to compare it to, but it's pretty cool. The first comedian we saw managed to finish off his set without being completely offensive, which is always a win. What sucks is how the lighting is really dim so you can't really make out the paintings on the wall donated by artists for exposure. That's like me donating my manuscript to a library only for it to be used as a doorstop.

Dylan returns with drinks—two ginger ales for Samantha and himself, a Pepsi for me, a lemonade for Mario—and we toast to our night out. It's been almost an hour and I haven't heard from Arthur yet. I even texted him a look who's late now joke, but no response. I'm going to give it another ten, fifteen minutes before I call him to make sure he's okay. I wouldn't be surprised if he fell asleep in front of his laptop while rewatching *Waitress* covers like he's been known to.

"Please welcome the Pac-People to the stage!" the host says.

"Woooo!" Samantha cheers, and Dylan keeps pumping his fist like he's at some sports game.

"Who are they?" Mario asks.

"Yo no sé times a hundred," I say.

"Patrick recommended them to me," Samantha says. "The Pac-People were trending on TikTok and he thought I'd like their sound."

"Patrick may be right about one thing," Dylan says.

"What about when he said he liked your man bun?" Samantha asks.

Dylan raises his chin indignantly. "I happen to disagree with him. Man buns are out."

I pay him no mind and focus on the Pac-People, who are setting up onstage. There's five of them, all dressed up in classic Pac-Man/Ms. Pac-Man and ghost colors—bright yellow, red, blue, pink, and yellow again. And once the music starts, it's so energetic, it feels like something you would hear during a really fun level in a video game. Mario hugs Dylan from behind and sways with him, and Dylan is not shy at all about dancing.

"Hold my drink, babe," Dylan says, handing his ginger ale to Samantha, which she double-fists like a champ.

"Sostén mi bebida, Alejo," Mario says, handing me his lemonade.

"Boys will be boys?" Samantha asks me.

"Mario and Dylan will be Mario and Dylan," I say.

They've been really chill with Mario tonight, and Dylan has only made ten you're-stealing-my-best-friend jokes. I need Dylan to step up his game because Samantha and I have five dollars on the line here on how many times Dylan harasses Mario on my move to LA by the end of the night.

"So cute," someone says as they pass our guys.

"Thanks!" Dylan says.

"He makes confidence look exhausting," I say.

"And exhilarating," Samantha says with a smile.

"I won't tell him you said that."

"I tell him enough."

"Samantha, you're feeding the beast!"

"I knoooow."

The Pac-People put up another song, and Dylan and Samantha turn to each other and cheer.

"'Ballad of Aphrodite'!" they say at the same time.

Samantha pulls Dylan away from Mario and they sway together.

"This sounds like Cupid created a song with only a harp and an electronic keyboard," Mario says.

"And it kind of works though, right?"

He holds out his hand. "Let's see if it works."

"How do you even dance to this?" I ask.

Mario grabs me by the wrists and moves me around like I'm some puppet. "Don't know, don't care. You just move."

And I move with him, laughing, up until his phone rings.

"It's my uncle. Mind if I get this?"

"¡Ve! ¡Ve!"

Mario turns to leave, but comes back and gives me a kiss before heading toward the front door. Between this kiss and the ones he's given me all week whenever we've greeted each other, this is what I've been missing with him the entire time.

While Dylan and Samantha are busy swaying, I call Arthur. It rings once before going to voice mail. It's immediately followed with a text: Be there in five mins, sorry!

Yay! I type back.

I'm watching the Pac-People finish their set when Mario comes back and drags me to the front door with the biggest smile on his face.

"I have news," Mario says. "I have *the news*."

"The show—"

"The show sold in a bidding war! It's all happening!"

Mario bounces around, almost like someone hammering the jump button in a *Super Mario* game. He stops and grabs my hands. "Alejo, I feel like my dreams are coming true. I'm going to get to work on a TV show and help bring some androids alive. Power them on. Whatever. Wow. *WOW!* I can't believe this."

He stands there, frozen. Like he's imagining his amazing future.

Now I'm doing the same.

Mario will go to Los Angeles and I'm going to follow him. This is the most exciting fresh start ever.

He grabs my hand. "There's more, Alejo."

"Oh my God. What?"

Maybe he'll be more than an assistant on the show.

"So Tío Carlos has a lot of industry contacts, obviously, and he's friends with this one film agent at UTA—the United Talent Agency. The agent Dariel is this queer man who loves fantasy stories. Carlos brought up *The Wicked Wizard War.*"

I'm almost sure I've heard him wrong. "Say what? Your uncle knows about that?"

"Of course. I told him how much I love it."

Mario really does have me on his mind, even when I'm out of sight.

"But I'm not done with my revision."

"You'll get there. Dariel is really into the premise and

could recommend some literary agents, too, if he likes the book."

This is really exciting and also really overwhelming. I feel like I should run home and get to work in case this offer has an expiration date.

I'm so grateful that I want to kiss him. When I lean in, I hear my name—out of Arthur's mouth.

"Sorry I'm late, but surprise!"

Arthur is holding Mikey's hand—the same Mikey who's supposed to be in Boston. My stomach drops. Seeing them together makes me want to cling to Mario even more.

"Wow. Hey, Mikey."

"Hi!"

I lead Arthur, Mikey, and Mario back to our table, right as Dylan and Samantha are returning to their seats. Dylan does a double take before he launches straight into Mikey's arms.

"Triple date!" Dylan shouts. "The very first in the history of the world!"

"That can't be right," Mikey says.

"What brings you back?" Samantha asks. "You here for another Broadway show?"

"I wanted to surprise Arthur. Just because."

"And surprise Arthur you did!" Arthur says.

"I'm going to grab a drink," Mikey says. "You want a Sprite?"

"Perfect," Arthur says. Then after Mikey walks off, he stares blankly at the next comedian to come onstage.

"Hey, you okay?" I ask.

"Perfect," Arthur says again, even though there are tears forming in his eyes.

I inch closer to him. "Do you want to go somewhere and talk?"

It's heartbreaking to see him like this.

Arthur shakes his head. "I can't. I mean, I don't need to. Everything is fine. I'm like that GIF of the dog in the hat who's saying everything is fine even though there's a fire. Except there's no fire."

I want to stop time and only talk to Arthur. No Mikey, no Mario. No one else. I want him to be honest with me so I can be there for him like he obviously needs right now. But he's not letting me.

He's acting like he's listening to the comedian, fake-laughing to jokes that Mario and Dylan are genuinely reacting to.

Mikey returns with drinks. "Sorry I took so long."

"No need to say sorry. You're banned from apologizing forever," Arthur says.

Seriously, what did Mikey do to him?

Or what did Arthur do to Mikey?

I can't get comfortable during the next couple sets.

Someone sings "Jingle Bell Rock." Mikey remarks how that's a choice and praises her singing. Then two people do improv, which is hard to watch, and Dylan is not having any of that shit either, so he turns his back on them.

When the host comes back to the stage, he says, "Next up is Mikey!"

Arthur's eyes widen. "Oh wow. Yay!"

The thing is, as much as Arthur loves Broadway, he's no actor. I can tell that he's not as enthusiastic as he's pretending to be. Whatever he's going through, maybe Mikey is doing this to cheer him up?

Mikey kisses the top of Arthur's head and walks to the stage. He grabs the mic and says, "This is dedicated to my boyfriend, Arthur. You deserve big moments, and this is the first of many more."

"Awww," Dylan says, rubbing Arthur's knee.

Someone begins playing the piano.

"'Arthur's Theme'!" Mario shouts. "Great pick!"

I've never heard this song before. I'm speechless when Mikey sings about getting caught between the moon and New York City. His voice is gorgeous and my eyes water at how beautiful this is. Under this spotlight, Mikey is so endearing as he sings into the mic, "*The best that you can do is fall in love.*"

I push my chair back and stand.

Mario smiles up at me. "You good?"

I mutter something about the bathroom, and then I get the fuck out.

I should be happy for Arthur. He deserves this, right? He deserves a boyfriend who will deliver personal Broadway-worthy performances and surprise him just because. I could never in a million years give Arthur the kind of moment Mikey's giving him right now.

And sure, maybe Arthur wasn't happy when he walked into the bar tonight. Maybe he and Mikey aren't perfect. But I speak Arthur's language better than anyone, and I know exactly what this sort of grand gesture means to him. Whatever the two of them were going through, I'm sure it all went out the window the minute Mikey stepped onto that stage. I'm sure they'll go home and have sex and make a bunch of big tearful love declarations.

That's totally fine. I can have my own do-overs, too.

CHAPTER TWENTY-SIX

ARTHUR

Friday, June 19

Nothing about this makes sense. Mikey doesn't do solos. He *definitely* doesn't do solos while standing on chairs in Tribeca coffee shops. And yet the guy who just sang his heart out to a roomful of strangers was unquestionably my spotlight-averse boyfriend.

His sweetly nervous expression makes me want to burst into tears.

"You're incredible," I say, not quite meeting his eyes. I grab his hand to guide him back to the table, and even that feels like a lie.

Dylan greets us with a slow clap. "Hot damn, Sir Mikes-a-lot."

Mario pushes his sleeve up to show us his goose bumps. "Fucking brilliant. Talk about a real, old-fashioned Hollywood grand gesture." So then everyone starts talking about how Mario should write it into a TV show, but I stop listening pretty quickly. Mostly because Ben's finally back from the bathroom, and his face is hijacking my brain.

"Well, speaking of Hollywood," Mario says, giving Ben a quick side hug. "Alejo, should we tell them the big news?"

"Wait, how big? I want to prepare myself." Dylan says. "Are we talking new Avengers movie, or is this more of a B-list—

Samantha covers his mouth with her hand. "Did it get picked up?"

Mario beams. "Ten hour-long episodes. Full fucking series order."

Samantha smacks the table. "Oh my God! You're a TV writer?"

"I'm a TV writer!"

Mikey's eyes widen. "That's incredible."

"Congratulations," I say, eyes flicking toward Ben. He looks a little bit dazed.

"Guess that makes it official," says Dylan. "My Benhattan is moving to Los Bengeles."

"Um. Yeah." Ben smiles. "I guess I am."

Mario nudges him. "Okay, now tell them what *you* have in the pipeline."

Ben blushes. "Like, the agent guy?"

Mario grins. "You mean the agent who wants to check out *The Wicked Wizard War* the moment you're done?"

"Yeah, because you and Carlos keep hyping it. Let's see what he says when he actually reads it," Ben says with an eye roll. But there's no hiding the current of hope in his voice.

"He'll love it," I say, trying to tack on a smile. "How could he not?"

I remember the night Ben let me read his draft, how sacred that felt. At the time, it seemed like the most intimate thing you could share with a person. Your unfinished heart.

But Mario's the one carrying Ben's dreams over the finish line. I may have been Ben's first draft, but Mario's his hardcover.

I guess that's how it goes, though. Sometimes happily ever afters aren't about your happiness at all.

Mikey holds my hand all the way back from the subway, and I feel like more of a liar with each passing step. I don't have a clue where to start. How does this even work when we're not fighting? How do you break up with a guy who hasn't done anything wrong?

"I can't believe you found a song called 'Arthur's Theme,'" I blurt.

Mikey laughs a little. "I already knew it. I've been sitting on that one for a minute."

Cool, cool. Good to know Mikey's been plotting gorgeous surprises while I've been wrecked over Ben. Good to know I'm an actual fucking monster.

"Well, thanks," I manage. "It was really sweet."

"You deserve to be serenaded."

My throat thickens. "So do you."

"Hey. You okay?" Mikey asks.

"What? Of course! Why?"

"I don't know. You're so quiet. You seem lost in thought."

"I'm—yeah, I'm fine." I pause in front of my building, releasing Mikey's hand to root around for my key. "Sorry. It's just been a weird week."

The entryway lights are off when we reach the apartment, just like we left it.

"No one's home," Mikey says. "I guess Jessie's date's going well."

"Ha. Yeah," I say without looking at him.

"Maybe we should—"

"Want to watch a movie?" I interject, practically divebombing the couch. I feel so jumpy and strange, a human hiccup. I grab the remote and start scrolling, but all the thumbnails blur together. Which is when I realize my eyes are wet.

"Arthur?"

I set the remote down and press the heels of my hands to my eyes. *I can't do this. I can't fucking do this. Not tonight.* "I'm fine," I say.

"You don't seem fine." His voice is so tender, I lose my breath for a moment. "You don't have to talk about it," he adds quickly. "But if you want to, I'm here."

My throat tightens—for a moment, my words can't break through. "You're such a good person," I say. It comes out husky and strained.

"No I'm not. I'm just in love with you."

I try to smile, but it falters. I press my hands to my face.

"Hey." Mikey pulls me closer. "You don't have to say it back. You know that, right?"

Tomorrow, I think, and I hate myself for it.

He kisses the top of my head, and my eyes flutter shut.

Last time climbing into bed beside Mikey. Last time he'll set his glasses on my nightstand. Last time I'll catalog his features in the semidarkness: his cheekbones, the slope of his nose, his snowy-blond eyelashes.

I'm the only guy he's ever shared a bed with. I'm the only one who knows he hugs a pillow when he sleeps. What am I supposed to do with that information? Where do I put it?

When he breathes, the pillow rises and falls with his chest—but then he opens his eyes, tilts his head toward me. For a moment, we just stare at each other.

"Can't sleep?"

I shake my head. "Not really."

"Me either." He rolls onto his side, leaving barely an inch between our faces. I try to smile, but somehow it's already skidding toward tears. "I'm so sorry."

"For what?" He wraps his arm around me, pulling me in closer. "Hey."

"For being an asshole."

"You're not an asshole."

"Mikey." I take a deep breath. "I don't even know how to say this. I was going to wait until tomorrow."

His chest stiffens against mine. "Okay."

"Mikey."

"Please just tell me."

I squeeze my eyes shut for a moment. "I think—when you told me you loved me." I pause, wiping a tear. "I was just—I didn't expect it. In that moment. So I kind of shut down. I don't know."

"Arthur, I know. I get it."

"And I love you. Obviously. I knew that. But I couldn't tell if it was the same kind of love, and I didn't want to say it unless I was sure—"

"And that's okay! There's no rush."

"I know, I know. You've been"—I swallow—"so wonderful and patient. I don't deserve it."

"But you do."

"I don't."

I meet his eyes, and it feels like I'm free-falling. His expression is like wood.

"Mikey, I want to be in love with you so badly."

He closes his eyes, smiling tightly. "But you're not."

I shake my head slowly. "I'm not."

A tear slides down the bridge of Mikey's nose, and he wipes it roughly away. Then he rolls away from me, onto his back.

"It's not—"

"It's not me, it's you. Got it."

"I know how that sounds, but it's true!" I sit up, hugging my knees to my chest. "You're the perfect boyfriend. I don't know what's wrong with me. I've been racking my brain trying to figure out what's not adding up. How I can love every single thing about you, but I can't make it click—and Mikey, you deserve a guy who can give you that. I feel like I'm holding you back from meeting him."

"So, what? This is just . . . it?"

"I'm so sorry."

"Wow." Mikey stares up at the ceiling.

"Like, I'm so fucking sorry. Mikey. I just want you to know how incredible—"

"I don't want to hear how incredible I am!" He sits up, burying his face in his hands. "God, Arthur. Can I just have a second to wrap my head around the fact that I just took a train here so you could dump me?"

I wince. "I don't like the word '*dumping*'—"

"I don't like being dumped!"

I start to cry again. "I'm sorry—"

"Can you just stop?"

I press my lips together, nodding.

"Do you want me to leave?" I say finally. "I can sleep in the living room."

"Please. Stop. You don't have to sleep in the living room."

"Then can we talk through this?" I ask.

"What do you want me to say? That it's fine?"

"No—"

"It's not fine." He tilts his head back, eyes fixed on the ceiling. "Where did this come from? Did I embarrass you tonight?"

"No! God—no, you were amazing! This wasn't a tonight thing. I've been trying to wrap my head around it for a month."

"A month. So, like, around the time you got to New York and started seeing your ex-boyfriend every day?"

"That's not why—"

"Really?" Mikey turns to face me. "Look me in the eye and tell me this has nothing to do with Ben."

All my words vanish.

"Got it." A tear streaks down his cheek.

"Nothing happened," I say hoarsely. "I swear to God."

"Nothing, like you didn't have sex, or—"

"Nothing like nothing! Mikey, I would never cheat, ever."

He just looks at me. "Did you kiss him?"

"No! Kissing is cheating to me." He doesn't respond. "Mikey, you've known about every single time we've hung out. And that's all it is. Not sex, not kissing, not holding hands. Just hanging out. And half the time, Mario's there."

Mikey presses a hand to his forehead. "If you're not hooking up with him, what are you even getting from this?"

"What? Nothing! He's my friend."

"Your friend who you were in love with! How long did you have to think before you said it back to him?"

I stare at my knees.

"How long did you even date? Three weeks?"

"Three weeks and two days," I say, without thinking, and Mikey looks like I've slapped him. "I was sixteen. He was my first boyfriend. What do you want me to say?"

"I'm so glad, Arthur. So glad you had such a special first love story. Want to hear mine? We shared a bed every night for three months, but he wouldn't call me his boyfriend. And then he dumped me two hours before the winter concert. That was great for me. I loved that."

"Mikey, I'm sorry. I wasn't—"

"Want to know how I spent Christmas? Crying my eyes out. Barely got out of bed. My mom was so freaked out, she skipped church."

I look up with a start. "But you said you—"

"What was I supposed to say? Hi, I know you just flew up to Boston for me, but let's talk about how you ruined Christmas—"

"You should have said that!" My eyes spill over. "I deserved it!"

"I was so in love with you, Arthur. Do you even get that? You think this summer was the first time I've wanted to say it? The first time I've felt it?"

I look at him, stunned. "I didn't know—"

"And then you show up on my doorstep on New Year's Eve saying you want to be my boyfriend?" Mikey presses both hands to his chest. "That's all I wanted. All I wanted was to start over with you."

"I'm so sorry," I say, so quietly it's almost an exhale. "I was so stupid and confused. I'd just broken up with Ben—"

"It's always Ben." Mikey shuts his eyes behind his glasses. "So, what, are you in love with him or something?"

"I—"

"I guess that's why you came to New York."

"No! Not at all. We weren't even talking!" I take a deep breath. "Mikey, nothing's happening. I swear. He's following his boyfriend to California. I have no idea if I'll ever see him again. That's it. That's the whole story. There's no epilogue where we get together." My voice is choked. "And yeah, I have feelings for him. They've probably always been there. I'm not good at this, okay? I thought I was over him, but apparently I'm not, and who the fuck knows if I ever will be. But you shouldn't have to sit around waiting for that to happen!"

Mikey's quiet for a moment, rubbing the bridge of his nose. "Then I guess that's it," he says finally.

I nod, the corners of my mouth wet and salty with tears.

He doesn't speak, but he does this long, shaky exhale that I feel all the way to my bone marrow. The urge to hug him is like gravity. My arms are halfway there before the thought reaches my brain. "Can I—"

Mikey nods, and I throw my arms around him. I don't think I've ever loved him more. Maybe in another universe, it could have been enough.

I don't remember how long we cried or when we decided to sleep. All I know is this: when I wake up, I'm alone. The blankets on Mikey's side of the bed are pulled up and neatly folded over.

Early bird, I think, though it's already past ten. I can hear the faint TV audio leaking in from the living room. Mikey's probably catching up on Netflix while he finishes up breakfast. Except—

The empty spot beside my dresser. His suitcase is gone.

I slide out of bed and cross my room to the door, feeling divorced from my body. A school bell chimes on the television when I step into the living room.

He's gone. Of course he's gone. And when Jessie looks up from the couch, I completely unravel.

"Fuck." She turns the TV off. "Are you okay?"

"I look that bad?" I try to laugh.

"Like absolute shit." She's already halfway across the room. "What happened?"

There's no start space. There's no first page to this story. I don't even know how to tell it. All I know is he's gone. I deserve it. I'm relieved. And I miss him. And I want to tell Ben, so he can touch my face and kiss me and say he's loved me all along. Except he won't, because he hasn't, and me breaking Mikey's heart won't change the fact that Ben's breaking mine all over again.

CHAPTER TWENTY-SEVEN

BEN

Tuesday, June 23

"This is not what I had in mind when I said let's hang out."

Dylan shrugs. "No, no, no, no, no. You were bitching and moaning about how I'm the sole reason you're leaving New York because we don't hang out. You don't get to bitch and moan when we actually hang out."

"You're not the sole reason. You're not even in the top three reasons."

"That's offensive, but I don't care about your pettiness right now because I'm anniversary shopping," Dylan says as we enter a flower shop here in Alphabet City. "Mikey was fresh out of a *Glee* episode with his solo, and now I've got to make sure that Samantha feels the love the way Arthur did."

I'm not sure Arthur felt the love at all. I don't know,

maybe I'm misinterpreting things, but I could swear Arthur was acting even weirder after Mikey finished his song. He was so quiet all night, almost completely checked out. I couldn't make sense of it at all. I was so sure Mikey's performance would have fixed the tension between them.

I keep almost texting him to check in, but I don't how to bring it up without making it weird. I mean, I'm not exactly dying for Arthur to know how much time I've spent obsessing over his relationship dynamics.

But it's probably all in my head. I probably imagined the tension. And even if they really were fighting, I'm sure they've kissed and made up by now. I'm sure Mikey's gotten his *I love you, too.*

I'm not exactly dying to hear about that either.

"Psst." Dylan leans in. "Being in this lovely flower shop has me wondering about what it must be like to deflow—"

"I can't believe Samantha has almost survived two years of you," I interrupt.

"There's no getting away now."

"You think you're untouchable from heartbreak?"

"You break my heart every day," Dylan says, reading the flower cards while the florist helps another customer. "But Samantha and I are happy."

"I can tell. It's nice to not be worried about you. On that front, at least. I'm definitely concerned you're going to out-Dylan yourself in front of the wrong person one day and get a beatdown. Here's hoping Samantha saves the day."

"Oh, please. I watch WWE. I wish someone would try."

Only Dylan would think watching fake wrestling is self-defense training.

He holds up some small white flowers bunched together. "What do you think of these?"

"They look like cauliflower."

"These are stephanotis, you fool!"

"How do you even know that word?"

The florist approaches us. "A fine choice," he says in his deep voice. He's Black with a thick white beard, and vines draped around his shoulders. He reminds me of this potion maker in *TWWW.* "What's the occasion?"

"Two-year anniversary with my girlfriend."

"Ah, mazel tov. Do you know her favorite flowers, or are we just looking to arrange something ourselves?"

Dylan pulls out his phone and opens his Notes app. "She's a fan of calla lilies and ranunculus."

"You have a cheat sheet of her favorite flowers? That's cute."

"You have to with names like these."

I shadow them while the florist takes Dylan around the shop.

Dylan points to some white roses. "B-Man, what do you think?"

"They're cool."

"Are you impersonating some straight bro? If you don't stop and smell some roses I will get a new best friend at the Pride parade."

"Be my guest," I say.

"You'll regret this. It's going to be a huge extravaganza. It's going to be like *The Bachelor* except we'll call it *The Best Friend* and all your people are going to woo me so hard."

"Can't wait to not watch that."

"You're cranky. I'm going to hang with Phil here."

I wish Phil the best of luck.

I text Mario, asking him how playing basketball with his brothers is going, and then I wander the shop while waiting for a response. There's a section called *Flowers for All Moods*. Smart move since you don't want to bring sympathy irises to date night. There are pink and red roses for love and joy. Bluish-purple daisies to wish someone better health. The bright yellow tulips are recommended to cheer someone up. It has me thinking about Arthur, though if I wanted to make his day, I'd deliver some wildflowers, which are his favorite. I almost sent him some in December after the Mikey breakup. But the only wildflower bouquet I could find was for funerals, and it cost sixty dollars, so instead I sent a link to some park's virtual tour of their wildflower exhibit. It was better than a bouquet, because we got to watch it together.

I keep thinking about last December. Arthur and I were

flirting so much you'd think we never got the memo that we broke up. Arthur was begging for a *TWWW* sequel, and around Christmastime, I was really thinking about a sequel of our own. I was willing to do the long-distance thing, especially after seeing how we were still so connected.

I was so close to telling him how I felt.

And then Arthur chose Mikey before I even stepped into the ring.

Now I don't even trust myself to know what's in his head. If he really was upset at the open mic night, would he even reach out to me?

If he did, I'd run out of this flower shop.

I'd skip the Pride parade, even though it might be my last in New York.

I'd even tell Mario someone important needs me.

But I doubt I could make Arthur smile the way I used to. I don't even know if it's my place to try.

CHAPTER TWENTY-EIGHT
ARTHUR

Friday, June 26

"He'll come around," my mom says. I picture her in her swiveling office chair, holding the phone up like a walkie-talkie. "I'm sure he just needs a little space to process everything."

"A little? He soft-blocked me!"

"That's very . . . I don't know what that is," she says. "Why is it soft?"

"It's not. It just means he made my Instagram account unfollow his account. And he's on private, so I can't even see his pictures!" I stare dazedly at my bedroom ceiling, hands pressed to my cheeks. Of all the things I thought I'd miss, who knew it would be Mikey's terrible Instagram photography. It's mostly random bodies of water and overexposed shots of his sister's cat, Mortimer, who has a bowel condition that Mikey references frequently in the captions, because apparently he's the world's first nineteen-year-old boomer.

And I'm not saying I miss the bowel updates. I just miss Mikey. I miss talking to him and teasing him and making him laugh, and I wish I could say sorry for real.

Once my mom hangs up, I sprawl on top of the covers, holding my phone aloft to stare at my under-eye bags in the selfie camera. I've slept like garbage all week, and it shows.

A week ago, Mikey was on a train to New York.

I can't wrap my head around any of this. I've barely told anyone about the breakup, which means it barely feels real. Yeah, Mom's called me every single day this week, and my dad keeps trying to FaceTime me at work. And Taj knows—he guessed it the minute he saw my face on Monday. But the only other people who know on my end are Jessie, Ethan, and Bubbe. And Bubbe's book-club friends and the guy at the deli counter at Bubbe's favorite grocery store and some woman named Edie from shul whose bisexual grandson is premed and single. But I haven't told Musa. And I definitely haven't told Ben. I don't even want Jessie to tell Samantha, because it would get back to Ben, and I'm not ready for that. I'm just not.

I tap over to Mario's Stories again, just to ride that misery spiral all the way down. Why the fuck not, right? It's

Pride Weekend Eve, and crying in my boxers about my ex's hot boyfriend is a deeply valid expression of gay culture.

It's only my fourth time watching this particular sequence of videos—tiny consecutive clips strung together, with the song "Hollywood Swinging" playing in the background. In the videos, Mario's drumming on cardboard boxes and sealing them shut with packing tape, and every so often he looks up to mouth the lyrics directly into the camera. His excitement's so infectious, it makes my heart hurt. The whole thing is filmed by someone offscreen, who says the word *wow* partway through the second clip. At least I know it's not Ben. I'd recognize Ben's voice in any universe, even from one syllable.

My phone rings, and I'm so startled, I almost drop it on my face.

It's Ethan. Love the guy, but I'm not in the mood, so I let it ring and head straight back to Instagram. But before I can even tap back into Mario's Stories, it rings again. This time it's some random number with a New York area code.

"Hello?" My heart's pounding.

At first, it's nothing but static and street noise, but after a moment, a muffled voice says, "Oh! Hi!"

My brow furrows. "Hi?"

"Um. Sorry! I'm outside. Can you hear me?" A horn honks in the background. "Oh, it's Ethan!"

"Sorry, *what*?"

"Ethan Gerson? Remember me? Your best friend since elementary school?"

"I'm not—you're where?" I peek at my phone screen, and it dawns on me: this isn't a random New York number. It's the someone-wants-to-get-buzzed-into-the-lobby number. "Outside, like—New York outside?"

"Exactly like New York outside. Want to let me up?"

I give a startled laugh. "Holy shit. Yeah! Buzzing you in—no, wait, I'll come down and—no, God, sorry, it's hot out. I'll buzz you in, but just stay in the lobby. I'll come down and get you. I just need to put on, uh. Clothes." I glance down at my boxers and yesterday's T-shirt.

"I know how to use an elevator. You're 3A, right?"

"I can't believe you remember that!"

"I didn't," he says. "I had a spy on the inside—"

I buzz him in before, God help us all, he starts rapping.

"You're actually here," I say, for the millionth time this afternoon. I'm supposed to be showing Ethan around Times Square, but I can't stop turning to look at his derpy tourist face. "I can't believe you took off work!"

"I can't believe your work gives everyone the day off for Pride," he says, tearing his gaze from a giant rainbow billboard. "Is that a thing in New York?"

I laugh. "I don't think so? But it's a queer theater, and my boss and his husband go all out for Pride. They dress up and march in the parade, and there are definitely feathers involved."

"Wow! So what's our game plan?"

"Well." I peer up Broadway, shielding my eyes. "We're at Forty-Second Street now, so I can show you some of the theaters if you want. Most of them are just—"

"No, I mean what's our plan for Pride?" Ethan says. "What's the gay agenda?"

"Ehhh, no thanks." I make a face.

"What? Why not?"

"I'm not exactly in the celebratory mood," I say.

"Uh-uh. Nope. Pride has nothing to do with Mikey!"

"You know Mikey's gay, right?"

"I mean, it's not about *you* and Mikey. It's about you and your identity, your community. I mean, look at this. It's incredible." Ethan gestures vaguely at the flags and streamers adorning the storefronts, the giant screens lit up with rainbows.

"Okay? Obviously, I'm glad it exists. I just don't feel like going to a big gay party a week after my big gay breakup."

"But this is a big gay opportunity to move on! What if you run into the guy you're really meant to be with?"

"Then he'll have to wait," I say. "Look, I appreciate the effort, but—"

"Or even the guy you're meant to hook up with. I can be your wingman!"

"I'm pretty sure the universe isn't weighing in on my hookups."

"Yeah? Then explain *this*," Ethan says, stopping short in front of a Broadway souvenir shop. There's a mannequin in the window wearing a shirt I know by heart, the word "love" written over and over down its front in every color of the rainbow.

"That's the Lin-Manuel Miranda quote—"

"Dude, I know the quote. Come on, I'm buying that for you." Already, he's pulling me into the store.

"Not necessary."

"Oh, I *absolutely* insist—"

"I mean I already have that shirt," I mutter.

Ben mailed it to me senior year of high school as a Chanukah gift. I still remember how it felt to see his handwriting on the package label.

"No way! That's perfect—"

"Ethan. Stop," I snap. "How many times do I have to tell you? I don't want to go."

"I know. I hear you, but—"

"Why are you so hung up on this?"

"I'm not hung up on it! Sheesh," he says, staring a little too intently at a snow globe display.

Which is when I remember that Ethan literally took a train up from Virginia to cheer me up. And here I am yelling at him in a souvenir store.

"Ethan—God. I'm sorry."

"No, you're fine. I get it."

"I'm just messy right now, with the Mikey stuff," I say. "But it's so unbelievably cool of you to come up here. Honestly, it's cool that you want to go to Pride! Like, not every straight guy is clamoring to play wingman at Pride for his gay best friend—"

"I mean," Ethan says, "I don't know if that's true—"

"It is. It's not lost on me. Not everyone has an Ethan. Talk about above and beyond. Surprising me in New York—and orchestrating the whole thing with your ex-girlfriend?"

"No, I mean." Ethan picks up a snow globe. "Okay, I guess I have a thing to tell you."

"A thing."

"A life update, kind of?"

"Okay . . ." My mind flips through the possibilities like a slideshow. *A life update. Something he wants to tell me.* It's funny, this reminds me so much of—

Two summers ago. When Ethan and Jessie announced they were dating.

My jaw drops. "You and Jess are back together!"

Ethan looks dumbfounded. "We are?"

"Okay, I'm not going to be an asshole this time. Wow! I knew you guys were talking again—"

"We're not back together," says Ethan.

"Hooking up—"

"You know I live in Virginia."

"Which is why you're in town! To win her back!"

Ethan bursts out laughing. "Arthur, wow. No."

"Then what's—"

"If you stop talking for a minute, I'll tell you." He shakes the snow globe, smile flickering. "So . . . I realized something lately."

My hand flies to my mouth.

"And I'm still kind of figuring this out. But maybe you can help me with that?" He lets out a quick, nervous laugh. "Okay, you look so excited."

I nod without speaking, grinning into my hand.

"So." He pauses. "Um. I think I might be bi?"

"I KNEW IT!"

Ethan looks startled. "You did?"

"Not like that—sorry, I don't mean I knew all along. You were just serving up some very strong coming out vibes just now. Ethan!" I shake my head, beaming. "What do you need from me? Can I be your queer mentor? Oh my God. Okay, I'm shutting up. Tell me everything."

Ethan sets down the snow globe, pink-cheeked and smiling. "Um. Well—"

"Wait!" I fling my arms around him in a full-on tackle hug. "I love you. But you know that. Okay, now I really am shutting up."

"I love you, too. And, uh, yeah. It's weird. Like I keep

thinking about prom, and how you'd already known for so long and were just figuring out when to say it. But this was like—sudden onset. Like an allergic reaction."

"You're allergic to monosexuality!"

He laughs. "Maybe? No, what I mean is—like, you know how you can have a latent allergy that's just kind of sitting in your system, waiting for the right environmental trigger, and then BLAM." He smacks his chest lightly. "Am I making any sense?"

"Definitely. Yup. I'm totally following. A bunch of science stuff and then more science stuff, and then you were triggered."

"Something like that." He grins. "I guess what I'm trying to say is that this thing, this epiphany or whatever, it *feels* really new, but it also feels like something that was already there? Like it was hidden in plain sight the whole time, and then two weeks ago, I'm like, *oh shit*."

"That, sir, is what we call"—I pause, grabbing a shirt off one of the Pride racks and thrusting it into his arms—"a bi awakening."

Which is literally what the shirt says, styled like *Spring Awakening* in a stamped red box.

Ethan laughs. "Oh my God, that's perfect."

"So did something happen? Walk me through it!"

His cheeks turn even redder. "Well. Funny you should ask, because. Uh, you get a lot of the credit here."

"Oh really?" I stand up straighter. "Tell me more."

"Do you really want me to?"

"Ethan! Yes!"

He nods, clutching the *Bi Awakening* shirt to his chest. "So. Remember when you called me from Dave & Buster's because you were freaking out about Ben's hot new boyfriend, and then afterward you sent me his Instagram profile so I could validate your need to be told you're hotter than him?"

"That is absolutely not—"

"Anyway. This guy Mario. I started looking through the pictures, and I'm like, yup, that's a good-looking dude. And then I'm like—wait. That's a *really* good-looking dude."

I stare at him. "Wait. So—"

"I don't know," Ethan says quickly. "It was like—something about Mario flipped this switch for me. It was wild. I started remembering all this other stuff I'd kind of brushed off. Like, all the way back to elementary school. Do you remember that kid Axel from Florida?"

I nod vaguely, but the truth is, my brain spun off the road the minute he said Mario's name. And now Ethan's running through all these details of recovered past crushes, and I just—I can't fucking believe—

Mario? Ethan's bi awakening was *Mario*? This has to be a joke. Sorry, but this takes universe fuckery into a whole new stratosphere.

"So." I blink. "You had no clue?"

"I mean, there were tons of clues. Like, it's so obvious in retrospect, but yeah. I had zero conscious awareness, because . . . I don't know? I like girls. I was ridiculously in love with Jessie. But I guess even when I was dating her, there were all these signs I was missing—and, Arthur, they were like *billboards.* But Jessie missed them, too? I don't know. Anyway, she's been talking me through it lately."

"Oh." I nod weakly.

"So, yeah. I feel—just. Thank you so much." He looks at me, eyes shiny.

"God. Of course. I'm so happy for you. And I'm buying you this." I snatch the shirt from his hands.

"You mean . . . *bi*-ing it?"

"Wow, you really are bi, aren't you?" I hug him again. "Fuck, I'm so *proud* of you!"

"Thanks." He smiles. "And sorry I was being pushy about Pride. I actually didn't come here with, you know, a bi agenda. I'm just still a little—like, this is a very recent line of inquiry for me. Hasn't been, uh, put under peer review."

"Okay!" I clasp my hands. "How about fewer nonsensical science metaphors and more finalizing the outfit for your very first Pride."

"No, seriously—"

"Nope. It's been decided. I'm *your* wingman now. And

you know what? You need a hat." I swipe down two beanies from the Pride display, holding up one in each hand. "Gentleman's choice! *Les Bisexuales* or *Queer Evan Hansen*?"

"Did we really just go from Surly Breakup Arthur to Queer Wordplay Arthur in ten minutes?"

"Get yourself a man who can do both," I say smugly, shoving the Evan Hansen hat into his hands.

CHAPTER TWENTY-NINE

BEN

Saturday, June 27

It's officially been over a week since I've heard from Arthur, and I guess I shouldn't be surprised. It's the same old magic trick: the better things are with Mikey, the more he disappears.

But I can't let my brain go there today. Arthur's not allowed to rain on my rainbow parade. It's my last New York Pride, and it already feels like a dream. Marching through the streets holding Mario's hand. Our cheeks painted with rainbows that we drew on each other. *I'm with Him* shirts that Mario made for us with colorful arrows pointing at each other, which is great since people keep checking him out.

"You've got a lot of fans out here," I say as we cross

through a crowded Union Square.

"So do you, Alejo," Mario says.

I've seen no proof of this, but it doesn't matter. I'm not trying to attract anyone out here.

I'm just trying to be present during this parade: brushing shoulders with people who may have had a harder time coming out than I did; listening to Mario as he sings along to songs blasting from a drag queen's speaker, like Robyn's "Dancing On My Own" and Carly Rae Jepsen's "Cut to the Feeling"; cheering as colorful confetti rains down from a rooftop; buying pronoun buttons from a vendor with blue lipstick; taking pictures of two Latinas with signs, one reading *Yay I'm Gay!*, the other *Oh My, I'm Bi!*; and joining the massive applause as a young teen grabs a megaphone and comes out as trans.

Why can't every day be as beautiful as today?

I've been keeping my phone buried in my pocket because I don't even care if Arthur texts me. I don't want to miss one moment. The sun is on my face and I'm ready for my freckles to pop out like a little Pride constellation.

And as much fun as I'm having with the community, it's hard not to laugh every time I see my favorite ally.

Dylan is wearing an *ALLY AF* shirt along with a rainbow headband, a rainbow peace-sign necklace, and rainbow wristbands. Basically, Dylan's aesthetic is GAY AF. And because he loves the attention, he's asking people to sign his shirt as a token for this day. None of us have told him that three different people have drawn dicks on his back.

"Everyone looks like they're auditioning for a Lady Gaga video," Dylan says.

Samantha twirls around in her high-waisted rainbow mesh dress. "Dylan!"

"It's not an insult! You're homophobic for thinking so."

The sun is a little on the hot side, but I get the feeling that even if it were below zero, some people celebrating today would still be walking around in nothing but underwear. All the power to everyone just living so hard right now, even if this is the only weekend they feel comfortable dressing—or undressing?—like this.

"I'm going to miss this," Mario says. "We just missed LA Pride, too."

"Make the most out of today, then," I say with a smile.

"Already am, Alejo."

Samantha kisses Dylan on the cheek, and he suddenly announces, "I require a piss break."

"Same," Samantha says. "But not as crudely worded."

"Form the Snake!" Dylan shouts.

He invented the Snake as a way to link us all together by hand so we can file through the crowds so "no man or Samantha gets left behind." We snake through the parade until we find a café down the block from Pa's Duane Reade, which you couldn't pay me to go inside on my day off.

Dylan and Samantha get on line, both of them looking like they're dancing as they squirm.

"How much cash you got?" Dylan asks. "We're going to bribe our way to the front."

Samantha reaches into her purse. "I have a twenty."

"I'm tapped out after buying the pins," I say.

Mario observes the line. "There's nine people ahead of you. I'll go break that twenty and we'll make it work."

He takes the bill from Samantha and runs toward a hot dog cart.

"Do we trust Mario with the money?" Dylan asks.

"Nah, he's a total mentiroso," I say.

"Total *what*?"

I smile as I step away, not translating *liar* for him.

I take in the passing crowd, wondering what everyone's stories are. What everyone has been through to be able to be here today. Who will be here next year. And the year after. Will I be back? Will I be back with Mario?

I'm not psychic, so I focus on the present.

There's so much life out here, it's explosive. And style like no other day. Someone really went all out in a Captain America costume but instead of red, white, and blue stripes, there's a rainbow flag. For the most part, people are representing the day in incredible shirts that I wish they'd wear year-round:

Sounds Gay, I'm In.

The "T" Is Not Silent.

Trans & Proud.

Space Ace.

Assume Nothing.

And then a short cute guy turns the corner in one of those Lin-Manuel Miranda *love is love is love* shirts.

Half a second later, I realize it's Arthur, and suddenly I don't care that he hasn't texted. My heart's pounding so fast, because this has to be the universe at work. Who knows how many people are packing these streets, and of course I zero in on Arthur Seuss. I'm so happy to see him that I jump up and down and shout out his name, but he can't hear me over the energetic crowd and loud music.

And then, just as I'm about to push through everyone to reach him, I see someone in a blue beanie sidle up to him, linking arms. It's got to be Mikey.

I feel like I've lost my voice and lost control of my muscles. I want to sink down onto the curb and hide behind the parade.

I don't even get how Mikey's still in New York. Did he quit his job and just move here? Are they seriously not capable of living apart for one summer? I think back to that weird night at the open mic bar, trying to imagine how everything must have played out. Maybe Mikey just couldn't bring himself to get back on that train. Maybe they spent the whole week having incredible sex. Maybe Mikey has been delivering personal encores of his karaoke performance every single night. That would definitely explain why Arthur hasn't texted me all week. It sucks, because I really thought Arthur and I were getting closer. But I feel further away from him now than I ever have before, even when we lived almost a thousand miles apart.

He could have at least let me know he'd be at Pride.

Then again, I guess I could have reached out to him, too.

I don't even know why I care. All I know is, this is why I'm so fucking ready to start over in Los Angeles. No more memories catching me by the throat every few blocks. No more turning corners and stumbling into exes with their new boyfriends who get the ultimate do-overs that I never did.

CHAPTER THIRTY
ARTHUR
Tuesday, June 30

What sucks is that I really thought I was fine—or at least I was getting there. Sure, it stung when I couldn't text Mikey about the *Animal Crossing* cosplayers at Pride, and I'm still checking in on Mario's Instagram like it's my full-time job, but at least my mouth was starting to remember the mechanics of smiling. There were even real stretches of time where I didn't think about Ben or Mikey at all. I was just a guy in a *Hamilton* Pride shirt, walking with my best friends through the rainbow-spangled streets of Manhattan.

And then Ethan went home.

I really need to start learning the difference between *fine* and *distracted*.

Yeah. So, it turns out, the world doesn't stop for heartbreak. I don't get to skip work because I look like a sleep-deprived ghoul, or because I feel bad about Mikey, or because Ben doesn't love me. I don't get to unravel nine days before our first dress rehearsal.

Nine days—and just eight more days after that until we officially open. Shouldn't I be at least a little bit excited about this? Here I am standing on a real New York stage, beneath a scaffolded ceiling and professional-grade lights. I'm not saying it's Radio City Music Hall—it's a black box, which is basically just a dark-painted cube, even at a top-tier place like the Shumaker. But the black box isn't the problem. I'm the problem. Because my brain won't shut up about the boy I'm not in love with.

Except when it remembers the one who's not in love with me.

"I'm not buying it," says Jacob. "Arthur—sorry—would you mind pushing the crib back a few feet? All I'm seeing is that creepy fake baby."

I roll the crib upstage, almost to the backdrop. "Here?"

Jacob surveys the new configuration for a minute, before sighing and turning to Taj. "Should we bring in a real baby? We're going to have to bring in a baby, aren't we?"

"You mean the crying kind?" Taj asks.

Jacob pinches the bridge of his nose. "Maybe we age him

up to three or four? I'll play around with the script—"

"Totally. I totally hear you. But." Taj's voice is unnervingly calm. "I'm wondering if there's a way we can avoid changing the entire script? Since we're, uh, less than three weeks out from opening night?"

I shift my weight from one foot to the other, gaze drifting down the rows of empty chairs—right to left, like reading in Hebrew. Fifty seats arranged on platforms, ascending like stairs. But the front row is level with the floor and the stage, and that's where Jacob and Taj are sitting.

"Yeah . . ." Jacob sighs. "Okay, why don't we press pause for a second. We'll circle back to this in fifteen." He stands and stretches, tapping the screen of his phone. By the time I reach the front row of seats, he's already halfway to the lobby.

"Yikes. Rough day for the GDB," Taj says, peeling the lid off a soy yogurt container.

I grab a pack of cheese crackers from my messenger bag and plop down beside him. "He's not actually going to age the baby up, right? Like, you'd have to rewrite the entire bedtime scene, plus anything in the park, and it's just so—"

"Bananas," Taj says. "It's the whole banana grove. But he really hates those dolls."

I turn back to the stage, currently set to resemble an apartment interior—living room, nursery, and kitchen. The design's more suggestive than literal—it's really just a few key pieces of furniture arranged in front of three canvas backdrops. Though when you see it with the lighting in place and the actors moving from room to room, it actually does feel like a home.

But even I have to admit: Jacob's right about the goddamn baby. I guess it's decently realistic for a prop doll, but you can't pretend it's not serving up some major corpse energy. Or lack of energy.

"There has to be an easier workaround," I say.

Suddenly, I'm out of my seat, crossing the few feet of space between the front row and the stage. I stare for a moment at the trio of backdrops. They're intimidatingly huge, but at least they're on wheels. I give the center panel an experimental push.

"Redecorating?" Taj asks.

"Just trying something."

Taj sets his yogurt down and stands.

Five minutes later, we've rolled the center panel back and pulled the side panels in, until the set's no longer three adjacent apartment rooms. Now it's just a living room and kitchen, with a hint of a nursery tucked behind them—just a foot of toothpaste blue backdrop and the edge of a crib. "So the baby's always *there*," I explain. "She's just a little bit offstage."

I watch Taj take it all in, following his gaze from panel to panel. It's wild how the simplest tweak can change the entire feeling of a space. The overall focus is tighter, and the added depth makes the apartment feel that much more real. Like there's this implication of life existing beyond the boundaries of these sets. No idea what Jacob will think, but I'm pretty sure I love it.

"Okay," Taj says. "Say we're Addie and Beckett, middle of scene eight, when they're arguing and Lily wakes up—"

"Right! So what if Beckett's actually offstage for that scene? Like we get a sound cue where she's crying, and you see him go into the nursery—"

"Huh!" Taj purses his lips. "So . . . we keep Addie in the living room . . . are they just talking between rooms? Maybe he pops his head around the side, so we feel him in there?"

"Exactly," I say—and for the first time since Ethan left, a light flickers on in my brain.

I usually feel like such a fuckup at work—even when I'm not dropping the ball, it always feels like I'm just about to. But something's clicking today in a way I can't quite explain. Taj keeps nodding when I talk and typing notes on his phone, like my ideas are worth writing down. Like I'm not just some dumbass intern. Or at least I'm a dumbass intern with *potential.*

"Oh, wow!"

Jacob's voice—my heart leaps into my throat.

"This is so interesting," he says, sidling up to Taj. "Walk me through it."

Taj gestures toward me. "It's all Arthur."

Jacob clasps his hands. "Taking creative risks. We love to see it."

"It probably won't work," I say quickly. "It's just a random idea—I haven't really had time to think it through. I was mostly just curious. Seriously, I can put everything back the way it—"

"Or," Jacob says, smiling, "you could tell me about it."

Ten minutes later, Jacob and Taj are off and running—photographing the stage from every angle, texting the stage manager, slipping into this whole second language of abbreviations and theater jargon. It's the kind of thing that makes me feel like such an amateur, normally, but today feels different. Today, it's just another piece of the magic I helped set into motion.

I watch from the front row, in dazed disbelief.

Jacob loved my idea. He actually gasped when I explained it. He called me a *genius.*

Yes, I'm a total disaster. Yes, Ben's moving. Yes, I fucked up with Mikey. No, I'll never be able to pull off a floral tie the way Taj can.

But.

Jacob Demsky. Called me. A genius.

When they wander back over, Jacob's cradling the GDB like it's his actual baby. "There's been a truce," Taj explains.

It feels so good to laugh.

"Arthur, you changed the game." Jacob leans over Taj to fist-bump me. "I'm checking in with Miles tonight to get a couple of new cues locked in, but I actually think we're in good shape. I don't know how to thank you."

"I'm so happy to help." I flush proudly.

"Seriously. God, take the rest of the day off. Or take Friday! Catch the Greyhound, surprise your boyfriend—"

Taj elbows him, and he stops abruptly, midsentence.

For a moment, no one speaks.

"Um." My voice comes out an octave too high. "I don't. Have one of those."

"One of . . ."

"A boyfriend. Not anymore."

"Oh." Jacob turns toward Taj and me. "Oh, Arthur. I'm so sorry."

"No, it's fine!" I add, a little too quickly. "I'm the one who initiated it. I care about him, but. I guess I realized I wasn't—I'm not in love with him. I really wanted to be."

"Then it sounds like you made the right call," Jacob says, so simply it cuts me wide open.

The whole story spills out. "It just sucks, because we were actually really great together, and now I miss him.

So much. But it's just not *it.* And how could I fix that? I don't know; maybe we could have gotten there eventually?" A lump swells in my throat. "I guess part of it was me realizing I'm still pretty hung up on someone else, which obviously wasn't fair to Mikey. He shouldn't have to wait around for me to get over Ben—that's my other ex. My first ex. But that's not happening either. Seeing as he's following his boyfriend to LA."

"Following him there, like moving there?" asks Taj.

I nod down at my messenger bag, and its brown surface seems to blur a little. "It's fine. It's just one of those things, right? The universe wasn't building toward an Arthur endgame. It happens."

"But you're not over him," says Jacob.

"Well, no. I'm in love with him." My voice breaks a little, and I wince. I don't know why I thought I could sound casual while dropping that bomb. I wrench my lips into something like a smile. "Kind of pathetic, huh?"

"No, not at all," says Taj.

"I'm so curious. What makes you think it's game over?" asks Jacob.

"You mean with Ben?" I glance at him sideways, and he nods. "Well . . . I guess the part where he's moving to California with his new boyfriend."

"Right, so. Boyfriend, not husband," Jacob says. "Is this move, like, a forever thing, or just for the summer, or what?"

"I mean, he *says* he's just trying it out for now, but it's not like he's going to hate living in California for free with his hot TV-writer boyfriend. It's a dream scenario."

"Sure, but—okay, look. I'm a writer. I have to look at this like a story. The guy you're in love with is moving to California with another guy. That's our narrative, right?"

"Pretty much."

Jacob nods. "So the obvious question is about perspective, right? Whose story are we telling? What's your role in it?"

"I'm the guy who figured it out too late?"

"Okay. Are you the obstacle? Is California the happily ever after? Or . . ." Jacob pauses. "Are you the guy running to the airport to stop him? Are you the protagonist?"

"I . . ." I blink. "How would I even know that?"

"Here's a hint." Jacob smiles. "It's your life. You're always the protagonist."

My heart flips, but I tamp it down. "Right, but. My ex is also his own protagonist. And so is his boyfriend."

"Absolutely," says Jacob.

"So it's not that simple. I don't just get to declare myself the protagonist because I want to be in this story."

"Sure. You can't control how it's going to play out, of course. And if Ben says no, that's that. But if you want to be in the story, go be in the story! Chase him to the airport!"

"I think he's driving."

Taj leans toward me. "It's a metaphor. He's saying you should tell Ben how you feel."

"Oh! God, no. That's—yeah, no. Ha ha. Absolutely not."

"Why not?" Taj asks.

"Because I'm not trying to shit all over his happiness?" I wince. "He's in a new relationship. I don't want to interfere with that."

"You're only interfering if he has feelings for you, too," Taj points out.

"I haven't even told him Mikey and I broke up. It's just not—" I cut myself off, heart pounding. "I'm just worried I'll make things harder for him."

Jacob looks at me. "Or are you worried he'll reject you?"

"I'm terrified he'll reject me," I say, without hesitation.

Pretty sure he already has.

Jacob keeps telling me to go home, but I'd rather throw myself into work—I barely even leave the stage until Jacob shoos us out at five. It's been hours since I've looked at my phone, but I feel it ringing in my bag before I even step outside.

It's Jessie, who usually texts, so I rush to accept it. "Hey! Everything okay?" I ask.

"Are *you* okay? You got my texts, right?" Her voice is both exasperated and concerned, and I realize with a pang that I've heard this combination before. Senior year, the first few weeks after Ben and I broke up.

"Totally fine." I root around in my bag for my earbuds. "Sorry, I was onstage all day. They were working on cues and stuff."

"Oh, okay. Sorry. I was just checking in about Sunday, but it's all in the texts. I don't want to repeat myself. Basically, I'm just wondering if we can bump the Friday night Grayson thing to Sunday dinner."

"Works for me. Can't wait to meet him." I slip in my earbuds, so I can see my texts while we talk.

"Me too! I think you guys will get along," she says, and the next thing I know, she's listing off restaurants. But I lose the thread completely when I see Dylan's text. Okay Seussical, Friday night escape room, bros night. Be there 😉

"So maybe sevenish?" asks Jessie.

"Sure." I stare at my screen. "Hey, so. Dylan just invited me to an escape room on Friday?"

"Oh, cool. Those are really fun. I did one in Providence."

"Yeah, but—" I step to the right to let a family pass me on the sidewalk. "You don't think it's weird that Dylan's inviting me to hang out? And to an escape room? Why would I want to be locked in a room with Ben and Mario? Unless he's trying to sabotage the California thing by—"

I stop short, trying to dislodge the tiny seed of hope threatening to take root in my brain. Because even if Dylan is trying to spark something, it's not like Ben has to go along with it. At the end of the day, Dylan doesn't get to vote on Ben's love life.

And neither do I.

"Oh yeah. Yikes," Jessie says. "I don't know."

"I should say no, right?"

"Sure, unless you want to go—"

"I absolutely don't." My voice booms so loudly, a dog drops his stick. "I'm done. I don't need to get tangled up in that whole group and all their weird enmeshed friendships. I just want to hang out with *my* people. Like you and Ethan. And I can't wait to meet Grayson, and—oh, I'm almost at the subway, but listen, I know Grayson can't be there, but if you still want to hang out on Friday night, let me know. I'm free. Obviously."

"Oh, um. Actually." Jessie hesitates. "I hope this isn't weird, but I'm . . . hanging out with Samantha that night?"

"Oh!" I nod—always a galaxy brain move on an audio call. "Yeah, no. Okay, cool. That's. Great."

I stare at the screen for a full thirty seconds after we hang up.

For the whole ride home, all I can think about is my last night in New York. My *first* last night, when Ben and I spent the whole evening studying chemistry. I remember how his mouth twitched every time he got a question right. Has there ever been anything as beautiful as Ben Alejo's face when he's proud of knowing something?

He told me the difference between physical and chemical changes—didn't even have to peek at the flash cards. Physical reactions are the no-big-deal kinds of changes, the surface stuff. But chemical reactions break bonds and forge new ones, until the composition of the substance is irrevocably changed. "For example, baking a cake," Ben had said. "You can nope out halfway through, but you're not getting your ingredients back. Chemical change."

See also: Jessie's friendship with Samantha. Dylan in my texts. And the fact that I can't go a single subway ride without thinking about Ben, because he's bonded himself to every cell in my brain, and I'm starting to think he's rebuilt my heart from scratch.

CHAPTER THIRTY-ONE

BEN

Friday, July 3

I'm ready to play.

It's been a while since I've done an escape room. I love games, but sometimes it feels like there's so much pressure to solve the puzzle, and I don't like being seen as someone who isn't smart enough. This insecurity is also why I hate Scrabble. Everyone swears I'll dominate that game because I'm a writer, as if I know every single word in the human language. Then I freeze up and play words like "stick" and "car." The only game of Scrabble that didn't make me want to break things was online against Arthur senior year. We both immediately lost interest and ended up screenshotting the board so we could write in a bunch of dirty words with the Paint app.

But, you know what? I'm pretty sure I wouldn't hate Scrabble with Mario either. I bet it would even be relaxing to play against him, because I know he doesn't care if my biggest contribution to Scrabble is a three-letter word. Just like he won't care if I don't contribute in this escape room.

We're all in the lobby, waiting for the infamous Patrick. Mario is texting away on the orange couch. Dylan is staring at the leaderboard, muttering about how there's no way we're going to win with Patrick on our team. I'm going through the basket of victory/defeat foam signs, excited to see how this all plays out.

"Unbelievable," Dylan says. "This guy is so late."

"Why'd you invite him?" Mario asks, looking up from his phone. "You seem to hate him."

"Because I love my girlfriend and—" Dylan puts up air quotes and mockingly says, "I have to be nice to her best friend because she's nice to mine." He rolls his eyes and points at me. "Who couldn't love this freckled angel?"

"For real," Mario says.

Those words hit me differently. Is he trying to say that he loves me? I mean, do people move in with each other if they're not in love? Do they move across the country for them if they're not in love? I've got to ask myself the same question: Do I love him?

I love spending time with him, I love how much we fit together, but do I love *him*?

I should know this.

The escape room employee, Liam, comes from around the counter, wiping his glasses clean. "Your time starts in three minutes. Is your fourth almost here?" he asks in an English accent.

"Fantastic question, Liam. Let me call that bastard," Dylan says.

He pulls out his phone right as a model-like guy walks in. He has black curly hair and a strong jawline and apologetic brown eyes and he's so pale I think I can make out some sunscreen on his face; he's like a sad vampire. "Dylan, dude, I am so sorry. I would blame the subway, but I should've left half an hour earlier."

It's Patrick.

"It's fine," Dylan mumbles.

"You must be Ben and Mario," Patrick says, shaking our hands with both of his. "Dylan talks about you all the time."

"He's said a few things about you, too," I say.

Patrick touches his heart. "Aw, that's sweet."

Mario's loud ringtone blares. "It's the moving company," he says. "Un momento."

"But—"

I know dealing with the moving truck is really important, especially because Mario bumped his move date up to Monday. But I really want this memory with him.

We put our belongings in lockers and Liam breaks

down the dos and don'ts of escape rooms while we wait for Mario—luckily, Mario already knows how to play. The rules are simple: we have an hour to escape and can ask for clues at any time.

"The theme is the Z-Virus," Liam says, running a hand through his blond hair. "A global pandemic is turning people into zombies. Very scary stuff. Your mission is to explore the abandoned laboratory and escape with the antidote. Or the world is over."

Patrick pretends to shiver in fear. "Ooh. We've got our work cut out for us!"

Dylan pretends to stab Patrick in the back.

"Are you ready to begin?" Liam asks, opening the door to the room.

"Oh, uh, Mario should be back any moment," I say.

Liam checks his watch. "There's a party coming after you. We really have to begin."

Dylan's eyes widen. "Uh. What happens if we don't escape?"

"How do you mean?" Liam asks dryly.

"I feel as if my question is clear."

"Narratively or in reality?"

"Both?" Dylan asks.

"Narratively, you die. In reality, we let you out."

Dylan nods his head, slowly, like he's digesting this response. "What if . . ." He turns back to the front door, where Mario is still outside on the phone. "What if we don't want to leave the room?"

"Are you stalling?" Liam asks.

"How dare—"

"Well, this is your reservation time. If you don't go now, we're still charging you. You have thirty seconds before I close the door."

Dylan does this low growl. He turns to me and Patrick. "So it's just us . . ."

Patrick rubs his hands together. "I'm so excited! It's my first time." He steps inside.

"Kill me," Dylan says.

"Ten seconds," Liam says.

"I'm going to grab Mario," I say.

Dylan grabs me by the wrist and drags me inside.

Liam closes the door behind us.

"D!"

"There's no way in hell I was going to be locked alone in a room with Patrick for a whole hour," Dylan whispers.

"And now I don't have Mario."

"You'll live." Dylan points at Patrick. "He wouldn't have."

This sucks. No leaving early without forfeiting. Maybe Liam will have a heart and break the rules by letting Mario in.

The laboratory has a flashing red overhead light with a

low alarm sound. It smells like Styrofoam and paint. There's some dried fake blood over some documents and a dirty magnifying glass. Patrick puts on a lab coat with a torn sleeve.

"This is so cool," Patrick says.

Dylan mouths-mocks him.

"Where do we start?" I ask, ignoring him.

Patrick picks up a first aid kit. "Maybe this is something."

"Doubt it," Dylan says.

I check out the first aid kit and there's a combination lock. This is definitely something. We search for the numbers we need and Patrick quickly finds them inside the bloody documents. I let him have the honor of opening the kit himself. We find gloves, a stethoscope, a vial, and a key.

"Ha, they locked up a key," Patrick says. "Clever." He walks off with the key. "We should find the lock."

"Sherlock Holmes," Dylan mutters.

"D, he's chill. Be nice."

On the other side of the room, Patrick tries opening all the drawers in the desk. Dylan and I check some cabinets.

"Sorry about Mario. The move stress is catching up to him."

"And now we have to survive the zombie apocalypse . . . and Patrick."

Nonexistent zombies and one of the nicest people on the

planet. How will we survive?

Some of us have real escapes we're thinking about.

I keep thinking about how hard it was seeing Arthur and Mikey at the Pride parade. I guess I always thought I'd be the one showing Arthur his first New York Pride. It's like I have a whole box of hypothetical Arthur moments tucked away in my brain. It mostly random stuff, like carving pumpkins or washing dishes. Or even just holding hands on the street, or linking arms the way Arthur and Mikey were.

Sometimes it feels like Arthur's already living the life I always thought we'd share together.

But I know those what-ifs aren't real. What's real are the memories I'm going to make in California. With Mario.

"D, I got something to tell you."

"I know you're gay."

"I want you to hear this from me first this time. I think I might leave with Mario on Monday." Dylan stops rummaging through the cabinet. "What?!"

"The road trip would save me a lot of money."

"You have never once shown interest in a road trip."

"I'm trying to change my life."

Dylan shakes his head. "You can't. There's a barbecue at Samantha's house next weekend and I need you there."

"Because of . . . ?" I point at Patrick, who is messing with the hands of a clock. "You'll be fine."

"No, screw him. You have to be there. You can move

after I'm gone, but I'm here."

I close the cabinet. "Dylan, don't you want me to have what you have?"

"Yes! But I also want you to . . ." Dylan takes a deep breath, then another, and starts counting down in cappuccinos. "Eight cappuccinos, seven cappuccinos—you can't go. Trust me, Ben Hugo Alejo. I need you here. I will get you the money to fly to Los Angeles after next weekend. But you can't leave me yet."

I'm getting nervous. He's not making any jokes about how he needs me around to make sweet love. And his breathing keeps increasing. "What's going on?"

"Just don't go."

"Tell me why I should hang around this city that's haunting me!"

"Because Samantha and I are having a surprise wedding next weekend because we're also pregnant—surprise! She's pregnant, I'm not pregnant, but you get it. And she's asked me not to talk about the pregnancy to anyone, not even you, because we've been trying to figure everything out. Her family has been all over us, but now you know, and I need my best man around for the wedding! And it would be wonderful if the best man didn't move to Los Angeles, since we're moving back to New York so our families can help us—including you, the baby's godfather!"

It's quiet except for the sounds of Dylan breathing and

zombies banging outside the door.

Over the speaker, Liam says, "Do you need a clue?"

Patrick shyly raises his hand. "Yes, please."

Dylan snaps around, talking over Liam. "Why aren't you invested in this bomb I dropped?"

Patrick cringes. "Samantha told me already . . ."

"WHAT?" Dylan's head might explode. "But I wasn't allowed to tell . . . Ben, you better show up to my wedding and *object*!"

"I'm not going to do that."

"Fine, I'll stand her up."

"She was scared," Patrick says. "I've known her forever and—"

"I've known Ben longer than forever," Dylan says.

"Is Samantha okay?" I ask.

"She's fine, baby is great, all that."

"Wait." I grab him by the shoulders. "You're going to be a dad."

Dylan tears up and I do, too.

My best friend is going to be a dad—and a husband!

Patrick solves a puzzle and a blast of steam sprays from the wall. "I opened a vent," he says, crawling into it and vanishing.

"You're not going to be here," Dylan says. "I always thought you would be here."

"Look, I won't go with Mario this week; don't worry.

I'm here. I just wish I could've supported you this entire time."

"Ben Alejo, I love you. I'd never do this without you. I mean, I *had* to do it without you, but I *couldn't* do it without you." Dylan grabs my hand. "You have been there during all the major steps. I had you try on a suit so I could get it tailored. The café tasting was for the reception. The open mic night was so we could see the band perform live. Flower arrangements were for the wedding. And this"—he gestures at the escape room—"is my bachelor party!"

His mind is so extra.

"Oh my God, there's going to be two of you."

Dylan smiles like that devil emoji.

"I'm sorry I canceled on you so many times. Between the obstetrician appointments and how drained we've been from fighting with her family and figuring out the move back home, it's been a lot. Mom and Pops have been frustrating, too. I hated not being able to talk to you about it, but I thought we weren't telling anyone until . . ." Dylan looks around. "Where's Patrick? Did the zombies get him?"

Patrick comes crawling out the vent with a little vial. "I solved the puzzle."

"By yourself?" I ask.

"Yup."

"Well done."

"Liam helped him," Dylan says.

Then Liam's voice comes over the speaker: "No, I didn't. You talked over me. Oh, and congratulations on the wedding and baby."

Dylan stares at the camera and mutters, "Congrats on your wedding and your baby."

"Not your best," I say.

"Daddy brain."

Patrick puts the vial inside a test tube rack and the door unlocks. "We did it!"

That wasn't exactly a group effort, but he's sweet to include us.

Mario is in the lobby and pops up from the couch when he sees us. "Alejo!"

"Hey. All good with the moving company?"

"It'll be okay, but I'm so sorry I missed the escape room."

I wrap my arm around Dylan's shoulders. "That's not all you missed."

CHAPTER THIRTY-TWO
ARTHUR
Sunday, July 5

I stare at Jessie, dumbfounded. "Pregnant, like *pregnant*? With a *baby*?"

"I mean, I hope that's what's in there."

"And they're getting married." I scoot in beside her on the love seat, tugging a shaggy brown throw blanket over our tucked-up legs and feet. My new favorite weekend morning routine: the Two-Headed Grizzly.

Jessie's hands are wrapped around a coffee mug. "Yup. Married. In less than a week."

"But they're our age! How did this happen?"

"Well, when two people love each other very, very much—"

I give her a swift kick under the blanket. "I just mean

how are we just now finding out about this?"

"They weren't even planning on telling anyone this soon. It was a whole thing. Like, we were at Samantha's parents' house"—Jessie pauses, sipping her coffee—"it's me, her sister, and a few other people, and Samantha's set up this whole video-game tournament. So we're about three hours into it, and Samantha's phone starts ringing—and at first she ignores it, because she's in the middle of pulverizing her cousin Alyssa, but then it rings again, right? So she steps away to investigate, and it's Dylan, and she's kind of sitting there on the futon talking to him, really quietly, and there's this moment where her face goes like *this*." Jessie rolls her eyes up to the ceiling, letting her mouth hang open. "So she ends the call, and for a minute, she's just staring into space—and obviously we're all a little worried. But then she laughs and says, 'I guess I have something to tell you.'"

My hand flies to my mouth. "Dylan proposed over the phone?"

Jessie just looks at me. "Arthur."

"You mean the *pregnancy*? How would he know before she did?"

"Is that a serious question?" I nod, and she slowly closes her eyes. "Your cluelessness is truly groundbreaking. You know that, right?"

"That sounds like a compliment, but I'm not sure it *is* one."

"It's not one." Jessie laughs. "Holy shit, I love you so much. Yeah, so Samantha, the person carrying the baby in her body, was aware of the pregnancy—"

"Some people don't know! There was a whole show about—"

"Do you want to hear this or not?"

I nod quickly and pantomime zipping my lips.

"Okay, so it turns out, Samantha's, like, four months pregnant, but they'd only told immediate family, because—long story, but basically the plan was to announce the pregnancy at their wedding, which was *also* a surprise—they've been telling people it's a barbecue."

I blink, thinking about Dylan's sudden interest in owning a fancy Bloomingdale's suit. "Let me guess—Samantha's cousin isn't getting married."

"Alyssa's twelve," Jessie says.

I press my hand to my cheek. "So why'd they decide to announce everything this weekend?"

"I don't think they meant to. Sounds like Dylan had a panic attack, maybe, and it just slipped out? He didn't, like, tweet it or anything, but he told Ben and Patrick and . . ."

Mario, I think—but I shake the thought away. "Is Dylan okay?"

"Yeah, totally, he just felt bad. But I think they're excited to finally be able to talk about it."

"Wow." I burrow farther under the blanket.

"I know."

"What are they going to do about school?"

"Not sure," Jessie says. "I don't think they've a hundred percent decided. Baby's due in December, so they're going to try to have a normal semester, I guess. But after that, no idea."

"I guess I should text her, huh? And Dylan."

But when I open my texts, the name I look for is Ben's.

Just heard the news!! omfg, I type. You were NOT WRONG about something being up with Dylan!!!!!!

Ben writes back immediately. I KNOW. It doesn't even feel real yet. So I'm Uncle Ben now?? Like the rice???

A moment later, he adds: I just have no idea how to do this. I'm at a baby store literally right now and it's aggressively cute but so overwhelming, like how do I know what this baby wants?? It's not even born?

I grin down at my phone. Haha no clue. I guess I should get something for them too at some point, huh

WAIT, Ben writes. Are you home rn? I'm on the upper west side, Columbus and 80th, it's like right across from the museum. Come meet me?

Baby shopping with Ben.

On a Sunday afternoon.

Like a pair of newlywed dads. What if—

Nope. Absolutely not. Butterflies, get the fuck out of my stomach. You know what I'm not going to do this time? Get my hopes up for some kind of capital-*M* Moment, when I know perfectly well Ben's probably standing right next to capital-*M* Mario at this very second.

Twenty minutes later, I spot Ben reading his phone outside a bank of expensive-looking boutiques. But he shoves it in his pocket and hugs me as soon as he sees me.

"Just in time," he says. "They were starting to side-eye me pretty hard in there. I think they think I'm a baby-store criminal?"

I laugh, feeling slightly dizzy already. "I hear that's a real problem in this town."

"Baby-store crimes?"

"They thought it would all be over once they caught the onesie bandit, but—"

"Cute." He pokes my arm. "Should we go in?"

"Sure! I mean—unless you want to wait for Mario to get here?"

"Oh—no, he's packing." Ben scratches the back of his neck, suddenly flustered. "I'll probably head over a little later to help him." He pauses. "Or not. I guess he's pretty much done? We—um. He was going to leave tomorrow, but he pushed the U-Haul rental back a week. Couldn't miss Dylan's wedding."

"Right." I follow him into the store, trying to ignore the pang in my chest. *We.* "You were right—this place is aggressively cute." I peer around the space, taking in the spherical light fixtures and bright white display tables, holding artfully arranged onesies and bedding.

Ben points to a stack of organic blankets, each patterned with a different illustrated print. "See, this is exactly what I'm talking about. Does the baby like macarons? Does it even have a digestive system yet? Who fucking knows!"

I smile. "Okay, but they have unicorns. And narwhals!"

"Absolutely fucking not. I'm not having Dylan mock me for another six months about how narwhals are real."

"Wait, Dylan thinks narwhals are real?"

Ben tilts his head. "They are real."

"Uhhh . . ."

Ben bursts out laughing. "Right? That's what I said! Arthur, it was so bad. I had this whole water scene mapped out for the *Wicked Wizard War* sequel, and yeah. So, I'm telling Dylan about it—this is Christmas break—and he's like, 'Benion, I love you, but I can't let you set a narwhal scene in the Caribbean.' So I start talking like an asshole about how it's my '*interpretation* of a fantasy creature,' and Dylan? Fucking loses it. Like, laughing so hard I thought he was choking. Because, as it turns out . . ." Ben pulls out his phone, types into a search bar, and holds it up to show me.

It's a photograph of a whale with a long, pointy horn.

"WAIT—"

"Absolutely one hundred percent real."

"I—had no idea."

Ben makes a face that's somehow split between a smile and a cringe. "We're the only two people on earth who didn't know."

"Life comes at you fast."

"Speaking of." Ben lets out a quick, breathless laugh. "Can you believe Dylan and Samantha planned a wedding right under our noses?"

"I know. True legends."

"You're going, right? Are you bringing Mikey?" he asks. "I don't know if Dylan talked to you yet, but you guys are definitely invited."

I freeze.

"Um. I—am not bringing Mikey. Because." I bite my lip. "We kind of. Broke up?"

Ben's hand goes still on a flower-print onesie. "You did?"

"Yeah. Like, two weeks ago. When he was up here?" Cool. Loving the upspeak I'm serving. King of confidence.

Ben opens his mouth, closes it, and opens it again. "Are you okay?"

"Oh, yeah. Definitely. It was after the whole open mic thing, and I just realized . . . I don't really want to get into it, but it just wasn't working, and so I told him, and . . ." I shrug. "That's pretty much it."

"I had no idea."

"Sorry. Yeah, I didn't want to dump that on you. You have so much going on."

"That's not—" Ben shakes his head. "Don't do that. You don't have to keep that stuff from me. I want to be there for you."

"I know. It's just complicated. But really, I'm fine."

Ben's quiet for a moment, brows knitted together. "Sorry, I'm just—" He studies me for a moment, almost like he's deciding whether or not to say something. "I could have sworn I saw you guys at Pride?"

"Wait, what?"

"Maybe I hallucinated it. It was by the Strand? We were waiting for Dylan and Samantha to finish peeing. Again."

"I was at the Strand! But not with Mikey. Are you sure you didn't see Ethan? He was in town that weekend."

Ben squints. "Was he wearing a hat? I didn't really see him too closely—"

"Yes! A *Queer Evan Hansen* hat!"

"Oh!" Ben's eyes widen. "Is Ethan—"

"Let's just say he had an epiphany." I smile.

"Good for him," Ben says—and then he looks up with a start. "Wait, are you guys—"

"Oh my God, no!" I burst out laughing. "That would be like you dating Dylan—okay, bad example, because I can *totally* see you dating Dylan—"

"Might I remind you that we are literally, right at this moment, picking out gifts for the baby he's having with his fiancée, who he's marrying next weekend—"

"Okay, fair enough, but I'm not dating Ethan. I am a single young intern."

Ben smiles. "Interns are cool. Also, wow! Less than two weeks until the show, huh?"

"Yup, the seventeenth! And the first dress rehearsal's in four days."

"Fuck. Are you freaking out?"

I laugh. "It's weird—I actually think it'll be really good? The ads just went live, and I'm obsessed with them. Want to see?" I pull the image up on my phone and hold it up.

Ben's eyes go saucer-wide. "Wait, is that—"

"Amelia Zhu and Em—"

"You're telling me . . . this whole time, every time you've mentioned Emmett and Amelia . . ." He shakes his head, looking shell-shocked. "Emmett Kester is in your play?"

"He is! He's awesome, and he's really sweet—"

"You've talked to him?" Ben's voice jumps a solid octave, just like at the diner with our waitress. Ben, the theater fanboy. I don't know if I want to laugh or kiss him or both.

Definitely both.

"If you come to the show, I can introduce you," I say, hoping my cheeks aren't as red as they feel.

Something flickers in his eyes. "Actually. Um. I think

I'll be in California by then."

"Oh." I try to smile, but it barely lasts a millisecond.

"Yeah. Sorry, I haven't really told most people yet, but I think I'm just going to head out there when Mario goes. After the wedding."

For a moment, neither of us speaks.

"You're really leaving, huh?" I say finally.

"It hasn't fully sunk in yet."

I grip the edge of the nearest table. "I guess we should figure out the baby stuff, then. You probably need to pack."

"Yeah . . ." Ben's cheeks go pink. "No, that's—"

"I'm going for the narwhal blanket," I say quickly, forcing a smile. "I'll tell Dylan you suggested it."

"Asshole." Ben grins.

We each pick out a blanket and take them to the counter to pay—me with a card, Ben with a rolled-up, rubber-banded bundle of cash. Then Ben skips the Seventy-Ninth Street subway station and walks me all the way to the front of my building.

I pause at the door. "I guess I'll see you at the wedding?"

"Definitely! Or sooner. Let me know what you're up to this week."

I watch him walk down Seventy-Fifth Street until he disappears, veering right at Broadway. Off to pack for California. So much for that fucking airport chase, right?

I feel totally empty, not a drop of air left in my lungs.

He's leaving.

I told him about Mikey, and it didn't matter. I don't think I even realized how much hope I was pinning on that. As if Ben would suddenly drop all his plans for Los Angeles. As if Mario was some kind of backup plan.

He's really leaving.

New York's going to be just another city without Ben in it. New York without any of its what-ifs. Why did I even come here? Why am I even trying to pretend I belong here? I'm not a fucking New Yorker.

I just want to go home.

PART THREE

IT CAN BE US

CHAPTER THIRTY-THREE

BEN

Sunday, July 5

I stare at the boxes in Mario's room.

He's packed up all his stuff in the basement. Most of it is following him to Los Angeles; some of it is winterwear his brothers didn't want that he's donating to a local shelter. I can't help but think about my history with the breakup box for Hudson, which led me to Arthur, who I sent back home to Georgia with a friendship box. Sometimes boxes are carrying goodbyes. And sometimes they're carrying fresh starts.

"Alejo," Mario says, acting like a shirt cannon.

I catch the shirt, unrolling it. It reads *LA Wizard* with a drawing of a wand underlining the words. "This is awesome. Gracias."

I can't believe this is actually happening. I'm going to be in Los Angeles. This could be the shirt I wear on the day we arrive. Then what does my life look like? Lying on the beach with Mario, reading each other's books and scripts could be amazing. We could spend more time at restaurants so I could try ordering our food in Spanish and let Mario come in with the assist when needed.

As fun as that all sounds, I'm nervous to say goodbye to everyone I know. Ma, Pa. Dylan, Samantha. Especially right as I'm getting my best friend back.

And then there's Arthur. I don't even know if I'll make it out of that goodbye in one piece.

It doesn't help that Arthur's making me question every single one of my choices. My head's been spinning ever since I learned he and Mikey broke up. I mean, it's obviously completely pointless. It's way too late for what-ifs.

But the what-ifs keep creeping in.

I'm taping another box shut when something catches my eye. It's the stuffed bear Arthur won at the Dave & Buster's claw machine and gave to Mario. That was the night I thought I'd be meeting Mikey.

I guess it's just hard for me to believe the Mikey breakup's going to stick. Like, I can't even let my mind go there with Arthur. I can't rewrite my next chapter just because he's single again. Where would that leave me when Arthur and Mikey inevitably decide to go for round three?

I tape the box shut and stare into space.

"¿Estás bien?" Mario asks.

"I'm fine. I mean, estoy bien. Just thinking about how you're the only person I'm going to know in Los Angeles."

Mario smiles. "There are worse people to know."

"Let's not meet them."

"We won't, but making new friends is part of the adventure. It's the experience you were wanting by going away for college. Everyone you love will be here when you get back. So what's scaring you?"

He's right. Back to my box metaphor, sometimes things go in storage for a bit. You don't take them with you, but you don't throw them away either. They're waiting for you when you get home. That's the case for my family. Dylan and Samantha.

But not everyone I love will be here whenever I come back.

"What if it doesn't work out?" I ask.

"What if what doesn't work out?"

"Us," I say.

I'm so used to being the one trying to remember a word in Spanish that I've never seen Mario speechless.

"It's just, we've never even talked about being boyfriends, Mario. And soon I'm going home to pack boxes to follow you across the country."

"I don't see it as you following me across the country.

It's you escaping the city that you've said numerous times is suffocating you."

"I guess I'm worried that moving somewhere else isn't going to help me breathe either."

Mario keeps starting sentences, then stopping. He definitely isn't prepared for this conversation. Even I wasn't planning on bringing any of this up. For so long I've wanted to make sure that I don't disturb our flow because I want him to want me, to see that I'm not complicated. It's so hard to come by guys like him. We're so compatible that it feels like we were made for each other. But then why doesn't this decision feel easier?

"It's not too late for you to back out," he says. "If you decide to stay here, though, I'm not sure I have it in me to do long-distance."

Am I going to have as many regrets about Mario as I do about Arthur if I don't follow him? I'm not sure I want to find out. It took so long to recover from that breakup that I don't want to find myself in another one again—official or not.

"I hear you," I say.

Then it's really quiet. It probably isn't even for that long, but it's uncomfortable. I feel like I've messed up. Like I should've shut up, been happy, and let everything play out.

"We can keep talking about this," Mario says.

"No, I'm good. It's just a big week with Dylan's wedding, too."

"You also just found out he has a kid on the way. It's a lot, Alejo."

"I'm scared of missing out on that, too."

"They'll be one flight away. It's Los Angeles, not Mars," he says with his first smile since this conversation took a turn.

The thing is, Los Angeles might as well be Mars. Not having the money to hop on a plane whenever I want might as well mean that my best friend is planets away.

"Totally," I say so I don't rock the boat anymore.

I'm going to make all of this work. I'll get a job out in Los Angeles. I'll create a special savings account specifically for trips to New York. I'll finish my book and hopefully sell it for a lot of money, and I can have the best of both worlds.

"It's your life to live, Alejo," Mario says, resting his hands on my shoulders. "Just make sure you're living it for yourself and not anyone else."

CHAPTER THIRTY-FOUR

ARTHUR

Tuesday, July 7

The evening drizzle turns to rain as soon as I reach Tompkins Square Park. I should have known the universe would come through with the perfect finishing touch on this shitpile of a moment. This could be the last time I'm alone with Ben Alejo for the rest of my life, and now I get to show up sopping wet and panting, like a sad, gay Mr. Darcy.

I make a run for the first structure I see—half gazebo, half statue, with the word "CHARITY" engraved in all caps near its roof. There's a water fountain in the middle, and the rain creeps in through its wide-open sides. But it's enough shelter to protect my phone and Ben's present, so it's good enough for now.

My hands are shaking, so I call instead of texting. "Hey!

Sorry—okay, wow, the rain's really loud. Can you hear me?"

"You okay?" Ben asks. "Where are you?"

"Tompkins Square Park, and it's pouring. But I'm in a gazebo, so I'm just going to wait it out for a bit—"

"A gazebo . . ." He pauses. "Is there a bronze lady on top?"

"Yes! And a bunch of virtuous words."

He laughs. "Okay, wait right there. I'll grab an umbrella and come get you."

"What? Ben, no—"

"Already on my way. See you in a sec!"

Staring at the rain lulls me into such a glassy-eyed daze, I don't even notice Ben until he's right in front of me, holding a peacock-patterned umbrella. He smiles when he catches me eyeing it. "It's my mom's. It's so extra, I know, but it's the biggest one I could find."

"No, I love it," I say. "Thanks for rescuing me."

"Of course," he says, lifting the umbrella so I can slip under. Then he pulls it back down about an inch above his head and half a foot or so above mine, like a little nylon-and-metal cocoon. I'm acutely aware of how close he's standing—only my messenger bag hangs between us.

I've barely stepped into this moment, and I already miss it.

"This fucking weather," he says.

I'm too tongue-tied to speak. We're practically out of the park by the time I cough up even the most inane of all questions. "How's the packing going?"

"Fine, I guess? Could be worse." Ben switches hands on the umbrella handle for a second to scratch an itch. "I'm not packing up my whole room or anything. And Mario's uncle's guest house is furnished, so it's just whatever clothes and stuff I want to bring with me."

"Better bring something for the red carpet."

Ben laughs. "I think that's getting a little ahead of things."

"Well, it's what you deserve."

"Thanks, Arthur."

We wipe our feet on the mat outside Ben's apartment, and he dumps the umbrella in a stand near the door. "My parents are at work," he says. In a different universe, I think, that could be an invitation.

He taps his phone, and music drifts from a speaker in what sounds like his room. But it's not until he opens his bedroom door that I recognize it. I look up at him, smiling. "Is that my Broadway playlist?"

"Got to soak in all the New York while I still can."

Ben's bedroom is a war zone of strewn clothing and books and a few half-packed cardboard boxes.

Box Boy, I remember, my heart panging sharply.

Ben surveys the chaos. "Sorry about all of this." He

crosses the room, swiping a black garment bag off his bed and looping its hanger through his window blinds. Then he sits back down on the bed, scooting to make space.

I hesitate. "Do you want help with any of this? I don't want to throw you off your packing game."

"Oh, it's fine. I can take a break."

I settle in beside him, glancing up at the zippered bag now hanging from his window. "Is that the Bloomingdale's suit?"

"My Best Man gift from Dylan and Samantha. I don't know how I didn't see it. Like, in retrospect, why on earth would Dylan drag me to Bloomingdale's, have me try on an expensive-ass suit, and *bring in a sales consultant* to get the fit right?"

I laugh. "Because it's Dylan, and he does stuff like that?"

"I know." Ben's face clouds over. "I still can't believe the timing. I'm moving across the country, and now he's having a baby."

"But the baby's not due until December, right? Maybe you could come back for a few weeks?"

"As long as I can find cheap tickets." He smiles, a little nervously. "It'll be my first time on a plane."

"I forgot you hadn't been on one."

"I'm, like, already scared of flying."

"Oh no! Don't be. It's weird—for most of it, you barely

feel like you're moving. You'll get used to it pretty quickly." I pause. "And you'll be with Mario, right?"

"I guess so? He'll probably want to spend Christmas here if he can, so . . ."

"That will help."

"Yeah." He scoots back to the wall, tucks his legs up, and sighs. "Okay, honest question. Am I the biggest asshole for leaving?"

"Wait—why?"

"I mean, how often does your best friend have his first kid?"

"Once? Unless all his other kids are do-over first kids?"

Ben's eyebrows shoot up.

"Okay, stop being morbid. First first kid is alive and healthy. And you"—I prod his arm—"need to stop rereading that YA book where everyone dies at the end."

He tips his palms up. "It's a good book."

"And you're not an asshole," I add. "You shouldn't have to put your life on hold for Dylan's."

"Yeah. No, you're right. I'm being weird." He stares at his knees without blinking.

"Let me grab your present," I say when the silence is a little too unbearable. I reach for my messenger bag.

"You really didn't have to get me anything."

"It's small. You'll see." I root around inside the bag for

a moment, managing to slide the envelope out of my work binder without even undoing the clasp. It's a regular white business-sized envelope—sealed and, thankfully, dry.

"Should I open it now?"

I nod, and he carefully pries it open, revealing a tiny full-color picture on photo-sized cardstock. Along the side, styled like a ticket, are the words: *Play It Again: Dress Rehearsal, Admit One.* "Oh, awesome!" Ben says.

"Turn it over."

He flips it, eyes widening as he reads the handwritten words out loud. "'Ben, Hope to see you Thursday! Yours, Em Kester.'" Ben turns to me, gaping. "WHAT?"

"Surprise!"

"Arthur! Fuck. This is *incredible.*" He flips it back over to study the ticket. "I'm—wow. I didn't even know they made tickets for dress rehearsal."

"They don't. I mean, they *do*, but just for the final dress rehearsal, and you'll be gone by then. But Jacob said you could come to this one. And I made the ticket so Emmett would have something to sign." I pause, heart pounding. "If you *do* want to come, I'm pretty sure I can introduce you to Em afterward."

"Oh." Ben does a few quick blinks. "Wow."

"No pressure though," I say quickly. "I know you have a ton going on, with the packing and the wedding, and—plus, you don't have to decide now. Or at all. Just. If you want to, you can."

"I mean, it sounds amazing. I need to figure out what I have going on this week—"

My cheeks flood with heat. "Seriously, don't even worry about it."

"This is such an amazing gift. Just. Thank you."

"No problemo!" I say, immediately cringing. "Wow, I did *not* just say that. Whatever you thought you heard . . ."

He laughs. "I'm going to miss you."

"Me too." I exhale. "Which is so ridiculous, because I don't even really live here. Literally, what's the difference, right?"

"No, I get it," he says, and my eyes start to prickle.

I stand abruptly. "Anyway, I'll let you finish packing."

"You're fine! Hang out as long as you want."

I stare at his face, trying to memorize all its details. I know I'll see him again at the wedding, and maybe the play. But Ben's face has always looked a little different when it's just us. "I should—I'll see you soon."

He jumps up to hug me. "Okay, well. Thank you so much. For just—yeah."

I nod into his shoulder, barely capable of speaking.

The door shuts behind me, and I can hardly catch my breath for a minute. I don't know what I even expected.

A big final-act kiss? A scorching rejection? It's the kind of thing that makes sense in movies, but it falls apart when it's real, when it's Ben, when his bedroom floor is covered with moving boxes. When he's telling me to hang out as long as I want to, but not begging me to stay.

I wonder how many love stories end like this—with an ambiguously long hug and a million things left unsaid.

I reach the staircase, staring down blurrily like I'm peering over a cliff. My phone buzzes a few times in my pocket, and I pull it out to find a whole long thread of texts from Ben. The first one's just a word: I'm—

Followed by a series of screenshots, each one zooming closer and closer on Emmett's handwritten *Yours.*

Yours. My breath catches.

He texts again. EM IS MINE??? 😭😭😭😭😭

His. Emmett's. Not mine. Not ever. Unless—

I'm barely aware of my feet springing me back into the hallway, barely hear my own knuckles on the wood of Ben's door.

Ben opens it, smiling. "What'd you forget?"

I step past him into the apartment. "Okay, listen," I say. "I'm not trying to make things weird, and I don't want to fuck things up for you. I don't even know how this goes, because I can't—I can't imagine saying this to you, but I also can't imagine walking out that door without saying it." I turn to look at him, finally, and my lips are trembling.

"Ben, I'm so fucking sorry."

He laughs, looking taken aback. "Why?"

I start to cover my face with my hands, but I stop myself, clasping them under my chin. "I'm not making any sense."

"Literally none."

I laugh, a little breathlessly. "Right. I just have to—fuck. They make this look so easy, and I'm—" I hold my hands up, and they're shaking.

"Okay, you're scaring me a little."

"I'm still in love with you," I blurt.

Ben's lips fall open. "Oh—"

"And I know I'm not supposed to be, and I promise I'm not standing here waiting for you to say it back to me. I know that's not . . . going to happen, but it's fine." I try to smile. "And I want you to know that I'm happy for you and Mario." I stop. "I mean. Sort of." I stop again. "Okay, you know what? Fuck that. I'm not."

Ben lets out a quick, surprised laugh.

"Look, I want you to be happy. But not with him, because he's—I mean, he's great." A tear slides down my cheek. "I actually really like him. But I want you to be with me." I press my hands against my chest, against my thudding heart. "And he's not me."

"Arthur—"

"Wait, let me just say the rest really quickly, before

I—just. I just need to say it, okay? I don't want to wake up in two years and have to tell the next guy I'm not"—my voice cracks—"I'm not in love with him. Because he's not *you.* And I know this is the part where I'm supposed to list out all the quirky reasons—like, oh, I love how fucking intense you get about video games—"

"It's not really the games," Ben says. "I just don't like—"

"Losing. I know." I give a choked, tearful laugh. "I'm just—I'm so *bad* at this. How am I so bad at this? You know what I did last night? I watched every love confession scene I could find, and every single one of them reminded me of you. All of them. *Notting Hill. Crazy Rich Asians. Ten Things I Hate About You*—Ben, I cried watching the end of the *Kissing Booth* sequel, because for me, it's always you. You're the point of every story."

A tear rolls down Ben's cheek, and he swipes it away with his fingers.

"And I want to tell you it's okay that you're leaving and that I'll get over you, I'm sure it is, and I'm sure I will. But right now?" I shut my eyes for a moment. "I don't even know what getting over you looks like. I can't even imagine it, and—God, I shouldn't be telling you this. It's not fair to you." I wipe my eyes. "I know. I know it's not."

"It's fine, Art. You're fine."

"You know what? I'm gonna go"—I gesture vaguely at

the door—"so you don't have to figure out what to say or how to say it. Just know—I get it. I do, and I'm going to find a way to not be in love with you. Eventually. So." I shoot him a faltering smile. "I guess I'll see you at the wedding. Bye, Ben."

I take a shaky, deep breath, and then I walk out the door.

CHAPTER THIRTY-FIVE

BEN

Wednesday, July 8

What was I supposed to say when Arthur confessed that he loved me?

Was *still* in love with me?

I've been speechless since last night. After he left, I just stood in the entryway, staring at the door he'd just shut. Thinking about the door he'd just opened. I couldn't wrap my head around it then, and I still can't. It just doesn't feel possible that he said those words out loud. To me. Here I was, so convinced he'd be in Boston by the end of the week, begging Mikey for a do-over. Just like last time.

But now he says he's not over me. He can't even *imagine* getting over me.

And I let him walk out.

I should have chased him.

No, I shouldn't have.

There's a time for big love confessions and it's not right before I'm about to leave for Los Angeles with someone I really, really like. I didn't ask for Arthur to swoop in like it's the last act in some Broadway show. I'm not a character. I'm a real person whose heart he stomped on when he got back together with Mikey.

I never told Arthur how I'd found a Greyhound bus to New Haven for fifteen dollars. I was going to try to surprise him. My first time leaving New York. I couldn't stop imagining the way his face would light up when I stepped off the train, imagining what it would feel like to finally kiss him again. I was so sure things were just about to fall into place for us.

And then he called me from the airport the day before New Year's.

It was like someone turned a knob and made the entire world dimmer. Like my heart was cracking straight down the middle. I'd never felt heartbreak like that before, not even when I watched Arthur walk away from the post office on his last day in New York. I spent all of January in a black hole. I don't even think Arthur knows that.

The thing is, Mario's the only thing that's made me feel almost normal in months.

Now all I can think of is Arthur with his hands pressed to his chest. *Because for me, it's always you. You're the point of every story.*

I keep drafting texts in my head, but then I triple-guess every word before I can even think about sending them. Knowing Arthur, he's dying to hear from me. But if I'm not reaching out to say *I love you too*, then what's the point?

I need time to figure out my feelings.

There's a knock at my bedroom door.

"Entra, por favor," I say.

My parents come into my bedroom. Ma has a plate of crackers smothered in peanut butter. Pa looks around at all the boxes, and I swear he's fighting back tears.

"Aquí estás," Ma says, handing me the snacks.

"Gracias."

I barely have an appetite, even after skipping breakfast. I just want to pack myself into a box and hide in the darkness.

"It's not too late to change your mind," Pa says.

I look up at him. "About what?"

"Moving?" Pa says. "We haven't rented out your room yet."

"Oh. Right."

Ma sits on the floor beside me. "I won't bother asking you if you're okay because I know you're not." She brushes my hair. "Talk to us, mijo."

I don't even deny that I'm not okay. I just avoid eye contact because I feel like I might crack and I'm trying to be stronger than this. I'm surrounded by boxes because I'm supposed to be—no, I *am* leaving for Los Angeles. Things are finally on track with Mario, and Arthur's confession is creating traffic so I can't move forward. That's not fair. Not after he got to have a whole other relationship before realizing he wants to be with me.

Pa joins us on the floor. "We're always going to be here for you, Benito, even when you're not here with us. Except you're going to be three hours behind us in California so do not call us after nine p.m. because your mother and I *will* be asleep." He pats my back. "Talk to us while we're all here together."

I've spent so much time lately wishing I had more space from them. Things will be different when I can't step out of my bedroom and find them on the couch.

"Uh. So . . ." I take a deep breath. "Last night Arthur said he's still in love with me."

My parents exchange a look. Like they're trying to figure out who responds first. Then I think it's more than that. It reminds me of a couple years ago when I came home with the news that I had to go to summer school. They knew my grades had suffered. They weren't surprised. And I don't think they are now either.

"How do you feel?" Ma asks.

"Like I don't know what to do."

"I'm not asking what you plan to do—I'm asking how you feel."

"There are no wrong answers," Pa says.

"There aren't any easy ones either," I say. "For so long I wanted Arthur to say everything that he said, and I kicked myself for not saying it whenever I had the chance. But it never seemed like we were going to make sense and it still wouldn't make sense now. Or could it? I'm clearly willing to move. But then I'm screwing over Mario, who hasn't done anything wrong. This would be simpler if one of them pulled a Hudson and cheated on me. But they didn't. And they're both amazing."

Someone is going to get hurt.

"Again, Benito, you're not answering the question. How do you *feel*?"

I don't know why Ma is so obsessed with getting this answer out of me.

"I'm scared I'll regret not taking this chance to make things right with Arthur. And I'm terrified that if it doesn't work out, then I'll have lost the only other person who wants to be with me."

"Don't worry about that," Pa says. "There's still Dylan."

"Very true," Ma says. "There are no vows powerful

enough to keep him away from you."

I give my parents the tiniest of smiles for trying to cheer me up.

Ma grabs my hand. "You have two wonderful young men who would be lucky to be with you and there's more in the world who would be privileged to have a shot with you. It's up to you right now to figure out what risk will make your heart happiest. You shouldn't rush into deciding."

"Though you don't have forever to choose either," Pa says. "There's a moving truck to pack soon. And once I help you load your stuff, my job is done."

"No pressure."

"There's some pressure," Pa says, surprising me. Most parents would lie. "This is part of growing up. You're not always going to be able to please and protect everyone you love. The best thing you can do when life is hard is try your best." He kisses my head and gets up. "I believe in you."

"Me too," Ma says, taking Pa's hand as he helps her up, too.

"Wait. Any chance you guys want to tell me which team you're on? Arthur or Mario?"

"We're always on *your* team," Ma says, closing my bedroom door behind them.

"Not helpful!" I shout.

It's very sweet, but I want someone to make this easier for me.

I grab my phone and call Dylan. I've been trying to wrap my head around everything before bringing it up to him because he's going to ask a bunch of questions. Hopefully he can help me answer them, too.

He sends my call straight to voice mail and follows up with a text. At the courthouse.

Why? I text.

Suing Samantha for telling Patrick the news before I got to tell you.

Translation?

Paperwork. Marriage is boring!

Haha. Well, have fun with that. Call me later.

Bet your sweet ass I will.

I'm patting myself on the back for more character growth. Instead of getting worked up over Dylan living his life, I'm respecting it. He's not ghosting or being weird. His priorities have shifted, and that's part of growing up. My best friend can't be around twenty-four/seven anymore. But I trust that when we do catch up, he'll be unhelpful and flirty for an hour and then come through with something wise before bringing up my sweet ass again.

It's too weird to bring up Arthur's confession to Mario. I will, but not yet.

I'm scrolling through my phone contacts, hoping someone can help me wrap my head around all this. Everything is changing, and I don't want to have any regrets.

I stop at someone's name.

This feels crazy, but.

I'm going to ask my first ex-boyfriend for love advice.

CHAPTER THIRTY-SIX

ARTHUR

Thursday, July 9

It's been thirty-nine hours since my shitshow of a love confession, and not a word from Ben. Which is entirely fine and not at all panic-inducing, other than the fact that I've been checking my phone every ten seconds for two days straight, because evidently my brain thinks Ben might slide in with an *I love you too* text at nine-thirty a.m. on a Thursday.

"You know what?" Jacob surveys the stage, fist tucked thoughtfully under his chin. "Can we get more of a build here on Addie for the monologue?"

The light brightens slowly on Amelia's face.

"Okay, nice." He pauses. "Hey, can I get some quick

photos from the back of the house? I want to see how this reads."

"On it." Taj pats my shoulder, and both of us stand, yet again—let's just say Jacob has no qualms about last-minute lighting cue changes. I snap a few pictures and almost forget to text them to Jacob, because I'm too busy checking my phone settings again. Just to make sure I'm not accidentally on Do Not Disturb.

I would very much like to be disturbed by Ben Alejo.

It's really the silence that's unbearable—even a straight-up rejection would be better. I just wish he'd say *something.* Though maybe the silence *is* the something, because what else could it mean other than Ben not loving me back? It's not a job application. He's not out there calling my references and weighing out my pros and cons. Loving someone isn't an informed decision. It just is. You just do.

Or, in Ben's case, you don't.

All I can do is plod through my longest-ever workday. Even if everything runs on time, dress rehearsal won't be over until eight thirty tonight. And thanks to the scheduling glitch, we have to strike the set right after and bring everything back to the studio for a week. It kind of makes me wonder why Jacob's bothering with a full dress rehearsal in the first place. So much effort and care poured into this thing that ends almost as soon as it starts.

I check my texts again. Nothing.

Pretty sure it's time for someone to take this phone away from me and bury it. Way past time. Pretty sure the right time was when my mom texted me a picture of my aunt's new puppy this morning and I cried, because apparently I've reached the fuck-you-puppy-you're-not-Ben stage of heartbreak.

Forty hours and counting. I think I might be losing my mind. Did my big rom-com confession even happen? Did I dream it? Is Ben trying to make me *think* I dreamed it? He's just never going to mention it, is he? Is that even allowed? Who would *do* that?

Something stops short in my brain.

Me. I would do that. In fact, it's exactly what I fucking did.

Three weeks. I went three weeks without giving Mikey an answer, and when I finally did, I was a wishy-washy asshole about it. And then he took a train to New York, grabbed a mic, and put his heart on the line in front of a roomful of strangers. At which point I promptly stomped all over it and never once looked back.

"So, let me know," Taj says brightly.

I look up. "Sorry—what?"

"Starbucks? Full offense, you look like you could use

it. Mocha frappe with extra whipped cream, right? What size?"

"Tall, I guess?"

"Let's go with venti," he says. "Just in case Jacob decides to change all the sound cues, too."

"Oh God. Why?"

"Because he's Jacob?" Taj shrugs. "You'll get used to it, though. Trust me, by next summer, you'll be anticipating his every move."

"Next summer?"

"He already submitted a grant application so we can pay you properly," Taj says. "If you're up for it, of course."

My mouth falls open. "Like a do-over?"

"More like a well-deserved encore," Taj says, ruffling my hair.

Forty-one hours. I'm staring at my text app again, but now it's Mikey's name I'm stuck on. The last dozen messages in our thread are all in blue. All from me.

I can't really blame him.

Intellectually, I've always sort of known Mikey was the one who'd fallen harder, but I'm not sure I fully believed it. It just seemed a little ridiculous that anyone could like me *that* much. I don't leave that kind of a mark. Or I didn't think I did.

I should call him.

Or not. Definitely not. I don't want to put Mikey on the spot. Texting's better. That way he can take his time with it, or reply with emojis or something. Maybe he won't even write back.

I stare at the empty text box for a full fucking minute.

Hey, I write finally.

No immediate response, but that's fine.

I keep going. I know you're probably busy with Robbie's wedding, so no need to respond to this right away

Or ever

Seriously, no pressure at all

I just wanted to say again that I'm so fucking sorry. The more I think about how I treated you, the more horrified I am.

And like

You were SO honest with me, and I can't imagine how it must have felt when I left you hanging. I wish I'd been braver

And more self-aware

Wish I'd taken better care of your beautiful heart

I'm so sorry, Mikey Mouse.

I press send—and as soon as I tap out of my texts, a notification pops up from my photo app.

July 9. Two years ago, today.

Skyscrapers, shot from such a low angle, they seem to tip over. A flare of brightness peeking through the background.

I remember this moment so clearly, I practically feel the sun on my cheeks.

The Arthur who took that picture didn't know he was on his way to the post office. He didn't know he was minutes away from meeting a boy with a box.

CHAPTER THIRTY-SEVEN

BEN

Thursday, July 9

I haven't been to Hudson's in almost a year and a half.

I buzz the intercom and I'm still surprised he's letting me in.

The lobby hasn't changed much. Packages left in front of the mailbox. A smudgy mirror. The elevator has maintained its lemony scent. The dim hallway leading to his apartment always smells like someone's making dinner, no matter the time of day, but fitting for this early evening. I ring the doorbell that's still as loud as ever.

My heart is pounding as the door unlocks and opens. Hudson is wearing glasses, which is a first. They look really good on him.

"Hey, Ben."

"Hey."

Hudson invites me inside, but doesn't open up his arms for a hug. I'm now incredibly uncomfortable inside this space that used to feel like a second home. But he doesn't owe me a super-warm welcome, especially when he knows why I'm here. I'm grateful he's not being so cold that he wasn't willing to talk about my love life. Especially when he haven't seen each other since last spring, when I bailed at the last minute on bowling for Harriett's birthday.

He starts to walk to his room, and I'm not even sure if he wants me following him, but he pulls out his chair by his desk and then he sits on his bed. That's as good an invitation as I'm going to get.

"How are things?" I ask.

"Things are things," Hudson says.

Really starting to feel like I came here for nothing. "Should I just go?"

"You do what you want," Hudson says. "Or don't want."

"So you're still upset about Harriett's birthday," I say.

"You mean when you turned your back on us when we were trying to fix things with you?"

"I wouldn't say either of you were trying particularly hard."

Hudson crosses his arms, definitely a little defensive. But we didn't have to touch any of this. I came here because of my business and he made a big deal about the past as if my crimes were bigger than his. He's the one who cheated on me. And he's still the one who gets to be happy in a new relationship, while my love life is a train wreck.

"So Arthur still loves you," Hudson says.

"Apparently."

"And you had no idea?"

"Not really. Arthur and Mikey seemed really perfect for each other."

"In what way?"

"They geek out over Broadway—"

"Liking the same stuff doesn't mean someone is perfect for you. It means you like the same stuff and that makes them good company." Hudson's whole vibe is *duh.* "You mentioned that you're thinking about moving to Los Angeles with your boyfriend."

"Mario's not my boyfriend."

"He's not your boyfriend." It's not even a question. Hudson is stating the fact and it stings even more. "You see what's wrong with that." Again, not a question.

I take a deep breath. "We want to give it a shot."

"I feel like Dylan has gotten it into your head that everyone our age is supposed to have some epic love story."

"Well, Dylan and Samantha are getting married and having a baby."

Hudson laughs.

"I'm not joking."

"I know," Hudson says. "That's so ridiculous. Dylan really dragged that poor girl into his insanity."

"They're really happy. It's real for them. Just like it was for his parents."

"There's no guarantee they're going to turn out like his parents."

"He doesn't want to be like his parents. He wants to be with Samantha."

"Ben, you sound like you have your answers already. If you want to take a risk, move to California with your *buddy* and prove me wrong. If you want to be with Arthur, be with Arthur."

This is not what I wanted out of this. I wanted some maturity. Hudson has taken some accountability, but he could also not give a shit whether I leave New York or stay. "Hudson, you're the only other person I've dated. You were my first love and that was real for me. I don't know how it was for you, but everything hurt so much. But I was able to move on and you did, too. That's great—I'm not trying to hang out with you and Rafael, but I'm not bothered by you guys."

"Because you have your choices now?"

"Because I want to keep it real."

I get up, not finding any of this helpful.

"Ben, it was for real for me, too," Hudson says. "It doesn't stop me from loving anyone else, or even getting excited about anyone else, but it was real. I still feel really shitty about how it ended. Cheating on you was the worst thing I've ever done. I just made a bad fucking choice, and I've always regretted it. But I have to live with it now."

"That's kind of what I'm scared of. What if I make the wrong choice? I don't want to live with regrets."

"It's not the same thing, though," he says. "It's not like cheating or not cheating. There's not an objectively bad choice here. You just have to figure out what you actually want."

"I just don't want to hurt anyone."

Hudson laughs flatly, shaking his head. "You're going to hurt someone! That's just how it is sometimes, and it sucks, but what's the alternative? Never make a real choice? Close yourself off completely? You have to be honest, at least with yourself. Ben, I learned that from you. Just be real! Either tell Arthur you're moving on, or tell Mario to move on without you." He gets up and walks toward me, and I think he's about to hug me. But instead he takes my hand and looks me in the eyes. "You're the writer, Ben. If you could write your perfect ending, what would it be?"

Someone is going to get hurt.

It really took hearing that from my cheating ex-boyfriend for that message to sink in.

No matter how many times I've put Ben-Jamin and the

crew through the wringer, the pain I'm about to deliver tonight is far worse than any seven-headed monster or magical fire. This will be real.

I've always hated the love-triangle trope—probably because I always thought of myself as the person who wouldn't get chosen. Now I'm someone with choices. Two incredible choices. I'm honestly tempted to not choose either of them, so we can all be alone and miserable together. But then three hearts get broken for nothing. That's pretty bad math in my book.

I'm on the train, one stop away from Mario's. I've spent the entire ride staring at the *LA Wizard* shirt he made me and Arthur's bootleg ticket to tonight's *Play It Again* dress rehearsal. These little gifts are personal reminders of how much these guys want me in their lives. It feels a little hard to believe, but I've got to exhibit some character growth. That's what I'm ready to do when I get off the train.

I don't drag my feet getting to Mario's. I text him to come outside, because I'm not ready to do this in front of his family.

My heart is pounding, like everything has been building to this very moment.

The front door opens, and Mario comes down the steps in nothing but overalls. No undershirt, no socks. One strap is hanging down, showing his bare chest. Mario doesn't seem fazed by how chilly it is. He only takes me in with his hazel eyes and pulls me into a minty kiss. And I keep our lips pressed while I run my hands along his arms.

I break the kiss and take a deep breath. "Hi."

"Couldn't stay away, Alejo?"

"Apparently not . . ."

Mario grabs my hand. "Well, why are we out here? Vamos."

"I actually can't stay long. I got to get to Arthur."

"Oh right! His show. I'm so excited for him. Aren't you going to be running late?"

"Story of my life." I squeeze his hand, scared to let go. "I got to open up to you about something." I take a deep breath. "Arthur is in love with me. He actually never stopped being in love with me."

There's silence. Like he's already dreading this conversation.

"So that's why he broke up with Mikey." Mario rubs his forehead. "When did he tell you all of this?"

"A couple days ago."

Then he's quiet. There's nothing but the sounds of passing cars and laughter exploding from inside the house.

Mario sits on the steps. "I take it he doesn't want you going to Los Angeles."

"He understands why I want to go. But when I read between the lines, he doesn't want me to move. Which still doesn't make sense, since he doesn't even live here."

Mario looks me in the eye. "Maybe there's another reason why it doesn't make sense . . . a me-shaped reason."

I sit beside him. "Of course you're the main reason it doesn't make sense. Everything else with Arthur could be figured out if that's what I want to do. But even with everything you and I have in common, there's something in the mix with you that I didn't have when I was dating Arthur."

"A stronger grasp on Spanish?"

"Okay, two things," I say. "The other thing was doubt, Mario. I don't know what the future holds for me and Arthur. I just know that when I was with him, I knew that he wanted to be with me. I can't say the same for you."

He nods. Another breeze rolls in and he rubs his arms to warm up. I want to hold him close, but now isn't the right time. There may never be a right time for us ever again.

"You deserve to know how someone feels about you," Mario says. His gaze is so intense that I almost look away. I can feel how much he cares about me. "But you guys gave it a shot already. What makes you think it's going to be different now?"

"It might not be different. It might not work. But you're special enough to me that I don't want to hurt you any more than I already am. And the truth is, I've spent so much time since the breakup trying to move on from Arthur. I practically lie to myself every day about how much I don't care about who he's dating, when in reality it breaks me. It's not fair to move away and start my life over with you when I'm still carrying some huge feelings for him."

"Do you still love him? No importa. Don't answer that. I don't need to know." Mario looks up at the sky, staring at the retreating sunlight. "I really think we could've been something great, Alejo. I hope I can be happy for you one day. But that's not tonight."

"You don't ever have to be happy for me, Mario."

"I know. But I want to."

We sit together in silence, and when Mario shivers, I hand him the *LA Wizard* shirt.

"Here. It makes more sense for you to have this now. Especially since you're going to make some incredible magic out in Los Angeles."

I really do believe this. One day, I'm going to see a billboard for a TV show that credits Mario as the screenwriter. And I'm going to take pictures like a proud friend, even if we've lost contact by then.

Mario stares at the shirt instead of putting it on. "I'm going to head on in, Ben."

No longer using my last name feels like an immediate downgrade from where we were romantically. And it's weird, but it's right for us.

"Can I hug you?" I ask.

"You better."

He wraps his arms around me first and I rest my chin on

his shoulder. "Gracias for everything good and lo siento for everything bad."

"De nada. Para lo bueno y lo malo."

He fights back a cry and lets go, turning so fast that I can't even see his face one last time. And then he's back inside his house, quick as magic.

I stand there for a moment, feeling too heavy to move. No matter what happens with Arthur, I know I made the right choice to end things with Mario. Hudson asked me about my perfect ending. But I'm going to focus on the beginning instead.

The do-over, to be precise.

CHAPTER THIRTY-EIGHT

ARTHUR

Thursday, July 9

Pretty sure my phone's just mocking me at this point. As if my gaping void of a text thread with Ben wasn't enough, now there's a fresh round of radio silence from Mikey. I wonder how many times you can swipe your lock screen before your thumb starts to blister.

I should go completely off the grid. I should move to a farmhouse in a postapocalyptic version of New Hampshire where almost everyone's dead and there's no cell service or electricity, because when it comes to the absence of text messages? Turns out, I'm a full fucking expert.

But it's cool. I'll just sit here rereading every line of this program like I'm Bubbe and her shul friends rolling in early from New Haven for a Sunday matinee. Because tonight has nothing to do with my phone, or boys, or the absence of boys. It's about the fact that I'm here in the Shumaker Blackbox Theater, one row back from my favorite director. It's about getting to see my new favorite play in its near-final form, and knowing I helped get it here.

Jacob murmurs something into his headset that makes the house lights flicker.

Then: a sweep of movement, the soft scoot of a chair. Ben sliding into the seat beside me with dumbfounding nonchalance, just before the house lights cut out.

I'm pretty sure my heart just leapt a full octave.

I squint into the darkness, my stomach in knots. Am I even awake? Is this actually happening? Ben shoots me a quick sideways smile, but it's cool, because who even needs lungs? Why are we all so obsessed with breathing?

It's completely surreal. The fact that he's here. Does he know I would have been singing dayenu over a text message? A single GIF would have been enough.

How am I supposed to act normal when my heart's pounding out eighth notes?

Time keeps tumbling forward—every time I blink, another scene goes by. Act One is apparently ten seconds long. Either someone's messing with the universe's speed-control dial, or my brain's short-circuiting.

When the show ends, Emmett and Amelia plop down

onto the stage like high school kids. I turn dazedly to Ben. "Did you like it?"

"For sure. It was great." He nods quickly.

I glance back at the stage, where Jacob and Miles, the stage manager, have scooted in next to Emmett and Amelia. "They're just giving the actors notes," I explain. "Shouldn't take too long, and then I can introduce you to Emmett."

"I'm not here to see Emmett." Ben's voice is unexpectedly intense. "Is there—can we go somewhere? Just for a second?"

"Yeah. Yes. Definitely. Let me just—here, come with me."

I lead him backstage, behind our black curtain backdrop and outside the back door. *Be cool, okay, be cool be cool be cool be cool.* But there's no cool. No such thing. Not for me.

I think my brain's tilting sideways. I feel like the sky before sunrise, the pause between *two*, *one*, and *liftoff.*

I look up at him. "Is this okay? Are you okay?"

"Yeah. I don't know." He lets out a slightly hysterical laugh.

"Ben, I'm sorry. I shouldn't have said anything. I don't blame you at all. You know that, right? Not even close. You're so—God, I can't believe you came to the show. I'm so glad I get to be your friend. That's not—"

"You really never stop talking, do you?" Ben says, smiling so affectionately, my breath hitches.

"Never."

He laughs a little. "Okay, well, my turn. I'm just—I haven't been able to stop thinking about Tuesday. Everything you said. Arthur, I had no idea. None."

"I know. I shouldn't have—"

"Nope." Ben shakes his head fiercely. "Listen. As soon as you left, I went back to my room, and I'm sitting there, staring at those fucking boxes, thinking—*oh my God, California*. Like, it's supposed to be this big reset button, right? I'm supposed to do my whole life over, twenty-five hundred miles from everything and everyone. Except you—Arthur, you're like this stowaway in my head. I don't know how to not bring you with me. Every time I think something weird, I'm like, *Arthur would get this*. Do you realize that every time, every single time anyone's smiled at me for the past two years, I've compared it to your smile? For *two years*. As if anyone else could win that game." He presses a hand to his forehead. "And the thing about being a writer is that it's not only about telling stories to other people, right? It's also about the stories I tell myself. Anything and everything I can say that'll make me believe I'm happy. But I'm done rewriting how I feel because I'm scared of getting hurt again. All that's going to do is break my heart later when I don't get my perfect ending. And the perfect ending to my story is with you."

"You're—" I press my fist to my mouth. "I'm going to cry."

"You're already crying. Literally right now." He lets out a choked laugh, grabbing my hands to pull me closer. Then he presses his lips to my forehead, leaving them there just long enough to turn me to liquid. "I love you. Te amo. I'm not moving. I ended things with Mario. Can I kiss you?" His eyes are wet. "Please?"

My hands are cupping his face before he even finishes talking.

I thought I remembered this feeling, but I must have remembered through glass. Because I wouldn't have survived the full force of not having this. Ben wraps me in and pulls me closer, hands pressed flat on my back and all I can think is *Oh. Right. This.*

This. The way he has to lean down to kiss me, how I have to tilt my head up like I'm looking at stars. I thread my hands through his hair, all these strands I haven't met before. Two years of haircuts, new skin cells, new freckles. So many updates to download.

He kisses my temple. "Remind me why this took us so long."

"Because we're dumbasses who can't see what's right in front of us?"

Our lips are so close, I can feel the warmth of his breath when he laughs. "This doesn't even feel real. It's like I'm watching myself in a movie."

"You mean *Arthur and Ben Reloaded*?" I ask. "*The Revenge of Arthur and Ben. Ben and Arthur*—"

"That one actually exists," Ben says.

"Yeah, but what about *Ben and Arthur, All Night Long*?"

"Sounds like an amateur porn spin-off—"

I kiss him again and he kisses me back, and suddenly I can't tell whose tongue is where, whose mouth is what. I step back, leaning against the building's back wall, pulling him along with me until there's no space between us. His lips find mine again without missing a beat, and I think, *Yup, this.*

"I love you," I say. "Did I say that yet? I love you, too. Te amo very much."

"Te amo mucho." The look on his face is so earnestly smitten, it leaves me short-winded.

"Te amo mucho," I say, wishing I still knew Hebrew, wishing I could say it in every language on earth. The words tumble out so easily when it comes to him, like being in love with Ben is just part of my infrastructure.

"What's wild is that you *knew*," he says suddenly. "From day one."

"I knew we'd make out behind my place of employment?"

"You knew the universe wasn't an asshole."

"Oh, no kidding. You know what day it is, right?"

"Thursday? July—" He stops short. "Holy *shit*."

"To the day. You can't tell me that's not the universe."

"The fucking universe. Wow." He lets out a laugh, short and breathless.

I smile up at him smugly. "Guess we saw how it played out."

"We were a basic-bitch love story all along." He ruffles my hair, and I laugh, but I'm also sort of buzzing.

And then we both speak at once.

"Okay, you know what—"

"Do you want to, like—" He cuts himself off, grabs my hands, threads our fingers together. "You first."

"No, sorry, it's fine. I was just wondering if you want to go somewhere. Like. Not behind a theater." I look up at him. "What were you going to say?"

"Literally that." He laughs. "Want to come over? My parents are out. Or, you know, they better be. If I tell them I'm bringing you home, I bet they'd clear out for us."

Us. I'll never, ever get tired of hearing that word on Ben's lips.

CHAPTER THIRTY-NINE

BEN

Thursday, July 9

The universe has finally given me a win.

The win.

Arthur and I waste no time making our way to House Alejo. We're holding hands the entire time, even on the subway despite that scary episode two years ago. If anyone is giving us dirty looks we'll never know, because our eyes are locked on each other as if we haven't seen each other since we broke up. There's some truth to that. For the first time since we said goodbye, we get to be *us* again.

This story hasn't been easy.

The meet-cute at the post office led to us searching for each other.

We kept trying to make our dates perfect when perfection is a myth.

Our breakup should've kept us apart, but we were virtually inseparable.

We reach House Alejo, and my parents are mercifully still not home. I practically drag Arthur to my bedroom like we're in my book and outrunning some wicked wizards. I bump into boxes, knocking them over. Not concerned, since there's only clothes in there, but I would throw my laptop across the room right now if it were in our way.

I fall back into bed first, kicking off my sneakers and unbuttoning Arthur's shirt while he's kissing me. We're finding our way back to each other with every touch, both of us more experienced than last time, and without meaning to, we're bringing those histories on top of the sheets. Even though I'm so damn ready to be naked with him again, I take my time undressing him.

"I missed you so much," I whisper.

He says he misses me back with another kiss.

Holding him feels like a dream. But this is real. I'm holding his smooth arms. I feel his breath on my face. His blue eyes see me. His lips keep visiting mine, and I want them to stay.

I've waited as long as I can when I reach for the condom in my drawer.

And as we embrace this do-over, I'm already excited to do it over and over.

The deeper I go, the closer we become.

With every kiss and every breath, I'm more and more confident that Arthur and I will never let anything separate us again. You could launch us to opposite ends of this solar system, and we'd find our way back to each other. The universe always wanted us together.

When we finish, I want to start all over. But I'm exhausted and poor Arthur is doing a terrible job fighting back his yawns.

"Go to sleep, Art."

"You're not going to be in LA when I wake up, right?"

"I'm not going anywhere without you."

"That's really"—Arthur fights another yawn and loses—"sweet."

"Everywhere you go this summer, I go. And I hope you'll follow me around too. Like maybe even to Dylan's wedding. As my date."

Arthur pops up like someone has dropped a bucket of ice cold water on him.

"I do—I will!"

Saturday, July 11

My best friend is getting married. And he needs deodorant.

"Benito Franklin, you were supposed to bring deodorant."

"No, I wasn't."

"As best man, you have to anticipate all my needs."

"D, if you're grown enough to get married, you're grown enough to pack deodorant."

We're using the guest bathroom in House O'Malley, which is a lovely property in Sunnyside, Queens. I'm scared that my pants are going to split as I search every drawer for deodorant. That's probably for the best. I'd be more grossed out about Dylan using a stranger's than his own smell.

"Should I use toothpaste?" Dylan asks. He's standing in nothing but boxers.

"D, it's this kind of thinking that has me really relieved that you're moving back here to raise your kid." I go into the shower and grab Dylan's soap. "Here. And don't ask me to help you."

Dylan dabs his armpits with the soap. "Worst best man ever." He already showered, but the nerves sweats don't care. He lifts his arm. "Better?"

"Your nose reaches your own armpit."

"Strike two, best man. One more and you're out of the wedding."

"Like, I'm kicked off the grounds, or I can go sit with Arthur during the ceremony?"

"You're obsessed with your future husband."

"Don't start," I say, tying my tie as Arthur taught me.

"Marriage is a wonderful thing, Ben. You'll love it."

"You're not married yet."

"Still time for you to make your move on me."

"I'm not going to be a homewrecker out of respect for Baby Boggs."

"Ugh, this kid is cockblocking me already."

We finish getting dressed and I help Dylan with his tie.

"Benny Rabbit?"

"Dylan Pickle?"

"I'm really happy for you."

"Shut up. It's your wedding day. I'm happy for you."

"I know. I love you and I'm Team Arthur. Lock it down!"

I shake my head. Marriage isn't on my mind just yet. But when that day comes, I know what team I'm on. "I'm happy you and Samantha are locking it down, D. I believe in you guys, and I'm so excited to hang out with your kid."

"You better make a *Wicked Wizards Jr.* for them."

We finish getting ready. Dylan looks so striking that he should really look into a modeling gig. His man bun is being held up by a medallion-yellow band that complements his pocket square. The black suit is a perfect fit.

"These pants do nothing for my ass," Dylan says.

Near-perfect fit, I guess.

"You ready to do this, D?"

"Been ready for years, Ben."

He holds my hand as we leave the guest bathroom, waiting a total of one second before thrusting at the air for his parents to see. Mr. and Mrs. Boggs, also known as Dale and Evelyn, are seriously two of the most normal people in the world. You can't even curse around Evelyn without making her feel weird. And here we have Dylan acting like we just had sex in the bathroom. He was probably switched at birth. Which means somewhere in this world there's a lowkey Dylan not living up to the crude humor of his wild parents.

I still wouldn't trade our Dylan for anyone else.

(On most days.)

"You look very handsome, Dyl," Evelyn says, fighting back tears. "You too, Ben."

"The pants are hiding my ass," Dylan says, like he's expecting his mother to fix that.

"We've very proud of you, son," Dale says, ignoring Dylan's complaint; he's had a lifetime of practice. He straightens Dylan's tie.

Dylan hugs his parents. "Thanks for showing that I can do this."

His mother cracks, crying her mascara off and rushing into the bathroom to clean up. His father squeezes Dylan's shoulder before following his high school sweetheart.

"That was really sweet, D."

"Special occasion. But that's it!"

"I hope you've saved some nice stuff for your vows."

"I'm going out there with a you're-pregnant-so-I-got-to-marry-you-now template."

Dylan looks over his shoulder at the side door. Pretty soon we're going to be stepping out there where the guests are waiting in the backyard. He's sweating again, and I dab his forehead with my pocket square. He relishes in it like a dog getting its ear scratched.

"Thanks, best man."

He hugs me. "I love you, D."

"My *D* loves you too," Dylan says. "So do I."

The bathroom door opens and Evelyn cries all over again seeing us hugging. This wedding is going to kick her ass. Instead of darting away this time, she pulls out her phone and takes a picture of us; I'm going to need her to text that to me later.

"So sweet," Samantha's mother, Donna, says as she turns the corner of the hallway. "I've got family and friends waiting outside and one gorgeous bride ready to marry you." She's been calling herself the wedding director, and I swear she must have a clone, because everything seems to be running smoothly. She's even fully dressed already in a cream dress with a light pink blazer. I don't even want to know what time she had to wake up to curl her auburn hair down her back so elegantly. "How are you feeling, Dylan?"

"Ready to see that gorgeous bride," he says.

"Let's get you out there, then," Donna says.

Dylan hugs his parents one last time before Donna escorts them to their seats outside.

This is all really happening.

My best friend's wedding is about to begin.

The processional song comes over the speakers. It's an instrumental version of "Into the Wild" by Lewis Watson, which Dylan would sing with his parents as a kid. Dylan steps outside, taking in the sun and the applause, which he only encourages, until people are cheering and whistling.

I'm right behind him thinking about why I'm becoming such a fan of the universe. One reason is that there wasn't enough time for Dylan to rehearse one of those dances down the aisle. But my favorite reason is sitting among the guests. This is my first time seeing Arthur in person today and he said there would be a surprise—he's wearing the hot dog tie from the day we met.

I almost forget that this isn't our wedding. I'm ready to run up and kiss him when I remember I'm here to be the best man.

Everything in good time.

For now, I smile at him. It takes me too many moments to even register that he's sitting between Jessie and my parents.

Standing under the canopy, Dylan and I are joined by Patrick. He's wearing a forest-green suit with simple black shoes. He smiles at us and waves.

"Psst." Dylan gets my attention. "He's trying to outdo my suit. The nerve of this motherfuc—"

"Dylan. Dude. He's not your competition. And even if he was, you're literally moments away from marrying Samantha. I think you win."

Dylan nods. "Damn right, I win." He smugly smiles at Patrick.

Down the aisle, all five members of the Pac-People exit a white tent, all of them in black shirts with their respective color ties and instruments. Everyone goes silent as the band begins performing the Israel Kamakawiwoʻole version of "Over the Rainbow."

All the guests rise, waiting.

Then the flaps of the white tent part again, this time revealing Samantha and her father.

Samantha is wearing a flowy white dress with lace sleeves and her silver key necklace. I already want to write this outfit into my book during a royal ball. But I couldn't write her smile as she first sees Dylan.

"I'm going to cry," Dylan says. He's trembling. "Don't let me cry, Ben."

I rest my hand on his shoulder. "Stay strong, D," I say as I fight back my own tears.

Samantha hugs her father before joining us at the altar.

Dylan immediately drops down to one knee. "Hi. You're beautiful. Marry me."

She laughs. "I'm trying to, Mr. Beautiful."

Once everyone's laughter winds down, the officiant begins the ceremony.

I can't believe I'm standing beside my best friend at his wedding. I thought this day was years away. But he's really following in his parents' footsteps and getting married young. I don't have any doubts about Dylan and Samantha succeeding. I'm only a tiny bit concerned about the baby and whether Samantha will be grounded enough to cancel out how extra Dylan is. Thankfully I'll be around to watch this kid grow up.

Samantha begins her vows. "Dylan, when you proposed to me on April Fools' Day, I never once thought you were joking . . ."

I'm so happy that I'm standing here with Dylan, but I'm looking forward to sitting down with him and Samantha soon and getting caught up on all the backstory on this secret saga of theirs. There's so much I missed. Like how in Samantha's vows she's talking about how she was so nervous to tell her family, but when Dylan told her it was going to be okay, she believed him because she's never trusted anyone the way she does him.

"I promise to love you, Dylan, even on the days when I want to power you down," Samantha concludes.

"Can I kiss her already?" Dylan asks.

"We're getting there," the officiant says with a smile. He passes him the mic. "Would you like to share your vows?"

Dylan spins the mic between his fingers. "Samantha, in honor of meeting you in a coffee shop, I thought about stacking these vows with puns. Stuff like how you're steaming beautiful and how I love you a latte and asking where you've 'bean' all my life? But that's beneath me. Instead, I'd like to go back to that April Fools' Day where I didn't have a ring to offer you, but I gave you a key instead . . ." He turns to the guests like he's a comedian onstage. "Why a key, you ask? Well . . ." He cups his hands around the mic and shouts, "BECAUSE I LOCKED IT DOWN!"

As everyone laughs, Samantha included, she snatches the mic. "Tell them the real reason or I'll walk away."

"You already vowed to love me!"

"Dylan . . ."

"Fiiine." He squeezes his hand around the key hanging from her neck. "This is the key to our dorm room, aka our first home together. And I told you I want to share more homes with you."

My hand shoots to my mouth with how sweet that is.

"Great, now everyone knows how sweet I am," Dylan says.

"It's humanizing," Samantha says as she brushes his cheek.

Dylan turns to the officiant. "For the love of God, can we kiss now?"

The officiant laughs as he wraps up the ceremony. Patrick

and I give our best friends the rings. Dylan's is a simple band and Samantha's gold ring comes from her grandmother.

"Now?" Dylan asks, dying to kiss Samantha.

"I now pronounce you husband and wife," the officiant says. "You may now kiss—"

Dylan wastes no more time as he kisses the girl he once called his future wife.

My best friend is married.

I've never clapped so hard in my life. Through teary eyes, I watch Dylan bow while holding Samantha's hand. Together, they walk down the aisle with all their family and friends cheering them on.

And I find Arthur turning to look at me like his eyes have been away from mine for too long. I'm so happy he's back in my life, and I'm ready for do-over after do-over to become the best us we've always known we could be.

I once wondered if we were a love story or a story about love.

I now know the answer.

CHAPTER FORTY

ARTHUR

Saturday, July 11

The only thing better than Ben beneath a canopy is the part where he walks straight to me when the ceremony's over. And the part where he kisses me with such casual certainty, I almost melt into the neatly mowed grass.

It's still so thrilling and strange—these quick, offhand kisses in front of grandparents and caterers and Dylan's hot uncle Julian. I've been out for so long, I don't even think about how much I hold back in some spaces. But the truth is, fifteen-year-old me barely dared to dream about kissing a boyfriend in public. I'm pretty sure thirteen-year-old me thought two guys kissing at a wedding was a thing that only happened in strangers' photos.

Ben takes both my hands, threading our fingers together.

"So. Like. How good was the best man?"

"The best. Best best man. Couldn't take my eyes off him. Was there even a groom?"

"Wouldn't know," Ben says. "I was too busy checking out some guy wearing a hot dog tie."

I smile up at him. "Special occasion, right?"

I swear, my molecules rearrange when he's near me. The air between us feels so thick, I could poke a hole straight through it. He leans in to kiss me again—I don't even know how I'm still standing upright.

"Ow ow owwwwwwwww!" Dylan howls into megaphone hands.

Ben and I break apart, flustered and smiling.

"Now, I don't want to interrupt—"

"Dylan!" I catch him in a full-on bear hug. "Mazel tov! How do you feel?"

"I feel like taking some naughty pics, is how I feel," Dylan says.

Ben mouths the word "wow." "That sounds like more of an after-wedding activity."

"Au contraire, my Best Ben. You're indispensable," he says, adjusting Ben's tie and giving him a firm pat on the shoulder. "Photographer's orders. And," he adds, waggling his eyebrows at me, "boyfriends *definitely* allowed."

Boyfriend—my stomach does cartwheels when he says it. That's how Dylan introduced me to his parents this morning, too. *Ben's boyfriend.* I'm trying so hard to keep my cool about it, since Ben and I haven't technically discussed it yet. But I can't help but notice that Ben didn't object either time.

He takes my hand. "Come with me?"

Like it's even a question. We trail behind Dylan, past three floral-decked tables and a makeshift dance floor strung with twinkle lights. There's a tree-lined alcove at the edge of the O'Malley property, where a woman in all black is snapping pictures of Samantha with various combinations of relatives. When she sees us, her practiced photo smile breaks into a full-beaming grin.

Samantha as a bride is still the weirdest concept, but there's no denying she wears it well. She's so beautiful, even I'm a little bit spellbound. Her dress looks like something straight out of a Jane Austen adaptation—high-waisted and flowy, with ivory lace and cap sleeves. *Maternity chic*, she'd called it this morning, tugging the fabric tight around her belly to show us just how fucking oblivious we've been for weeks.

The photographer pulls Dylan into the tableau, in between Samantha and her grandma. I lean in closer to Ben to watch her bustle around, snapping a million pictures from every angle, periodically pausing to add or remove another O'Malley relative.

"I keep thinking about how these are Dylan's *wedding*

pictures," Ben says, smiling faintly. "Like, we're witnessing the creation of an image that's going to be passed along to their grandchildren."

I watch Dylan stretch his arms up languidly—and then stop short to sniff his armpit.

"For the grandchildren," I say.

Ben kisses my cheek before squeezing in next to Dylan for the wedding party photos—followed by a full best-friends photo session at the groom's request.

Samantha cuts across the grass, straight to me, arms outstretched for a hug. "Arthur! I'm so glad you're here. Thank you so much. Just. For everything."

"Are you kidding? Thank you for inviting me. This wedding. And you!" I press both hands to my heart. "You've ruined me for all other brides."

"Sucks. Guess you shouldn't marry one."

I laugh. "I guess not."

"I'm so happy for you guys." She glances down at Ben and Dylan, who are currently reenacting a *Twilight* pose on the grass. "I've never seen Ben glow like that."

My heart does this quick, tiny flip. "Really?"

"Arthur, he's head over heels. You see it, right?"

"Hey, current wife," Dylan calls out, hoisting himself back up to standing. "Come back here."

"Wow. Not into that—"

"Excuse me." Dylan clears his throat over the noise of

Ben's laughter. "My *forever* wife."

Samantha breaks into a grin.

"You too, MacArthur Seuss Award. Get in here."

Samantha grabs my hand. "Our paparazzi awaits."

It's the kind of joy that's almost too bright to look at straight-on. How could I ever ask for anything but Ben's hand on my waist and the click of this camera? Documented proof that this moment existed, that Ben and I belonged to each other.

Evening fades into night, one happy blur of food and flowers and dancing. I spend all of it in Ben's arms, already missing every single moment that passes.

"Want to walk somewhere?" he asks, sometime after the cake's been cut—which is how we end up back in the tree-lined alcove at the edge of the yard, where the posed photos were taken. The music sounds almost otherworldly from here. We're completely alone, face-to-shadowy-face. Nothing between us but our own intertwined hands.

I wish I could stay here. I want to lock myself inside this moment. I keep imagining future me, alone in my dorm room, trying to dream myself back into it. I wonder if Ben will miss me this fall. Will we still be together by then? We could make it work this time, right? Long-distance isn't the end of the world, and Connecticut is so much closer than

Georgia. We'll just do the train thing . . . for three years.

"Hey." Ben tugs me closer. "What are you worrying about?"

"Oh, I'm—just. I don't know. I'm glad to be here." I smile up at him. "I still can't believe it."

"That Dylan and Samantha are married?"

"That too." My heart skitters. "But no, I mean *us*. That we're, you know, back together . . . I guess?"

"You guess?" Ben tilts his head, and I laugh.

"I don't know! Are we? How does this go?"

The music shifts—and even from across the yard, I recognize the song from the very first measure. Pretty sure I'd know this one in my sleep.

"Marry You." Bruno Mars.

Ben bursts out laughing. "Wow, is there, like, a flash mob coming, or . . ."

I cover my face. "I didn't plan this. Oh my God. Universe, what the hell? Take a day off every once—"

Ben kisses me.

I look up at him, startled. "Okay, then."

He kisses me again, his hands running down the sleeves of my jacket, leaving fields of goose bumps in their wake, even through layers of fabric. My arms hook beneath his, hugging him closer, holding his lips against mine, because air is good, but Ben's breath is better. His hands change course, trailing back up to my shoulders, to the back of my neck, and I can't stop thinking about how many stories these hands have told on tiny square keys. His fingertips find the skin just above my collar and just beneath it, tracing around the tag of my shirt—didn't even know that was a move, but it definitely is.

The way his touch lights me up, leans me forward. I think he's italicizing me.

"Look," he says, his voice breathless from kissing. "Here's the thing about do-overs. You have to try something different, or—you know. There's no point."

My heart sinks. "So you don't think there's any point—"

"No—God. Sorry. What I'm saying is—Arthur, fuck." He draws in a deep breath. "I'm saying yes—holy shit—I want us to be back together. We never should have broken up. Arthur, we chose wrong last time. Let's try again. I don't care about the distance. We'll make it work, okay?"

"Yeah. Let's—yeah." Suddenly, I'm crying and laughing all at once. "Here's to do-overs, right?"

"Here's to us," he adds, hugging me. I bury my face in his jacket.

"I'm so happy." My voice, muffled by fabric, is a jumble of tears and choked laughter. "This is my favorite day."

"Favorite until tomorrow," says Ben.

I wipe a tear from his cheek with the heel of my hand. "Please tell me you can spend the night tonight," I say.

"Does Dylan need you for . . . I don't know—"

"His wedding night?"

"Look, it's Dylan."

He laughs. "I'll tell him I'm needed elsewhere."

"Good, because Uncle Milton's horse paintings have been asking about you."

"I'm into it," he says. "And you know what else I'm into? Not being surrounded by my entire wardrobe."

My heart squeezes happily, like it does every time I remember he's staying. He's staying he's staying he's staying. "I'll help you unpack first thing tomorrow."

"You don't have to do that—"

"Hi, you gave up California. For me," I remind him. "And the fact that I get to keep you on my coast? I'll clean your whole room every day until school starts. I don't even care."

He laughs. "How long's the ride to Wesleyan again?"

"Two hours or so by train. It's like twenty-five bucks, but there's a discount if you buy a bunch of tickets in advance. Like, if you know you're going to visit a lot." I smile. "We should visit a lot."

"Okay, but—" Ben turns to me, suddenly, with an expression I can't quite decipher. But when his eyes meet mine, they're practically shooting off sparks. "What if we don't?"

EPILOGUE

THE WORLD FALLS AWAY

BEN

Four Years Later

Brooklyn, NY

Not every story has a happy ending.

Sometimes you try and try, but it doesn't come together. You end up wasting so much time by trying to force something that will never work, instead of moving on to the next best thing. It's a really tough lesson, especially when there's years of comfort and happiness involved. It's even tougher when big dreams are involved. But saying goodbye can be really freeing and open new doors for you.

That's certainly the case for *The Wicked Wizard War.*

I really, really wanted it to sell. It was the book I started in high school and dropped out of college to finish because I believed in it so much. Even though my wicked wizards were able to charm my literary agent into representing me, the book didn't quite cast the same spell when it reached publishers. My agent, Percy, encouraged me to start the next book. It was popular advice, but I didn't have it in me. I thought I was going to be the exception to every rule, and I felt totally powerless when I couldn't make my wildest dreams come true.

But I found my power again because of my biggest fan.

My incredible boyfriend, Arthur Seuss.

When I followed Arthur to Connecticut at the beginning of his sophomore year, I rented a bedroom near Wesleyan and RJ Julia, where I got a job as a bookseller. Arthur knew how pathetic I felt after *The Wicked Wizard War* didn't sell. But he didn't let me give up on writing.

The idea for my contemporary novel seemed to come out of nowhere. I remember Arthur's head was resting on my shoulder when I opened the blank document and started writing. Ten months later, when I finished that brutal first draft, Arthur was already begging to read it. When my agent called a few weeks ago with the news that *The Best Us* sold to a publisher after a four-house auction, Arthur popped open a bottle of prosecco and we danced around our tiny Brooklyn apartment.

I would have called my parents and the Boggs Squad the next morning to share the news, but then Arthur had a pretty amazing idea to announce my book deal in style. I haven't even begun officially editing the book yet, but

Arthur thought it would be cool if we hosted a gathering where I could read a couple pages. He called it a dress rehearsal, because he's always got Broadway on the brain—especially since Jacob hired him for real right after graduation.

So for tonight, we've converted our apartment into a small coffee shop—Café Bart.

Our home doesn't even feel big enough for the both of us, let alone our border collie Beauregard, who gets really hyper whenever we return from anywhere, even if it's down the hall to throw out trash. But it's a straight-up fire hazard now, with how many people we're hosting.

It's a little overwhelming. But everyone seems to be having an amazing time.

Arthur is with his parents and Ma and Pa, who are still gushing over how much they loved last night's show. Arthur and the whole Demsky Theatrics team really put their all into *Out in the City*, and it's paying off. The critics who attended the premiere are giving it really great reviews—and I've managed to distract Arthur from seeing the one that was kind of so-so.

Ethan and his a cappella boyfriend, Jeremy, are on our makeshift stage—the ottoman with a secret compartment for Beauregard's toys—and they're singing "Here's to Us" by Halestorm. They've got Abuelita; Bubbe; my Connecticut roommate, Yael; Jessie and Grayson; and my bookseller friends mesmerized. And Taj is being an absolute hero recording them for Ethan and Jeremy's joint TikTok account.

My bedroom door opens, and my four-year-old godson Sammy comes running out with a glass clock from the set of the pilot of the TV show Mario and his uncle wrapped filming last month; fingers crossed the show gets picked up because it sounds amazing. Only fifty of those clocks were made, so I'd really appreciate it if Sammy doesn't break it like he did my Nintendo controller.

"Sammy, hey, bud," I say. "Can I see that clock?"

Sammy stares up at me with his mother's blue eyes that glint with his father's mischief. "You can buy it."

"Buy it? It's mine."

"But I have it."

"That's not really how that works, but okay. How much do you want? A dollar?"

"Eleven dollars and seventeen cents."

"Eleven dollars and— That's so random. Where did you even come up with that number?"

"I don't know."

I do. Genetics.

Dylan and Samantha come out of the bedroom, sneaking up on Sammy. I discreetly lift a finger, telling them I got this.

"How about if you give me that clock, I'll take you to

the bookstore tomorrow morning."

Sammy makes duck lips while considering this. "Zoo. And I want cotton candy."

"Deal."

We shake on it and he hands me the clock. Then he runs off to terrorize my father.

"Don't bring him home until the sugar has worn off," Samantha says.

"Or leave him at the zoo with the other snakes," Dylan says. His phone buzzes and he lights up with a smile. "It's Patrick. One second—Patty! How's Cuba, you sexy bastard?"

Samantha shakes her head as Dylan walks off to talk to his Third Best Friend. "Please let me move in, Ben. I'm so tired. I know Beauregard doesn't use his bed."

I laugh and offer her a hug.

For the longest, Dylan kept calling the fetus Cider. It actually grew on me a little bit, I'm not kidding. Samantha didn't have any name she loved, but when Dylan saw everything she did to bring their son into the world, he said they should name the baby after her. It's funny how she never lets anyone but her mother call her Sammy, and then she named her son that. Maybe it'll become some new tradition.

One hour in, I think everyone who's going to be here has arrived.

I squeeze through the crowd and take Arthur's hand.

"Excuse me," I say to all our parents and lead him to our bedroom. "We should probably get started before our neighbors complain."

"I don't understand why they can't enjoy the show," Arthur says. "I'm practically bringing Broadway to Brooklyn."

"Sometimes Broadway should take a night off," I say, kissing his cheek.

"Blasphemy," he says. "Also, Mondays."

We go into our bedroom, and I grab the cardboard box with my manuscript that Arthur printed and bound at Staples. I couldn't believe that I was holding a physical version of the book when he brought it home. We return to the living room, where Arthur gets everyone's attention. He stands on the ottoman and speaks into a prop microphone that's off.

"Welcome to Part Two of the Arthur and Ben Special," Arthur says. "Thanks to everyone who made it out to the show tonight, and thanks for coming today to hear about Ben's big news . . ."

"Did you get another dog?" Sammy asks, petting Beauregard.

"Nope. Just Beau for now."

"Get another."

Dylan points at Sammy and turns to his wife. "Control your namesake."

"Control your DNA," she says.

My legs are trembling as I realize everything that's about to happen. How differently I'm about to be seen in front of all my loved ones. How this day has finally arrived and everything I went through to have a moment like this.

"So I've been keeping really quiet about something. I've been writing something so personal that it scared me. I didn't want to talk about it because I was really humiliated when my fantasy book didn't sell. But . . ." I reach into the box and pull out the manuscript.

"You finished!" Ma says.

Everyone is clapping. And I turn to Arthur, who is giddy with excitement.

"I didn't just finish writing the book," I say. "I got a book deal . . . I'm going to be a published author."

My parents lose it. Dylan and Samantha cheer louder than anyone, and Sammy is just yelling to yell. Everyone is so happy for me, but I'm still shaking because of what comes next.

"Arthur thought it would be cool if I read the opening pages for you all. It's bound to change, but this is the version that sold . . ." I open to the first page and stop. "Actually, I can't."

"Boo!" Dylan says. And of course Sammy chimes in, too.

"Arthur, would you mind reading for me?" I ask. "I'm too nervous."

Arthur looks surprised. "But I haven't rehearsed. Can I have a second to get into character?"

"I love you, but absolutely not."

We swap spots on the ottoman again.

Arthur opens the book, and I'm waiting, but he reads, "Chapter one . . ."

"Wait. Art. I think you skipped a page."

He looks at me. "Did you sneak in a prologue? I thought you were anti-prologue—"

He flips back to the dedication page.

"To Arthur," he reads. "My forever husband."

His blue eyes water as everyone gasps.

I get down on one knee and pull a ring out of my pocket. "Do you have any edits?"

ARTHUR

Two Years Later

Middletown, CT

What do you call a moment that's so perfect, you're scared you dreamed it?

I'm close enough to make out some of the faces in the crowd, and it's the strangest patchwork of people. Musa and his wife, Rahmi, sitting next to Ben's author friends. Mrs. Ortiz from up the block making kissy faces at one of Jacob's toddlers. Juliet and Emerald. Namrata and David. So many relatives, too—like Uncle Milton and his Special Lady Friend from upstate, not to mention the ultimate old-lady power duo: Bubbe and Abuelita. All these people, from every era of our lives.

No ex-boyfriends, though. We weren't surprised when

Hudson and Rafael declined our invitation, and we were even less surprised about Mikey and Zach. Mario's the only one who seemed crushed he couldn't make it—he couldn't get away from his writers' room, but he sent us a video message with lots of congratulatory kisses from his lucky *I Love You Beary Much* bear.

An instrumental version of "Marry You" starts playing, and Ben steps into the aisle. I'm not close enough to make out his expression, but I can picture it—the little self-conscious half smile when he knows people are looking at him. I call it his book-signing face. He's flanked by his parents, and they're moving so slowly, probably because Isabel keeps clasping people's hands as she passes.

"Still breathing?" my mom asks.

I shake my head. "I'm getting *married*."

To Ben. To the guy I've been in love with since I was sixteen years old.

Ben and I haven't seen each other for hours, but we woke up early so we could wander around Main Street together, just us. Ben signed stock at RJ Julia, and we had brunch at Ford News Diner. And of course we hit up the Bark-ery for homemade dog biscuits, since it's our first time leaving Beauregard with anyone other than Ben's parents, and Ben's not taking it well. I did manage to talk him out of FaceTiming the dog sitter from inside the store, so Beau could see all his options. You could say I have a pretty good idea now about what Ben's going to be like as a dad.

Is it weird that I can't wait?

The song switches to "Only Us" from *Dear Evan Hansen*, which is apparently Sammy's cue to full-on somersault down the aisle. Literally no idea where his ring pillow is, but it's cool, because we've got the actual rings in our pockets. Past Arthur and Past Ben knew way better than to let someone with that much Dylan DNA anywhere near them. Sammy throws his fists in the air when he reaches the chuppah, like a fighter entering the ring.

My dad pats my back. "I think it's go time. You ready?"

The sound that comes out of my mouth definitely isn't a word, but he just laughs and straightens my tie.

Then my parents hook their arms through mine, and I'm vaguely aware that a hundred faces have turned around to watch me.

But all I see is Ben. The way he's standing so straight in his dark gray suit—I think he's too nervous to slouch. Our eyes lock, and he presses his fist to his mouth, like he's trying to hold back a sob.

I legitimately can't believe I get to marry this person.

Ben tries to kiss me hello as soon as I reach the chuppah, but Dylan bops him on the head with a rolled-up sheet of paper. "No spoilers!"

"It's a wedding," says Ben.

"You're not married yet!" Dylan turns back to the crowd.

"Friends! Enemies!" Then he pauses, bowing slightly. "Lovers."

Samantha shakes her head incredulously.

"I want to begin," Dylan continues, "by calling upon the godlike scriptures of my church, the church from whence delivers . . . universal life. Fellow wanderers, I've been challenged! I've been tested! My road to celestial fulfillment has been one of great tribulation! But since the day I submitted my information unto that holiest of online contact forms, I have been"—he shuts his eyes briefly—"a man of unshakable faith."

Ben looks at me, and I bite back a laugh.

"Thus, it is my divinely anointed pleasure to welcome you here for the holy gay matrimony of Benjamin Hugo Alejo and Arthur James Seuss. This is—no exaggeration—the most homoromantic occasion in the history of humanity." He pauses dramatically. "So without further ado, I'd like to turn it over to our grooms, who have taken a vow of writing their own vows. Go ahead, Ben. Make my day—no." Dylan smiles, gesturing grandly at me. "Make *his*."

The next thing I know, Ben's pulling a slightly crumpled sheet of paper out of his jacket pocket, making a noise that's somewhere between a laugh and an exhale.

"As we all know, I'm not—" he begins, voice shaking a bit. "Sorry, can I—let me start again." I squeeze his hands and smile at him, and he smiles nervously back. "Okay, do-over time. As we all know, I'm not the fantasy author I thought I was going to be. That was a rough time. But I got through it because of you—you're my biggest fan and my biggest champion. And you prove over and over how the real world is more magical than anything I could ever write because you're in it."

I lose my breath. This much joy can't be survivable.

"There are so many days when I still can't believe you're in my life. What if I hadn't gone to the post office that day? What if you hadn't come back to New York? What if I had left? Then when I think about how horrible my life would look without you, I think about everything I'll do to keep you. Like letting you sing show tunes before bed despite complaints from our neighbors. And never abusing the courteous five-minute period of lateness you've so generously granted me."

I laugh, wiping my eyes.

"Arthur, I love you and I'm so excited to write this next chapter with you," he says. "And every chapter."

"Seussical, holy *moly*," Dylan says, shaking his head. "What are you gonna say to *that*?"

"Yeah . . . remind me why we let the published author go first?"

Ben grins, and I grin back.

"You're lucky I'm not easily intimidated," I say, and then I pause. "Or that I'm so easily intimidated that I'm *used to* being intimidated, which is kind of like not being intimidated, I guess?"

A few people chuckle, and I unfold my paper, feeling strangely removed from my body.

Deep breath.

"Dear Boy from the Post Office."

I sneak a glance up at Ben, who's already wiping his eyes at the corners.

"Eight years ago, we talked for a few minutes at the post office on Lexington. I was the guy with the hot dog tie. You were the guy mailing stuff back to your ex-boyfriend. And now I'm marrying you."

There's a collective *awwww*, but it must be a million miles away, because right now it's just us. Me and Ben.

"Much like a narwhal," I say, glancing back down at my paper, "I can hardly believe this moment is real."

Ben laughs, and it makes my throat go thick.

"I'm so in love with you. I always have been. You know that. And I know I'm supposed to be vowing stuff, but I don't really know where to start." I breathe in. "I just want to make you happy," I say. "But I'll be there when you're not happy, too. If you're sad, I'll sit inside it with you. I know I'm going to mess up sometimes, too, but I promise to say sorry a lot, because that's what people do when they want something to work."

Ben nods, blinking really quickly.

"Ben, I want to fall asleep next to you and start every day with you. I want infinite do-overs. I want to make you laugh and know everything about you. I want to see what you look like when you're old, and I'm not even talking about, like, dad old. I mean *old* old." Ben laughs again and wipes another tear. "I want your whole entire story. And the bonus footage. And the blooper reel. I just—I love you more than I thought was even possible. Like, it's honestly kind of ridiculous. And I just keep thinking about that first summer in New York, and how I was actually homesick." My voice breaks. "But now I know you're my home."

I fold my paper up. Exhale. Ben and I look at each other.

Dylan dabs at his eyes with the cuff of his sleeve. "Folks, I don't know what to tell you. They're not straight, but they came straight for our hearts." He clutches his chest for a moment. "Yeah, I better seal this deal, stat. Whip it out, guys!"

"The rings," Samantha cuts in from the front row. "He means the rings."

Ben's hands are shaking, I notice. And then I realize mine are, too.

The next part is a blur. *With this ring. As a symbol. From this moment forward. Without reservation.*

I do.

I do.

"Then with the power vested in me by the internet, by

God, and by the state of Connecticut, I now pronounce you husband and husband!" Dylan declares, blowing a kiss in our direction. "Do the thing."

And all I can think is: sometimes what-ifs come true.

ACKNOWLEDGMENTS

As Ben Alejo once said, this story hasn't been easy. Deadlines, virtual elementary school, misaligned schedules, and our own messy brains made this a very different process than *What If It's Us*. But amid all the fog and chaos, one thing's always been crystal clear: we've got the world's greatest people backing us up, and there isn't a universe where we could have done it without them.

In particular:

- Donna Bray, who walked us through many rounds of do-overs with the most brilliant editorial guidance. Thanks for bearing with all our ups and downs (and the occasional wedding-themed PowerPoint presentation). Your patience and sense of humor are unparalleled—which just might come in handy now that you're Dylan's mother-in-law. (Lo siento for all the spitting, Donna!)

- Andrew Eliopulos, forever one of the biggest stars in Arthur and Ben's universe.
- Our agents, Jodi Reamer and Holly Root, who (as Dylan would say) LOCKED THIS BOOK DOWN. We can't thank you enough for your endless support and advocacy throughout this entire process. Infinite gratitude as well to our teams at Writers House and Root Literary (with special shout-outs to Alyssa Moore, Heather Baror-Shapiro, Cecilia de la Campa, and Rey Lalaoui)
- Alexandra Cooper, Alessandra Balzer, and the rest of our incredible team at HarperCollins, including: Shona McCarthy, Mark Rifkin, Erin Fitzsimmons, Alison Donalty, Allison Brown, Sabrina Abballe, Michael D'Angelo, Audrey Diestelkamp, Patty Rosati, Mimi Rankin, Katie Dutton, Jackie Burke, Mitch Thorpe, Tiara Kittrell, and Allison Weintraub.
- Kaitlin López and Matthew Eppard, who run the show (and should probably run the universe).
- Our team at UTA, who make what ifs come true: Jason Richman, Mary Pender-Coplan, Daniela Jaimes, Orly Greenberg, and Nia Nation.
- Dana Goldberg, Bill Bost, Blair Bigelow, Stacy Traub, and Ryan Litman for the do-over of our dreams.
- Our amazing international publishing teams, who have brought so many readers into this universe (with special

shout-outs to S&S UK, Leonel Teti, Christian Bach, and Kaya Hoff.)

- Jeff Östberg, for a cover that was love at first sight.
- Froy Gutierrez and Noah Galvin for sharing their unbelievable talent with our boys yet again.
- Jacob Demlow, who is even more iconic than his fictional counterpart. Their wisdom, insight, and wealth of theatrical knowledge made this book so much richer.
- Mark Oshiro, who pulled the ultimate Mario by schooling us in Spanish and making this book a hundred times more super.
- Frantz Baron, for the ultimate virtual tour of Bloomingdale's.
- David and the Arnolds + Jasmine and the Wargas. We wish these bands existed, but we're mostly just glad these people do.
- The book community. Truly, this book wouldn't exist without the support *What If It's Us* received from readers, bloggers, booktokkers, bookstagrammers, booksellers, librarians, and artists, and we're so grateful.
- So many friends—SO many. When finishing this book felt impossible, you carried us through. Though this short list barely scratches the surface: Dahlia Adler, Amy Austin, Patrice Caldwell, Dhonielle Clayton, Zoraida Cordova, Jenn Dugan, Sophie Gonzales, Elliot

Knight, Marie Lu, Kat Ramsburg, Aisha Saeed, Jaime Semensohn, Nic Stone, Sabaa Tahir, Angie Thomas, Julian Winters, and the Yoonicorns.

- Our families, who we love in every universe. So grateful to every single one of you Jews and Puerto Ricans (and all the rest of you, too). Special shout-outs to Brian, Owen, Henry, Persi, the Riveras, and baby Max.
- And finally: Willow and Tazz, who sacrificed so many head scratches so this book could get written. Heroes.

DON'T MISS THE LATEST FROM

BECKY ALBERTALLI & ADAM SILVERA!

A buoyant rom-com about BFFs, shared crushes, and daring to step into the spotlight.

Two siblings put brotherhood, love, and loyalty to the test during a magical war generations in the making.

FROM

KATE IN WAITING

OVERTURE

It really feels like an ending, in every way possible. With the curtains pulled closed, the stage might as well be another planet. A well-lit planet full of giant foam set pieces, inhabited only by Andy and me—and Matt.

Coke-Ad Matt.

"It's now or never," whispers Andy. He doesn't move an inch.

Neither do I.

We just sort of stand there, in the shadow of a papier-mâché Audrey 2.

There's nothing sadder than the end of a crush. And it's not like this was one of those distant-stranger crushes. Andy and I have actually talked to this boy. Tons of words, on multiple glorious occasions. No small feat, since Matt's the kind of gorgeous that usually renders us speechless. He's got one of those old-timey faces, with blond hair and pink cheeks. Our friend Brandie collects Coca-Cola merch, and I swear the vintage ad in her bathroom looks exactly like Matt. Thus the nickname. The ad says, "Thirst stops here." But in our case, the thirst doesn't stop.

It's basic Avril Lavigne math. We were the junior theater counselors. He was our cute townie vocal consultant. You truly could not make it any more obvious. And for a full six weeks, he's been the sun in our solar system. But he lives up the road from camp, in Mentone, Alabama.

Which is just about a hundred miles away from Roswell, Georgia.

So Andy's right. Now or never.

Deep breath. "Hey. Uh, Matt."

I swear I can feel Anderson's surprised approval. Damn, Garfield. Just going for it. Get yours.

I clear my throat. "So. We wanted to say goodbye. And. Um. Thank you."

Matt slides a sheet of music into his tote bag and smiles. "Thank me?"

"For the vocal consultation," I say. "And everything."

Andy nods fervently, adjusting his glasses.

"Aww, Kate! You too. So cool meeting you guys." Matt hoists his tote bag over his shoulder, shifting his weight toward the door, just barely. Exit posture. Crap. I'm just going to—

"Can we take a selfie?" I blurt. I'm already cringing. You know what would be cool? If my voice would stop shaking. Also, Anderson. My dude. Anytime you want to step up, be my guest.

“Oh, sure,” Matt says. “Let’s do it.”

Well then.

We squeeze into the frame, curtain tickling our backs, and I stretch my arm out at the up angle, just like Anderson trained me. And we smile. I mean, I’m trying to. But I’m so flustered, my lips are trembling.

It’s worth it. Even if I come out looking like a dazed fangirl, it’s worth it. Raina and Brandie have been begging for photographic evidence of Coke-Ad Matt’s cuteness, and God knows Instagram’s yielded nothing.

But this picture isn’t for the squad. Not really. Honestly, they’re both just going to make fun of us for having yet another communal crush. According to Raina, Anderson and I are enmeshed, which basically means we’re codependent. Apparently some people believe falling in love is a thing you’re supposed to do on your own.

FROM *INFINITY SON*,
BOOK ONE OF THE INFINITY CYCLE

ONE
BROTHERS

EMIL

I'm dead set on living my one life right, but I can't say the same for my brother.

No one's expecting Brighton to be full-grown when we turn eighteen at midnight, but he needs to step it up. Long gone are those days where we were kids acting like we have powers like all these celestials roaming the streets tonight. Their lives aren't all fun and games, but he stays ignoring the dark headlines we see every day. I can't get him to see the truth, but I can check myself. I'm done dressing up as the heroic Spell Walkers for Halloween, and I'm done watching celestials and creatures wrestle in steel cages with their natural-born powers. I'm done, I'm done, I'm done.

I got to chill because we're close as hell, don't get me wrong. You step in his face and you'll find me in yours, even though I can't swing bones for the life of me. But man, there's been a few times I wondered if we're actually twins, like maybe Brighton got switched at birth or is secretly adopted. That nonsense no doubt comes from all the comics about chosen ones I've read over the years.

He's running wild at this all-night block party, trying to score interviews left and right for his online series, Celestials of New York, but no one's about it. Everyone's busy celebrating the arrival of the Crowned Dreamer, a faint constellation against the dark sky, which is hanging around for most of this month and then goes back to sleep for another sixty-seven years. No one really knows how far back celestials have existed or how they first received their powers, but all signs throughout history point to their connection with the stars. Like maybe their eldest ancestors fell out of the sky. Whatever the truth is, constellations are always a major event for them.

It's good to see celestials partying for a change. The only time I see gatherings like this lately is to protest the acts of violence and injustice against them, which have doubled in the last nine months. Being gay isn't rainbows and sunshine all the time, but ever since the Blackout—the worst attack New York has seen in my lifetime—people have been treating celestials like terrorists.

Tonight reminds me of when I attended my first Pride

parade. I was out to my family and friends, and all was good there, but I couldn't pretend there wasn't still a knot in my stomach from wondering if strangers would be cool with my heart; reading minds would've come in handy. During the parade, I felt relief and security and happiness and hope, all tied up like an indestructible rope that bound us together. I breathed easy around strangers for the first time.

I wonder how many celestials are taking that breath tonight.